Change Of Momentum

LIANA BROOKS

FLEET OF MALIK

Bodies In Motion
Change of Momentum
For Every Action (forthcoming)

HEROES AND VILLAINS

Even Villains Fall In Love
Even Villains Go To The Movies
Even Villains Have Interns
Even Villains Play The Hero
The Polar Terror

ALL I WANT FOR CHRISTMAS

All I Want For Christmas Is A Werewolf
All I Want For Christmas Is A Reaper (2020)

SHORTER WORKS

Darkness And Good
Fey Lights
Prime Sensations

OTHER WORKS

Find other works by the author at
www.lianabrooks.com

Change Of Momentum

LIANA BROOKS

AUSTRALIA

Print ISBN: 978-1-925825-82-4
eBook ISBN: 9781393187523

www.inkprintpress.com

National Library of Australia Cataloguing-in-Publication Data
Brooks, Liana 1982—
Change Of Momentum
582 p.
ISBN: 978-1-925825-82-4
Inkprint Press, Canberra, Australia
1.   Fiction—Romance—Science Fiction 2. Fiction—Science
       Fiction—Military 3. Science fiction—Women authors

Summary: An unknown enemy forces ex-enemies Rowena and Hollis into an uneasy partnership. Love is a battlefield, and on Malik III, war is in the air.

First Edition: April 2020
Cover design © Clare Williams

DEDICATION

This book is for anyone
who ever needed a second chance.

NEWTON'S SECOND LAW OF MOTION:

$$F = m*a$$

An object that is at rest will stay at rest
unless a force acts upon it.
An object that is in motion will not change
its velocity unless a force acts upon it.

$$F = \frac{\Delta(mv)}{\Delta t}$$

A NOTE TO READERS

When I sat down to write *Change Of Momentum,* I knew I was writing the story of two people who had survived some of the most horrific experiences a human could survive, namely war and the loss of their loved ones. For anyone to move past those kinds of traumas and be able to embrace a better future requires that they address what happened. For Rowena, who was groomed by a sadist to take his place, this means looking at what she could have become.

Chapter Eighteen contains a frank discussion that touches on the topics of abuse, torture, emotional abuse, and sexual assault. While it is important to the character's emotional journey, I would encourage readers who may be sensitive to these topics to skip over that section of the book. Your mental health and wellbeing is more important than a story, and you'll be able to catch up in the following chapters.

RANKS WITHIN THE FLEET

Because the Fleet of Malik was cobbled together by treaty and agreement between disparate groups, it does not follow the rank structure most people are familiar with. This is an isolated, military culture that combined ground troops, air support, and non-military vessels into something like a homogenous culture. The officer ranks are as follows.

Empress of War (*extinct*): The official title of the Empress of the Fifth House. It was an honorary title only and has not been used since the fall of the wormhole and the end of the Empire.

Fleet Marshal of the Sun of Malik (*currently in abeyance*): The Fleet Marshal of any solar system is the military leader for the entire system and is usually selected by the military themselves from the ranks of senior officers. The rank has never been used in the Malik System.

Commodore (*once in abeyance, now considered extinct*): The rank of a senior space station commander. In the Malik System, the rank is exclusive to the space station *Eden* and has not been used in the past 800 years since the station became a joint military-civilian command. Since the loss of the *Eden* some five hundred years ago, the rank has been listed as extinct.

Admiral (*currently in abeyance*): The rank of Admiral is held by senior members of the Fleet Marshal's Council. This rank is by appointment only and had not been used in the Malik System.

Joint-Commander (*currently in abeyance*): The rank assigned to both civilian and military commanders of a space station or repair station. The rank has not been used since the period of isolation that began five hundred years prior to the events of this book.

Armada Captain: The highest extant rank within the Malik System, an Armada Captain (commonly referred to only as Captain) is the commander of a crew's entire fleet of ships. An Armada Captain sits on the Captain's Council to judge matters of importance to the fleet, and is legally obligated to assist the Starguard and defend the citizens of the Malik System.

Fleet Captain: The commander of a large vessel (heavy courier or larger), or the second-in-command of an armada. Commonly referred to only as Captain.

Sub-Captain: The commander of a smaller vessel (light courier or smaller), or the second-in-command of a large vessel.

Commander: The lowest rank of field-grade officer. Commanders tend to be staff officers and make sure the ship is running smoothly. Do not ask them about the paperwork.

Lieutenant Commander: The senior rank of company officers. Lieutenant Commanders are usually found running individual sections, flight teams, or fulfilling other necessary roles.

Lieutenant: Mid-level officers who get all the dirty work.

Lieutenant (2nd Class): The youngest and most junior officers. They are young, green and eager to work (or else).

Yeoman: Technically not an officer, but not enlisted either, the yeoman are assistants to senior-level officers. They fill an odd gap between Warrant Officers, NCOs, and everyone else. Their job is to fill in the gaps and clean up the messes.

Cadet: A trainee officer between the ages of 14 and 19. For most of the history of the Malik System, the cadets have trained at the Fleet Academy. After the Landing, the Academy was re-organized in Enclave in the training houses.

Noncommissioned Officers (NCOs) and enlisted personnel exist within the fleet structure. Unaugmented crew members (those without mechanical implants) who cannot complete the officer training at the Fleet Academy are referred to as Crew Officer, Tech, Engineer, or other ranks depending on which crew they belong to. These members of the fleet often serve as gunners, instructors, trainers and boarding parties during times of war.

1

MALCOLM

THE HYPERTRAM FROM RYUN to Kytan was running three minutes late, a silver-blue moonbeam racing across the golden desert. It was one of the little inefficiencies that made Malcolm Long hate ground travel. That and the other passengers, of course.

Waving off an offer of food from the refreshment cart, he settled into a seat on the port side of the tram and bullishly stared out the window as they rushed across the barren rock between the city-states.

High overhead, a shining Koenig-1-11 caught the sunlight as it turned for a landing in Dreyun to the north.

Long's lips twitched into a frown as he pulled out his ever-present palm pad to take notes. The one-elevens were supposed to be phased out by now. Blue Sky Air Transport had been sold off six weeks ago to Lethe, and Lethe was replacing the one-elevens with the Koenig-360, a plane with a fabulous interior and fuel consumption that made him wince.

He assumed that was why Lethe had contacted his offices two days ago to request this meeting. They were paying for his travel, and had offered a consulting fee that was generous without being obscene.

The whole set-up made the hair on the back of his neck stand up.

Senior engineers at small research firms did not generally get attention like this. Especially since he hadn't published anything in over a year. His team had been busy, and he'd been juggling too many projects to finish anything of substance.

If this was about the Koenig-360s, he could handle the matter in a couple of weeks. If it wasn't...

An old fear clawed up his throat.

For a moment the crowded tram was silent, devoid of oxygen, cold as the dark between stars. Memories of pain and rage threatened to destroy him. His heart raced as he fought the fear. Pulled it under. Drowned it in the memories of today.

That had been another life.

Another name.

A time of power and cruelty—because the two always went hand in hand. But it was the past. He'd left the islands and there was no way Lethe could know who he had been.

Lips twitching into a grim smile, he checked his watch as the rocks gave way to the cultivated terraces of Kytan. Red rock formations ringed what were laughably called terraformed plateaus, bordered first with grain crops dividing the desert from the cultivated countryside, and then the land rippled inward past pools of pale pink water lilies, and into a sea of blue-green iridescent irises that sparkled like a dragonfly's wing.

Kytan was famous for the blooms that appeared for six weeks during the height of the Descent wedding season. Right now, the city-state was overflowing with tourists who wanted to wander the parks and young couples taking engagement photos for next summer.

The tram went straight to the hanging gardens hiding the terraced buildings at the heart of the city. The air was cooler there under the shade of the vines, effervescent with the scent of falling water, and the crowd hurried past him to catch the city transports while he walked, briefcase in hand, along a stream-lined road.

The artisinal waterway was filled with silvery-blue fish that swam through the sun-dappled water against the current flowing down from the step pyramids at the city center.

The original home of the Imperial Governor of Malik IV, designed to match the legendary summer palace of Emperor Insei Qui the Third, the pyramids in the center of the city were an architectural wonder, covered in towering waterfalls and fronds and vines of greenery. Great stone mountains built in the desert plain and covered with a deep green jungle, with flowers of brilliant white and pink burning along the branches like captured stars. The whole city sparkled like the dead emperor's scepter, exactly as the first arrivals from the old Empire had hoped.

"A thousand years of freedom and still we bow," Long murmured to himself. He couldn't remember the rest of the poem now, but he remembered when he'd first heard it, in the halls at school spoken by a girl who'd both captivated and challenged him.

She would have appreciated the architecture of Kytan. Probably had the opportunity to, considering her family and wealth.

Or perhaps not.

With the powerful families on the first continent, it all depended on who you knew and who you were allied with.

The Longs were a small family with no allies, unless his mother's book club friends counted, which he personally didn't feel they needed to. A family name, the right genes, a pittance of an inheritance, and an acre of land somewhere out in the wilds between city-states. It had been enough to get his family off the islands along the edge of the second continent and earn him a scholarship to the most prestigious university, but it wouldn't keep him alive if the Lethes wanted him dead.

Especially not here in their capital city.

"I suppose I should have asked for a bodyguard," he muttered to himself. One of the lab interns had the height and reach to be a good shield—but also the personality of a frightened rabbit, which might have made the graceless man more a liability than an asset.

Long followed the streams to the step pyramid and walked up the wide steps until he reached the main entrance. The arched glass doors opened into a chilled atrium, where the light passing through the waterfalls outside rippled and splashed over the dark marble floor.

Jewel-colored hummingbirds zipped past, chasing each other to the background music of a drowsy orchestral melody.

He felt he should applaud the theatrics, but restrained himself instead to a small half-smile.

The Lethes didn't sound like the kind of people who would enjoy his sense of humor.

A man in the Lethe colors of deep purple and slate gray approached him, white hair slicked back to an opalescent sheen. "May I help you, sir?"

"Doctor Malcolm Long. I have an appointment."

"Certainly, sir. If you'll please follow me."

He gestured to a bank of black lifts behind a discreet marble reception desk. The greeter stepped around and peered at a screen that Long had the good manners not to peek at.

Or at least not to get *caught* peeking at.

"You're a few minutes early, sir," the greeter said, glancing up at him with a moue of censure.

"My apologies. I have the day free if you would like me to wait." He must have rushed. *And now I look too eager*, he berated himself. On time was on time. Eager looked weak. Late was disrespectful. It was these little social mores that kept the culture of Descent afloat.

The greeter shook his head. "No, I apologize, sir. The computer recalculated the time based on the tram delay. You have arrived on schedule, but a few minutes later would have been acceptable as well. If you'll take lift number seven, sir, it will take you to your meeting room."

That wasn't much information to go on.

Today's invitation had come from Lethe Corp, but without a signature. It was one of the annoying habits of the business people on the first continent that they used to keep their rivals guessing. Not knowing who he was meeting with meant he couldn't study or prepare for the meeting, not unless he wanted to study the several hundred middle managers, division leads, and board members.

He stepped into the mirrored elevator and tried to avoid glancing at his reflection, afraid he'd catch himself glaring and remember what a bad idea it was to get caught up in the machinations of political fanatics.

The mirror image glared back anyway.

For good reason, too; he should have worn a touch of Lethe purple somewhere to show a willingness to work together. The dark gray suit with a white shirt was a little too neutral. Long jerked the edge of one cuff straighter, an expression of annoyance tugging at his lips. He suppressed that too. This was a stupid risk to take. But declining, he suspected, would have proven fatal.

The door to the lift opened to a long, wide room with a row of slit windows overlooking the city. The only furniture was a white stone desk, carved to look like it had grown out of the stone floor. The walls were lined with silent waterfalls that pooled around the edge of the room, filled with small green reeds that had either been genetically engineered for the poor lighting or were fake; he couldn't tell at this distance.

At the desk, a woman was silhouetted by the window light, her pale hair swept up into a coiling, sleek up-do and held in place by a pin with a dripping chain of amethysts that matched her silk shirt. She was framed by the jungle outside, a pale diamond in the city of jewels. The effect was stunning, albeit contrived.

Long waited in front of the lift for her to acknowledge him as a dark suspicion formed.

Several minutes crept by before the woman finished her work, turned off her screen and stood. Recessed lights in the ceiling turned on as she moved, spotlighting Sonya Lethe, the sole heir of the Lethe fortune.

Fear crawled down his spine with cold fingers.

This is what a fish feels like when it sees a shark. I always wondered.

"Doctor Long, please, come in," she said from behind the desk. "I'm delighted you could make time in your schedule to come to Kytan today."

"The delight is mine," he said, repeating the proper polite phrasing. "I've been looking for an excuse to come to Kytan."

"Wedding season," Sonya said with a slink of a smile. "Is there someone you were hoping to show the flowers to?"

"Much to my mother's dismay, there is not."

Sonya walked around her desk and perched on the front edge. "Yes, she is Nettie Amherst of the Northland Amhersts, isn't she?"

"The last of that line to bear the Amherst name, yes." Sonya had done her homework, both a threat and a show of strength. Or maybe she thought it put them on equal footing. After all, any schoolchild raised on Descent could name the Lethe heirs back to the first ship.

"Perhaps your future spouse will see fit to revive the name. Long is...." She pursed her lips as she looked him up and down in an appraising way. "...Perhaps a little generic?"

He let the insult pass with a smile. "My father says it's a dialect word from the Grizhjan System meaning 'dragon'. I make it a rule never to argue translations with a linguist."

Sonya laughed. It was a calculated move, the arch of her neck, the degree of her smile, the uplift of her breasts, all mathematically designed to hide the fact that the muscles around her eyes never moved. She wasn't amused, she was manipulating him.

There were few things in the world that felt worse.

Long waited her out. Social graces did not require him to laugh along with her, so he didn't.

"Doctor Long, you look so grim. I do not like grim faces at business."

"Forgive me, Miss Lethe, I wasn't sure what response you anticipated. My name is not often a topic of conversation."

She smiled with an apologetic head tilt. "Engineers. You're always so delightfully focused, aren't you?"

"It's been mentioned before."

"Excellent." Sonya nodded. "Focus, I believe, is something this project needs. Please, take a seat." She brushed her hand along a control set in the stone desk and a chair materialized to one side, perfectly set to give the occupant a view of both the city and Sonya at their best angles.

Long regarded the chair with quiet suspicion. It was a trap, that much was obvious, but he wasn't sure exactly what kind.

Days like this, he thought about throwing it all away and moving back to the islands.

But then he'd never be able to fly again. And flying again was the only reason he kept breathing. Everything else was lost to him, but maybe, one day, he could reclaim the sky.

"It's quite safe," Sonya assured him as she took her own seat behind the desk. "The matter transporter is something new our research and development team is working on. It could replace all travel one day."

All the more reason to hate it.

Aloud he said, "I'd heard of research along those lines, but I thought we were decades away from a breakthrough." Unless someone was getting tech from the space fleet that had landed on the third continent. He, like most people, wasn't privy to the fine details of the treaty the planetary representative had signed with them, but he felt certain the tech they'd brought with them was off limits.

"This can only move objects a few feet. But it is fun to bring a chair in from the closet at the touch of a button. There's an awe factor I appreciate." She sat back with a smug smile, the empress on her throne.

"I can imagine." He took a seat and dutifully surveyed the view of the city.

Sonya sat in the chair across from him, blonde hair framed by the shimmering blue flowers. "Tell me, Doctor Long, do you have your father's gift for languages?"

The question blindsided him and he let a frown slip. "No. Some, I suppose. I speak all the regional cants of the first and second continents and can read the Journals Of

Discovery in the original Imperial Script, but that's a talent any well-educated person on Descent can boast of." Especially since the dialects only changed a handful of slang terms between all of them. Calling them languages was a bit of an insult to the idea of diversity, really.

"You claim to have no gift for languages, but you broke the hardest cipher we know while at university." She laughed. "What a shame everyone isn't as lacking in gifts."

"Ah," he said, shrugging one shoulder in dismissal. "Cryptography is a ghost from my misguided youth." And he hadn't broken the cipher alone. The key to the whole thing had been in an obscure text his classmate had found.

Technically, he should have credited her, but that would have required finding her after the move to Descent, and he hadn't had the resources. And she was unlikely to want to speak to him ever again anyway.

"I work exclusively in aeronautical science now. That was why I thought you'd called me in, to solve the fuel efficiency problems with the Koenig-360?" He let the opening dangle.

Sonya waved the comment aside. "Planes are relics. We can burn all the fuel we want. In a few years the new matter transporters will be the foundation of Lethe's transportation division. Let the Koenigs fly. This project is much more time sensitive." She held up a datcube, black and small enough to be concealed in his fist.

Long raised an eyebrow in question.

"This belonged to one of my employees. At the time of his death he had no heir, so the data became company property."

How convenient for Lethe.

"My techs have been able to decrypt a portion of the data on here, but the rest is beyond them. We've applied to other experts Lethe already has a working relationship with, but neither were able to decrypt it. Both experts mentioned you." She held the datcube out to him.

It was heavier than its size suggested. Someone had coated it in the anti-theft paint that had been popular for the past two years—which meant it wasn't too old to be recoverable—but on one side he felt an indentation, as if someone had pierced the cover with a fingernail.

It was all too easy to picture the previous owner holding this in a death grip in their final moments.

A sense of inevitable dread settled over him. It had been a mistake accepting the Lethe's offer. A mistake to be found on their radar at all. If he couldn't untangle himself—quickly—he would undoubtedly meet the same fate as the dat-cube's luckless owner.

"Have you considered the possibility that the information is corrupted?" Long asked. "I can guess which experts you would speak to, and who would recommend me, and there's very little I could do that they wouldn't have. There's no point in wasting your time if the data isn't salvageable."

Sonya shrugged. "I give it a twelve percent chance of being corrupted. It might be a keyed cypher, but the balance of probability says it's most likely an encryption."

"And the data?"

"Time sensitive only because of the employee's death."

A thin thread of hope appeared. "I realize it's tactless to ask, but is this datcube part of an ongoing investigation into that death? My clearance for several of my projects requires me to steer clear of the Jhandarmi and all local constabulary." *Please say yes.*

Sonya gave him another calculated smile, this one undoubtedly meant to make her look innocent and charming. "The employee died because of a burst heart. The coroner ruled it death of natural causes."

The coroners of Descent would rule a stab wound death by natural causes if the right people asked. It was a line of thought he didn't dare to follow. "The best I can offer is to look at the encryption. Without seeing it I can't tell you anything more."

"Can you have a status report to me by the end of the week?" Sonya asked with a polite smile that said 'No' wasn't an acceptable answer.

Three days to unlock the datcube and analyze the contents was a tight timeline if he wanted to focus on his other work, but it was doable. He nodded. "A status report, but nothing more. Do you have a copy of the cube that I can take with me?"

Her lips slipped into an uncharacteristic grimace. "That is our only copy."

"Ah." He set it down on the desk between them. "That makes security problematic."

"Your lab is secure?" she asked.

"The research lab is, but the outer office is designed with client comfort in mind."

Sonya nodded in understanding. "The datcube will be sent by armed courier. Lethe can offer you the standard security fee for priority technology as well as a consultant fee." She twisted the screen on her desk he could see the numbers.

Standard fees, nothing that raised any red flags, although the whole affair seemed suspect.

"If you are able to decode the data, there will be a sizable bonus. Have you ever worked with Lethe before?"

"I've never had the pleasure." Just as he'd never had the pleasure of being burned alive before. It was one of those little life-threatening things he'd made sure to avoid.

She pulled a paper contract from her desk drawer. "This is our consulting contract. While working on this project, you are not considered a Lethe employee and will not receive shares, benefits, or protections from Lethe. You will be paid commensurate to your skill level, and at the rate agreed. The contract terminates automatically after six weeks, unless both parties agree to extend the contract. Before, during, and after this project you are forbidden from disclosing the focus of the project with anyone other than your Lethe contact. Do you have any questions?"

Long looked over the paperwork. "Do you have the work of the previous groups that tried to decrypt this cube?"

"Would it be useful?" Sonya tilted her head.

"Knowing what they tried and what failed will save me time." And it would tell him who she had trusted.

Another small frown. "The other experts said they didn't want to be influenced by other people's processes." There was a hit of censure in her tone.

"We all approach work differently," he said. "I will probably look at it before reviewing their notes, but I don't feel the need to reinvent the wheel. Appearing like a genius to the world usually involves standing on the backs of geniuses who came before. It's how I did the decryption that I published in university."

Sonya gave a small nod, but he could see that she'd deducted a few points from the imaginary tally. "In that case, I'll make their work available to you. The records and a machine to process it on will arrive tomorrow. It goes without saying that everything stored on the computer becomes the property of Lethe after the contract is over."

"Of course." He made a mental note to scrub the machine for spyware and keep it away from his work lab and notes when it arrived. Lethe hadn't made their empire by playing fair.

Sonya stood up. "Then all is in order."

Following her lead, he stood too.

She posed, probably trying to look seductive. "I look forward to working with you, Doctor Long."

"And I look forward to working with you." As much as he looked forward to being eaten alive by ant lions. It was a trap, and the only way to escape was to move forward. If he could get Sonya the information maybe—just maybe—he'd escape with his life.

2
ROWENA

ROWENA STEPPED BACK, DODGING her attacker's punches. He was unbalanced, feet spread too wide on the green training mat, leaning on his shield and hers.

So she dropped her shield for a millisecond.

Stepped right.

Brought a new shield up as he fell.

She dropped in for the kill.

Her opponent rolled, using his larger body mass to grab her and pin her with her arms over her head.

Hollis Silar grinned down at her in victory. Dark red hair slicked with sweat framed a chiseled face with a patrician nose and wide, golden brown eyes filled with delight.

The foolish boy thought the fight was over.

With a little growl, and a tight smile, Rowena backed up. Using the telekyen in the mats that allowed for tech-assisted telekinesis, she flipped Silar off her.

He stepped away, reassessing the situation. Sunlight streaming through the large cargo bay door highlighted a tanned and freckled body made of carved muscle. He'd lost his shirt, earlier, tossing it aside as the training gym grew warm, leaving only a pair of black running shorts to work out in. Silar chuckled, cocky and sure of himself as always. He should have known better.

Rowena followed, catching him with a flurry of punishing kicks and punches that pushed him to the edge of the training ring, where slack-jawed cadets stood watching.

Silar punched, but she pivoted away.

Her gray knife came out, and she tapped him twice on the side of the neck.

"Combatant down." The deep, male voice of the gym computer echoed around the training facility.

Rowena nodded. "And, with that, there's one less enemy in the world."

Several of the cadets snickered. A few red-headed Silars crossed their arms and scowled.

"Now, that wasn't a real fight. You can tell by a couple of things. First, no bruises." She stood up and held up her forearms.

Silar followed suit.

"We both had training shields up, so no one was injured. Second, what would we do in a real fight? Besides kill each other?"

The cadets, the fleet's new officer-candidates, stared at her mutely. Three weeks into drilling them on close-quarters combat, and still they sat there like she was a holovid for their entertainment.

She sighed. "Guardian Silar, can you help the cadets out?"

"If this were a real fight, we would have worked to take down our opponent's shield," Silar said with an infuriatingly calm but cheerful voice that masked every emotion and drove her mad. One day, she hoped to rattle his hull as much as he rattled hers.

The man destroyed her peace of mind. If he would just vanish—or if she could just use the knife while she had it at his throat—life would be simpler.

Rowena nodded, keeping her thoughts in check. "In a real fight, the shields would probably spark." Spinning, she turned and stabbed at Silar with a dull practice knife. A flurry of green and blue sparks flew off their shields as they clashed, and the knife stayed in mid-air when she released it. "Pretty enough, but useless. What you need to do is take down your enemy's shield."

It took thought and focus, but she had Silar's shield now—he'd finally repeated the cycle. She forced it to break, feeling it crack in her mind and kicked his feet out from under him so he landed on the mats with a thump. She dropped, one knee on his bare chest and a knife at his throat. "That's how you kill someone."

Silar grinned and put his hands behind his head like he'd planned on lying down to relax.

A light globe appeared over one of the baby-faced cadet's heads, a virtual construct projected by the chip implants most members of Fleet had, designed to politely indicate a question.

"Yes, Cadet Daunfar?"

He blinked his tiny, dark eyes a couple of times. "How did you break the guardian's shield so quickly?"

That was one of things she'd been hoping no one noticed. Or, if they noticed, she hoped they would think it was staged. "I didn't break his shield quickly. When the guardian walked in, I started working on it." Which made her look criminally inept, because Hollis had started haunting the edges of the class over thirty minutes ago.

She rolled her eyes to the ceiling and prepared to do something she detested: compliment a Silar.

Ugh.

"Because the guardian is combat trained, he was cycling his shield, both before the fight started, and during the fight. After the demonstration was over he dropped to a single-layer personal shield and that's what I broke."

Silar jumped to his feet in a fluid move that had half the class gawking and the other class mentally stripping his shorts.

"How many times did you cycle your shields?" Rowena asked for the class's benefit.

"Thirteen times in the two minutes we were fighting," Silar said, standing at-ease beside her, and still smiling.

The urge to crack his jaw and shake that smile loose was becoming overwhelming. She'd been in the gym for four hours, working out and then training cadets, and she still had a full day of duties aboard the *Danielle Nicole*. It wasn't fair that Silar still smelled freshly showered and was completely unfazed.

"It helps if you've been trying to kill someone for the better part of a decade," Rowena said. "The random pattern generators on your shield aren't truly random. Patterns repeat. Most people will use patterns they've learned from other shields."

Another cadet's globe lit up, her blue eyes narrowing in her dark face.

"Yes, Cadet Ukuroh?"

"Is it true that you can sync shields?" The girl's voice managed to drip unsubtle suggestion while being entirely wholesome.

Silar coughed as he hid a laugh.

Rowena leaned over to him and whispered, "Is one of those books making the rounds again?"

"Yes." The guardian grinned with impish delight.

Nishu books were handwritten literature passed around the fleet, a vestigial tradition usually titillating in nature—gruesome war stories or erotic romances, it didn't matter. When one of the books got loose in the general population, it was like an uncontrolled engine fire.

At least this one wasn't about her.

Hopefully.

She rolled her eyes. "All sex-ed questions can be saved for the guardian after class. Does anyone have a question relevant to the demonstration?"

Another light, this time over a young man with dark hair and quiet, steady eyes.

"Cadet Moren?"

The boy frowned at her and Silar. "If you've been trying to kill him for so long, why isn't he dead?"

"Too many witnesses," Rowena said without thinking. "The guardian is actually intelligent enough not to meet me in a dark alley."

Silar coughed again and gave her a warning look. "And, we're at peace." There was a subtle emphasis on the last word. "The disadvantage of a long conflict is that your enemies can learn your habits, and that makes you easier to kill. It's better for everyone if we can resolve conflicts without combat." He put on an overly cheerful smile. "Right, Drill Instructor Lee?"

"Of course, Guardian Silar." She faked a smile too. "Hit the showers," she told the cadets. "You have tomorrow off, and then we'll start on paired sparring. Ancestors help us all," she added under her breath.

As the cadets ran off, Silar stayed. "That was a nice touch of bravado at the end. You're going to have the cadets looking over their shoulders after dark now, worried that DI Lee is after them."

"Good. It makes up for the fact that I have to deal with their little romance dramas. If the guardians need to know who the age seventeen cohort finds attractive, I have a list of requested sparring partners." She stretched, arching her back and trying to work loose some of the knots.

"Aw, kids." Hollis grinned. "They haven't learned that a good sparring partner is the one who actually challenges you."

Rowena nodded agreement as she picked up the dull practice knives they had been working on holding today. "Speaking of which, how'd you get tickle fight duty over here again? I thought it was Herra's turn."

Not that Meryem Herra could hold her own in a knife fight, but Silar had taken over as Rowena's training partner four months ago when her regular partner had moved to a different work shift. It was hard to imagine Silar volunteering to come see her more than required.

"Carver asked me if I wanted to roll around with a hot woman and have her hands all over my body."

Rowena snorted in amusement. "How's that working out for you?"

He didn't even bother doing the whole look-the-body-up-and-down-suggestively thing. But his brown eyes sparked gold when he smiled. "I wasn't going to say this in front of the cadets, but..." He crowded her personal space, trapping her between the raised platform of the green mats and his body, and leaned in. "If you want to caress me that much, you should at least ask me out to dinner first."

"You want a broken jaw?" Rowena demanded, throat tightening. Silar was a big bastard. Tall, with broad shoulders and a dominating presence. The smell of his sweat and his crew's oakmoss soap surrounded her. Ancestors, but he made her fists itch. "I'm more than happy to oblige. I was pulling my punches in case you forgot to shield."

"You were dropping your guard on your left side, too." His voice was low and smooth, somewhere between a threat and an invitation.

"It's called 'leaving an opening'. I didn't want you to embarrass yourself." She tossed her head and almost smacked him with her thick, black braid.

Silar sidestepped the attack, giving her an escape route. "Yeah, you left an opening so big I could have flown a squadron through it. If I get this detail when I get back, I'll take that opening."

"When you get back?" She stopped and looked at him in confusion. "Where are you going?"

"Ah, that's something I needed to talk to you about. I'm headed to the Jhandarmi survival training in the mountains. Sciarra said you'd done it." Silar grinned apologetically. "Want to tell me what torture the grounders have planned?"

She dumped the practice knives in the cleaning bin and shrugged. "It's pretty easy stuff I guess. You're supposed to use your implant as little as possible, because if you're trapped anywhere on this planet it's because your implant is broken and you can't teleport home. Well..." She shrugged. "For me. I don't know what your teleport range is." It was a not-so-subtle dig.

"Far enough that I could get home from the mountains on minimal power."

Ugh. Of course he could.

"But don't use it to balance hormones or keep your muscles going," Rowena continued. "That's the main difference. Half of fleet have their nanites cleaning up lactic acid and they can't turn their implant off without getting sore in an hour or two."

He nodded, probably taking notes with his implant.

"Other than that, I don't know what to tell you. The instructor I had was good looking. The grounders were friendly enough until they figured out what crew I was from. You won't have that problem."

"Were they rude?" he asked, a touch of warning in his voice. The guardians could be very prickly about perceived insults to the fleet.

She shook her head. "No more so than anyone I meet. The Lees aren't going to be popular again in this generation. That's our fault for backing the Baulars and being Warmongers. In hindsight it was a bad move, but with the intel we had at the time, that was the only choice to make. It's life. We made mistakes. We're getting punished for it."

Her more than the rest of the crew, but that was a different matter.

Silar didn't look too pleased with her analysis. "The Sciarras are back on track," Hollis said, referring to the black-skinned, green-eyed Warmonger crew known for their lethal knives.

Her best friend, Titan, had been second-in-command there until he'd married Captain Selena Caryll, breaking the strict delineation between Allied crews like the Silars and Warmongers like the Lees.

"Their crews don't have Hoshi Lee as captain," she said, and then regretted it. That was crew business. "And the grounders don't care. They gave me extra stuff to carry, didn't talk to me much, but that was it. They weren't cruel."

Rowena sat down on the edge of the training ring, trying to remember anything useful. Hating Silar was as natural as breathing, but he was still fleet, it went against all her training to send him to enemy territory unprepared. "The worst part of the survival training is the quiet. I thought sleeping outside would be bad, and it is, it feels like a hull breach and the first night you'll have trouble sleeping. But the quiet is the worst. No crew checking in, no information adding to your implant, no sense that someone is nearby."

She stared at the now-empty gym and shivered at the memory. "The grounders like it. They say they enjoy the space. But to someone born in the fleet? It was torture. Not the worst two weeks of my life, but I didn't enjoy it. I could do all the physical stuff, but mentally being away from everyone?" She shook her head.

Silar grimaced. "I'm only going for a week."

"And the grounders will probably talk to you." It seemed Hollis Silar could get along with just about anyone, except her. They weren't exactly at each other's throats the way they'd been in their younger years, but they were light-years away from being friends. The best she could hope for—from anyone—was tolerance. Friendship and family were things lost to her for good.

Hollis sat beside her, shield to shield, just another way of turning every moment into a competition. He wanted to make her flinch. The gym was her domain: if she left first, he won. "So, now that I've made you miserable, are you going to the flight show this afternoon?"

"Um, no." She laughed as she forced herself to stay close. "I have cleaning duty and a 2000 curfew."

He frowned. "What? A curfew?"

"One of the crew is courting, so everyone the captain has listed as a trouble maker is on curfew and extra duty so we don't embarrass her."

Silar bumped her shoulder with his, invading her space. "Ah, come on. You might be trouble, but you're a fun kind of trouble." There was a gleam in his eye. The one that had seduced half the fleet into falling for his charms. She'd never quite understood why, but people loved Hollis Silar as easily as they hated her.

"Really?" She glared at his shoulder until he scootched away. Point to her. "You want to do survival training with broken bones?"

Voices of cadets returning from the showers saved Silar from whatever idiotic thing he was about to say.

He looked over her head with an expression of minor panic, then back at her. "All right. Kiss me!" Another intoxicating smile hit her at full force.

And bounced off her shields. Rowena raised her eyebrows. "Excuse me?"

"Before the cadets get here, kiss me. Otherwise I'll have children following me around all day peppering me with questions about how erotic shields can get." He nodded. "Right now. Please."

She laughed. An honest-to-ancestors belly laugh. "Oh. I wish I had the day free to follow you around and watch this." She stood up, still laughing. "Poor Hollis," she said mockingly, pretending to reach for him. "Chased by teens with raging hormones and zero common sense! Whatever shall you do with all that adoration?"

His teeth champed together as he snapped his jaw shut and scowled. "Lee..." He put a spin of menace on her name.

"You're on your own, fly boy." She walked away.

Silar took the escape route of many a trapped fleet officer and teleported away before the cadets could catch him.

They'd dressed for flirtation, summer skirts and light shirts purchased in the grounder city of Tarrin outside Enclave. Several of the girls had their hair loose. One had gone so far as to dry her hair and give it a bit of curl.

For a minute, Rowena tried to picture herself in the grounder clothes, her black hair falling free. It didn't work. Skirts never had enough pockets and loose hair got caught in gears. Impractical had never been her style, even if it was a good way to attract attention these days.

The younger generation—the ones who had been too young to fight in the war—were finally realizing they were going to grow up here. Groundside. The ships parked in the

Enclave like a forest of metal fungi and the stars out of reach.

They seemed okay with it. Even if most crews insisted they learn basic combat skills before being allowed to go to the university in the city.

Who knew? In another year or two maybe one of them would get adventurous and venture outside Tarrin to one of the other city-states on the planet. They might even be welcome on the first continent, Descent, if they were from the right crew and the grounders solved their housing problems.

But there would never be a home for her on this planet.

She sighed. After her students left, she did a final sweep of the training gym and headed back to the *Danielle Nicole*, the Lee flagship—and her home.

The late summer sun was pleasantly hot on her face as she walked from the gym to the shade of the smaller ships that made the outer ring of each crews' territory. They towered over her, obscuring the sunlight as she walked past landing gear wide as a grounder car and taller than most the buildings in the nearby city of Tarrin.

There was a hint of brine in the air from the rocky seashore at the edge of Enclave that was slowly washing away the metallic scent of space travel. If she could, she'd find a way to escape to the *Danielle Nicole's* outer hull so she could enjoy the sunshine, stretch out on the hull and let the heat work out some of the aches from training. There was probably a sensor there that needed fixing. Or she could break one. It wasn't like anyone else on the crew knew how to run her ship.

They'd made her a Yeoman as punishment. Stripped her of rank and made her a runner for the whole crew. But she'd still managed to take over engineering. Eventually, she'd find a way to take over the rest of the ship.

The problem wasn't the recent war, as everyone outside the crew assumed. The problem was that the Lee crew had been fundamentally split for the better part of the century. Her parents had been on one side, aggressive and totalitarian. The Captain had been on the other side.

Hoshi was quiet, slow to show others what he was thinking, with mercurial moods that changed as easily as the weather and a penchant for holding grudges.

That was what no one else understood.

It didn't matter what she did. It didn't matter if she were the best engineer or pilot in the fleet or if she sat in the bilge drinking shanty, Hoshi hated her parents, so he hated her. And everyone from his side of the family hated her.

She'd never be promoted. Never be recognized. Never escape. It was as hard to swallow as broken glass, but what other choice was there?

The war had left most her family and friends dead. Those who had survived treated her like a jinx—except for Titan Sciarra. But he'd gone off, become a guardian, and fallen in love with Selena Caryll, of all people. She'd feel utterly betrayed if he wasn't so disgustingly happy.

"Happiness." She tasted the word and it was as alien as the planet she was living on.

She let the thought go as the angular shadow of the *Danielle Nicole* fell between her and the sun like the maw of an abyssal beast. Home sweet home.

Ish.

The ramp was being watched by Minsu, a third-cousin on her mother's side and not in Hoshi's good graces. He sighed in relief as he saw her and ran over to Rowena on the rocky path. "The captain's looking for you with war on his mind."

She checked her internal clock. "I'm less than sixty seconds behind my normal schedule. What broke?"

"Nothing. You have a visitor."

"Minsu!" Captain Hoshi's bellow echoed from the shadows.

Her cousin grimaced and ran back to his post.

Rowena trudged after him.

It was a shame Titan was over on Descent, in the completely wrong time zone to make bets with, because she was betting Hoshi was going to lend her out to someone. If nothing was broken on a Lee ship, that's where she wound up, spending hours in the bowels of someone else's vessel. This time of year it was usually to repair an environmental coil and keep the ship from turning into an oven.

"Yeoman Lee!" Hoshi stood at the top of ramp, hands on hips.

He wasn't an ugly man, despite his personality. He'd probably been considered quite handsome in his younger years, when his black hair had less gray. He wasn't tall, but none of the Lees were, and he was taller than she was. But the years of scowling had taken their toll and now his face was a wrinkled prune of disapproval.

"Captain?" She saluted, hiding all of her thoughts behind a blank stare and a heavy shield.

"You're late."

"I apologize, sir."

"There's a minister from Tarrin waiting for you in the main war room. Teleport there immediately and apologize to him for your tardiness."

Rowena snapped a second salute. "At once, sir."

"Dismissed."

She blinked out of Hoshi's reach and landed in the empty grey metal corridor outside the war room. Teleporting in on grounders tended to startle them, and if this one was already insulted because she was running on schedule and didn't know about an unscheduled appointment, they were probably the kind of person who would feel insulted if they were startled.

Thankfully, she pushed the door open and instead of finding a Tarrin politician, she found the Jhandarmi regional director. He was a bullish man with a shaved head and a permanent expression of mild surprise.

Despite all that, she liked him. "Tyrling."

"Agent Lee." He nodded and went back to picking things out of the ornamental fruit bowl. He held up a green orb with a dark interior. "What do you think this is supposed to be?"

"Winkli fruit from the Gewfyn System. One of the plants was given to a Lee captain seventeen hundred years ago as a wedding gift. There was one growing in the hydroponic gardens of the *Ginger Kerrick* until she was shot down in the first war. The only other vessel known to carry the fruit was actually the space station *Eden,* last seen over six-hundred years ago when the fleet and the planet chose isolation."

Tyrling chuckled. "That's what I like about you, Lee. I ask a simple question and you have an encyclopedic answer. Most of the Jhandarmi would simply say: fake."

"I thought you could figure that out on your own." She took a seat at the polished metal conference table and put her feet up. "Pardon the sweat, I just finished teaching cadets how to hold fake knives."

"How's that going?" he asked as he took a seat opposite.

"They won't survive a real fight with anyone who fought in the war. But maybe that's the point? We train them enough that they don't get killed in a park, but not so much that they can actually hurt anyone."

He smiled. "Well, they're young yet. Right?"

"Seventeen."

"Most people haven't had to fight to the death at seventeen."

Rowena kept her mouth shut. The infighting on the Lee ships had been so fierce in her younger years that going to the Academy had seemed like a vacation. For her, the war started when she was ten.

Tyrling's eyebrows went up. "I won't ask."

"And I won't tell."

They smiled at each other in understanding.

"So," she said, "what does the Jhandarmi want with the fleet's least favorite person today?"

"Oddly enough, since we're talking about death, I need you to come examine a corpse."

Rowena shook her head. "I'm an engineer with flight training, not medical training. I can *make* corpses but I don't do anything past that."

Tyrling waved a hand. "I know, but in this case my coroner is stumped. I want you to come in for weapons identification."

"I'm assuming you want me to tell you what killed this person instead of identifying a gun they're holding?"

"Right."

She sighed. "How soon do you need me?"

"Within the hour if possible. The gentleman's family is coming in from their home town and we'll need to release the body in the next twenty-six hours. I've cleared it with your captain, if that helps."

"It does. Immensely. Uniform?"

Tyrling winced apologetically. "I don't suppose you have something in your wardrobe that screams 'Distinguished Scholar', do you?"

She didn't hide her grimace. "Do scholars wear coveralls with a lot of pockets?"

"No."

"Then no. But I can get something from the guardian's day-trip wardrobe."

Tyrling smiled, and as he stood pulled a paper card from his pocket. "Coordinates for the Tarrin morgue, since I assume you'll teleport there."

Rowena nodded. "Do you need a lift out?"

"No, thank you. I have to stop by the OIA and check in with Marshall and Carver. The guardians have volunteered to help with crowd control at the air show, which means the Tarrin police force is giddy and trying to prove they've got bigger balls, which means there'll be a Jhandarmi presence to keep everyone in line. We don't expect trouble, but there's more than one group pushing for Tarrin to reclaim the spare building material going to waste in Enclave."

"The what now?" Rowena almost laughed. There wasn't spare space to *use* any spare building material in Enclave. Some of the crews had run out of ground and landed their smaller shuttles on the upper hulls of their warships in an effort to house the growing population. There was nothing for the grounders to reclaim.

Tyrling nodded to the bulkhead. "The hulls. One of your large warships could be the seed for a decent sized city-state. They hold a lot of people."

"I know, they're holding people now." The largest warships were still in orbit, and they could hold well over a hundred thousand people. The largest ones in Enclave could hold a third of that.

"How many of them are half empty?"

"None," Rowena said a touch defensively. She knew Tyrling had worked with the fleet long enough to respect them, but he needed the facts so he could argue on their behalf. "Even if they were, they belong to people. They're dowries and futures. They can be repaired."

Tyrling tilted his head to the side. "But they'll never fly again."

Rowena's chest tightened. "They will."

"How will you do that without fuel?" His brows drew together.

"It's a problem I'm addressing."

The door opened without warning and Hoshi stepped in. He nodded politely to Tyrling, and scowled at her. "I assume you've some new excuse to avoid work today."

Rowena stood. "No, sir. I can refuse the request for assistance from the Jhandarmi." It wasn't like her rank with them was official. They'd offered, but Hoshi saw it as an insult to his family line that Tyrling hadn't offered one of them the job.

"Is loaning Rowena to us a problem?" Tyrling asked.

The captain's mouth twisted with disgust. "Not at all." His look could have frozen a star. "When you return, I expect you to clean sections C and D to repay the crew for your absence."

"Yes, sir. Of course, sir." She saluted.

With a sniff of disapproval, Hoshi walked out.

Tyrling made a noise of disagreement. "Charming man, your captain. If this is too much of a problem, I can get someone else to look into it."

"It's not," Rowena assured him. "Hoshi just likes throwing his weight around. It's nothing I can't handle." She clicked her tongue. "About those arguments for seizing Enclave..."

"It'll be handled," Tyrling promised. "We might have a housing crisis, but we're not going to solve it by stealing homes from the fleet. I know that. So do most people when they stop to think about it. But scared people say stupid things."

She nodded. "If it comes up, try to find a way to politely remind the grounders that the fleet will go to war before they give up their ships. No one wins in that scenario."

Tyrling nodded in agreement.

With a smile instead of a salute, Rowena said, "If that's all you need, I'll go change for the morgue."

"See you soon," Tyrling said.

Rowena teleported to the safety of the engine room and stared at the wall where she'd carved the names of her dead family. Hoshi wouldn't allow their names on the memorial in the quiet rooms at the heart of the ship. He said they were traitors. That she was a traitor.

They would understand her choices though. Survival was the only thing that mattered now. Whatever she had to do, whoever she had to work with, it was worth every sacrifice. The engine room—*her* engine room—was where the work got done, where she kept the crew running through back-channel trades and calling in old war favors. Hoshi took the credit, but it was her name that kept the Lees alive.

Her deal with the Jhandarmi was more of the same. They were allies now, and keeping them strong meant the crew would weather whatever political storm was brewing on the horizon.

They had to. She'd couldn't lose anything more without losing her mind.

3
HOLLIS

IF HOLLIS HAD KNOWN AT SIXTEEN that acing a tactics exam would catch him a lifetime of paperwork and organizing in the fleet, he would have skipped the test and taken up dishwashing duty. Ancestors bless Perrin Carver, he was a good man but he had the organizational skills of a concussed walrus. The sheer amount of files sitting on the desk waiting to be sorted made Hollis's eye twitch.

His oversized, transparent black desk with three screens were drowning in stacks of color-coded datfiles. More of them were marked red for Priority than he cared to count. The space behind his chair had been filled with lockers of things Perrin felt were important but that the commander didn't want cluttering his own office. Weapons. Restraints. Spare parts for various computers.

But oddly no blankets. Perrin had taken those away after he caught Hollis napping on the long black couch that took up the second wall.

The other two walls were tinted windows that let him look into the Guardian's bullpen. Right now, the labyrinth of underground tunnels the Starguard used as office space was quiet.

Hollis triggered the Guardian Veil program on his implant to count life signs. Two junior techs were down in the gym, there was a squad meeting in the secondary bullpen, and that was it for the underground. Upstairs, the OIA offices were lively, filled with crew filing reports and collecting passes to the air show.

But there wasn't a single peon he could dump the paperwork on.

He checked the time on his implant and wondered if it was too late to chase Lee down and pick a fight. It would get him away from the desk work and it would be fair payment for siccing the cadets on him. Plus, he'd have the pleasure of getting a reaction out of cold-as-dark Rowena Lee.

The Silar cadets were keeping a running tally of her sneers and eye rolls. If any of them got a tight-lipped smile from her, they'd consider it a momentous victory.

Lee had given him a smile on the sparring mat. Granted, it was the only warning at all that she was going to break free and try to snap his spine. But, all things considered, this was progress. A year ago, there wouldn't have been a warning.

"Guardian Silar!" one of the junior guardians screamed from the front desk as a door slammed at the top of the stairs. "Guardian!"

Hollis rolled his eyes skyward and wondered if anyone would notice if he accidentally force-teleported a junior officer to vacuum.

Guardian Tejan opened the door to Hollis's office, heart-shaped face suffused with panic. "Sir, we have a problem up front."

Hollis sighed as the smell of fried chicken and lime soap wafted in. The Tejans were Silar allies. Making her vanish would cause trouble. "What kind of problem?"

"Vaneer is arguing with a woman up at the front desk. She's requesting a day-pass from him but her crew doesn't have her listed. She's asking to speak to you." Tejan's face was wrinkled with more worry than the situation sounded like it merited.

"Is she a pretty woman? A cadet? Someone I shouldn't talk to?"

"She threatened to leave Vaneer smeared across the tile and give his eyeballs to his captain if he didn't find you immediately."

"Hmmm. Off-hand I can only think of two women in fleet likely to make that threat and follow up on it. It's not Marshall, is it?"

"No, sir. She's, um, a Lee I think? Maybe a Gonbar. Short, black hair, round face."

From up at the front desk, Guardian Vaneer pinged Hollis's implant with a panic code.

"I'll go check." Walking through the office would waste precious seconds, so he teleported, stepping directly from his office to the front desk.

The offices had once been the main hub of all interstellar trade in the Malik system, a spaceport capable of refitting gravity-capable warships while unloading new settlers and running a major trading port. At the height, the spaceport had seen thousands of people and hundreds of space craft crossing the marbled floors every day.

Overhead, the summer sun came through the stained glass dome that had once been the central terminal for the Tarrin spaceport.

A small circle of blue-white light marked the edge of the Guardian's reception area. Two junior guardians stood barricaded behind a half-circle stone desk as if it could lend them the authority they needed to win this battle.

Rowena Lee was glaring down his junior guardian. She'd showered and pulled her night-black hair into a tight bun at the back of her head. All the softness she allowed during training was replaced by the olive green Lee uniform with a sculpted collar that hid and protected her neck.

Under the sharp angles of the yeoman's rank she wore on her shoulder, she wore the same faded ship's patch for the *Danielle Marie* that he'd singed during one of their battles. They'd first crossed paths when that patch was new. Back when they'd both been lean, hungry teenagers.

She'd been a few centimeters shorter, but she was the same unflinching fighter he'd first met at the Academy, hovering in Mal Baular's shadow looking for throats to slit. The Lees were still considered a minor crew back then, tech experts who made decent weapons.

Somehow, in the bowels of their monstrous warships, they'd forged her as a gift to the Baulars. To be Mal's wife and protector.

Rowena was the Warmonger's perfect weapon. Cold. Ruthless. Brutal.

Beautiful.

If she were a ship, he would have stolen her in the war. If she were a knife, she'd be at his side every hour of the day.

But instead she was his... something else. Not quite enemy. Not quite ally.

A rogue planet with no orbit, or a flaring sun, it was hard to say.

The ruling council thought they'd broken her, but he saw slips of the old Rowena still. A flash in her eyes during training that said she was thinking about killing him. A sneer on her lips that said she wanted to see him die the way his brother had.

He kept a tight shield up and walked calmly toward the front desk, waiting to see how far Rowena had slipped from civilization this time.

"Sir!" Vaneer looked like he was going to pee himself in relief. "I've told this woman twice that her captain hasn't authorized her leave." The junior guardian had the good sense to hide behind the long desk and keep his back to the long wall of windows.

"And I told your officer twice that this isn't a matter of leave." Rowena turned, arms crossed, eyes cold as the black between stars. "I'm going to the Tarrin morgue and need a shield pass."

"Depositing or picking up?" Hollis joked, trying to defuse the situation.

Lee looked unimpressed, lips moving a fraction of a millimeter into a condescending sneer. Her shield gave her ship and rank, and marked her as being on official business, which was all the junior guardian really needed to know.

Vaneer missed all that and smirked. "She threatened me, sir. Said she'd leave me all over the floor." He chuckled like that was a hilarious idea.

Hollis glared at Lee. "Really? You were going to leave me with sex-crazed cadets *and* a crime scene? That's a little unfair."

"I can bury him alive or drop him in the black with a teleport," she said blandly. "No mess. No paperwork." For Rowena that was practically pacifistic.

"You couldn't!" Vaneer protested.

:Don't kill him.: Hollis ordered Rowena over a tight, localized beam.

Rowena's jaw tightened a fraction, the only sign she'd heard him.

Grinning so he didn't yell, he walked over to Vaneer. "You see this woman? This is Rowena Lee. Put her face on your implant with a warning signal. Lee might be ranked a Yeoman right now, but she was a commander in the war, she's a decorated fighter pilot, an engineer, and one of the five most dangerous people walking around Enclave. She could kill you. More worrisome, she *would* kill you and she wouldn't apologize. If your crew complained, she might kill them too. The guardians would catch her, eventually, but we'd lose people in the fight. You don't have the firepower for this battle. The reason you're alive is because she's a nice person, not because she's weak."

Rowena took a breath and some of her softness returned, a gentling in the tightness around her eyes that said she was willing to let this insult go. "Don't lie to him, Silar. He's alive because I don't have time to play children's games."

Vaneer's eyes went wide with panic. Good. Maybe the kid would learn some survival skills.

Hollis smiled. "Thank you for your patience, Yeoman. Would you please step into my office so I can help you? Vaneer is only authorized to hand out passes for the airshow, and I understand you're not going."

He watched her closely, trying to see something. A flicker of the eye that might be regret or distress that she was not going. A glance at the passes. Any sign that there was an emotion there.

There was nothing.

If there wasn't fury and rage, there was a blank mask, a boundary he wasn't allowed to cross.

He followed her into the guardian's bullpen and waited for an explanation.

She walked into his office before she spoke. "I need a pass to Tarrin and I need something that makes me look like a Tarrin professional."

"A professional what?" Hollis sat on the edge of his desk, pushing back a stack of datfiles.

"The Jhandarmi want me to identify a weapon that was used in an apparent homicide. The family is coming to collect the body today, so I need to look like someone you would trust with the deceased and the investigation."

"What happened to the pass Sciarra gave you when you started working with the Jhandarmi? That shouldn't expire until the new year."

There was a slightest narrowing of her eyes, a hint of anger. "Captain Lee did a quarters check and said I wasn't allowed to have it."

"Your captain approved of your training with the Jhandarmi and working outside Enclave."

"He approved that, but not of me leaving Enclave without express permission each trip," Lee said, voice dangerously calm. "Captain's prerogative."

Hollis rolled his eyes. It wasn't his place to question how other crews ran, it really wasn't, but there were times he wished he had a clear shot at Hoshi Lee and an excuse to pull the trigger. It was criminally stupid to tie Rowena down to one ship. "All right. I'll get a new one ready for you. And I'll walk you down to wardrobe since I don't think anyone else here has the code."

She could probably break in if she was feeling motivated, but that wasn't something he wanted to encourage. People asked questions when he let other people break locks for convenience.

Hollis led Rowena down the hall with unmarked Eden-green doors at odd intervals. "You know, if you'd let Carver officially swear you in, they'd give you a code of your own so no one had to escort you down here."

If it were possible, the temperature around Lee dropped, but he was fairly certain the chill off her was hovering at zero Kelvin as it was. Telling her she wasn't a bother would probably make it worse. He didn't need a favor from her and he wasn't trying to curry one. So he tried to think of something else to discuss. "Have you see the new holovid going around Enclave?"

"Which one?" she asked with a hint of annoyance.

"The one the younger Daunfars smuggled in from Tarrin? One of their senior officers brought the Starguard a copy to have it checked against fleet standards."

Rowena's eyebrows went up in confusion. "We have holovid standards? I thought anything not filmed in an empty cargo bay was considered a masterpiece."

"Fleet moral standards," Hollis said loftily as he unlocked the room where the guard kept their grounder clothes.

None of them had ships with ample closet space and the since no one had gotten particularly attached to any of the styles, the lot of it had wound up moldering in a closet. It had taken the new recruits two weeks to clean, sort, and hang everything. The end result was a space nearly as large as the training gym with rows of clothing sorted by size and color. It smelled of dust and a lingering floral perfume someone had tried several weeks ago.

"What passes for fleet moral standards these days?"

"Whatever Perrin says, I guess." He turned on the light and smiled as Rowena grimaced. "Smallest sizes on the left, largest on the right."

Her lips twitched in what might have been a silent curse, but she squared her shoulders and marched to the left.

Hollis followed. "The vid was about grounders who used fleet tech to reanimate bodies. Bring them back from the dead, sort of. But then the dead attacked the living and the city burned down."

Rowena pulled a pair of heavy pants with four pockets off the rack. She paused for a moment, her black eyes staring off unseeing as she accessed her implant. There was a hint of green in her eyes, then purple.

He hid a smile. So far Rowena was the only person he knew of whose eyes glowed two distinct colors when pulling up data. He suspected she was accessing two different data bases, one public and one private, but he'd never been able to prove it. Asking wasn't likely to get him anywhere, but she always did have the best gossip.

She shook her head. "We don't have any tech capable of doing that."

"No, but it's meant to be a fun, scary movie." He held out a hand and pushed the pants back toward the rack. "That's a uniform for a dock worker."

Her lips twitched in the hint of a grimace. "Dock workers can be well-educated consultants for the Jhandarmi, can't they?"

"Try these." He offered her a pair of graceful black slacks with a matching jacket.

Rowena held it up. "I think the neckline's a little low."

One glance said that the jacket alone would reveal more skin that was practical, or than Rowena was likely to ever let anyone see and live. Still...

"Still..."

"This is business, Silar! I'm not you. I'm not trying to seduce anyone."

"I'm just saying you could if you needed to. Here," he pulled a dark gold blouse from the rack. "This should look fine with it."

Rowena regarded it skeptically. "It looks... shiny."

"Metallics are very popular in Tarrin right now. You'll look like someone with a comfortable amount of wealth, a basic understanding of classic Tarrin fashion, and it'll give you freedom of movement."

She rolled her eyes, but took the clothes and stepped behind the curtain someone had thrown up. "I am going to a morgue."

"Where the dead could rise up and attack you," he teased, listening to the sound of fabric over skin.

"Silar, if I get there and this dead person wakes up, I swear you are going to meet your ancestors a lot sooner than you planned." She stepped out, black hair falling in soft waves to her waist, a scowl etched on her face.

He ordered his implant to save that memory for later. When was reaching his second century he wanted to be able to recall this moment like the fine art it was. But not share it. "Hair up, I'd think. You don't want viscera on you."

Her hair curled up on its own, manipulated by telekyen.

It was very tempting to pull a strand loose just to see her reaction. But he quashed that. Their interactions over the past year had grown friendlier, but she looked close to her breaking point. "It looks good. Your boots work, but I think we have some office shoes on the far wall." He looked across the room, implant pulling data from the telekyen tags, until he found what he wanted. "Here. Black, with a slight heel. You can run in them and they'll give a little height."

Rowena's eyes widened at the perceived insult. "Are you saying I'm too short to examine a corpse?"

"They're weighted so you can kick in someone's head easily, and the heels give you a better reach." He grinned.

Her mouth opened with an objection then snapped shut, teeth snapping together as her jaw clenched. :You're ridiculous.:

"True. But they'll fit. So..."

Rowena took the shoes and put them on. "How do I look?"

Hair pinned up, the suit with the gold, sleeveless blouse on... She looked devastating. Dangerous. A dark goddess incarnate come to destroy the last remnants of humanity.

If she were anyone else, even another Lee, he would have tried for more than a look. But, Rowena?

"Silar? Did you die?"

"No, no... I'm trying to find a suitable response." He crossed his arms and shook his head.

"It's not that bad," she huffed, turning to look at herself from all angles. "It's not very practical, but I look like a grounder."

He measured her reach and took two steps back. "You look gorgeous."

Rowena snapped him an angry glare filled with confusion.

Hollis held up his hands to placate her. "Please remember that the grounders don't know you, they don't know your reputation, and one of them might try to approach you and flirt."

She shrugged. "So? People have flirted with me before."

"How many had broken arms after?"

"That's unfair!"

"All I'm saying is, please don't add to the morgue's collection of corpses while you're gone." He had to tease her, had to make it playful, because if Rowena realized how beautiful she was she'd run and hide again. The fleet needed her to crawl out of her shell. Needed her to be the confident, competent officer she'd been during the war. She was the strongest Warmonger still alive, and, although she didn't see it, many people in the fleet still looked to her for guidance. If Rowena could make peace with the fleet, the civil war that had broken them and brought them to die on this planet would finally end.

"Don't break any treaties. Don't break any arms. Got it." She looked up at him. "I've done the training, you know. I might step into the occasional bar brawl, but I can control my temper."

He narrowed his eyes, all thoughts of coaxing her back into fleet politics forgotten. "Occasional bar brawl? In the last month the guardians had to break up seventeen 'little brawls' you were in. You tried to take out my knee cap in one of them."

"You were off duty."

"Seventeen, Lee. Seventeen!"

"I didn't start them. Not unless you think breathing in public is enough to start a fight." She crossed her arms, the metallic shirt rippling interestingly.

In that outfit, breathing could start a fight.

"Besides," Rowena said, "that's here with the fleet, not out there with the grounders. I know when I step outside Enclave I represent the Lee crew and the fleet."

Hollis looked her over once more. Forget flirting, someone was going to fall in love if she went out like that. "I think you need to change. Maybe the dock worker uniform."

"This one is fine!"

"That, on you, is enough to bring a dead man back to life."

Rowena rolled her eyes. There was a slight twitch in her lips, the barest hint of a ghost of smile.

Mentally, he awarded himself a point.

"I'm gorgeous, Silar, but I think the dead man is likely to stay dead."

"And… the living who try to ask you out?"

"I'm on duty and, although I'm flattered, I'm not available." She held her hand up like she was taking an officer's oath. "I promise not to kill any grounders…" She put her hand down. "Unless they attack me first."

"Actual attacking though," Hollis said seriously. "Not just grabbing your shoulder to get your attention or invading your personal space."

The corner of her lips twisted up in a satisfied smirk. "We both know that I know exactly what to do with someone in my personal space."

Hollis smiled back. "Yes, but the grounders don't have shields. Cushion them as they fall, please."

A ping on his implant told him the things Rowena needed for her excursion were ready.

He snapped his fingers as he focused on what he wanted and teleported the pass card from the main office. It hung in mid-air for a second, then dropped into his hand.

"All right. Pass for the shield." He handed it to Rowena as he led her back to the main hall and locked the wardrobe door behind them.

Rowena turned the card over. "This doesn't have an expiration date."

He shrugged. "Do you know when the Jhandarmi will close the case?"

"No."

"Then it stays open. You can teleport in and out at need. And there's a shield code for you. It allows the Starguard to know which side of the shield you're on, and if someone needs to leave you an urgent message, it'll be waiting for you when you cross the shield."

"Anyone who needs to send me an urgent message can use my personal code," Rowena said.

Hollis nodded. "Yes, if they have it. Most people don't."

"All my friends do."

Which meant Titan Sciarra and maybe a few of the Lees.

He grinned anyway. "I don't have it."

"You don't need it." Her tone was venomously sweet. "We're not friends."

Hollis let that one go. Technically, he needed a way to contact her if there was an emergency because she was signing out under his authority. But Rowena would dodge that by saying she was under Jhandarmi authority, or her captain's, or some other side rule that meant she wasn't going to share anything she didn't want to.

With a tight smile, he pointed at the pass. "This is one of the cards given to field agents. Break it, and a guardian will be on site in seconds."

She eyed it thoughtfully. "Like the one I had when Titan went missing. You don't hand those out to everyone?"

"Not since one enterprising young officer decided that being cold and lonely one night was an emergency. She went to her quarters, stripped her uniform off, and broke her key to see who would show up."

Rowena's eyes lit with amusement. "I bet you had fun."

"Hardly. Sciarra was on duty and not too pleased to be pulled away from clocking out for the night to go home to his wife. Even if it had been me, I would have been on duty and given the officer the same lecture. We've been more careful about who gets the right to summon a guardian on a whim since then. I figure you're responsible enough not to do anything shenanigany."

"I'm absolutely positive that's not a word."

"Shenanigan. Shenanigans. Shenanigany. It declines." He held out the obsidian knife he'd loaned her once before. "Here."

Rowena held out her hand in surprise. "You sure?"

"In case something goes wrong. It never hurts to have a backup weapon. You could be trapped in the morgue with the undead!" He widened his eyes in fake shock and alarm.

She rolled her eyes in exasperation, then looked around. "What?"

Black eyes met his. "Too many witnesses."

He looked down the hall. Sure enough, three guardians were loitering there, waiting to see if a fight broke out. "They're probably taking bets on who's going to throw the first hit."

"Probably." She looked at the floor.

"We could really mess with their minds you know…"

It wouldn't even take something as scandalous as a kiss. If he made Rowena laugh in front of witnesses, all of Enclave would be talking about it by noon.

"We're not trying to kill each other, isn't that paradigm-shifting enough?" Dark eyes looked up at him through long lashes.

Hollis shrugged. "Mmmm, we could do more." He watched the guardians as they milled in a circle.

"Not everyone exists so you can get a reaction out of them, Silar."

Hollis shifted his full attention back to Rowena. "But it's so much fun to get a reaction."

She lifted her chin a fraction as she squared her shoulders. That was a look of annoyance he knew well. Rowena was done fooling around.

"I should stop talking and let you get to the Jhandarmi," Hollis said quickly. There was a limit to his good luck.

"That's what I would prefer."

"Well, have fun. Good luck identifying the mystery weapon. And don't die. Everyone knows I get to be the one to kill you."

Rowena chuckled softly, sending a pleasant little frisson through Hollis's body and probably starting a wildfire of gossip in the process. "Not if I kill you first." There was a flash of a smile before she teleported out.

Hollis dragged a hand along his chin. He'd just let Rowena Lee loose on the world and there were really only two ways this could go.

Either the world was going to end, and it was best if he hunkered down behind the thickest hull in the Silar armada.

Or the nature of the universe was going to dramatically realign, and the smart thing to do was grab a good snack and find a seat to watch the fireworks.

Whichever, Magnetic Storm Rowena was on the horizon.

4
ROWENA

THE JUMP COORDINATES FOR THE downtown morgue landed Rowena in a small building filled with dust, old pipes, and a newly installed computer screen that logged new arrivals. She'd seen it once before from the outside, an overgrown gazebo in the corner of a park. From the outside it was an unremarkable piece of the landscape, but that made it ideal for people like her who were, technically, crossing borders.

Tarrin was a sovereign city-state with an expansionist government that was barely holding on to power. If they weren't careful, at least in appearance, the isolationists would gain control of the senate and increase the tensions between the fleet and the grounders.

Which meant that if the Tarrins saw someone coming from Enclave to assist on a Jhandarmi case, they'd want to be looped in. It nearly violated several of the newer treaties between Enclave and Tarrin. Which Tyrling knew.

The fact that the Jhandarmi regional director was willing to risk political fallout over this intrigued her. It also meant she would tread very, very lightly. There wasn't a margin for error.

A recessed door pulled back and slid aside to reveal a woman in a brown Jhandarmi officer's uniform, her lavender hair pulled into a neat bun. "Commander Lee, I assume?"

"Yes," Rowena said. Yeoman hadn't translated to the Jhandarmi rank system. Sergeant would have been better, but somehow she'd wound up wearing the title of Commander when she was with the grounders. She strongly suspected that 'somehow' was Titan and Selena's fault. "Thank you for inviting me."

The officer shrugged, part apology, part welcome. "Director Tyrling is inside waiting for you." She held out a visitor's badge for Rowena.

"Thank you. Main door or back door?"

"If you take the gravel path it leads to a side door. Your badge will unlock it. There are Tarrin officials in the front lobby. This wasn't a quiet incident and already people are saber-rattling." She rolled her brown eyes. "You know how it is. One prominent citizen dies and suddenly everyone's demanding reparation. Money, lands, trade deals, it's the unending cycle of politics."

Rowena lifted a shoulder and dropped it. "The alternative is worse."

"Boredom?" the Jhandarmi officer guessed.

"War."

The officer made the quick, brushing sign of warding off ill-sayings, running her fingers over her thumb twice. A tell that the officer was from one of the northern city-states of the third continent.

Rowena tucked the fact away on her implant in case she ever needed it. It was strange being away from Enclave and cut off from the constant data flow. Most people in the fleet leaked data. Not intentionally, of course, but their com streams were too wide, or their shields were too weak. Her secondary implant was programmed to pick up all the data.

It meant she had all the good gossip first, and enough leverage to survive.

Walking down the white gravel path, Rowena tried to ignore the uncomfortable silence that came with being around grounders. There was only a single shield over the morgue, a static one gifted to the Tarrins when they allowed the fleet to take back the old space port on the rocky beach. The people here were all unaugmented. They couldn't communicate mind-to-mind, or lift anything with a thought. They couldn't access data without an outside device. They didn't display their rank, name, and familial affiliation in a neat ribbon of light.

The only comfort to be found was cataloging the information that was available. The gravel was white rock mixed with shells, an import from the west coast. The city building had columns and squared, red bricks rather than rectangular ones, a style from some three hundred years earlier.

As Rowena approached the silver door, her badge beeped, and the light next to the door handle changed from yellow to green.

She walked through the door and ran her hands down her unfamiliar clothes once more. The metallic gold shirt was... unsettling. Technically, no crew wore metallic gold, but it wasn't her Lee greens and it wasn't the black training uniform. At least the slacks and jacket were comfortable, softer and silkier than her uniform, but light and comfortable in the summer heat. The only thing that felt completely right was the knife holstered on her thigh, and accessible through a slit in her pocket. That probably said more about her mental state than any psych eval the Captain's Council would ever use.

Not that she was going to appeal her case again.

The last court meeting had made it very clear; if she wanted her rank back, she could either convince Hoshi to promote her, or join a new crew. The Council wasn't holding her back any longer. Her loyalty to the Lees was.

The door shut slowly behind her, locking her in the quiet government building with the chill air.

For a terrifying moment her mind seized on the emptiness, the lack of shields and pings. Her worst nightmare was a derelict ship and that's exactly what this place felt like: a grave.

Complete with dead people in the basement.

Unbidden, her implant brought up the memory of Silar teasing her about the dead coming back to life.

That was unhelpful. She set a new parameter for searches in her implant so that Silar's undead commentary wouldn't come up as a valid information source.

Heavy footsteps startled her, and her battle shield snapped into place as her heart jumped. It would have been embarrassing if anyone from fleet was around to see her.

Everyone knew Rowena Lee wasn't scared of anything.

"Except Rowena," she muttered to herself. Too long living on the edge of disaster was not good for her nerves.

"Lee?" The familiar voice of Director Tyrling from the Jhandarmi bounced down the hall, warping as the sound waves were absorbed.

"Here, sir." She walked forward, chin up, all fear hidden behind a passive mask of quiet interest.

Tyrling stepped around a corner at the end of the hall, light gleaming off his polished, bald head. "Thank you for coming down so quickly." He looked her over, one eyebrow lifting slightly as his mouth creased in a frown.

"Problems?"

"No. Nothing. I wasn't expecting this kind of wardrobe is all."

"The guardian who assisted me assured me it was appropriate." And if she'd got caught in one of Silar's misguided pranks, he was going to be eating through a straw for a week, field training or no.

Tyrling shook his head. "It's perfect. If I didn't know where you were from, I would have never guessed. There's still a slight accent"—she grimaced at the rebuke—"but most people would think it's from Descent." He shrugged. "The pitch range is wrong, but most people won't talk to you enough to notice."

Rowena nodded as if she understood. In her mind, she sounded like Fleet. Maybe more Lee and Warmonger than some of the others, but it didn't matter. "Where's the body I'm meeting?"

"The first body you need to meet is Dr. Keen." Tyrling led her through the large main atrium and past a guard desk to where a woman waited for them.

She looked like a dusty grounder: dull brown hair, brown eyes, brownish skin a few shades lighter than Rowena's, and a beige pant suit over an off-white cream blouse shot with white metallic threads.

The doctor nodded. "A pleasure to meet you, Commander." She held out her hand.

Rowena reached out, letting the grounder take her palm in grounder fashion and trying not to show how unsettling it was. Fleet favored tapping the backs of hands, to test shields and exchange information in greeting, and even that was more touch than Rowena liked with a stranger. "Rowena Lee, doctor. You can call me Lee. Most people do."

"A crew name, correct?"

"Yes," Tyrling said. "Similar to a family name." He smiled. "I'll let you two proceed to the morgue while I sort out jurisdiction and prep the paperwork for the man's family. Dr. Keen will fill you in on the details." He held out a second security badge to Rowena, gave them another nod-and-smile, and walked away.

Dr. Keen took that as her cue to turn toward the morgue. "Do you know much about death, commander?"

"Enough." Rowena fell into step with the woman as her implant mapped the security.

Tarrins either had odd views about who was allowed to see the dead, or they were very concerned that someone wanted to loot the morgue. There were security cameras on the wall spaced a meter apart, four layers of security doors, and live guards in black and blue uniforms at every turn. She'd have to ask Tyrling about that later.

"Is this dead man important?"

"Not that I'm aware of," the doctor said. "There is a family though, and he is likely of importance to them. But he doesn't vote on the hospital budget committee or for Tarrin politicians, if that's what you mean by important."

Rowena scanned her badge at a door leading to a ramp and the cool air of a basement. "The security seems tighter than I remember last time I was in town."

"Civil unrest," the doctor said. "People are disappointed with the failure of the land purchase on the north end. Didn't you vote on the ballot measure?" Her tone suggested that not voting was a grave sin.

"I'm not from Tarrin," Rowena said.

"Ah." Doctor Keen pushed open heavy metal double doors that swung back and locked in place behind them. "This building houses multiple government offices. No one would attack a morgue, but they might go after the vote counters upstairs."

They passed through a wide room under a network of narrow, brown staircases leading up to various offices. The walls sucked in the sound, swallowing their footsteps as the floor slanted down to the underground morgue.

Doctor Keen nodded to the guard as they approached a set of bullet-proof glass doors. "With the citizenry unhappy, there have been complaints. Certain individuals feel a show of force is the best way to end the tide of complaints."

Rowena shook her head. "I've seen that tried. It's like putting a blanket over a sucking chest wound: sure, it's out of sight, but eventually someone will need to go pick out the shrapnel."

The doctor tilted her head to the side. "What a very odd metaphor. I had not heard that one before." She blinked, and with a facial shrug dismissed the conversation as the morgue doors slid open.

The outer room had a faded orange couch that smelled of stale grease and an aging computer sign-in screen on the wall that Doctor Keen brushed past without noticing. "The patient is Harlan Briceno, of Sandur by birth. He currently resides with his wife in her home city-state of Harstud. They have three grown children, no grandchildren. Briceno is a builder by trade, apprenticed, trained and such."

Another set of gray double-doors with a sheen of curling, bronze paint opened into a wide, low-ceilinged room with slate gray tiles and banks of silver freezers for the decedents. The air tasted of leaking freezer coolants with a bitter mint and citrus smell that clung to her.

"According to his public works file, he was a project manager for Serhiem and Wyte until two years ago, when he ran for city office. He won, and worked for Harstud as a building inspector and sat on the growth committee which approves new roads and buildings within the city-state. He's behind door number four."

Rowena nodded. A building inspector was a respectable job, and the growth committee for a city that hadn't expanded in over a century wasn't atypical. It was usually an uncontested appointment that would have given Briceno a small government paycheck for a few days of work a year. "Age?"

"Sixty-three, barely middle aged for someone born on the third continent." Dr. Keen opened up the large metal door and rolled out a pallet with a body under a shimmering white shroud. "This is my one thousand, nine hundred and third autopsy, and the first one where discerning the cause of death has proved problematic." She pushed Briceno's pallet to the crescent-shaped central work station and locked it in place. "There's no obvious signs of attack, no signs of exsanguination, scans for cranial injury or heart attack all produced negative results. However, the scan did locate a foreign object in his chest."

She flicked a hand across the morgue control panel, dimming the outer ring of lights and bringing a diagnostic screen online. Pulling back the shroud with detached professionalism, the doctor revealed the decedent.

Harlan Briceno had been a pale man, body layered with the extra fat that accumulated with age. Deep lines around his mouth and eyes spoke to an animated, passionate personality, and his arms were lined with thin scars from his work. His flesh was still pink enough to make it look like he was sleeping off a good dinner.

Dr. Keen turned on the overhead light.

"How long did you say he'd been dead?" Rowena asked.

"He was last seen alive three days ago. Liver temperature suggests he was dead a full day before the local police found him."

Rowena frowned. Taking a set of plastic gloves from the work station, she poked at the dead man's arm. "He still feels warm. Were you keeping him in a cooling chamber?"

"We were," Dr. Keen said. "It's been seven hours and the body temperature hasn't changed. But there's no blood flow, no heartbeat, and no brain wave activity. I triple checked."

She was the type to. Thorough and careful. Exactly what a crew looked for in a doctor. Rowena felt her shoulders relax a little. Dealing with grounders often felt like flying through a minefield there were so many social norms, but Dr. Keen had a personality she could understand. "Do you object to me performing another scan?"

"Not at all," the doctor said. "It will be recorded."

Rowena nodded agreement and took off her gloves.

"How long will it take you to retrieve your equipment?"

Flexing her fingers, Rowena reached her bare hand over the corpse. "I don't need to retrieve anything." It took a thought to turn on her medical scanner. Telekyen on her skin and nanites in her blood combined to create a telekyen vapor that enveloped the body in a faint, green light. Slowly, she walked the length of the body, getting a full scan of the man.

Dr. Keen's lips formed a thin line of disapproval. "You belong to the space fleet?"

"Yes."

There was a sniff of disapproval. "An interesting choice for the director to invite to the investigation."

"The foreign object in his chest, your scans show it around the heart?" Rowena said, ignoring the doctor's frown.

"Near the heart, yes. It doesn't look like it's blocking anything though."

"It looks like it's enveloping it. Did Briceno have surgery of some kind?" Turning her palm upward, Rowena projected the image of her scan for the doctor to see it. "Grounders use something similar to regulate hearts with irregular beats, don't they?"

The doctor leaned in to peer at the scan. "The design is alien to me. And even an exploratory surgery would be listed on his medical records. Those are not public, but the coroner's office has full access in the event of suspicious death."

Rowena switched views, trying to see what the object was made of. She inhaled sharply. "There's orun in there!"

"Orun?"

"Orun crystal, it's the fuel source that powers the space fleet." Mentally she had to backtrack and try to remember how a grounder might understand. Orun crystals were as integral to life in the fleet as oxygen. If you were fleet, there was no explanation needed. "It's, ah, a yellowish mineral found near the event horizons of black holes. Very difficult to acquire, except in the Imperial System where there were large deposits found throughout and in the ocean off the coast of Seahome. There's a large deposit there, but it's unmineable."

Manipulating the data she'd taken from the corpse, she showed Dr. Keen the sliver of orun that was powering the device in Briceno's chest.

"It looks like amber," the doctor said.

The yellow shard was thick as two strands of hair and barely longer than her thumb nail. "That is enough orun to power my fighter squadron for three battles. It's more than most ships have right now." Ancestors, what a waste!

"Doesn't seem like much."

"It is when that crystal is keeping your oxygen flowing and your water clean. This is life and death. We fought wars over orun. People died trying to steal less than this." Rowena took a deep breath. "If… No. Ancestors protect me— there are still people in the fleet who would kill for this much orun. No one in Enclave has this much. If someone on the second continent has found a way to access the orun…"

…It would mean war. Everything she'd done would be for nothing.

She couldn't survive another war.

Everything Titan had suffered just to find happiness would be ripped away from him.

She stared into a bleak future filled with destruction. No one could know about this. Not ever.

Dr. Keen frowned in puzzlement. "How can it be that important? What does it do?"

"It… does things to light?" Rowena said slowly, trying to pull away from her fears. "Ah, sorry. The shortest essay on the properties and functioning of orun is six hundred pages of complicated math and very tiny text.

"The simplest way to think of it is that it is powered by the interactions of wavelengths of light. The larger a crystal it is, the more light it can bounce around, and the more power it generates. Over time, the crystals decay. The outer layers are destroyed by the radiation."

"Radiation? Could that have killed Briceno?"

Rowena shook her head quickly. "It's not enough radiation to hurt anyone. At most, even a large crystal would barely generate enough heat for your hand to feel warm if you touched it. Which, you wouldn't, because the oil from your fingers would degrade the orun faster. Even before isolation touching orun was enough to earn you time in the brig. Stealing it is an offense punishable by death."

The doctor frowned in confusion. "Then what is it doing in a dead man's chest?"

"I have no idea." Data flashed in front of Rowena's face. "Only two ships have orun this size on their inventory and both of them are listed as destroyed in battle—parts unsalvageable. Unless the engine core fell to the planet and somehow survived, this isn't from fleet."

"Do your eyes always glow like that when you think?" Keen asked with clinical interest, her datpad open for notes.

"Only when I access data. Look, I need to remove the device from his chest. This isn't tech I can identify with an non-invasive scan."

"It was understood that you'd be staying for the autopsy."

Rowena forced a smile. "Right. I was just expecting something a little more... common."

"If it were common we'd hardly need an outside expert," Dr. Keen said primly. "Are you ready to start? We have a selection of medical coats, face masks, and gloves. The doors are locked. The recording devices are on."

"Do we need locked doors?" Rowena forced a smile. Locked doors still made her a little panicky, even when she knew she could teleport out.

Dr. Keen shrugged. "It limits unwanted interruptions. The last time I forgot, a courier walked in while I was cracking open the rib cage. He fainted, hit his head on the floor, and was in the hospital for two weeks."

"I can see where that would be a problem." Rowena took a white coat off the rack and a pair of blue surgical gloves.

"If something urgent happens on the outside we can be reached over the building's intercom system. But, really, this is one of the safest places in the city. The morgue bunker can withstand a tsunami, gale force winds, and space debris impact."

As Dr. Keen pulled on her white lab coat, Rowena scanned the defenses. The shield over Tarrin could indeed withstand a short orbital bombardment, and the building was stable. She also found the exit. If there was an emergency, she could teleport Dr. Keen and herself to safety with a thought.

A distant scan pinged against her implant. :Problems?: The code said Starguard but it was Hollis's voice she heard in her mind.

:Routine security scan.:

There was the flash of a green acknowledgement sign off, and then a silence that became an absence.

She shivered.

Dr. Keen looked at her, eyebrows raised. "Are you cold?"

"Mmm? No. It's nothing." *Just living in my nightmares is all.* The fleet was too far away for comfort.

The doctor flipped on the overhead diagnostic screen and a recording device. "This is Doctor Atia Keen with Commander Rowena Lee of Enclave attending as witness for the continuing autopsy of Harlan Briceno. Date and time are noted in the file. At this time we are preparing to cut the thoracic region to access an unknown item located in or around the decedent's heart."

She lifted her scalpel and cut the corpse's skin in a clean Y-cut.

Rowena took a steadying breath and patted the knife on her thigh. There was a slit in the pocket of her slacks, but under the lab coat it felt too far away. She slid it out and tucked it into the lab coat pocket, where the weight bumped gently against her leg as she fidgeted.

"Commander, if you're scanning, could you please verbalize what you see for the auditors who watch the autopsies?"

Rowena nodded, glanced at the cameras, and focused on the task at hand instead of her unease. "My implant has detected a device of unknown origin that contains an orun crystal. The device is inact—" She stopped and blinked. "Pulsing? Dr. Keen, it's sending out a very faint signal."

"A tracking device, perhaps? Those can be controlled remotely."

"That's not a logical place to put a tracking device. The extremities are easier to reach. If you're worried about the target cutting a limb off, the neck or head is still better than the heart."

"Unless the person is tracking the heart specifically," Dr. Keen said as she extended the cut past the man's sternum. "I recall a case in Sandur where the debt collectors were micro-chipping organs that the victims had agreed to sell if their debts weren't paid in time. Or when the victim died for other reasons."

Red blood welled up along the edge of the cut.

"Barbaric," Rowena murmured.

"There are worse things," the doctor said. "It all came out in the court case, naturally. A debt collector sued a bookie who shot the debtor in the abdomen, ruining a perfectly good liver." She stepped back. "This is very odd. There shouldn't be blood at this point. Not blood like this."

Rowena stepped closer. "The device is contracting the heart."

The corpse's chest heaved as it inhaled.

Dr. Keen took a quick step backward. "That's not right. That's not right at all. This man was dead. Very, definitely dead."

"Right," Rowena agreed as the corpse sat up. She grabbed the doctor's arm and sent the code to teleport them to the gazebo outside.

Nothing happened.

She sent a distress signal, but it hit a wall. "The device is cutting communication lines. I can't teleport us out or call for help."

"Intercom," Dr. Keen said breathlessly as the corpse swung his legs off the morgue slab, his eyes staring vacantly ahead. "We have the intercom." The doctor rushed to her medical board. It died as she reached for it.

Utter blackness filled the room as the lights failed. The only sound was the breath of the living and the steps of the dead.

Rowena pulled on the stored energy in her implant to create a nimbus of pale green light around her. "Dr. Keen, if you'd kindly step behind me."

"Oh, naturally. That seems like a logical—a logical solution."

"Doctor, do I have permission to handle the body as I see fit?"

"Try not to destroy it, if possible," the doctor said a shade tartly. "The family will want him returned."

In the pale green light, Briceno was a swollen mess. The cut folds of skin and muscle flapped off his chest like a jacket. Coagulated blood, thick with decay, dripped from him like the ichor of the dead gods. His eyes glowed, not in the natural way of an augmented fleet officer, but with the cracked and fragmented light of a broken engine.

The smell of death grabbed at her, choking her as it brought memories she wanted destroyed.

Cold bodies weighing her down as she fought through smoking wrecks. Rotting corpses pulled from their broken fighters because she needed parts. She blocked it with her implant, having the nanites cover her scent receptors so she could stay in the moment.

Briceno's steps were stuttering, but intentional; he was moving toward them.

Rowena put up her best shield, trapping the man at the back of the lab so she could access the doors.

Briceno stepped through her shield, pieces of flesh burning as he did, filling the room with the stench of burnt hair.

"Crack my hull." She wove another shield, excluding large carbon arrays, orun signatures, and methane.

The corpse lurched through the new shield, layers of skin stripping away. The orun crystal caught, faltered, and surged, throwing Rowena to the floor.

Her head throbbed as her implant drained of power.

"Are you all right?" Dr. Keen asked.

"Fine," Rowena lied, pushing to her feet. "The tech in his chest is giving me a bit of a problem. But, you know what they say, brute force heals all wounds."

"I don't think anyone says that," the doctor murmured.

Rowena slammed the corpse with a punch of telekyen-backed air, sweat trickling down her back from the exertion.

The bloody cut across his shoulder glowed with energy.

"That is not supposed to happen." She stayed between the doctor and the corpse. Keen had to stay alive at any cost. Her loss could start a war between Tarrin and fleet.

"The device seems to be taking energy," Dr. Keen said.

With every step, Briceno glowed brighter.

"Kinetic energy being converted for use by the device? Okay. I can work with that." Rowena's implant alerted her to an energy draw. The cracked corpse was pulling on her resources, too.

Whatever the device was doing, it was meant to combat standard fleet augmentations.

"Where do you stand on the debate between desecrating the dead and survival of the living?" Rowena asked, wiping away blood splatter from her face.

Dr. Keen made an odd sound. "At the moment, I believe firmly in the rights of the living. If the family sues me, I will counter-sue for emotional trauma and damage to the city morgue."

Making a note to look up her own legal responsibilities in this case under Tarrin law when she had time, Rowena drew the black stone knife. The memory of Silar's teasing shot through her mind, leaving an icy rage in its wake.

He wouldn't do something like this... Probably.

And she didn't have time to guess how or why he would have set up a prank like this if he did do it.

"Doctor, if you can make your way to the door. I think I saw an emergency override on the lock. We should be able to force the door open without damaging the building too much." The other option was to punch a hole in the morgue wall, but the probability that Briceno's corpse would escape was too high.

Plus, despite four years on the planet, Rowena had an officer's aversion to damaging a structure. Hulls were hard to replace.

The corpse lurched toward her. There really was no other word for it.

Dr. Keen moved, and the corpse turned to follow. Not just the head, like an intelligent creature might track something, but the whole body turning, angling the device in the chest to follow the movement.

He sped up.

Rowena stepped forward, intercepting him. "Hi."

In life, Briceno hadn't been a small man. He didn't look like the type who would have fought while breathing either, but in death mass was all that mattered. His fist hit her shield and drove her backward.

Catching her balance, Rowena spun around, kicking his legs backwards. They crunched, but it didn't slow him down.

"The locking mechanism is stuck!" Dr. Keen shouted. "I can't get the door open."

"Does the panel go through the wall?" Rowena asked as she moved around the morgue slab, trying to buy time.

"Yes."

"Push the panel out and yell for help."

The corpse lunged at her.

Rowena brought her knife up to block and sliced through the decaying arm. Flesh and liquid splattered her. The smell was worse than a ship running three days with no air filter. That was all it took to take her back to the decks of *Theano* as the engines and crew died. Her lungs stung at the memory of the smoke. Her eyes watered.

She stepped backward and bumped into Dr. Keen's tool tray.

The knife wasn't enough. There had to be something...

There... The hooked hammer for separating pieces of the skull.

Grabbing the heavy hammer, Rowena smashed the man's ribs, twisted the hook into the rotting flesh, and pulled away the ribs to expose the device.

She stabbed with the stone knife, speared the heart—and tore it from the dead man's chest.

The device tumbled to the ground.

Rowena stomped on it. Hard.

For a moment Briceno stood, lifeless. Then the muscles slowly went lax and he fell to the floor.

The door opened with a screech and a shout from Tyrling. "What happened?"

"Sir, there was a mechanical device that caused an anomaly during the... the initial autopsy." Dr. Keen's voice waivered. "I feel ill."

Covered in blood and body fluids, Rowena turned to the director, her fists clenched to hide the shaking. "I'll have a report to you by morning."

Tyrling looked at her and then down to the dead man on the floor. "Ah..."

"Tomorrow." Her implant returned to life. *Twenty percent.* It was enough.

She teleported directly to Silar's office. Even if she hated him, he'd need to know what the Jhandarmi director was talking about when he called in the morning.

The office was dark and empty. Cool air that smelled of sweat and rushed meals brought her back to the moment.

Somehow, she could still hear the screams of the dying.

"Focus."

There were six forms to fill out. A couple of reports to file.

And all she could think of was the smell of death, seeping into her skin. If she didn't shower right now, she was going to lose her mind.

Rowena took the knife and slammed it into Silar's desk. There. Report filed.

She'd been attacked.

She'd survived.

She was filthy.

She was going to take Silar's head off if it turned out he was responsible.

He could read that all off a knife.

If he couldn't, well, he could find her on the *Danielle Nicole*, using up a year's worth of soap allowance to get the dead man's blood out of her hair.

5
HOLLIS

MORNING LIGHT ROSE AT THE EDGE of the horizon, rolling over the concrete runways and the bright red fixed-wing planes that made up Tarrin's aerial display team, all of them finally silent.

One last sweep of the Tarrin fairgrounds and small airport and he could go home. The flight show had run all night with crowds running under neon lights between tiny pop-up shops. Even now the tang of the biolipid fuel cells for the jets and cooking grease hung in the air, caught in the fog rolling up from the distant river.

It was a pretty area, by grounder standards. A nice flat field with rolling hills at the edge and then the mountains in the distance.

His implant overlaid a screen between his eyes and the view that he tagged with as many relevant labels as he could think of. Hill. Mountain. Yellow flower: *Ranunculus acris* –

toxic – do not eat. When he got back to the *Veronica Guerin* he would upload the images for the rest of the crew.

Hollis stretched as he counted the sleepless nights. His implant could keep him running for up to six days, but tonight he really needed to sleep. Ancestors willing, it would be a quiet day.

He grabbed the shirt he'd bought from a vendor and waved off the last few Starguard who were prowling along the flight lines between the grounder planes. The primitive machines were cute, in their own way. Not capable of reaching even low orbit, but fascinating in their limited capacity. The large passenger planes were the strangest, and had drawn the most attention from the fleetlings. Hollis counted it a success that none of the children had managed to hijack anything from the air show.

The first joint mission with Tarrin law enforcement had been a success.

"Daydreaming or just dreaming?" Tejan asked as she bumped her shield against his. Her brown hair still had an easy, beachy wave to it even after pulling a twelve-hour shift, and her eyes were bright with anticipation.

He stifled a yawn. "Neither. I'm fine."

"I knew that." She gave him an appreciative look, eyes roving from his head down to his belt and back up again. "You're fine at so many things. What's in the bag?"

"Gift for someone who couldn't make it."

"That was sweet of you." Her voice curled around the statement in an unasked question. Of course Tejan wanted to know who the gift was for.

And he wasn't telling.

"Back to the bullpen, Tejan." He teleported back to Enclave, knowing she would follow.

The building was blessedly quiet. It was too early for the morning shift and too late for the evening crew to be anywhere but at their lockers packing up to go home. A tiny, domed cleaning bot scuttered across the polished floors, leaving a behind the wispy scent of lime cleaning solution that didn't quite cut through the smell of dirty, sweaty, harried guardians who had worked an eighteen-hour day.

"Never again," Tejan vowed as she dropped a bag of high-visibility vests into the bullpen cleaning bin. "I spent all day retrieving lost toys and telling people where to find the washrooms. If the Tarrins invite us back next year, we're sending the juniors." She rolled her head and rubbed at her neck. "I need a massage."

There was a nudge at Hollis's shield as he opened the door. "Sorry, Mireia, you'll have to find someone else to indulge you." He smiled to take the sting out of his rejection.

Tejan sighed. "You used to be fun."

"I used to have less work." A unfamiliar scent tickled his nose. Something sour, putrid.

Tejan wrinkled hers. "What is that?"

"I don't know. Maybe my waste recycler's broken again." His implant brought back memories of the war. This was the warning smell that had seeped out of his brother's life pod when they found him. The smell of death that filled empty decks after battles.

"Want me to call a tech in?"

He flipped on a light. It glittered violently off the obsidian handle of a knife embedded in his desk. "No. It's just a prank. Looks like my cousins were here," he lied as he reclosed the door so Tejan couldn't see. "They left a mess for me."

"Too bad," Tejan said. "I'm going to get breakfast at Cargo Blue and then go get some sleep. If you change your mind about wanting company, you know how to find me." She winked before spinning away, long brown hair flying behind her.

Warm brown skin, light brown eyes, sun-streaked brown hair, long legs, beautiful smile... Tejan was, he admitted, very much his type. Dark hair and dark eyes with a stunning smile always worked for him. Hermione Marshall had the same brown-on-brown coloring.

And Tejan's cousin Diego.

And over half the fleet that he wasn't related to. He did have standards, but for casual companionship he kept an open mind.

Except for this past year, when no one had caught his interest.

No, that wasn't fair.

It wasn't that he was bored of relationships and it wasn't that he hadn't been interested. He'd observed, weighing every potential lover against some intangible metric, and they hadn't measured up.

Lovely to look at and all, but as he'd watched he'd felt no need to take someone home with him anymore.

The metric seemed mercurial as his moods lately. There was something he knew he wanted, knew he needed, but he couldn't find the calculations to determine what his subconscious had fixated on.

He opened the door to his office again as Tejan left, and assessed the situation.

There was something gooey pooling on his desk. The smell of rotting flesh filling the room suggested that a closer examination would only turn his stomach. Rowena's trip to the morgue must have been eventful.

Shame she hadn't seen fit to leave a report.

Hollis didn't need to run a sweep to know where she was. This early in the morning Rowena was in the gym running drills. It was probably good they were going to have this fight in a public place. This was going to fuel fleet gossip for a month.

The cadets were practicing basic hand-to-hand blocking maneuvers and counter attacks in the training gym when Hollis walked in.

Rowena stood at the far end of the long blue sparring mat with a full shield up, showing her rank as Drill Instructor and the list of things the cadets were meant to be practicing.

Hollis sent her a ping, letting her know he was in the room.

The answer was a practice knife, flying up at his head from the bucket by his side. Good to see she was in a mood to match his. He knocked the knife to the ground and waited. It was always fun when Lee was looking for blood.

Hollis stretched, warming his muscles in case she decided to use him for punching practice again, and watched the cadets. Their clumsy attempts at fighting took some of the edge off the battle memories. :If we ever go to war again, we're in trouble.:

On the instructor's platform Lee's smirk looked forced, as if war were still a threat. :How is it that none of the little Silars can punch like you?:

Saying that there weren't enough Lees to practice on was too cruel. Rowena's sister, Aronia, had lost one child during the war and almost lost a second last year. Pushing that button would bring the apocalypse. :I wanted to leave you something to do.:

Her response was a memory of the late Mal Baular, ancestors forgive him, rolling his eyes and saying, "Can you stop talking, Silar?"

:That didn't work for Mal, and he had a prettier smile than you.:

The practice knife shot back toward him. She wasn't even looking and her aim was good.

Hollis batted it aside. :Finish up with the cadets. We need to talk.: He added an official Starguard emblem to the thought so she'd know it was business. Not that it would change much. Lee and he rarely found a way to talk without fighting.

It took over twenty minutes before Lee was satisfied with her class's performance and released the exhausted cadets to shower and leave. Most of them didn't even have the energy to teleport out.

Lee stepped off the central platform, expression blank. "Be quick. I have a meeting with my sister in an hour."

He took out the knife and floated it to her. "You left this in my desk."

Lee snatched it from the air as she reached for a cleaning rag. "If I'd found you last night I would have left it in your skull." There was no emotion in her voice. "But I've had some time to think, and it seems unlikely you were involved with the incident."

His teeth ground together in frustration.

"You wouldn't do anything to endanger the current treaty," Rowena concluded, as if that was all he needed to know.

"Incident?" A hot wash of fury rolled over him. "Incident? Lee?"

She looked up, face expressionless. "Yes."

"Do you know what usually accompanies an 'incident'?" He filled the word with all the venom boiling through him. "A report."

"You got a knife. That should have been enough to tell you that the person who had the knife—me—was back in

Enclave, and that it had been used. What else do you need to know?" Cold, flippant, dismissive words. Not the least bit apologetic.

Red fury burned in his blood as his shields locked into place. "Were you hurt? Was someone else hurt? What happened? Why did you use the knife, Lee?"

She snapped up a sound shield, blocking anyone else from listening, then raised an eyebrow. "Nothing major." The words crawled out through barred teeth. "I went to the morgue. There was a minor attack. The Jhandarmi are handling it. No new corpses were added to the collection, just as I promised. The treaty is still intact and that's all you need to know."

Hollis's hands tightened to fists. All he'd heard was that a fleet officer had been attacked. "Who attacked you?"

"A dead man."

That was the first comforting thing she'd said. "I assumed anyone who attacked would be dead. Who were they before they attacked you?"

"Dead." Lee shrugged. "The corpse on the autopsy table was the one that attacked me. There was a device attached to his heart and central nervous system. When I ran a scan, it activated, and the corpse attacked. Then I stopped him from attacking. Problem solved."

The red-gold of battle blurred his vision. Hollis sucked in air like he was dying, muscles knotting as he fought his training to stay still and calm. To keep his temper in check. "You were in a liaison mission between the OIA and the Jhandarmi. You were in the field under my authority. Was it an attack on the fleet? On you? On the Jhandarmi? I need to know these things."

"It was a Jhandarmi op in grounder territory. I reported to the appropriate people. You weren't one of them." The lack of emotion in Lee's voice was a twisting knife.

She was cutting him out. Ruthlessly dismissing him.

And she wasn't responding to his temper.

"What if you were hurt?"

"The grounders have medical teams." That wasn't an answer.

"Ones your crew would approve of?"

Her eyes narrowed, letting him know that what her crew approved of was not of consequence. After all, half of them would applaud her attacker.

Taking a deep breath, Hollis dropped his battle shields. "You should have given me a report."

"Why? Because you need more work?" She shrugged. "There was nothing actionable. Nothing you could do."

His lips curled into a snarl at the phrase.

Rowena lifted an eyebrow. Point to her. "Protecting me isn't your job."

"It is. It literally is." He tugged at the jacket of his Starguard uniform. "This isn't a costume, Rowena. And we're not twelve anymore."

She took a step forward so her shield sparked against his. "When I'm with the Jhandarmi, they take care of me. Not you." An echo of a much older argument; he'd been assigned as her partner for a mock battle the first year in the Academy, but she'd turned to Mal Baular for help.

Afterwards, as he'd cursed her, she'd run into Baular's arms. *He takes care of me. Not you.*

The flash of memory made his fists ache for a fight. She'd been right back then. But Mal wasn't here to protect her anymore. No one was. "Unacceptable. When you leave Enclave under my authority, I get a report."

"If you need one, you'll have one." Rowena lifted her chin in challenge. "You should trust your field operatives enough to let them make a call on whether or not a situation needs your oversight."

His implant matched the tone and words to arguments they'd had dozens of times before. Everything between them was loaded with pain and memories.

Hollis shook his head. "Trust? You? No. I've known you too long for that. You wouldn't report a broken bone, let alone a major incident, if you thought you could handle it on your own." And she almost always could. "The Starguard needs to know these things before there's a war brewing."

Lee's jaw tightened and her mouth pinched into a mew of acknowledgment. "I left the knife."

"Not enough." He ran a quick surface scan. "There are fresh skin cells on your arms. How were you hurt?"

"I got that playing with the filters on the *Janu Faun.*"

Unbelievable. The sheer arrogance of lying to a senior officer. "You went to do repair work last night but couldn't leave a note to explain the situation?"

"My captain promised our allies my help. The *Faun's* crew has children and repairing their air filters was time sensitive." Rowena's eyes were filled with challenge.

"It's something any officer should have been able to do." Every Silar knew how to repair a filter. There was a time when every Lee knew how to too.

But it wasn't about skill. It was about giving Rowena a thankless task as punishment. If their crews had been allied, he would have offered her a berth. Ancestors only knew why the Sciarras hadn't yet. The Lees were toxic.

Or maybe they had offered and Rowena had declined.

"I will report back on the situation when I have something you can use," Rowena said. There was something in her voice that made him want to put his battle shields back up.

His jaw twitched. "Expected delivery time?"

Her eyes lit up, purple and green auroras glowing in a sea of black. "I'll be in Tarrin proper in forty minutes, and

I'll follow up with the Jhandarmi. I anticipate something from that."

"Is it likely to lead to another, similar incident?"

She tilted her head, face softening as she ran the calculations. "Not enough information. But I presume it is unlikely." Her eyes returned to their normal black. "Most dead people stay dead."

"Mmm." Lee *would* be the person to find the exception to the rule. "Keep the knife," he ordered. "If you're attacked again, contact me directly."

"I thought you were leaving at the end of the week."

"Tomorrow, but I won't be out of coms range. Not unless you've gotten worse over the years." It was a direct challenge, and it got the reaction he wanted.

Lee's sneer was a thing of beauty. "If your help is required, I'll send a message." She teleported out, not waiting to be dismissed.

Hollis dropped the rest of his shields and looked up at the training gym ceiling. *If.*

Was there anything that Rowena Lee would consider a situation where he was required? Probably not.

He needed to find another way to take control of this situation.

6

MALCOLM

BENNU INDUSTRIES SAT ON THE eastern edge of Ryun in the Helios Business Complex, three polished concrete buildings with a sparkling white sheen from the local dust and large, black windows that overlooked all that remained of the original marsh, like a temple to modern aeronautical engineering.

It was fitting, really. Bennu had been the ancient avatar of self-invention, rebirth, and creation. Now, a golden heron symbol hung over the main door, wreathed by the Latin words *Surge Claritate*, Rise In Brilliance.

It was equally fitting that Malcolm's second life began with a scholarship from Bennu Industries, then only a struggling startup with a dream and feverish focus. The scholarship had led to an internship, and finally to a job.

Here, in the sprawl of metal and white marble buildings and the lingering smell of stagnant water, he'd found a life where he could fly free.

Malcolm watched the sun come up, the sky burning pink, then orange, until the fiery rays of the sun shot out over the horizon and rebounded off Bennu Industries' engine testing facility to break into rainbows over the fountains out in the main plaza.

Climbing out of his car, he locked the door, then followed the sidewalk—white with glittering mica chips—around the fountains, past the pond, and down along the river walk.

It was all artificial. Six years ago, all of this had been some rather damp real estate with a few worthless houses on stilts and no prospects—until Mikell Yaeger bought it cheap and transformed it into the most exclusive business district in the greater Ryun area.

Bennu bought in early, when Yaeger was still making a name for himself, and it had paid off. The company now owned half of the land in the industrial park, and last year the land was worth more than the company.

That had changed in the last few months.

It was Malcolm's research that had moved Bennu from up-and-coming start-up with big ideas and shallow pockets to the frontrunner in low orbital flight. His engine was going to revolutionize travel.

Maybe.

If the sales went through.

He adjusted his tie as he approached the side entrance. There were always too many people in the main foyer, even on the days he arrived before five in the morning.

Pressing his palm on the door lock, he waited for the familiar warmth that was the scanner, then stepped into the first scanning room where he was checked for weapons or metals associated with the spacers from Icedell, and then into a second antechamber where a retinal scan and a voice-print analyzer waited for him. After that, it was smooth sailing through empty, industrial metal halls that smelled of commercial cleaner to the windowless office where he spent most of his time.

Originally he'd had an office upstairs with a view of the river, but it had made him too homesick. Not for the islands or any place in memory, but for the life he might have had.

So he'd asked for a sound-proof office down by the testing room where he worked. Ostensibly so he could keep an eye on the engines from his desk, but really to escape the memories of what could have been.

Now, he sat down and went to work, and he was still drawing designs and filling out work order requests when the office door opened.

"Malcolm?" Henry Harringworth, the regional director for Bennu Industries and the supervisor of the complex, walked in. "I thought you must have snuck in early again this morning." He was wearing his red checkered vest with an obnoxious yellow-and-mauve bowtie that didn't match, a sure sign he'd spilled something on himself earlier in the day, or late last night.

Harringworth was an engineer first, management goon second, and had the lamentable habit of eating at his desk while he worked at night. It led to a rather rotund appearance and bright pink cherub cheeks that, regrettably, made the director look like an overgrown, gray-haired cherub escaped from an Imperial Era painting.

Malcolm glanced at the clock built into the corner of his desk. When he was working, it wasn't uncommon for him to lose track of time, but it was only mid-morning and there were no appointments scheduled. He looked at Harringworth in patient expectation.

"Were you anticipating a guest today?" his supervisor asked, fiddling with his gold-rimmed glasses. Harringworth had somehow got the idea that the Longs were a much wealthier—and more powerful—family than Malcolm ever let on, and so had decided that Malcolm must have a secret life.

Being invited to Lethe's main stronghold probably hadn't done anything to kill the rumors that Malcolm spent his evening hours freelancing as an international spy.

"I wasn't expecting anyone this week," Malcolm said. "Is it a reporter?"

"No, it's a businessman who asked for, and I quote, 'That smart engineer you have.'"

Malcolm sighed in relief. "There's a number of brilliant engineers here, Harringworth. Why don't you find the most photogenic one and throw them at him?"

"He specified a blond."

"This isn't a dating service." Malcolm bit the words off. *Diplomacy.* These things required diplomacy. "But I'll see him, if that will make you happy."

Harringworth relaxed visibly, going from a pudgy pillar of upright thinking to a gooey puddle of a man. The man's spine was only on display when his precious research budget was threatened.

Closing and locking the protective shield over his digital desktop, Malcolm stood up and brushed an invisible speck of dust off his gray trousers. It was a nervous habit he'd picked up in school, but showing his nerves put everyone else at ease, so he repeated the ritual with a smile.

Then it was a tug at his gray vest, and a moment to straighten the tie that was only a few shades darker. There wasn't a mirror nearby, but Malcolm didn't need to check to know everything was in place. "Lead the way, sir."

With a genuine smile, Harringworth led him away from the safety of the engines to the central corridor.

A large window overlooked the southern view of the plaza and the central fountain. The eastern wing of the building was filled with official offices. Marketing was on the north end on the third floor overlooking the glass atrium. Wide stairs cut the building in half and flowed out into the company promenade with a set of tiny cafes, a shop full of merchandise printed with the Bennu Industries logo, and two smaller shops with essentials and trinkets. Fake trees with white branches and pale yellow-green leaves hid tiny, uncomfortable tables with equally undersized benches.

Out of habit, Malcolm surveyed the situation and counted the exits.

"Don't rabbit on me," Harringworth muttered.

"You've been talking to my mother again."

"Only because we happened to be at the same charity gala last weekend. The one you swore you would attend. The one you bought the blue suit for."

Malcolm wrinkled his nose. "I lost the suit."

"It's hanging in the closet of your office," Harringworth said. "I saw it myself."

"I needed to run tests on the Gamayun engines. The report is due this week and there were anomalies in the results."

Harringworth fussed with his yellow bowtie and plowed on through the mid-morning crowd of marketers coming for their second stimulant fix of the day, leading Malcolm to the front desk.

Several secretaries in conservative suits in a range of neutral colors chosen to not offend the aristocracy nodded to him as they very intentionally ignored the man drumming his fingers on the marble counter.

"Is this the one?" The man had the expensive clothes and subtle makeup only the obscenely wealthy bothered with. His silk suit had probably been a pale lavender before it had been assaulted by an over-achieving toddler carrying water colors. Green and lavender was a choice, not one Malcolm would make, but a choice nonetheless. And the fake eyelashes brought out the blue in the man's eyes but were a terrible choice for a morning look.

No house colors though.

The man's face underneath the pale foundation and silvery tint on his lips was unremarkable. Washed-out blue eyes. Artificially lightened blond hair. Rather unfortunately wide nose that made Malcolm's fist itch to break it.

It was like looking at the cheap, knock-off version of himself. If the man claimed he was a relative, Malcolm was going to vomit. On the intruder. Because punching someone was considered assault in this city-state.

"Doctor Long, if I may introduce you to our guest—" Harringworth began.

"Kedic Athfer Winn," he said, pronouncing his last name 'Whine'. "The fourth."

Four generations of Whiny Dicks? That was a terrible fate to heap on humanity. The corner of Malcolm's lips twitched up in a sneer that he forced into a smile. "Mister Winn, to what do we owe the honor?"

"A friend of a friend recommended I tour the place with you." Winn looked around in dismay. "It's not much to look at, is it?"

"It's certainly not the art district," Malcolm agreed. Sonya had said she'd send the datcube by armed courier. This wasn't what he'd had in mind. There was a subtleness to the plan that he could appreciate though. Armed men with bullet-proof briefcases drew more attention than casual visits from wealthy new friends.

"Not quite the red light district either." Winn surveyed the secretaries again and Malcolm could hear them grinding their teeth in a collective fume.

"Our staff are hired for their intelligence."

"Intelligence gets in the way."

"Is that a family motto?"

"What?" Winn frowned at him not understanding the insult. "The family motto is *Ex Fortitudine Fatum.* It means Blessed With A Beautiful Fate."

"It means From Courage, Fate." Malcolm glared at Harringworth's back as his supervisor slunk away.

Winn's nostrils flared. "It is my family motto. I think I know it better than you."

"My father teaches languages at the university and I'm fluent in the Imperial language." His fists were burning with the desire to rearrange the stranger's face. "Would you like a tour, Mister Winn?"

"Lord Winn," the man corrected. "My family are seventh generation nobility in Wellden."

Naturally. Only seven generations of in-breeding could produce this level of assured stupidity. "Lord Winn? Follow me." Malcolm steered him past the crowds. "Is there anything you'd particularly like to see?"

"It doesn't matter. Sonya asked me to come visit, so I'm here, visiting."

"Right. Why don't we step into the conference room?" Malcolm led him down the side hall that ended in a door to the back parking lot. There was a small conference room where the company kept applicants—when they were accepting them. Some days it smelled heavily of sweat and sex. Today it smelled of stale air and grease from someone's late night snack. "Please, make yourself comfortable."

Winn reached into his pants pocket and pulled out the datcube. "Here. This is what Sonya sent. She said you'd know what it meant."

Malcolm took it carefully. "Considering the contents, I expected this to arrive with more fanfare. Why you?"

Winn snorted in amusement. "I'm the only heir to the Winn fortune. Everyone in Wellden knows me. Everyone who is anyone on Descent respects me. Who would dare to accost me?"

Malcolm looked at the man's clothes again. "Someone who thought your pocket money would keep them fed for a year or two? Ryun is not a small city-state. And not everyone here is living in the lap of luxury." Ryun had three times the population of Wellden and nearly half that amount sprawled on the plains around the city. "You should have been more careful."

"My name is all I need," Winn said with a sneer. He turned away with a casual wave and left Malcolm with the datcube.

Twisting the cube in his hand, Malcolm took the back stairs to his office. As soon as the doors were locked and the privacy filters over the floor-to-ceiling windows were in place, he called Sonya.

"Doctor Long, has the gift arrived?"

"Yes." He placed it on the desk. "Tell me, the man I just met, are all the people around you like him?"

"Didn't you get along?" He could hear the smug smile in her voice.

"Not at all."

"Don't fret, doctor dear. Kedic is a useful pawn and nothing more. I'm sure you've heard the last of him."

"Thank you."

"Repay me by unraveling all the little gem's secrets as fast as you can. I will make it well worth your time."

Malcolm put the phone away slowly. Tangling with the politics of Descent was dangerous. But if the price was decrypting this for Sonya, he'd pay it. Better this than his family's blood.

7
ROWENA

ROWENA TILTED THE GLOSSED piece of metal sheeting she was using as a mirror and compared the image to the one she'd downloaded as a reference for Tarrin business clothes. The shirt was a stretchy, ribbed material cut with a high collar, no sleeves, and dyed a color called Deep Cranberry. The slacks and jacket were cut like the suit from her first encounter with Dr. Keen, but this time dyed a deep hull-metal gray with metallic accents threaded in.

On the grounder model it looked elegant and intimidating. On her it looked... Rowena glared at her reflection. Well...

It was clothes.

It wasn't a uniform. It didn't allow for the same movement her coveralls did. But the jacket did hide the knife sheath hidden under her belt at the small of her back.

She tried letting her black hair down and grimaced. Too easy to grab.

Even if they were meeting at the doctor's office and not in the morgue, it was too risky.

Her implant pinged with a distress code, a bright red flare and Aronia's signature image of a bowl of black berries and white flowers.

:What's wrong?:

:I need you here for a few minutes.:

Rowena tagged the Enclave shield as she teleported to her sister's house in the university district of Tarrin. She landed in the small living room with a tiny beige couch and a faded green blanket from the *Danielle Nicole's* ship stores with a metal rattle she'd fabricated for her nephew. The off-white walls were bare except for a layer of dust.

Aronia hurried toward her down the hall, the only thing delineating the living space from the kitchen and dining space, and shrugged apologetically. "Thank you for coming. Ki isn't sleeping well these days." She held up the nearly one-year-old baby as proof.

Ki glared as best as a child could from under a thatch of dark hair, his pudgy cheeks and lips chapped from drool. Aronia had told her about teething babies and it looked as horrific as it sounded.

"I can take him later this evening," Rowena said. "I don't know who's scheduled for family duty, but he can come play with me while I run diagnostics. Couldn't you?" She held out her hands to the baby.

Ki's lower lip trembled as his eyes filled with tears.

"That's not the problem," Nia said. "I need you to check on Yunjin."

The mention of the name brought up Rowena's file on the cadet. "I saw her this morning. Her shields need work, but she's doing all right in class."

"It's not class I'm worried about. Hoshi has started handing out assignments for the cadets. Their first training berths."

Rowena blinked. How had she missed that? "It's a bit early for that. They aren't near graduating yet."

Nia lifted a shoulder in a tired shrug. "You know how he is."

"I know there's only one Lee in my class, and that's Yunjin. Who else is he giving assignments to?"

"Some of the kids on his side."

"Ones who didn't make it past the fleet screening tests to get a slot in the Academy classes?" Rowena asked in disbelief. "What kind of cre—" She cut off her sentence. "I told him that I would work with those cadets on crew time and help them. A few weeks working with me and they could pass the next round of evaluations. Catch the next training cycle."

Nia nodded. "Hoshi has been training them."

"Idiot." She looked at Ki. "Sorry, I shouldn't bad mouth a captain in front of a future officer."

Nia tucked her son's head under her chin as she held him close. "Tay is upset. So am I. We're..." Nia blinked back a tear and Rowena caught the emotions she was hiding behind a tight shield. "We're thinking of handing in our commissions. Both of us. We can raise Ki here in Tarrin, away from the fleet."

"What?"

"I'm a lieutenant, but no one listens to me," Nia said. "I haven't been promoted in four years. I don't have my squad's respect. I can't even get a meeting with my captain for anything. Not even an officer evaluation, and I'm supposed to have those yearly."

Rowena sucked her cheeks in.

There was still time before her meeting with Tyrling.

Killing Hoshi wouldn't take more than a few minutes.

"Don't," Nia said, seeing her expression. "Don't even think about it. Tay's family is still on board."

"Then tell them to get off board!"

"Yunjin is a good officer!" Nia's voice cracked with emotion. "She's so bright, Ro. So sweet. She's going to make an outstanding officer, if Hoshi just lets her try. And she wants it so much. Tay's family has never had a senior officer in their line."

Rowena perched on the back of the couch. "We can get her into another crew. I have friends, a few favors I could call in... The Carylls need junior officers aboard the *Persephone*."

"She's a Lee!" Nia said. "She shouldn't have to give that up."

"Then what do you want me to do?" Rowena looked at her sister, emotions bubbling across the family link. She'd do anything for Nia. Anything.

Nia looked guilty. "Could you... can you talk to Hoshi about giving her a good berth?"

"Me? What alternate reality did you come from and where's my sister? Hoshi Lee isn't going to do anything I want!"

"Couldn't you get your own ship?" Nia asked. "Start a new Lee crew?"

Her sister had been reading the fantasy nishu books again. "How? I don't have time to rebuild a hull. I don't have the resources to trade for it."

"You have the *Danielle Nicole* as dowry." Nia said, cheeks blushing. "If you married someone you could—"

"M-marry?" The word filled her throat, choking her. "Aronia Shiyang Lee! Have you lost your hull-cracked mind?

Nia looked away, holding her son tight. "We can't afford an internal war and no one wants to break away."

"What poor person were you going to sacrifice to be my spouse?" Rowena tried to keep her voice level, but it wasn't working. "Spouses expect things. Like... touching, and comfort, and love, and all those things I am no good at."

Nia grimaced. "I was hoping you'd outgrow some of that."

"I haven't." Rowena rubbed a hand over her eyes. "Look, I need to go meet with the grounders. I will do what I can for Yunjin. Talk to some of the sub-captains at least. They're all waiting on repairs and I can trade expedited repairs for a request to Hoshi for Yunjin." She took a deep breath. "Are you really going to resign your commission?"

"I might," Nia said. "I don't want to, but the fleet's made it clear there's no career for me there. There are good engineering firms here on the ground. I have an internship with the hypertram company next month."

"Lethe?" Rowena asked in surprise. She shook her head.

"I know what you think, but it's local stuff. Nothing to do with the Lethes. Or Sonya. Or whoever is in charge."

"Still..."

"I'll be fine," Nia promised. "And I'll wait a bit longer. Finish the schooling here at least, before I leave the fleet. But, Rowena, I can't wait forever. And I don't want to leave you. If you can't find a way to get promoted, I want you to come with me. I want you to leave the fleet."

The cold of vacuum squeezed Rowena's heart. What was she supposed to say? Nia needed her. Baby Ki needed her. What she wanted didn't matter. "Okay."

There were more important things than her dreams.

Doctor Keen's office was divided into a visitor section with couches and low, stone table, and her work area with diagrams of human bodies and red stone desk piled with books. It all felt very... organic.

Tryling had been waiting for Rowena outside with one of his junior officers, a thin young man with close-cut brown hair who looked too young to be at this meeting. Maybe it was seeing baby Ki. She was feeling old.

Rowena sat on one of the short couches listening to the doctor explain how the rest of the autopsy had gone. Names of muscles and surgical cuts droned past without needing her attention.

"This is the only possible cause of death," Keen concluded as she lay a small silver and blue orb no larger than a hazelnut on the table between them.

"Interesting design," Tyrling said before passing it to his second.

The Jhandarmi officer passed it to Rowena and her implant pinged off the telekyen and orun. She held it up to the light. The central part was a blue glass of some kind, with something inside cradling the sliver of orun. Plasma possibly. Or a liquid. The metal caps on the orb were silver in color, cold to the touch, and veined with nanite wiring.

"The materials are ones we use in fleet," Rowena said. "But the design isn't anything I've seen before."

Her implant could find nothing similar in the records. Which didn't rule out some sort of priority tech, or expunged and redacted tech. But there was something else. "It feels... grown? Fleet likes to make things symmetrical. If I made something like this, I'd start with the innermost layer and work out. The outer layers would be the newest. This feels like the outer layer is the oldest."

"How could you possibly tell?" Keen asked. "Unless the center was replaced, it was all made at the same time."

Rowena rolled the orb in her hand, testing the weight of it, felt the heat of the orun and energy inside. It was heavy for its size and still generating more heat than the orun crystal could account for. "There are techniques for measuring age." And a process. Her implant brought up engineering techniques of the Third Wave of Colonization. "The metal flowers of the Arborian Moons."

"The what?" Tyrling looked at her in confusion.

"It's an old story that came with the Marshals, the old Fleet Marshals. One of their ships was from the Arborian System, the *Willow Bough,* and it had a garden of growing metals. The ship was destroyed in one of the early wars, but the lore says they could manufacture telekyen objects the same way a plant pushes out blossoms."

The Jhandarmi officer held out his hand for the orb. "Could it be that old?"

"Sure," Rowena said. "There isn't a hull in the fleet that is younger than a thousand years. The Malik System is metal-poor. Ninety-seven percent of the metals you see every day were shipped in while we were still in contact with the Empire. Everything has been made to last. Retrofitted, repaired, but never wasted. Never lost."

"It doesn't explain what it was doing in my patient's body," the doctor said. "It was molded around his heart. Flattened out somehow. I tried squeezing it, but..." She gestured towards the hard metal sphere.

Rowena nodded. "It's telekyen, which means it can be manipulated."

"By someone with a fleet augmentation?" Tyrling asked.

She hesitated; that was sticky political ground. "I could do it. Most officers could. But there are other ways. Before we adopted standard augmentations, the fleet and colonists used telekyen for a number of things. There are machines that could manipulate it."

"But, how would a native find the machine?" the Jhandarmi officer asked. "It's not like they're common."

"Every print and shipping office should have one," Rowena said. "Those shops where you order something and the machine prints the item or pieces for you? All of those can manipulate telekyen. Any shipping office would have a fabricator that morphs telekyen to create specialty-sized shipping containers."

Tyrling grimaced. "That doesn't exactly narrow it down."

"Sorry." She shrugged apologetically. "If you give me some time, I might be able to break it down and figure out how it works."

"Time is something we have in short supply." Tyrling exchanged glances with his officer. "We'll do it the old way. Send people to track down what Briceno was doing before he died. Talk to friends, family, co-workers. Check the cameras and retrace his steps. Lee?"

"Yes, sir?"

"Can you find a way to track devices like this?"

Rowena checked the satellites available to her. "I could do it right now. That's a matter of coding. But if you want a way for the Jhandarmi to do the search without me, that will take some time. I would need to find a way for you to use a fleet scanner without triggering the shields over Tarrin."

Taking down the shields and doing a quick sweep would be the easiest solution, and also the most obvious.

"No one knows we have this yet, do they?" Rowena asked.

Dr. Keen shook her head. "I found something with a similar density and slipped it into the decedent. It's inert, but the family was planning to bury him at sea as part of one of the living reefs. It's unlikely anyone would notice the difference."

"Unless this is a way of smuggling data," Tyrling said. The Jhandarmi were still reeling from the loss of priority information the year before, and it had sensitized them to the ways data could be stolen and smuggled

Rowena took the orb back and scanned it. "If there was data, it's not there now. All I can find is an instruction code for protein releases. And... this is still active. It's operational." Too late she realized that by dismissing it as a grounder device she'd ignored the potential threat. The whole mission would be compromised if this were a listening device. She put a heavy shield over it to block any further transmissions.

"What kind of protein releases?" Dr. Keen asked. "Could it trigger muscle movement?"

Rowena nodded. "This could be as simple as an experimental heart monitor. Or something meant to regulate an irregular heartbeat."

"Something to ask the family," Tyrling said. "They didn't mention a cardiac condition when we spoke, but people can be notoriously tight-lipped about that sort of thing."

"Experimental medicine isn't shameful," Dr. Keen said with a fierce glare that made Rowena smile.

"But being too proud to use the standard healthcare would look bad, politically," Tyrling said.

The doctor frowned. "Was Briceno looking at a political run?"

"There are rumors," Tyrling said. "But, at the moment, those are only rumors. We need facts before I can dismiss this case as medical negligence. Besides, heart monitors don't generally get corpses moving again." His tone suggested that he doubted it was medical at all.

Rowena was inclined to agree. From what she knew of the grounder scientists, she couldn't picture them letting a patient die and not following up. Dr. Keen should have had calls from the patient's attending physician within hours of the death announcement.

The silence was damning.

"There is another possible method," Rowena said slowly. "I might be able to track the movement of the device. If we compare that path to Briceno's, it would at least tell us where he picked it up."

Tyrling raised his eyebrows. "How could you do that? I was told telekyen was untrackable."

"Telekyen is too common to track, but orun isn't. Each orun crystal has a slightly different pattern of vibration. It causes disruption patterns at a quantum level that allow you to track the path of crystal. The problem is that the disruption pattern lingers for decades. In space, it's useless. The ships have crisscrossed the solar system so many times that there's too much noise. But on the planet?" She shrugged. "Orun is rare. Theoretically, I can re-task a satellite to track the crystal's movements."

She'd have to beg a favor from Titan and sweet talk the *Persephone* into listening to her. Loop him in on this. Risky, but of all the people she knew, Titan was one of the few she could trust. He wouldn't let word of orun mining get around fleet.

Tyrling nodded. "Get on it. Report in as soon as you have anything."

Rowena acknowledged him with a smile. "I will."

8

HOLLIS

ON A TORN SHEET OF PALE FABRIC, images of the past danced to a music no one could hear. The file, an old family memory stored in the Silar archives, had been corrupted when the *Ida Wells* had taken damage. Hollis watched it anyway.

In the hollowed-out wreckage of the *Nanny Maroon*, he sat on a worn couch, watching his parents celebrate their anniversary. His three older brothers were there, and him, and Gen barely two years old. His own memory of the event had faded. He hadn't been old enough for even a gauntlet that day, but he remembered the atrium of the *Ida Wells* where his father had worked. Somehow, Marcin Silar had convinced his CO it was okay to have a family party amid the plants that provided oxygen and food for the crew. A faded blue blanket sat on the floor between stands of trees with bright green leaves and pale orange blossoms. He could almost smell the oxygen-rich air and the loam enriched by the ship's fish supply.

His father had died there only a few years later when the Baular's *Errol* had opened fire. His mother had died in her fighter while defending the evacuating shuttles. After that, they'd gone to the *Veronica Guerin*. His oldest brother had been surrogate father, seeing everyone off to the Academy and remembering birthdays.

Until they'd gone to war again, and Trace had come back in a funeral capsule, a recording of his torture and death coded to infect every nearby mind when the capsule was opened.

That memory was all too clear. All too cruel.

Closing his eyes, Hollis ordered the family video to rewind and replay from the beginning.

There was a soft knock of knuckles on bare metal hull and a familiar touch against his shields. *Hermione.* Not his first lover or his last, but once upon a time she'd been his everything. The sun at the center of his orbit. Beautiful, brilliant, dangerous… loving her was addictive and exhilarating. Watching their relationship burn on the pyre of war had taken something from him, hardened him against whimsy and hope for a time.

What they'd formed out of those ashes was something unique in his experience, a friendship built on a perfect love, and a perfect understanding that they didn't love each other well enough to be happy together.

Not that he hadn't tried to convince her otherwise more than once. But, like everything else over the past year, he'd lost interest in pursuing her heart again. "Come on in," he said, not turning around. He moved, making room on the couch for Hermione to sit and lean on his shoulder.

"How are you?" she asked, taking his invitation and cuddling into him. The couch was a little too short for a pair as tall as they were, but she curled her long, brown legs in and managed to make herself comfortable.

Hollis kissed the tight curls of her hair that smelled of gardenias and sea brine. "I'm good."

"Really?" Her melodic voice was filled with skepticism. "This is the third night in a row you've come over here to watch memory files."

"Gen told you?" Typical. His baby sister had two best friends in the whole fleet, and one of them just happened to be the one willing to goad a dragon in its den. If Gen ever bonded with Rowena he'd be outnumbered and out-gunned.

"You should be happy your sister still worries about you." Hermione paused the memory, freezing the screen on an image of his family smiling back at him from the past. "One night is fine. Two is not unheard of. By the third, you're usually trying to drown the memories in dopamine with whoever you can find who's up for an athletic romp in the sheets."

"So?"

"So why are you here, alone, instead of picking fights and flirting over at Cargo Blue?"

Hollis shrugged and tugged at Hermione's dark curls. "Didn't feel like it. I'm leaving first thing in the morning for training."

She looked up, beautiful brown eyes filled with worry. "When's the last time you took a lover?"

"It's been a bit." He'd erased the countdown timer months ago and archived the memories, as unexceptional as they'd been. "Why?"

"You're playing with my hair again. It's a sure sign you aren't getting enough cuddling and sex."

He forced himself to drop her hair. "I've been busy."

"That's a lie."

"I haven't been interested?" he tried.

Hermione frowned. "Really? Or is everyone shooting you down?"

"I can count the number of people who have turned me down, and aren't related to me, on one hand." He ran the names through his head. Yes, five from his cohort. All of them had been pleasant lovers. Not as good as Hermione, but fun, satisfying. The relationships had been good while they lasted, but weren't worth pursuing now. "I'm just not interested in a casual relationship right now. No particular reason why."

"Gen and Perrin's marriage isn't a factor? You don't think seeing your sister married hasn't made you think about finding a spouse for yourself? Someone you could cuddle with every night?" Hermione had known him too long.

He slouched into the couch, giving himself space. "Maybe. Probably not though. I'm just... homesick? Maybe? Can you be homesick for the past?" His mother was staring straight at him, smiling, happy in the eternal moment of memory.

Hermione reached out to stroke his hair and he leaned away. It wasn't her touch he wanted.

"I'm fine. Really. Just tired."

Hermione rested her head on the crook between his shoulder and chest. "It's Trace's birthday today, isn't it?"

Hollis nodded as he moved Hermione's shoulder and resettled her so she lay against his chest. "Ten years older than me. But he never got to be as old as me."

"I'm sorry." He knew she was. She'd mourned his brother as much as he had. Held him through the dark times when all he could see was death. Stayed with him long after she stopped loving him.

"Thank you." The silence swelled around them, a heartbroken, heavy moment. Hollis closed his eyes and fought to pull himself out of the past. "How are you? I haven't seen you all week."

Hermione chuckled bitterly and closed her eyes. "There's a high-profile missing persons case on Descent. I've been running around trying to get the city-states to cooperate with each other. The Jhandarmi aren't taken as seriously over there, and a lot of the older families still feel they are above the law."

"Sounds fun."

"About as fun as sitting in an empty wreck of a ship talking to ghosts."

"It's not empty! The lower decks have been refitted as workout and training rooms. There are people downstairs swimming, and playing games, and having fun. Some of the year sixteen cohort are having a party."

"And you have a big shield up, keeping all of the fun away from you." Hermione pinched his side. "You're getting to be a grouchy old man, Hollis."

He squeezed her closer. "You're older than me."

"By a month!"

"Still older." He bumped his head on her curls with a smile.

She looked up at him. "There's the Hollis we all know and love. I missed your smile."

"Sorry I made you work for it."

Regret filled her eyes. "There was a time when I could make you smile by walking into the room. Now, I can barely hold your attention when I'm curled up in your arms."

"You were my sky and stars," Hollis said. "My light. My gravity. My whole world orbited around you. But it wasn't enough. I wish it had been. You're beautiful. Intelligent. Caring. Wonderful."

"So are you."

"But that wasn't enough, was it?" He sighed and leaned his head back, looking at the distant darkness overhead. "We did it all wrong. Somehow, we did it all wrong."

Hermione sighed too. "I wish I could have loved you the way you loved me. Being the center of your attention was amazing. Intoxicating."

"But not enough. I never had your full attention, or your heart."

"You had most of it."

"Mmm." He twined his fingers through her hair, enjoying the rough texture. "I was mostly your type."

She laughed. "I have a type?"

"Oh, yes. Intelligent, powerful, dominating."

Hermione nodded agreement.

"A leader, a doer, someone who is on the frontlines of the fray, but given to introspection and brooding. Sometimes pouting."

She slapped his leg. "Unfair!"

"Fond of strategy, math, and self-sacrifice, just like you."

"Of course."

"Blond." Hollis watched Hermione's face for a reaction.

She didn't even hide her eyeroll. "I liked redheads once."

"Mmm, no. You played with redheads once. You liked blonds."

"Not all blonds!"

"One particular blond genius. A pilot and fighter extraordinaire." He sighed at the memory of losing her to a man he'd hated. "You could live a hundred lives, and I'm convinced you'd always only have eyes for him."

Hermione's posture changed ever so slightly, a little tension in the shoulders, the tiniest frown drawing down her lips, an infinitesimal tightening of her jaw as she prepared to lie. "You know that's not true. Besides, he's dead."

Hollis gave her hair a tug. "We still love people after they leave for the Lost Fleet. Nothing's changed. Dead or not, you love him. More than you ever loved me."

She relaxed and grimaced. "I'm sorry. I really am. It would be so much easier if I could make myself love you."

"You don't need to," Hollis said. "We're good like this. Side by side, as friends, we're great like this. Happier. Healthier. And I will happily watch when you fall in love. Ready to cheer you on, or kill him if he makes you unhappy."

"And you? When do I get to cheer your courtship on?"

"Um... how does six weeks after never sound?" He smiled. "There's no one that wants to deal with me long term. I'm too much effort to civilize."

"You're very civilized."

"You are the only person who thinks that."

Hermione kissed his cheek. "I have to go, and you should too. Head over to Cargo Blue and have some fun. You need it."

"I'll think about it."

"Go, Hollis. If I get back and find you haven't, I'll drag you out myself."

He smiled in forfeit. "I'll go. Promise. Promise!"

Hermione left him with a smile.

Reluctantly, Hollis shut off the projector. Cargo Blue sounded unappetizing. Going to his bunk would result in a sleepless night grinding his teeth, and wandering Tarrin wouldn't settle him down.

He looked at his to-do list for tomorrow. When all else failed, there was always paperwork. Reports to file. Training schedules to review. Classes to schedule.

Classes.

Academy.

Trace.

Hollis squeezed his eyes shut, trying to focus on something other than the war and the heartbreak, but it was all too close to the surface.

A quick scan told him the training gym was empty; he could go hit the punching bags until exhaustion carried away the pain. It was as good a plan as any.

9
ROWENA

ROWENA TELEPORTED TO THE quiet of Enclave in the wee hours of morning, still smelling of the perfumed smoke she'd gotten caught in leaving a museum in Dalmine in the north. Infuriating grounder festivals.

Every scan for orun traces had led her to documented antiquities.

She sighed and watched the sun rise, a red stain over the seawall. Heavy waves rose and slammed against the shore in an angry tattoo as if they too understood her frustration.

Silence wrapped around the forest of landing gears, punctuated only by the sound of heavy fists pummeling a sand bag in the gym.

Checking her calendar, she frowned; today was an all-crew off day. No one should have been in her gym. Confused, she crossed the courtyard to see who was putting in the extra hours. She needed the space to work without Hoshi's interference, so whoever it was could get ready to take a beach run to cool down. The large bay door had been left open, leaving the fighter bathed in the crimson light of dawn.

The color suited him.

Hollis twisted, kicking high and sending the sand bag flying across the room. He was stripped down to training shorts, russet-red hair slick with sweat, with his shield on full war mode. Through the filters of her implant she could see it spiking and twisting like a storm, golden and opal-white tendrils writhing around him and then striking out like vipers. As he reached for another sand bag, he caught sight of her.

He turned, bag forgotten, and glared. His eyes were molten gold, the whites completely lost behind his war shield so he looked like some mythical war god. "What are you doing here?" His voice was gravely with anger, the rumbling warning of an avalanche in the mountains.

"It's my training gym," she said, the instinct to defend herself against his aggressive stance making her jaw tighten.

She didn't need to check the date to know why he'd fallen back into the battle memories. The anniversary of Trace's death was always hard. Obviously Hollis hadn't found a pack of warmongers to pummel this time. Maybe he was finally letting the pain go.

"Get out. It's an off day." He turned back to the sand bag.

Rowena crossed her arms and watched him devastate another piece of training equipment. If he noticed she was still there when he took a third one, he didn't say anything.

Or maybe not. He was going to destroy half her training equipment before he even slowed down. If she didn't stop him, she was going to spend a week filling out requisition forms. "Wouldn't you rather have an opponent who can hit back? Or are you feeling cowardly?"

A wave of energy flared across the warehouse, slamming into the walls with a sharp crack.

She let it fly past her, shields redirecting the energy like a stone under angry waves. This was the downside of implants. Sometimes the stored memories took over. It became impossible to separate past from present and suddenly you found yourself reliving a moment—or a war—with no escape.

Dumping the memories into permanent storage was the best solution. But for someone who had lost so much, the need to let go was constantly at war with the fear of forgetting everyone who mattered.

Hollis pivoted, shields glowing, creating a protective aura around him the same color as his eyes. "Get. Out."

"No."

He stalked forward, the ground shivering under every telekyen-enhanced step.

She lifted her chin. "I'm your training partner. You want to fight? Let's fight." It would save her gym. Besides, if he got loose in this state, she was the one the Starguard would call anyway. Carver and Marshall would only feed his rage. She could give it focus.

The air between them grew hot. That was a Silar special she hadn't seen since the war.

"I don't want a friendly fight."

"Good." She smiled. They didn't need another training fight. She teleported a knife to her hand. "Let's fight, Silar. Winner gets to hide a body."

With a thought she moved herself to the large battle platform at the center of the gym and pulled her shields up, a protective net around her. The outer layer was laced with a high energy charge meant to burn or shock, depending on where her enemy was careless enough to hit. Under that she had an obscuring field, swirling like muddy water. And under that, another layer controlling the air, temperature, and cushioning her body from projectile attacks.

Hollis didn't bother with a polite tap against her shields. He came in like a magnetic storm, slamming her defenses all at once as the platform shook under them. Phantom colors flitted across the gold of his eyes. Wherever he was, it wasn't in the here and now.

He was lost in some war memory, buried in a place where she was an enemy.

They'd gone toe-to-toe, no-holds-barred only once during the war. She'd led a raid on the damaged Silar ship *Aquila* to retrieve orun, only to find Hollis there trying to bring the ship to safety with a tiny crew and pure stubbornness. He'd set off an EMP bomb to keep her from using her implant, and for six hours they'd fought, sniping at each other, beating each other back into a desperate stalemate.

This time they had shields.

He sliced at those first, cutting through her outer layer as the obsidian knife danced between his fingers. "You can run."

She ground her teeth. "Lees don't run."

Hollis lashed out with a whip of energy that disrupted her diffuse second shield. He followed it with a quick punch, followed by a front kick.

Rowena dodged, then fell into the fight with a flurry of low kicks. She moved around him, trying to gauge his defenses.

Her shield flickered under a brute technological assault and she caught a low kick to her right hip. Rowena followed up with hard left kick to his ribs.

Silar raised his shield, leaving her kick bouncing off air. But it bought her space.

Growling, she attacked with her fists, punching high and low.

Nothing landed and Silar circled away, rapidly recoding his shields.

Rowena took advantage of his distraction, throwing a hard left leg kick to his lead leg. It connected and Silar stumbled down.

He teleported back to an upright position and brought out a second knife.

Pressing her lips into a grim line, Rowena pulled up another layer of shielding. If he wanted a rematch, he'd get one.

She'd been angry back then on the *Aquila*. Made mistakes out of fear and fury. Now, she was in control.

Her shields shimmered a deep black-green with silver streaks that flashed red when Silar probed them.

As reached he out, she sent a tendril of code that flowed back with his shield. The worm infiltrated his defenses silently as death, breaking his shields down, disrupting his rhythm.

Silar switched tactics, driving her to the corner of the platform with a series of punches.

Rowena fell back, stumbling and landing hard. She only just managed to keep a basic shield up as Silar rained down brutal punches and augmented fury on her shield.

She kicked, not something clean or graceful, but it gave her space to move again, and she scrambled to her feet.

He went for her legs, trying to knock her back down into a kill position.

There was a dirty joke there about Silars and floors, but she couldn't find the breath for it. Sweating, she slipped from his grasp.

They circled, testing one each other, flirting with quick strikes and brute strength. When she went one way, he took the other, but they were always moving, his knives never still, always spinning.

The air grew hot again. Underfoot, the mats crinkled and smoked in the heat.

Rowena poured energy into her inner shields, letting the outer one weaken under Silar's attack. He should have been slowing down by now. War memories rarely lasted long enough that an Elite fighter couldn't simply wait them out.

Hollis stalked forward, pushing against her shields until—with a grimace—he stepped into them. The outer layers crackled, snapping with angry energy as they roiled together.

Fear tightened her throat. *Crack my hull.* :Silar?: The ping bounced off a multitude of shields.

He was going to kill her.

The ancestor's bedamn'd bastard was really trying to kill her.

Common sense said she should teleport out. But she knew Silar. Once he locked on, he'd follow wherever she fled. They'd trade the relative safety and anonymity of the training gym for somewhere with civilians.

She had to kill him here. Or at least knock him out.

A fist broke through, knife-blades shrieking as they collided. Silar was done punching.

They broke apart, both breathing heavily. Silar's eyes still blazed with battle fury.

Rowena circled to his right to get outside foot position, avoiding his dominant side. She had to slow the fight down, bring him back if possible.

But quickly.

Fights were meant to be short. Even with the implant there was a time limit before muscle fatigue and the heat took her down.

Silar threw a right knee, missed and stepped away.

Rowena circled to his left for a better angle and shot a hard kick to his left leg.

Silar pushed Rowena against the ropes. His knee hit her rib cage. He had mass on his side—but she had sanity.

She grappled with him, throwing a leg kick to his injured left thigh as she tore at his shields. She added an audio attack, sounds blaring all around him as she cocooned him in confusion.

Stepping back, Silar shook his head and tried to pull his shields up, but she kept them down and fired off another kick.

Silar didn't even block. From somewhere, he pulled a reserve of power and threw up a fire shield that burned her eyes and face. Silar fire. That was a trick she'd have to learn one day.

For now, she fell back, arms blocking the light as she pulled a cold shield into place, her force of will freezing the air molecules.

Golden tongues of fire licked her shield. The knife was ripped from her grasp.

She took his metal one, shattering it with a thought, but the obsidian knife stayed. Typical. That knife was always between them, one way or another. She could hold him off for a few more minutes, but the heat was sucking the life out of her. She had to end it, quick.

Her worm found the code, and she gritted her teeth in triumph.

Taking his inner shield was child's play; he was focused on the outer ones and let the inner shield code cycle with too many repetitions.

Leaving an opening, she pulled Silar in, teasing him closer as she ruthlessly peeled away his shields one by one.

She kicked his thigh, trying to knock him nerveless, but he held firm.

He drove his knee into her body and then latched on, falling with her and landing on top.

The black knife flashed in his hand as his eyes burned gold. He sliced down.

Rowena smiled.

10

HOLLIS

BLACK HAIR AGAINST A BURNT mat. The image over-rode the memory of the *Aquila* burning. Burning plastic and perfume tickled his nose as he focused on a fluttering pulse under golden skin under a black blade.

Hollis licked dry lips, picturing what would happen, the skin splitting as bright red blood fountained out. His gaze flicked up from his opponent's neck to their eyes. To see the fear. To see the remorse.

Rowena smiled, dark eyes soft and relaxed.

It wouldn't take any effort to drain the light from her eyes. His arm knew the motion. He could cut her out of his nightmares. Rage made his muscles shake.

His implant flashed a warning: he was losing power rapidly, about to be vulnerable. If he didn't kill Lee now, he might never have another chance.

He twisted. Slammed the knife hilt-deep into the green padding of the training mats and rolled away cursing. Rushing blood drummed in his ears as he stared up at the cross-beams of the ceiling.

Something cold nudged his bruised ribs. "What? You're quitting?

"Quitting?" He turned his head to look at Rowena, heart pounding. "Why were you smiling? I was about to kill you. What were you doing?" She was lying on the charred mat, hair pulled back, with a ridiculous grin on her face. He wanted to pick her up and shake some sense to that thick Lee skull of hers. "You've lost your hull-cracked mind, Lee."

He pressed the heels of his hands to his eyes and checked his implant. Two percent. He couldn't even teleport to safety.

"I had a close shield. You were going to strike and the force would have made your knife bounce back up. I figured breaking your own nose might knock some sense into you." There was the scratchy sound of slow movement and a shadow fell between him and the lights.

"I nearly killed you, and you're laughing?" He'd held her shields, been ready to strip them off her… It was so easy to see the knife sliding through her throat, bright red blood spraying in the air.

He'd slit dozens of throats in war. Cut them and moved on, because there was no other choice. They'd needed food, or water, or orun. They'd needed to repel invaders or defend the ship. And at the end of the day he'd gone home, erased the memories of those fear-filled eyes and told himself he was still a good man.

Gradually his heartrate slowed and the gymnasium swam into focus. The smell of burning flesh and the screams of the dying replaced by the smell of melted plastic on the mats, and Rowena. He let his head flop back. There was nothing left to run on without the battle rage.

What did I do?

The last thing he remembered was his mother's smiling face on a screen and Hermione telling him to get to Cargo Blue.

"Hey. Silar." Rowena moved closer, the heat of her body warming him in the sudden chill. "Feel better now you've gone nova in my gym?"

He shook his head as sunlight arced across the ceiling. *Sunlight?*

How long had he been lost in the battle haze?

He tried to remember, but all that came to him was Rowena pinned under his body, smiling up at death. The anger returned full force. "What were you thinking?" he demanded as he sat up. "Did I look like I was rational?"

"You're Hollis." Rowena shrugged. "By default, I assume you're insane."

She was so cheerful about it.

His metal knife clattered across the ground and settled by his knuckles in a response still coded from when he was at the Academy.

Looking unimpressed, Rowena picked up the knife and threw it so it stuck in the far wall. "You tried that already. I'm still here."

"Yes."

Of course it was her standing there watching as he lost his mind.

Any normal person would have run for cover, or at least gotten help. Rowena was the only one crazy enough to go head-to-head with him. He rolled his neck, working out the ache of tension and rage.

Falling backward, he let himself slam into the warm mats. "You can leave now. I'm good. Just leave me here to die." He closed his eyes. Several minutes slipped past, the mat cooling under him.

He opened one eye.

Rowena was still sitting beside him, black hair falling loose of her sloppy ponytail. Her clothes finally registered, not training gear but slouchy civilian-wear. Completely unprepared, and she'd still challenged him.

He tried to read her expression, but it was even more opaque than usual. "Where were you at?"

"A museum, looking for something for the Jhandarmi."

A vague and useless answer. Her voice was level, perfectly relaxed and non-judgmental.

Which was unfair, considering he felt so empty he wasn't sure he had tears left for his murdered brother. He was shaking from exertion, dehydrated, head pounding and already cataloging all the rules he'd broken. Rowena should have been writing up reprimands and demanding he be stripped of rank, not just sitting there.

She raised an eyebrow.

He looked her up and down. There wasn't any major damage, but she wasn't sitting there because she liked his company. "So? Why are you still here?"

"I kinda need the gym back. There's work I need to get done."

"If you wanted me to leave, you shouldn't have left me gasping for air. What did you do to me anyway?" He felt boneless, and not in a fun way.

Her smile grew wider. "You'll have to figure out that trick for yourself. You should recover in a few minutes. I can wait."

Silence settled around them.

Animosity and atmosphere, that's what Rowena always said was between them. But times like this, it was something else. Something almost like kindness. Or forgiveness.

He ran his fingers through his hair.

"Keep breathing, Silar. You survived another one of our annual fights."

His dry lips cracked as he grinned. "You sure you don't want to finish me off while I'm lying here?" Ancestors knew she would have a year ago. A year ago he probably wouldn't have stopped himself from killing her, either.

Rowena surveyed him with a grimace of disdain. "The mats are trashed, so I guess a little more blood wouldn't hurt, and no one would notice you missing right away, but..." She wrinkled her nose and shook her head in dismissal. "Too predictable. Too quick. There'd be no time to savor my victory." She sounded so smug.

"Just admit I'm too cute to kill." Hollis gave her a grin that regularly ended fights and won over reluctant enemies.

There was a snort of laughter as she rolled her eyes. "No. You're not cute. Small, fluffy things are cute. Chubby babies are cute. Tiny gears are cute. You are... something else. Muscled. Hard-bodied. Carved. And cuddly, which is an odd combination." Her eyes met his. "Sorry, Silar, you're never going to be cute. If squat tugs are cute, then you're a fighter jet, full of fire power and raw energy."

"Makes me a helluva ride." He waggled his eyebrows.

"And a helluva fun fight." She smiled smugly. "Too bad you pulled out. I was having a good time."

"I won that fight!" Hollis protested.

She laughed and shook her head as she stood up. "You quit the fight."

The panic returned like a tsunami. "I was on top with a knife at your throat." He grabbed her ankle so she wouldn't walk away. "I was going to kill you."

"No, you weren't." Rowena leaned over him, eyes holding him. "Pinned down isn't dead, Silar. You walked away from the fight too early."

Hollis tried to articulate the frustration seething inside. She looked far too calm for someone who nearly died at his hand. Calm. Collected. *Trusting*.

It was a knife wound he couldn't heal.

Black eyes bored into him. "Stop lying down there hyperventilating. You weren't going to kill me. Even if—and this is a big if—even *if* you took my shield down, you wouldn't have killed me. Lost in a battle memory. Angry. Choked with rage. It doesn't matter what you feel, because it's not happening, Silar." She sounded far too confident.

He stood up, enraged. "What are you saying? That I can't?"

Rowena lifted her chin, attitude making up for the height difference. "I'm saying you won't. Not on accident. You don't lose control like that. If you ever kill me, it will be because you are calm, collected, and you made the choice to get rid of me."

"Really?" He wasn't sure he trusted his temper as much as she did.

"Mmhmmm, the same way I'm choosing to get rid of you right now. If you can argue with me, you can walk out of here."

"Ah, the mess…" He scratched at his temple, half wincing. Some of the mats were melted, and there were curved indentations in the ground where someone had been knocked down and their shield had compacted the concrete floor. Grounder buildings just didn't hold up the way ships did.

"I've got it. The mats were showing wear anyway."

"How are you going to explain the damage?"

Rowena raised her eyebrows and looked around, green and purple auroras flaming across her eyes. "Training accident?"

"A hot night of sex?" He winked.

"In the training gym?" A look of revulsion crossed her face. "You and me?" She shook her head. "You could do better."

He wasn't sure if she meant he could find a better lover or a better lie. And he wasn't sure either was true. But he let it go.

"Go find a shower, Silar. You smell worse than the incense I walked through."

He gave her a mock salute. "Good night, Lee."

Rowena looked pointedly at the sunshine outside. "Good morning, Silar." She made a little shooing motion as the devastated gym equipment lifted itself off the ground and vanished into whatever recycling hold Rowena had teleported it to.

At the edge of the gym, he stopped to watch for a moment, trying to articulate what he felt. Rowena always left him with such conflicted emotions: fury and admiration, hope and hate. Gratitude warred with grim reality.

It was the *Aquila* all over again. A stalemate.

Maybe this was the curse of war. Not the first brutal deaths or the blood that drowned out every dream, but this slow, sad slog through an eternity of battle lines. Never being able to change course. Never being able to make the choice a second time.

They were trapped in a prison of their past grudges.

There was no difference between Rowena being a breath away and in the Lost Fleet with the dead. As long as they kept marching to this cadence, they would never, ever be free. They'd never find a way to each other across a battlefield filled with ghosts.

11

MALCOLM

THE ISLAND CITY-STATE OF RYUN housed over twenty million people, most of them within the ring of hills designed to defend the city from the driving desert winds of Descent, and the rest across the river in the satellite villages. As always, the first thing Malcolm noticed when he drove across the river leaving the city was the lack of trees.

Ryun's architecture was interwoven with a lattice-work of fruit trees, flowering vines, berries, and edible landscapes that provided over a quarter of the food consumed by the citizens each year. Even now there were people at the hedges picking the first fruits of the season.

Tree-lined hills flowed into the wide river, and everything outside the island of Ryun was flat grass plains. Water was expensive, and a family's income could be guessed simply by the amount of lawn they kept. The poorest families had small yards of packed dirt. Closer to the city center and the safer transit lines, the homes had formal rock gardens, carefully cultivated mosaics of river stone and polished glass.

Malcolm turned off the major highway and through a cut between hills to the tiny vale, where a carved stone had the words 'River Willow' painted on it in gold.

Large, well-tended lawns of bright green grass were shaded by tall deciduous trees. Flowering vines hugged trellised sanctuaries along public walking paths. There was a park with a little fountain and a gazebo where a band played on Founder's Day.

All of it screamed wealth to the people of Ryun. This was where the affluent but disconnected lived. The cadet branches of powerful families. The independent entrepreneurs. The forgotten ones who, like his mother, had a small inheritance and no connections.

Straight on Glade Promenade, right on Fawn Drive, left on Hillside, and his parents' house was there, third house on the right. A one-story home, modest by any standard, with neatly trimmed shrubbery framing the golden-maple colored brickwork.

The lights in the front room turned on before Malcolm turned his car off. The door cracked open and his mother's silhouette appeared in the white light.

"Malcolm?" Her long black hair streamed behind her like a cape as she stepped into the night.

He waved as he got out of the car.

"I was so worried! I thought you'd been caught up in that dreadful traffic jam on the loop."

"I was in mid-town for a meeting," Malcolm said. "Missed the loop entirely and took the sixth street bridge. What happened on the loop?"

"Didn't you hear?" His mother grabbed the bag of pale white ghost cherries he'd brought for a peace offering as she herded him inside. "Someone jumped off the hypertram a few days ago."

Malcolm nodded to his father as he stepped into the small living room. "I thought that was cleared up already." Bookshelves filled with his father's collection of antique literature covered the far wall. By the front window, there was a narrow wooden table with a glossy black vase filled with roses—red, pink, and dusty rose-gold—from the garden out back. The wall separating the living area from the dining room didn't have family pictures, but instead a giant replica of the original survey map of Descent, marking the oases created by terraforming. He hung his suit jacket behind the door and took off his black tie.

"It was," his father said, closing a book of languages and tucking it back on the shelf. Lucas Long was no longer a young man, and his pale blond hair was going to snowy white, but he still had an imperious build; Mal had got his height from his father. His stony gray eyes stayed riveted to the screen. "The investigator reopened it. Apparently there were questions about the suicide. The man was an heir from Wallden."

Warning bells went off in Malcolm's head.

Sonya wouldn't...

Sonya couldn't...

If Sonya had...

He rubbed a hand across his mouth to keep from cursing. If Sonya had killed Kedic Winn, he was in much more trouble than he'd anticipated.

His mother touched his shoulder lightly. "Darling? You look worried."

Malcolm shook his head quickly. His mother wasn't raised the Amherst heir. That had been a mid-life surprise when the census on the islands decided to offer a genetic testing component so people could reconnect with their families on the mainland. To his mother, Descent was a beautiful haven, safe, comfortable, and welcoming.

They'd agreed when they moved to Descent that the painful past needed to be forgotten. It was behind them. Whatever future trouble he might get himself into, his parents deserved peace and quiet. "It's nothing. I'm just thinking of the traffic problems a dead heir can cause. He should have been polite and killed himself between the cities."

"Over the river would have been better," Lucas said as he poured a glass of wine for everyone. "Over the loop is messy, but at least the killer had two more stops on the train where they could get off. I'd charge extra if I had to go to Wallden for a contract killing." He sipped his red wine, pale gray eyes fixed in the distance. "Yes, the loop works, if you want to send a message. Over the river is a narrow window of opportunity, but then the victim just disappears."

Mother cleared her throat. "Dearest? You're a professor now."

Malcolm's father shrugged. "It was a thought exercise, dear. I wasn't suggesting I give lessons in murder to strangers." He sniffed. "Anyway, it's of no importance to us. Is it?" He skewered Malcolm with a knowing look.

In return, Malcolm put on a pleasant smile. "It has nothing to do with me. I'll take River Drive to work for the next few weeks. It's a bit longer, but the scenery is much more pleasing." That was true if the driver enjoyed looking at hills, drought-resistant scrub brush, and vistas of the plains. Personally, Malcolm preferred cities, spires of steel and glass, and the dome of a starry night.

But it didn't matter. There was steel and glass enough at work. A few days of looking at plants wouldn't kill him.

His mother seemed to guess his thoughts and wrinkled her nose. Nettie Amherst-Long loved plants. She always had. Even before coming to Descent, she'd been dedicated to botany.

In Ryun she'd, well, bloomed. Her garden was the envy of the city-state.

"Let's have supper," she said. "It's been so long since you visited."

"Work." The excuse didn't even require thought. "Harringworth thinks the company might sell off parts. The boss is looking at new ventures, and Bennu is stable."

His father set the dinner plates at the table as his mother brought over a box from one of the nearby restaurants. Nearly five years of this and none of them had learned to cook a proper meal.

"It's an odd way to run a business," Lucas said. "Build it up and then sell it off."

"Build a building, hire workers for the crew, and hand it off?" Mother shrugged. "Some people like starting things and not finishing them."

Malcolm heard the twist in her voice. "Some things are better unfinished."

"Of course, darling. Did I say otherwise?" Her smile was dazzling.

But he'd seen it all before. His mother had survived an abusive father by smiling sweetly, agreeing when necessary, and being ruthless the rest of the time. For years Lucas had been her only ally, until Malcolm was old enough to be groomed as her protector.

He didn't begrudge his mother his missed childhood. If she'd done anything less, they all would have died.

Now that the threat was gone, his mother's interests had focused on other things. Like...

"Did you hear the Felli girl is getting married? Such a pretty heiress," his mother said as she piled pasta onto his plate.

...Marriage.

Malcolm sighed as he sank into his chair at the dinner table. "How delightful for her. I'll be sure to send a gift."

"You could go to the wedding," his mother said. "We're all invited. The hostess will provide you with a seating companion—unless there's someone you'd like to bring."

The trap dangled in front of him.

"My love," Lucas said, "you're being too obvious. If our son wanted to tell us about his current conquests, he would." He poured the drinks.

Nettie slammed her hand on the table. "What have I said about calling them conquests?"

His father waved the criticism aside. "His dalliances? His interests? What do you want me to call these people our son fails to bring home to meet us?"

"How about the women your son is failing to talk to at all?" Malcolm suggested as he filled a side bowl with salad greens. He smiled at his parents. "I haven't brought anyone home, Mother, because there is no one in my life you need to meet. There's no one important to me."

Too late, he realized the second trap was waiting.

His mother's day planner was on the table and his father's phone was out.

"Blondes?" his mother asked.

"He prefers brunettes," Lucas said without looking up. "With darker skin if I remember."

Malcolm closed his eyes. "I thought this was dinner, not a matchmaking meeting."

"It's dinner and a date planning," his mother said with just a bit of tartness. "What about Kattina's daughter?"

Lucas frowned as he tried to remember. "The chemist? Oh no, a terrible match. She'd drive him mad."

"A little madness makes love exciting."

"No." Lucas looked up from his phone. "What about Marshall's daughter?"

Nettie blinked and Malcolm could see her lips move as she tried to remember the girl's name. "The professor?"

"I don't want to date a professor," Malcolm said.

His mother ignored him. "The father is a professor. The mother does... what?"

"Politics," Lucas said. "As does the daughter. She works at the embassy. Very pretty."

Malcolm was already shaking his head. "No politics. And no daughters of your friends."

His parents slammed down their devices in perfect unison.

"One grandchild," his mother said. "One. Is that too much to ask?"

"At the moment?" His thoughts turned to the dead man on the loop. "Yes."

Much later in the evening, Malcolm looked down on the empty street below his apartment as he shut his curtains. Everything was serenely quiet. He didn't trust the silence. There was a weight to the air, the pressure before a storm, the hush before battle. Black shadows of the night crawled along the bare walls of his apartment.

The original owner of the datcube was dead. The courier was dead. How long could it be before Death came for him too?

He closed himself in his work room. It had been intended as a closet, but with a few modifications, he'd managed to create a place to run his computers without the worry of spytech. The datcube sat alone, isolated on a shelf in a small Faraday cage. The idea of letting it near his other work awoke a primitive fear that he couldn't escape.

"If you do this, you're climbing into bed with Lethe," he told himself.

Revulsion warred with curiosity.

Curiosity won.

He turned off his main computer and took the datcube out to download the contents onto an empty frame. The screen filled with lines of binary code. The first layer of decryption flipped those into letters and numbers. Most of it was so jumbled it meant nothing. But others... he knew.

A cold chill of memory wrapped around him. The phantom taste of stale air and death. Memories of an island and a crash. Stars exploding in the heavens as the forgotten fleet in the sky fought.

The datcube wasn't grounder tech. It didn't belong to Lethe. This belonged to the strangers in Enclave.

He placed the datcube back in the faraday cage.

Did Sonya know what she was asking of him?

12

ROWENA

IN THE CORNER OF THE TRAINING gym, there was a barricade of desks, screens, and fitness reports that divided Rowena's world from the astringent smell of new mats and the paperwork that stank of bureaucracy. Maps of Malik IV were spread on every available surface as she compared the readouts from the *Persephone* with the list of orun-using machines the Jhandarmi had found for her.

A shadow crossed in front of the sunlight let in by the half-open bay door. Rowena flashed an orange warning sign on the shield around her desk, letting the gym's visitor know that she was there and working. If she didn't, there was always the risk that some amorous pair might wander in, thinking they were alone.

The person whistled a tune that had been playing in Cargo Blue all week, and it grew louder as they neared her. There was a tap at her shields.

Closing her eyes, she schooled her expression into one of polite disinterest, and looked up.

Hollis Silar smiled at her, wearing his Guardians all-blacks and holding folded black fabric and some documents.

Crack it all. He probably actually needed to talk. She dropped the outer shield and waved him over. "Yes, guardian? Are the update schedules not near the front door?" He looked better than he had a few hours ago. Maybe someone had knocked some sense into him and made him get some sleep.

"This isn't about schedules."

"Aren't you supposed to be leaving for the mountains to train with the Jhandarmi?" Going away? Giving her space? The thought was the bright point of her day.

"In an hour. There's something we needed to take care of first." He tilted his head to look at the map. "What's that?"

Nothing he needed to be interested in, but she'd planned for intrusions and curious onlookers.

"Plans for a unit on navigation and survival in low-tech environments. The fleetlings aren't supposed to use their implants while we're out, so I'm checking the physical maps for accuracy and making a threat list." Not a complete lie. The fleetlings were scheduled to do field training and knowing where there was orun would be an important part of the navigation portion of the class.

"Anything interesting?"

She turned one the maps around so he could see it better. "This is the north end of Seahome, the second continent. Tropical, volcanically and seismically active, it's the site of the original terraforming drop, which means the species diversity is high, as are the mutation rates for the local flora and fauna.

"Threats include, but aren't limited to, pit crevasses that drop several hundred meters, often populated by *Pandinus imperator albinius*, the pale emperor scorpion that grows up to four meters long, and *Daeodon malikus*, which is a tusked, carnivorous mammal that weighs over six hundred kilos and measures over two meters long. And then there are spiders, snakes, lava flows, poisonous fauna, and—oh, my favorite— the Bloodiers, mutated hunting hounds brought in by a wave of enthusiastic settlers who thought they could hunt the new species. *Canis dirus sanguis*, nearly hairless, obsessive when hunting, and fond of running down live prey. Large packs roam the jungles of Seahome and are completely feral. It's a joyful place."

"Four meter scorpions?" Hollis sounded interested despite himself. "Is that even physically possible?"

"Apparently, if you drop the genetic material of a large scorpion into the terraforming seed mix it's possibly. They aren't true scorpions in the way the Empire would have classified them, but they are scorpion-esque enough that the name's stuck."

He grimaced. "Let's never do that again."

"Well," she tilted her head in thought, "since we don't have the terraforming technology, and we don't have a fleet capable of flying us to other planets, and we don't have another planet worth terraforming in this system, I'd say we're safe. Problem solved." If only all problems were that easy.

"And you're taking the fleetlings to this death trap alone?" He sounded dubious.

"Are you insulting my intelligence, Silar, or questioning my planning skills?" She should have broken one of his bones during the fight. "No, I'm not taking the cranky murder children alone. Half of them want to see me choking on my own blood, and the other half are feral. I'll be gathering volunteers from the crews, possibly from the Starguard, and, if I can make it happen, I'll have a scout patrol from the nearest city-state to lead the teams. Pre-dawn here is full dawn there. If all goes well, we'll leave early and be back in time for them to shower and eat supper with their crews."

Still too many ifs for her liking.

Doing low-tech training was a necessity now that they were grounded, but it wasn't fun. She'd rather deal with a hull breach drill any day of the week.

Animals? Why, dear ancestors, did anyone think seeding the planet with animals mid-terraforming was a good idea? They could be living somewhere with only domesticated species right now, but no, someone had the brilliant idea to put wild animals on the planet.

And speaking of unwanted menaces... "Why are you here?"

"A couple reasons. First, a report courtesy of the Jhandarmi." He dropped the paper folder on her desk.

She took it with a frown. "You weren't supposed to read this."

Hollis shrugged. "They should have encrypted it better. Where is Kydell?"

Checking her implant, she said, "On the southern tip of the second continent. Why?"

In the folder was a printout of images of Briceno walking past columned buildings with a woman who looked vaguely familiar. The face didn't match any fleet files, but it matched a Jhandarmi sketch of a Person Of Interest from a murder in Clyde River at the start of the year.

There wasn't much on the woman, only a picture of a round face, black eyes, and black hair cut to the shoulders, but Rowena added it to her Immediate Attention file anyway. If she saw the woman again, she'd know in an instant.

Hollis clicked his tongue to get her attention. "I skimmed the report Tyrling sent over, since you're so loathe to share information. Briceno, whoever that is, broke his pattern and went there to do some gambling. The Jhandarmi thought you needed to know what their resources were for the area."

Her implant lit up. There were multiple orun sources in the area around Kydell. *Interesting.*

"Are you going to tell me why you need that information?"

"No." He was hiding it well, but she knew he had to be exhausted. There was no reason to add to his list of worries. "What was the second thing?"

He tossed the shirt at her. "Saw it at the flight show and I thought you might want to add it to your grounder wardrobe."

Warily, she unrolled the black fabric. There was a cartoonish picture of an atmospheric plane and a round-faced woman with black hair wearing a flight suit, underscored by the caption, 'Save An Engine Ride A Pilot.'

Rowena looked up. "In what alternate universe would I wear this?"

"Don't know." He shrugged. "She reminded me of you though."

Right... "I guess I could use more cleaning rags in engineering. Anything else?"

Silar smiled and dropped a fleet datfile on her desk. "The Captain's Council had a vote, and gave the OIA orders, who then in turn gave the Starguard and Academy committee orders, and now the orders are yours."

"Orders for what?" Rowena used telekyen to pick the file up and charge the electric pages. "Syllabus for a Sexual Information class? What?" She looked up in horror, blinked, and re-read. "*What?*"

"Carver gave it to me this morning and asked me to pick an instructor. Several of the age seventeen cohort have gone to their captains with questions of a personal nature," Silar said in a tone that sounded perfectly reasonable, which meant he was up to no good. "Normally a captain would tell them to ask their parents. But—"

"But most of this cohort are war orphans." Rowena cursed under her breath. When war was originally proposed, everyone made it sound glorious or necessary, the only path to survival. No one ever mentioned the fallout. Or the aftermath. Or said that the cost of war was more than blood and tears.

Lost Fleet kick Old Baular in the balls for his sins.

"Still... why is this my responsibility? Can't they do crew training on this?"

Silar nodded. "They could, but the captains felt it would be better if this cohort was given training by an adult they trust."

"That should rule me out immediately." Rowena pushed the report back at him. "Like I said, half of them would happily dance over my corpse. Why don't you do it?"

He pushed back with telekyen. The file shivered in the air, suspended between their warring wills. "You're their primary instructor. And, as you said before, I'm already very busy."

"Crack in the hull! What am I supposed to tell them? 'Sex is a thing that sometimes happens between consenting parties and certain people enjoy it?' This is not my field of expertise." She let the report drop to her desk.

This was not news to anyone in the fleet.

Sexual attraction was something she understood on an intellectual level, but rarely experienced. Even she wasn't sure if those brief moments counted. It certainly wasn't the same as what she saw in her crew or friends. And since she was generally touch-phobic, even on a good day, she'd managed to convince the Captain's Council that in their genetic plans for future generations, they could count her out.

Unless she knew the person well enough to trust them with her life, she wanted nothing to do with sex.

Silar knew that.

She looked up at him again.

He knew it.

He was her training partner and nemesis.

He knew all her weaknesses and strengths.

He wouldn't smile as he asked her to teach something she was unqualified for, not unless there was something else he wanted from this.

Someone else might have thought that, with Silar's history, he was trying to find a way to offer a casual sexual encounter. But they both knew that was never going to happen. Whatever their relationship was, from classmates to antagonists to very reluctant co-workers, there was nothing casual about their interactions.

Gold fire crossed Silar's brown eyes as his grin widened. He knew exactly what she was thinking.

"What do you want?" Rowena asked.

"Hmm?" His eyes widened in feigned innocence. "Want? Whatever could I want from you?"

What...? *Oh.* "Reports?" She raised an eyebrow in speculation.

Silar offered an exaggerated shrug.

It was the reports then. She sat down in her chair. "We both know I'm not the right person for this job. So cut to the chase, what do you want from me so you'll handle this?"

He picked up the file. "Full reports on your operation with the Jhandarmi." His tone had switched from deceitfully playful to the no-nonsense tone of a senior guardian. "Who you are with. Where you are at. What threats you might be facing."

"I can't get the Jhandarmi to read you in on this."

"I said full report, not official. You know the difference."

She did.

"When you leave Enclave for this I want to know what area you'll be in and what trouble you expect to find. When you get back, I want to know you're here in Enclave, and a medical scan proving you aren't injured."

That last bit was going to be a sticking point. "Injuries happen on the job. I can't always throw a shield up or teleport out of a situation, not without causing a panic. Not every grounder is as accepting of our tech as the ones in Tarrin."

"Fine, I'll accept a medical scan with the understanding that you'll go see your ship's medic if you're injured."

She made a noncommittal noise. The *Danielle Nicole*'s chief medical officer was closely related to her captain, and as much a risk to her life as any murderous grounder. "I'll make sure I get patched up. But this is only for movement related to my Jhandarmi consulting work. Nothing more."

"Nothing more," Silar agreed. "If you go out with friends, meet a lover, or anything during off-duty time, I don't need to know. Go have fun."

Rowena nodded, but she wasn't giving in that easily. "I can work with that. If..."

"If?"

"If you carry a scanner with you while you're in the mountains."

Silar's eyes narrowed. "What scanner and why does it need to go to the mountains?"

"It's small and light. All I need is to see if it can scan for orun traces in the mountains. I'm tracking some illegal tech for the Jhandarmi." That was more or less true, for a given value of true.

"I have to teach sex ed *and* carry the scanner? That seems like a bad trade. What else are you giving me?"

Rowena cocked her head to the side and pretended to consider her options. There was really only one concession left to make. "I'll keep your knife with me."

"And the emergency card to call a Guardian."

That was more than she wanted to give, but she accepted with a grimace. "Fine."

"Thank you." He didn't smile in victory, which showed he'd matured over the past few years, because this was a rightful victory he could hold over her head.

The thought made her fists itch. No matter how many times her pride took a blow and she lost, it stung.

"It's a win-win situation," Silar said as if he guessed her thoughts. He probably could. "Anything I need to know about the fleetlings before I prep the class?"

At least he was letting the conversation slide back to neutral ground. "If you do an open forum session, you're going to get at least two questions about coping with the death of beloved ones. The worst off is the Mirtoll boy, Kada. He was on the *Karff* when Old Baular attacked it at the end of the war. Most of his age group didn't evacuate on time. He was twelve, and it was his first love."

For a moment Silar's jaw tightened in memory.

The Mirtolls were a C-class crew, unallied, and poorly armed. The Baular's *Slibinas* had attacked them, demanding food and fuel. When the Mirtoll captain refused, the attack had destroyed nearly everything.

"Why'd he come to you? You're Warmonger."

"Because I lost my first love to the war," Rowena said. "Or as near to love as I'll ever get. He wanted to know how I coped with Mal's death."

Silar turned to her, a note of concern in his eyes. "Did you cope?"

Did she cope? The question was deeper than that.

Did she heal? Did she forgive the Council for banishing Mal? Did she forgive the grounder who planted a bomb in his car and killed him?

"I've seen a trauma counselor."

Silar's look could have frozen planets in their orbits. "Seeing them doesn't help. You need to actually talk to them."

She wrinkled her nose. This was not a discussion they were going to have.

Silar sighed in acknowledgment. "Acknowledged. That's a no fly zone. Anything else I should know about before I teach your group?"

"Don't be shocked when several of them show up wearing uniforms they outgrew last year. They've determined that Guardian Silar, the Elite-ranked warrior, is single again and eligible for pursuit."

"Ha!" He laughed with a genuine smile. "Oh, ancestors." A red blush flushed his cheeks. "Oh, ancestors, no. Can you pass the word along that anyone too young to fight in the war is too young for me?"

"We were too young to fight in the war."

"We were." He sighed. "Still... try to convince them that I'm not what they want."

Rowena smiled. "I'll do what I can."

It was a little hard considering he was the ideal fleet officer—handsome, kind, efficient, and, even when he was pushing the limits of her patience, she had to admit he was fun to look at. It wasn't sexual, he was just that pretty. Perfectly proportioned and classically built. And, when he wanted to, he could look at a person like they were the only thing that mattered in the universe.

The fact that he was single was not related to a lack of interest.

His tongue flicked out, wetting his lips. "You know, if you'd kissed me when I asked the other day, your fleetlings wouldn't be chasing after me."

"Or they'd kill me to take out the competition!"

"Eh, you could handle them." He grinned, and he had that look in his eye that invited her to forget everything else and let him make her the center of his orbit for an hour or two.

She gave him a tart smile. "I could handle them, but I don't want to handle you." *I don't want to deal with the fallout when you get bored.* "Shoo. I need to finish this before someone breaks their environmental system in this weather."

The heat in his eyes became a warm glow of comradery. "Fine. I'll go. And, Lee, the reports?" He raised his eyebrows. "I expect the first briefing today. Data on my desk before breakfast."

"Already sent," Rowena said. She put her shield back up as he left, feeling like she'd dodged a kinetic round.

One of these days she was going to have to take Silar out, or do something to put their issues to rest. The state of constant uncertainty, never knowing where they stood or how much of his flirting was real, was taking up too much of her mental energy.

"Should have killed him last year," she muttered.

Too late now.

Now, Titan was married to a Silar ally. And Silar was proving himself useful. If he was dead, she'd need to find a new training partner and someone to handle complicated emotional questions from her class.

It was tantamount to admitting she needed him.

She made a face of disgust.

Maybe it was time to get away from the fleet, or at least the gym. There were too many memories and emotions here for her to think clearly.

She looked over at the squeaky clean new combat mats, remembering Silar's teasing request for a kiss. She should have said yes just to watch him run in fear.

Grinning, she turned back to the maps. Now... what were the teleport coordinates for Kydell?

13
HOLLIS

AN INSECT LANDED ON HOLLIS'S arm and he squashed it before he lost any more blood. He'd been toying with the idea of letting them fill up and then activating the nanites so all the little buggers would explode, but he wasn't sure if the species of biting, winged vermin needed to be kept alive.

The mountains looked so organized at a distance, but once he'd arrived he'd found a thriving ecosystem that the grounders seemed to understand but that left him dataless. What was the word for it? Bewildered, perhaps?

Being in the wild, bewildered, yes—that seemed to scan.

The air smelled of strange herbs, verdant pines, and midsummer fruits. Unfamiliar animal sounds surrounded them: clicks, and chirps, and sharp screeches from birds soaring overhead. Even the dirt smelled different, more complex than the dirt in Tarrin and with more hints of detritus.

He was following a narrow trail between weedy trees made thin by lack of oxygen as he silently cursed his agreement to go train with the grounders. Three more days of this hiking seemed pointless.

After two full days of training together and practicing mountain rescue techniques that were obsolete for anyone with a working implant, the Jhandarmi had split into groups all headed to the same campsite for the evening. The goal, as Hollis understood it, was to familiarize himself with the mountains paths and practice map reading.

Both things he could have done in a picosecond scan of the area.

When he got back, he was going to petition the Council to give grounders basic implant tech. Again. It was like living in the stone age.

The only mildly interesting thing that had happened all day was when he'd picked up the trail the orun detector was pinging off, and Agent Erach Dolos had volunteered to follow it, claiming he knew the area well.

Hollis gave him an appraising once over as Erach led the way.

His companion wasn't fleet-fit, and he was hairy in a way no one in the fleet was, but he wasn't bad looking. Dirty blond hair, hazel eyes, a good tan on his skin from working outdoors. He was a touch shorter than Hollis usually preferred his men—Perrin-height was what Gen called it—but not bad overall. At least Rowena had been right about the view not being bad.

Erach stopped a few paces ahead to take a drink from his canteen. "You're a quiet one, aren't you?"

Hollis took a moment to remember his parched tongue needed to do the work. "Just trying to find a word to describe this place." One that wouldn't offend anyone, at any rate.

"Mountainous?" Erach suggested, looking around with a grin. "Steep. Rocky. Hard on my calves. Looks like any mountain on Icedell." He nodded to the valley ahead of them that was barely visible through the treeline. "This is part of the Winter Reach mountain chain. You can see the peaks of Glendown and Frostright over there and there. What more is there to say?"

"It's a new experience for me," Hollis said. "My first mountain hike."

"Do we need to slow down?" Erach asked. "I mean, no offense or anything, but do you even walk around much?"

Hollis frowned, trying to show his puzzlement. The grounders weren't good at reading fleet facial expressions and he found himself trying to exaggerate every reaction to compensate. "How else would I get around?"

"I dunno. Maybe you space people fly in your ships. Zero gravity or something. Or have zippy little space cars like they have in cartoons." Erach shrugged broad shoulders and gave him a forgiving smile.

"Even in space we have artificial gravity, and we don't need space cars. We walk or we run." No wonder the grounders had been staring at him all day.

Erach looked disappointed at the news. "So much for my dreams of what goes on in your city-state."

Hollis chuckled. "For me, it's mostly paperwork."

Erach started walking again and Hollis fell in beside him.

It was quieter than he liked out here, Rowena had been right about that. Turning off his implant meant cutting off the constant data stream from the *Veronica*, the Starguard, and his friends. The first night out, the only thing that had made it bearable was the quietly pulsing device Lee had given him to track the orun trail.

"Is it weird," Erach asked, "being out here instead of in those ships?"

Hollis shrugged. "A little. I mean, I was past twenty the first time I had to consider that I might spend the rest of my life on a single planet. It's bigger than a ship, but it still feels confining. You know?"

"Not really," Erach said. "I never thought I'd get to leave the planet. But I have moved between city-states. I was born in Kytun, over on Descent, and then moved to the islands as a kid. Now I split my time between the Jhandarmi offices on the second continent and coming over here for training. It's safer."

"Safer?" With his implant powered down Hollis couldn't ping it for references, but there was a memory from his discussion with Lee. "Second continent has all the weird animals left over from terraforming, right?"

Erach laughed. "I wouldn't say they were weird, but yes, there's lots of large animals. Icedell is safer, here only gravity can get you." He pulled the branch of a bush aside to show Hollis the drop down to the valley floor.

"Not a short cut I plan to take." Although teleporting down would mean his legs would stop screaming in protest. Nanites handled the lactic acid build-up usually; without them he was feeling the workout. He stretched his arms out. "Last time I felt this sore, I was with a woman."

Erach laughed again. "Wow. Way to brag."

"Oh, no." Hollis shook his head to chase off the thought of a marathon session in bed with Lee. "We were fighting. Both our crews ran out of food, and we found an abandoned ship with a storage locker still intact. We both went after it, and we spent the day trying to kill each other."

"I guess you won."

"Let's call it a draw."

Erach shook his head. "What happened to the woman? She still mad about that?"

"Not that in particular, just angry in general." The memory of Rowena watching him as the hull of the *Aquila* ripped apart was still vivid in his mind's eye. Black hair falling around her, framed by fire, glaring at him like she was a vengeful goddess ready to crush the cosmos to destroy him… He huffed out an angry breath as he tried to shake loose the tangle of emotion that the memory evoked.

"Women." Erach shook his head in dismissal.

Hollis looked up in interest, waiting to feel something other than general appreciation for the human form. They were alone. There were plenty of excuses to stop and touch each other, not the least of which would be a massage that Hollis was ready to pay someone to give him. And still… He shook his head with a sigh. *Nothing.*

Something in his head had to be broken. Maybe it was time to see the ship's medic and figure out why no one was appealing to his carnal side anymore.

Erach looked over his shoulder. "Problems?"

Hollis tapped his head. "It's so quiet, my brain is working overtime. It's been months since I didn't have a stack of reports to file or reviews to do. I guess my mind is trying to fit everything I haven't been thinking about into the time we have. Why don't you talk? Distract me." He hit Erach with a smile that worked on everyone but Rowena Lee.

Erach grimaced then grinned, eyes crinkling with delight. "Okay, but I have to warn you, I'm pretty boring."

Was this how grounders flirted? He'd have to ask Perrin later.

"What do you do for fun?" Erach asked as he turned down the left fork of a trail.

"What do grounders consider fun?"

"Ground—oh, us? Mmm, sports, games, stuff like that."

Hollis studied the right fork of the trail. "Were we supposed to go this way?"

"No, the trail washed out last year and hasn't been repaired. It was nice too, there was a bridge over the waterfall. But, unless you can jump a twenty meter gap, we're going this way. There was a rockslide a few years back, but it's mostly stable."

"Mostly stable isn't the encouraging trail review I want to hear." Twenty meters was nothing if he turned his implant on and teleported.

Even Rowena wouldn't give him a hard time for making that choice.

"Do you think we should try another route?" he suggested diplomatically. Teleporting Erach without his consent would probably cause some tension. The last thing he needed was Rowena taking another stab at him because he'd upset the Jhandarmi.

"We're not likely to die." Erach grinned.

Hollis groaned. He knew that tone of voice. "You need to meet Perrin. He said the exact same thing to me once. And then I nearly died." Risky behavior and near-death experiences were exactly Hollis's type. He paused to watch Erach moving ahead and waited again to feel anything.

Still nothing.

It was a good thing Rowena wasn't here. She'd be laughing so hard right about now. Although she would have seen reason and teleported down.

Erach laughed and broke down a branch obscuring the trail. Bright sunshine filled their view. "Perrin sounds like my kind of guy."

"Don't get your hopes up. He has a spouse."

The Jhandarmi officer's cheeks turned bright red. "Oh. No! I didn't mean it like that."

Oh. So, it hadn't been flirting. Erach was one of those people who didn't like men or women.

Hollis filed that tidbit away and wondered if that meant a shoulder rub was completely out of the question. There didn't need to be physical attraction to rub someone's shoulders.

Erach laughed uneasily. "Are you, um...?"

"Perrin's spouse?" Hollis guessed. "No, he's married to my baby sister. Which might be worse, honestly. I still see her as a little kid and now she's talking about maybe having kids someday." He looked across the rocky field and pinged the orun-tracker. Whoever had brought the orun into Tarrin had crossed here. "You want to lead or should I?"

"I'll take point," Erach said. "My brother and I used to hike this every summer with our dad. After he died, Mica and I came alone."

"Came, past tense?" Hollis asked as Erach stepped onto the first shifting stone. Small pebbles bounced down the mountain.

Erach took another wide step, landing on a large boulder that looked relatively stable. "Mica died last year. Killed by a migrant worker that came to our city-state. The guy said it was an accident, he was driving tired and Mica was crossing the street at night, but there's transit laws, you know?

"We didn't allow cars in the downtown proper until three years ago. Everyone lived within walking distance of the city transports. But, there's too many people. That's the problem. Too many people and not enough housing for all of them."

Hollis thought guiltily of the apartments Selena Caryll had sitting empty. Logically, a few dozen apartments waiting for fleet to move to Tarrin wasn't going to change the world, but it felt greedy.

Rocks slipped under his feet and Hollis resisted the urge to use his implant. It would take nanoseconds to put a shield in place to keep the rocks from sliding. If he had half an hour, he could fuse the rocks and make a functional bridge. It was tempting. But it was also cheating.

"Come on," Erach said. "There's less than a kilometer of this, and then we'll be back in the shade."

Hollis risked a look down.

The rock field ended abruptly at what looked like a cliff. "Does this go all the way down to the valley floor?"

"Not quite, the cliff face eroded away. That's what triggered the rockslide in the first place. But it goes most the way. We're not as high up as it looks."

Hollis glanced at the rockslide overhead and resisted the urge to calculate the weight that could potentially drop on his head if the mountain slid again.

"Silar, you okay? Not getting cold feet, are you?"

"Cold feet?"

"It means to get scared."

Hollis smiled. "I'm not scared, I was doing the math. I've never seen something like this. I don't have a threat matrix for it."

"Now it's my turn to be confused," Erach said as he stopped mid-field on a boulder. "What's a threat matrix, exactly?"

"It's a mathematical way of measuring how much it will hurt when something attacks you."

Erach looked up at the rubble. "Good news, the mountain isn't sentient or seismically active. We're probably safe."

"Probably safe. Not likely to die. You say the most reassuring things, Agent Dolos."

This was such a bad idea. Poorly thought out. Poorly planned. He could practically hear the lecture Rowena was going to give him when he told her the route she needed crossed this path.

He stepped out onto the first rock, carefully balancing as his boots sank slightly into the loose rocks. "If nothing else, this saves Rowena the trouble of trying to kill me again."

"Who?" Erach asked as Hollis made his way across.

"Rowena, she's the woman I mentioned. The one who didn't quite kill me last time."

The Jhandarmi agent laughed. "You should take her hiking up here."

"Yeah?"

"There are lots of places to hide bodies up in the mountains."

Hollis snickered. "No, everyone knows we're enemies. If she went missing on a hike, I'd be the first person they investigated."

"It's easy to make a death look like an accident. Slippery rock face. High winds. So many risk factors." Erach grinned.

A fist-sized rock slithered down the slump and careened into the valley below. "Are you *sure* this is the best choice of trails?" Hollis asked.

Erach laughed. "Do you always whine like this?"

"I'm not whining, I'm expressing an opinion."

"Which is what? I didn't hear it in all the complaining." Erach took off again, heading for the far side of the broken trail.

Hollis snarled good-naturedly at the man's back. "I don't love this mountain."

"Ooo! You're going to hurt its feelings!" Erach reached over and patted the mountainside. "Don't listen to that mean ol' spacer. He doesn't know what a beautiful mountain you—"

Rocks slipped.

Erach balanced for a second—and then fell.

It seemed like a breathless eternity where time slowed. There was a rushing sound, like wind, but it was the clatter of rocks.

Something hit Hollis's side, and he was falling, reaching for Erach and pulling on the energy in his implant.

Hollis got a shield up just as a boulder smashed next to his head. The momentum pushed him faster. Red and brown rubble and dust surrounded him, the smell of it clogging his throat. He made a guess at where Erach was and tried to shield his companion.

And then there was a ringing silence, like the world was under water.

Light and shadow traded places, swirling together.

"Silar? Emperor's pants, Silar? Are you okay? Stay there. Stay there. I'm going to get help."

14
ROWENA

WHEN TYRLING SAID THE JHANDARMI presence in Kydell on the second continent was light, Rowena had envisioned a small office with a handful of overworked agents. She hadn't anticipated a single, moldy corner of the main political building with a lone receptionist who informed her that the Jhandarmi officer who worked there was gone for the week, and that business hours were four hours long minus a break for lunch.

That meant no back up while Rowena wandered the hilly, coastal city.

It was the far side of the same ocean Enclave sat near, but it smelled different. Maybe it was the warmer air or the encroaching forest attacking the city on three sides with the port on the fourth, but something made it stranger. The air clung to her with an unnatural stickiness and the scent of strange flowers itched her nose.

Kydell was an impossibly uncomfortable city. Too chill in the morning and too hot by noon. The sooner she could escape it, the better.

All of the Jhandarmi's list of possible orun orbs were held in the wealthier end of the city, on the hilltop overlooking the small peninsula and the deep water port that was Kydell's major source of income. Ships crossing the channel from Descent unloaded their heaviest cargo here to be moved by the hypertrams, northward through the swampy jungle to larger city-states.

A day spent tramping between small museums and bribing servants to let her into attics had gotten her nowhere closer to finding anything useful.

Another significantly larger bribe had bought her a rumor about an information merchant who was in town.

Walking down the hill towards the port, Rowena took the time to notice the buildings. Higher up they were white stone with seashells used for decorations along high stone fences. But here and there the shine of metal was visible. Hulls of colonial ships that had been hammered into shape and carefully maintained over the centuries. A few even looked new, although she couldn't be certain at a distance.

The cost of a metal fence twice her height made of metal native to the Malik System was beyond what she wanted to calculate. Like orun, metal was rare. Buried too deep to safely extract and in such low quantities that most grounder homes only had the thin strands of copper and gold needed to keep their tech running.

The path split in front of her, widening to the left as it led past wooden buildings to the port, to the right narrow and muddy as it led to the warehouse district.

Rowena turned right, ignoring the empty glass bottles and abandoned wrappers left over from someone's midnight debauchery.

The warehouse district was on the edge of the jungle, long, low buildings half-overgrown by vines. There were burnt patches where it looked like the locals had tried to tame the jungle with fire. It hadn't worked. Even in the failing sunlight of evening she could see creepers winding through the grass, ready to set root and grow.

She followed a path made by foot traffic across a field to an unmarked, rectangular building with a sliver of light gleaming through a crack in an industrial-sized door that looked like it could be pushed aside for trucks to enter a loading area. This was where the locals were rumored to have a semi-illegal fighting ring.

Entering, Rowena circled the outer wall of the building, made from the same flattened hull metal she'd seen in the upper city. The interior of the warehouse was dirt and rock, heavy with the smell of fresh cut wood. Maybe there had been a loading area at one point—she could feel the cement underfoot—but it was covered by sand that had been heaped up and circled with a lashed-together wooden fence.

People were crowding the fence, watching the fighting ring, but keeping to distinct groups that didn't seem to overlap.

There were small clusters of toga-clad Kydellians hunched together on the east side of the ring, talking and exchanging money. The upper class had embraced a romanticized version of some archaic pre-Imperial fashion that resulted in children barely old enough to be second lieutenants wearing brightly striped bedsheets in public.

She captured the memory on her implant to share with the Lee fleetlings. Yunjin needed a good laugh.

The other group was working class—if they could be judged by their clothes, a slightly ragged array of items dyed cheaply into earthy colors—and kept to the west side, talking, watching, and waiting. They were wearing the pant-

and-shirt combination commonly accepted worldwide, the stained-and-torn variation seen at every dock. Local skin colors ran from light brown to dark with black or multi-colored dyed hair. She could have fit in with the workers if she'd dressed like she usually did.

But she wouldn't have gotten into the museums dressed like a ship's engineer, so she'd taken a navy-and-gold outfit similar to what she'd worn to the morgue. Hopefully there wouldn't be any corpses to worry about tonight.

Grimacing at the thought, Rowena hung in the shadows, listening to the conversations.

The word *Rowdy* was in frequent use, as was *Bruiser*.

She leaned against a metal beam and wondered what Tyrling would say if she just grabbed one of the men with a gold-dipped credit stick and interrogated him for an hour or two. Torture was unreliable, but it would have been so satisfying to punch the smirks off the Kydellians' faces. There was something about the rich grounders that made her blood boil.

"You… Pretty lady?" The sour smell of the man's breath hit her before he crept closer. He wore the loose shirt and heavy work pants of the rowdies. And though his dark copper skin seemed healthy, and his black hair was thick and wavy, he moved in the jittery, anxious way of someone very ill.

Rowena raised an eyebrow and stood up. "Yes?"

"You have a bruiser?" The man eyed the current, bloodless fight with hungry anticipation.

The fighters moved across a floor covered in sand, swinging their fists at each other. Any ten-year-old in the fleet could fight better than they did.

"Not yet. But I should be fine."

He shot her a look of pure disgust. Obviously navy slacks and a sleeveless gold blouse didn't inspire faith in her fighting abilities. "You a bruiser or a fine lady? Can't be both 'round here." He rubbed his chest, head twitching to the side.

"Are you all right?" Rowena ran a quick visual scan. It wasn't easy, he didn't have nanites or a significant amount of telekyen in his body, but it was good enough for now. Putting up a light shield, she asked, "Why can't I fight for myself? Because I'm a woman or because I'm betting?"

"The rich don't use their hands. It's how you know they're rich."

She looked over at the Kydellians in their obnoxiously bright colors and ridiculous blankets draped over their shoulders. "You mean the fact that they look like they're wearing curtains isn't enough of a hint?"

The man smiled at her. "You're not from around here." His accent sounded a touch more cultured, a touch more focused.

Her implant pinged with the scan results. It was easy to see why he was fidgeting non-stop: his body was pumped full of adrenaline and there was a metal marker in his chest. The energy from the orun crystal pinged off her implant like a beacon. *There you are.*

"Do you have a name?"

"Jae is good enough." He nodded to the ring again. "Let me fight for you. I'm good for it. I'll win you whatever you want."

"Shouldn't you be negotiating for your payment right now?"

He started to nod than shivered and shook his head at the same time the device in his chest pulsed. "Don't care about pay." His speech slurred back into a more rustic structure. "Let me fight. It's got to be. Got to fight. I need it."

His pupils dilated in anticipation.

"Okay..." Rowena said, drawing out the word. A drugged fighter controlled by an unknown factor was not what she needed to bet her mission on.

But on the other hand, a victim of these orun-run devices was exactly what she needed to find.

For a moment she weighed out the risks. *Someone* was going to hire Jae tonight; he was already looking at other spectators, ready to beg them for a chance to fight. And if she hired him, she could shield him in the ring, keep an eye on him, and it wouldn't be breaking any treaties. Technically. Stretching them, yes, but not breaking them.

"Consider yourself hired," Rowena said. "I'll go make my bet."

Jae licked his lips and nodded.

Behind him, a young woman glowered from across the sands.

Rowena nodded to her, and then sauntered over to where the heavy betting was happening amid the fumes of floral perfumes. Whatever happened to a good, old-fashioned shower?

She took the blue glass chip she'd bought from a local broker out of her pocket, holding it at her side for everyone to see. Laser-engraved into the glass was the seal of Kydell: a fountain under the stars.

A heavyset man built like a Baular enforcer, big and cruel, nodded to her. "What's your pleasure, lady, money or information?" he asked with breath that reeked of sour beer.

"Information."

He nodded to his associate, a man barely shorter and no less dangerous looking, who spread out printed images of faces. "Safe crackers, wet works, couriers, data merchants, we've got them all, one win is information to contact one person for one day."

Two faces jumped out at her. One was of a square-jawed man with pale hair and stormy gray eyes. Her implant didn't need to do a visual match for her to think of Mal. He was dead, and she didn't know what good seeing his doppelganger would be, but part of her ached to see his face again. To hear him say it was okay to move on.

But those were words and comfort a stranger could never give.

Rowena tapped the face of the wet works artist, torturer and assassin, a woman with short dark hair, and enough other similarities that she might have Lee blood back in her family line. A match for the woman who had been seen with Briceno and who was also tied to the murder in Clyde River. "This one."

"You fight my bruiser," the first man said with a nod to the ring.

Rowena looked over. The data merchant's bruiser was easily over a hundred kilograms and had fists the size of her head. She could have taken him down, shielded and healthy, but Jae was in for a fight.

"Who are you putting in the ring?"

"Jae," she said with a nod to where he was watching the next fight start.

Anyone not looking for it would have missed the look of satisfaction that slid across the merchant's greasy face.

"You're up next. May the water favor your goals."

She walked away with a nod, keeping her body relaxed so it didn't seem like she was scrutinizing the fight as she quietly moved through the crowd.

The data merchant's Bruiser was up against another rowdy, someone leaner than Jae and more harried.

The rowdy moved aggressively at first, but a minute into the fight he stumbled and wobbled as if he were suddenly drunk.

He dropped his fists to his sides and grinned as Bruiser moved in.

Blood sprayed across the sands.

The rowdy fell, and Bruiser went down after him, mercilessly crushing bone until there was nothing left of the fighter's face but blood.

Jae watched, mesmerized.

"You sure you want this?" Rowena asked as the bettor called for a second round with a new fighter.

"I've fought worse," Jae said. "I've fought him and won."

She didn't doubt it. In a fair fight Jae would move faster than Bruiser. "Have you been to the doctor recently? Any medical exams?"

Jae rubbed his chest unconsciously. "Only the police exam like usual. Got done for loitering after curfew. New boss didn't want to pay, so he kept us late, promised to pay up, and called the police instead. Bunch of us were rounded up."

"The man who was just in the ring, was he rounded up with you?"

"Sanger? No. He's a painter, not a dock worker. Addicted to anything that'll kill a brain cell." A remorseful frown crossed Jae's face like a storm cloud. "He shouldn't have been fighting. He likes to gamble, but usually he only bets on the side, never gets in. The fighting's good, it's the way it is, but the last few nights..." He shook his head.

"What are the odds of us getting a fair fight?"

Jae looked at and she saw anger, resignation, and fury burning in his eyes. "We're rowdies. It's never a fair fight."

"Win anyway," Rowena said. "The man has information I need."

"You'll get a good fight." The rowdy's eyes burned with a lustful, unhealthy hunger.

She wouldn't.

Without knowing where the controller was there were very few ways to keep the device in Jae's chest from betraying him. And most of the ways she could think of would leave the rowdy dead. She drew her thumbnail across the thin skin of her wrist, pulling blood, and reached over to pat Jae's head.

"Fight well." It wasn't much, a few thousand nanites at most, but it would give her something to work with, and an anchor for a shield.

Jae smiled. "You got a name?"

Rowena smiled back. "I do. Win the fight, and I'll tell you what it is."

He chuckled and went to the starting line as the second fighter's lifeless body was pulled off the sand.

"You're going to kill him." The voice behind her was filled with anger.

Rowena spun. Crack these foolish grounders who snuck around with nothing to track on them.

The glowering girl from earlier was standing just behind Rowena with a knife hanging from her belt. She moved like she could use it.

"Who are you to Jae?" Rowena asked. It could get bad if he had a lover in the crowd who'd seen her casually touching him.

"A friend," she said. "One who's been keeping his head on straight. He's been acting weird, picking fights, yelling. Tonight he wants to fight even when Nolotitus is here."

"Is that the data merchant? Nolotitus?"

The rowdy woman nodded.

"Do you know how he's rigging the fight?"

"No, but I know he is!" she protested.

"I know he is too. And I intend to find out how. Watch his men for me," Rowena said. "One of them will have a control box of some form. If you can tell me who has it, I'll pay you."

The woman crossed her arms. "How's that help Jae?"

"Jae'll be fine for the fight. I paid. It'll be fair."

She looked doubtful, but nodded. "I'll watch. If he lives, I'll tell you what I find. We'll work out payment later."

Rowena nodded and walked up to the wooden fence as Jae walked into the sands. It took effort to keep the lights out of her eyes while accessing her implant, but she needed to see everything that was happening without alerting anyone that she was fleet. The colors of room muted as she switched to watching energy currents.

The orun crystal in Jae's chest stood out like a brilliant fire. The dead fighters lined up outside burned brightly, too.

Every single one.

She didn't even want to calculate the orun that had cost. There was something deeply perverse about using the lifeblood of the fleet to murder people.

Nolotitus, the controller, was wreathed in the cold viridian fire of telekyen, with flecks of orun traces. A weedy-looking man sitting in the back corner tallying bets had tech in front of him and in his pockets.

The nanites she'd slipped into Jae were tracking his blood flow and chemistry. The adrenaline was wearing off far too fast.

Bruiser came up swinging as the fight bell rung.

Jae was slowing down, his body temperature cooling as he became lethargic.

Rowena pulled a shield up around him, tugged his arms into position to block. It was like moving a very heavy puppet with thought alone. She needed Jae's brain to work, even if his fists didn't.

Forcing Jae to step back and circle the Bruiser, she sent an order to the nanites to break the device in his chest. A reminder built into her implant pinged, stating that this could be viewed as a violation of standing treaties and negatively affect the status of her probation if this was reported.

As if she would report this to anyone.

The weedy man in the corner reached into his pocket and suddenly Jae's body filled with adrenaline. The four-way fight was on.

Bruiser stretched, taunting Jae into circling back, but the device couldn't switch blood chemistry that quickly. Jae would be feeling cold and cautious right now.

Narrowing her eyes, Rowena looked for a place to insert her own commands into the data stream controlling Jae. There wasn't a constant flow that she could find. That probably meant the device was sending single burst commands. Simple binaries—on-off, slow-fast, impulsive-depressed— would be the easiest to code and design.

She leaned against the wooden slats that made a fence and added a layer of shielding over Jae's body. A tight shield to protect his muscles, a flex shield a few inches out that would slow Bruiser down and put him off his rhythm. A fleet officer would expect it, but a grounder wasn't going to. It would be so much easier if she could step in and fight herself. She could take the hits. A little more pain was nothing to her.

Jae shook his head as the nanites registered a spike in adrenaline. He was trying to fight the delirium.

Bruiser grinned and punched.

Dodging, Jae dropped and swiped at Bruiser's feet.

Bruiser stomped down, missed, and they both backed away.

"The numbers man in the back has something in his pocket," the woman whispered as she stepped up next to Rowena. "Want me to get it?"

"Not yet." Jae was cooling again.

Logically there had to be a way to shut off the device, but she couldn't find it. Rowena used the tight shield to pull Jae's arms up to block another punch.

Bruiser staggered back, looking at his bleeding knuckles in confusion. Hitting a tight shield was like hitting a stone wall. The man was lucky he hadn't broken his fingers.

His shock bought Rowena a moment to reach in her pocket for a dot tracker. "Take this, slip it onto the device where it won't be noticed. I'll pick it up later."

The woman bumped her shoulder. "And Jae?"

"He'll live through tonight. And I'll pay you back by making sure he isn't vulnerable again."

Out on the sand, Jae sagged. His body registering fatigue and low oxygen. He should have dropped to his knees but the tight shield was an exoskeleton around him. His muscles were too weak to protest.

Rowena suppressed a smile. It was time to take Bruiser down.

The big man circled, grinning as he registered the dazed expression on Jae's face. But even with all of that, Rowena registered muscles twitching, readying to fight.

Without her, Jae would have still been pushing. He was trying to fight himself, trying to fight the body that betrayed him.

"Sorry," Rowena muttered under her breath. Using a shield like this was unethical at the very least, a direct breach of her oath as an officer to protect and defend the helpless, and it was going to leave Jae feeling miserable and confused. But vulnerable was better than dead.

She sunk the tight shield into his muscles and took control.

It wasn't an easy thing to do. There was barely enough telekyen, and this wasn't a move Fleet taught. She'd only learned it so she could steer dead pilots back to their ships after battles. The corpses hadn't resisted.

Jae barely fought. His panic registered, an uncomfortable scraping sensation in her mind, but his limbs stayed loose.

Straightening Jae's spine, she forced him to circle Bruiser. A quick punch to the throat would bring the big man down.

Jae's muscles twitched in a different memory.

She played it out in a simulation. If Jae's body was capable of responding to his brain, he would take out Bruiser's ribs. That worked. She maneuvered him into place and followed the moves Jae wanted, putting telekyen weight and force behind the blows.

A jab to Bruiser's abdomen. A kick to his rib.

Another kick. Bone cracked.

Bruiser fell to his knees, cursing.

Jae thought of another set of movements: knee to nose—fist to ear.

Rowena executed them and Bruiser crashed into the sand, unconscious and bleeding.

She let Jae stagger back to the sidelines and ordered the nanites to emit a death burst. It wouldn't destroy the device in Jae's chest, but it would keep it from receiving orders for a few hours. Hopefully that would be long enough for him to get away.

With the smile, she sauntered back to Nolotitus. "Good match. I was worried for a moment there, but my bruiser had been watching the fights. Who took your guy's rib out?"

"One of the early matches," Nolotitus muttered. "I didn't think Jae would fight that smart."

"I paid him well," Rowena lied. "Now, for my winnings?"

Nolotitus handed her a piece of paper. "Your specialist is Galeri Kygna. Torture, surgery, and assassination are her specialties. She'll be in Tarrin for the next eighteen hours on a contract. Then she's all yours. She'll pick up orders from the tram station locker number one-sixty-one. Leave your contact information and a date that you want the work done. She'll contact you with the price. If she already has a job that day you'll get in a bidding war for her time."

Rowena nodded. "And if I'd rather not be in a bidding war?"

"Win another fight and I'll tell you when she's booked."

"I'll consider that. Thank you."

Tarrin. Briceno's killer was in Tarrin. She had to get back to Enclave and alert Tyrling.

15
MALCOLM

BINARY CODE ILLUMINATED THE walls in soft blues and greens. Malcolm sat beside the projector drinking in the numbers, reading the most primitive of technical languages.

To someone untrained, there were nothing but 1s and 0s scrawled on the wall. But he saw the pattern. The little flourishes. The rhythm behind the coder's thoughts. The story not of what the code could do, but of how it was created.

It wasn't a Lethe code, no matter what Sonya said.

It wasn't from any of the major families of Descent either, which surprised him. He'd half expected to see something from the Marshalls in the code. Or the Felli family. The way his luck was going, it seemed inevitable that his interests would clash with his parents' desires for a stable social life.

Alone in his apartment, he didn't put on an act of surprise. The thought occurred to him—*touch your mouth to signal a secret, pull down your eyebrows in mild confusion, lean forward to show interest*—he'd been taught how to behave in a culture where body language was a large portion of communication. But he dismissed the thought just as quickly.

Things like that quickly became habit, and showing every thought was dangerous. Even more than it had been in the past few years.

Sonya Lethe... The easiest solution was to kill her discreetly. His mother's garden had many poisons. A slow, rare toxin that would take months to kill her would work best. She'd fall asleep after a party having had a little too much wine, and the coroner would rule it alcohol poisoning.

There were risks inherent to that course, though. Not the least of which was that Sonya was unlikely to be acting alone. No—he considered it—there was a better than seventy percent chance she was working with someone, and an eighty-four percent chance she was leading whatever group she was working with. Not knowing exactly what she planned, it was impossible to determine the risks her death would pose.

That meant stepping away was the best choice. Hand her the data. Apologize. Admit to failure.

Revulsion turned his stomach and the thick taste of bile coated his throat.

He'd failed a few times in life, but the one time it had meant everything, his failure had cost too much. The smell of drying blood drifted out of his memories, haunting him. Death curled around him, whispering to his pride that it had been a victory. A chill and taunting victory that tasted of defeat.

Malcolm shook his head. That was years ago. Another life. Another time. Another him.

Still, there was something to be said for conditioning. If instinct brought the memory of that death to him, then it was best to remember the price of it. The indifferent calculus of safety said stepping away was best; his subconscious felt otherwise.

That led to a third, far riskier, path.

He could stay close to Sonya, not giving her the data, but not leaving the battlefield yet. With time, he could gather information, fill in the missing variables, find a better solution.

His phone rang on schedule.

"Long."

"Malcolm," Sonya's voice was a honeyed alto, sweet with an undertone of biting bitterness. "I called to see how that little project you were working on was going."

The code on the wall continued to scroll past. Names. Dates. Security rotations.

"The project has proved problematic, Miss Lethe." He knew she'd hear only sincere honesty in his voice. "Your earlier experts were on the right path. I believe Levin had the right encryption family."

"But?" Sonya prompted.

"The encrypted data was itself corrupted. I've been trying to restore it using the base encryption. Thus far my efforts have been fruitless."

There was a thorny silence on the other end of the line. Miss Lethe was not used to disappointment. Their relationship was certainly going to be a learning experience for her.

"Was there something in the encryption that caused the corruption?"

"At first that seemed likely, but after various permutations it seems possible that the data was corrupted prior to encryption."

"How frustrating."

"It could have been accidental, or the result of pulling data from a failing drive. There are algorithms I can run to fill in the gaps if I know what sort of data was lost, but without that to build the probability sets, it's nearly impossible." He let the possibility of recovery dance in front of her.

She made a thoughtful sound halfway between a hum and a laugh. "The datcube was recovered from a very loyal employee. It is possible that, with effort, I could find out what project it was tied to."

Sonya Lethe lied poorly. It was the way her voice dipped and rushed over the lie like a river hitting a rock. The man she'd taken the datcube from had either not been loyal or not been an employee, and she knew exactly where it was from, but not the contents.

Interesting.

A string of binary made him stop the scrolling code. New calculations ran through his head.

"I'll prepare the base codes for the restoration program, Miss Lethe, in anticipation of your success."

Sonya laughed with delight. "Such faith in me!"

"You're a very intelligent and resourceful woman," he said to the name on the wall.

"Such flattery," Sonya said. "I appreciate it."

You would.

"As it happens," she continued, "I have a little side project that should yield some interesting facts very shortly." There was the click of computer keys on the other side of the line, followed by a murmur of voices. "An expert has been sent in to retrieve information. I'll share anything applicable shortly."

"You're most generous, Miss Lethe."

A hum of agreement. "Remember my benevolence, Doctor Long. In time, I'm sure you'll agree it is my finest quality. You will have what you need shortly. Then we'll schedule time for another meeting. I'm looking forward to it."

"As am I."

He let the phone go silent.

Another meeting with Lethe. Perhaps it was time to look into the range of legal weapons sold for personal defense. Or start going to the gym more than twice a week. His very quiet life was on the verge of becoming very complicated.

"Why do you do this?" he asked himself, but he looked at the name and knew.

There were still people in his life worth fighting for.

16
HOLLIS

IT WAS DARK. NOT THE COMFORTING darkness of home, with old blankets piled onto a thin mattress and the sound of a living ship cocooning him. Not the hushed darkness of the Starguard bull pen, with the smell of leftover food and the sound of hushed conversation. Not even the unfamiliar darkness of a lover's boudoir, scented with perfume and lust.

This was an ominous darkness.

A violently silent darkness.

A cold and creeping darkness that cut at his skin and clawed into his bones.

Hollis tried to open his eyes and failed. He tried to lift an arm but it wouldn't respond. Straining, he pulled on his arms, flexing his muscles, but it was like he was trapped in his own body.

There was a weight over him, a whole planet's worth of gravity pushing him down, holding him still.

He rechecked his implant. Tried to pull up a shield. Tried to fight the darkness holding him tight. Nothing was working.

Impossible.

He pinged the nearest fleet sailor.

There was nothing.

An empty vastness of oblivion.

His implant cycled through all the major frequencies—and found no one. The weight squeezed him tighter, made it hard to breath.

He ran a check on his implant as his heart raced.

Power loss.

No geolock. No location.

No allies nearby.

All he could hear was the blood racing in his veins like the roar of oblivion.

That was... not good.

Very not good.

Hollis tried to process the situation, but there was no memory or piece of training for this scenario. The fleet always assumed that communication and movement would be available. On the rare occasions that coms were down, or an implant drained, there were visual and audio forms of communication.

Which assumed that there would be someone to communicate with.

Terror flared, a brief thought that everyone was gone.

Or maybe this was death. Maybe there were no ancestors waiting in the Lost Fleet for him. Maybe that rock had won.

If this was death, he wanted no part of it.

He took a breath, and an odor he'd ignored caught his attention. It smelled like... onions?

He sniffed again.

Onions, meat, chilis, pastry... There was a mobile food vendor in Tarrin that sold meat pastries that smelled like that. It was a smell that didn't belong in the mountains, with the pine trees and the rocks.

So... Not dead?

Not in the mountains.

Hollis relaxed a little as a draft of air crossed his bare chest. Someone had taken him from the mountains, taken his shirt, but he couldn't teleport or communicate, which meant someone was blocking the larger bandwidths.

Time to try the dead channels.

They weren't truly dead; forgotten was a better word. They were the thin frequencies on the outer edge of fleet coms. Channels used by dead crews and dead officers.

He had a list saved from the war, and he went through it sending out an OID—officer in distress.

At least some of them felt like they'd managed to break the barrier around him. One pinged back Officer Deceased. Someone's implant still had a charge, even if their heart wasn't beating. Their corpse was out in the black, on a wreck or between the stars out of reach.

Another pinged back Ship Destroyed.

Hollis reached the bottom of the list. :OID. Assistance required.:

:MAL?: The response was immediate, filled with grief and hope, and sent with a bitter-sweet image of a flowering tree in the moonlight.

:Lee?: *Oh, ancestors, no.* Hollis withdrew. The last thing he wanted was to feel Rowena's hope right now. Her emotions flooded the channel: hope, longing, disbelief, despair.

:Mal?: The emotions faded into a profound sadness. :Not Mal.:

Death would have been kinder. :I'm sorry.: He sent his signature image, a golden sun rolling across a fiery desert.

:Hollis.: The word came with a mental sigh of resignation. :Why are you flashing OID on dead channels?:

:I ran into a bit of a problem...:

:I doubt you ran at all. This seems like a situation where you fell into trouble.: There was a hint of amusement in her tone.

His arms tingled, then burned with the pain of trauma. :I can't move. I don't know where I am.:

:Working on that.: She didn't sound too concerned about his predicament. Though it was still better than the grief-filled longing he'd felt from her just before. He shuddered, unable to erase the touch of it from his mind.

:Work faster. My implant is below forty percent and losing power.:

There was a sensation of curiosity. :Is it broken or being drained?:

He ran another diagnostic. :Looks like an external power drain, but I can't find a cause. Power is dropping three percent every ten seconds. If you're going to come find me, now's the time.:

The image he received was a memory of Lee giving someone a very bored, very disdainful look.

:You already know where I am?:

:Of course.:

:Any chance you're going to help me out?:

:What would be the fun in that?:

Anger pushed him to full awareness. His arms and legs were clamped down under something heavy, metallic, and telekyen free. There was a foreign substance in his blood stream that his nanites couldn't seem to process. There was a needle falling out of his skin, and something clamped to his fingers that was draining the energy from his implant.

And there were voices.

"Is the wet work operator here?" The voice was young, angry, bitter.

Not the thing he'd hoped to wake up to.

"She's here getting ready. What about the lord?" The second voice was lower, older.

"Prepped. Drained. Ready to be sliced."

:Lee, this is not a good time for games! I'm losing power! Get someone in here. Now.:

Hollis heard a door open. He fought the drugs to open an eye a few millimeters.

The wet work operator was a short woman with black hair cut above her shoulders, light brown skin, and a narrow chin. She peered over the shoulder of a fair-skinned boy with shaved head and a vest hanging loose over his under-nourished shoulders, and then turned to inspect Hollis.

Her eyes were black and cold as death... :Rowena?: There couldn't possibly be two women in the universe so unflinchingly cold.

A stolen glance was his only confirmation.

:I hate what you've done with your hair.: His lips twisted into a snarl as she lifted a knife for inspection.

:And we both know exactly how much I care about your opinion.:

:I'm about to lose coms.:

"When will he be ready for interrogation?" Rowena asked. She sounded far too comfortable for his comfort. Far too excited.

Hollis tried to move in the chair, but whatever they'd built it with, he was secure. He was completely at Rowena's mercurial mercy. If she wanted to kill him she could now, and no one would say a thing. He would have died on a mission.

Enraged, he switched his sight to the Guardian Veil.

Overhead, a bright gold net of energy spun around him. Six different layers of shielding, spinning, twisting, and twining as the shield kept him isolated. The rest of the room was telekyen free, except for Lee and a bright red thread. It stretched from her arm and slowly snaked toward him, dancing between the layers of the shield.

A telekyen filament, no thicker than an atom, a direct and physical link to Lee.

He watched it settle against his skin. Felt a pin prick of cold as it burrowed in. Watched as the red thread wrapped around his implant, stopping the drain and slowly cutting off the electronic leech.

:What was that?:

:A temporary fix.: She shot him an annoyed look. :You are causing me problems. I need to run an op, find out what these people know and what they have planned. The information the Jhandarmi got from the assassin before she died was that the victim was already critically wounded. I'm not here to save anyone.:

A silver knife danced in her hands, catching the light and slicing it.

:Sorry. A mountain fell on my head and I woke up here.:

Rowena tilted her head and dragged the knife blade along the edge of the table, carving out a curl of wood. "How much internal damage does our patient have?"

"Very little," the thin man said. "We thought the mountain would do most the work for us, but he got lucky."

Rowena made a small sound that could have been a laugh or a snort of disdain. "What's your plan for him?"

The grounders whispered to each other and the older one shook his head. "If the surgery goes well, then we can release him. If not..." He shrugged.

Hollis closed his eyes. :Best day of your life.: *Crack the hull.* Would Lee even hesitate to kill him? A year ago she wouldn't have. But the past year had to count for something. His implant sorted through their interactions…

Fights, insults, verbal digs, sparring, more fighting, bruised ribs and a sore jaw.

:Playing the highlight reel?: There was no shield between them, no way to block the amusement and satisfaction she felt.

:Go suck vacuum, Lee.:

The knife blade tapped a staccato rhythm on the chair. :Just doing my job, Commander.: Scenarios were playing out in her mind and he could hear them, almost see the blood spray. It would take two steps to bring her to the thin young man; his throat would be slit before the older man had time to raise a weapon. But there were guards outside.

:Teleport out.:

:Can't. Not from here. Not without blowing a lot of covers and the entire op.: There was a dragging sensation of resignation. :The people with the most information are the ones hardest to keep alive. Why is that?:

:Because the universe hates you,: Hollis said. He tried to build a shield, but she was there, under his skin and in his blood.

A cool hand ran across his arm and trailed over his fingertips.

With the touch came an understanding, a series of unfiltered thoughts and emotions. He got the sense that Lee wanted to make a play for information, but she was willing to kill them all and get him out in the next thirty seconds if that's what he wanted. It was a strange feeling, a sensation of being powerful without holding any power. He was helpless, too weak to fight. But Rowena was willing and ready to step in to defend him.

The amount of trust she was asking for was staggering. The risks were too high. But...

He took a breath. :You want to run a reverse interrogation with me in the chair?:

:If you're up for it.:

:All I have to do is lie here, right? I can do that.:

:Tell me if you need to get out.:

He opened his eyes and gave her a little nod. :Let's play.:

17
ROWENA

IN ROWENA'S MIND, THERE WERE three screens running. One tracking the movements of the grounders. One focused on the visible reality she was stuck in. And one tracking Silar's vitals and mental condition. He was shaky, angry, injured, and it felt irresponsible to keep him away from the medical bay even a second longer than necessary—but he was stable.

The grounders had hidden him in a blackened box of a room with a one-way mirror looking over a burned out office building at the northern edge of Tarrin. It had been the victim of a business rivalry gone too far that the city-state had let fall to disrepair. From the outside, it was nothing more than a hollow place with grass growing in the parking lot and sunken roof.

On the inside, the group she was infiltrating had created a maze of tarped-over, smoke-choked passages. The inner rooms where they'd hidden Silar were well protected, covered in fresh layers of cement that held the scent of the engines from the machine they'd used to lay it. There was a long, thin corridor that made a perfect kill box, a wider room filled with abandoned factory equipment, and the small torture chamber with tinted glass where Silar lay barechested and strapped to a chair.

If Tyrling hadn't listened—if they hadn't caught the torturer before she arrived—the day would have gone very differently.

Without knowing exactly what to look for, none of the fleet scans would have done any good. The Jhandarmi patrols passed this place every day without ever noticing the changes. There was no way Silar could have given an accurate description of the place from what he could see, and it was only chance—a perverse sort of fortune—that Silar had used Mal's long-dead com code to contact her.

Rowena rolled her shoulders and tried to look happier about the situation than she was. It had been nearly ten years since the Baulars had dragged her to watch her first torture session—training, Old Baular had said. Mal wouldn't even look her in the eye when it was over.

Even on her worst days, she'd never wanted to see another Silar like this.

A machine made ticking noises and a paper fell out.

:What was that?: She looked around at the hodgepodge of desks covered in an array of monitors, screens, and loose wires.

:Low tech communication.: Silar opened an eye just long enough to glare. :Are you tracking the security in this place?:

She wanted to roll her eyes and glare at him. :What am I? Three? Of course I'm tracking the security. I have names and histories of everyone in this room. I know all the exits. Would you like to review my battle plan, *sir*?:

Walking out and leaving him to the mercies of the grounders was almost tempting. It would be hard to explain, but if everyone thought she was incompetent she might as well live down to their expectations.

Along the thread of telekyen, she felt frustration and an unhealthy amount of fear. Silar had seen his brother die like this.

Mentally berating herself for making him feel worse, she sent him the information she had.

"Let's get started." She took the concoction of drugs from the kit she'd stolen off the dead torturer. "This will do most the work for us. Flayed skin tends to excite the authorities." She jabbed the needle into Silar's arm as he glared at her.

The older man stepped closer to inspect her work.

:Jan Bakker, born to a rich woman on Descent who was having an affair, sent to a family subsidiary in the city-state of Kydell for an education and a job. Thinks his bloodlines make him important.:

:Not like anyone we've ever met,: Silar said with a sardonic twist that made her stomach flex in a laugh that wasn't hers.

"Is he ready?" The younger man was Oliver Emerson. He looked at her with beady, blue eyes and an expression of lust-fueled anger.

:This one likes hurting people.:

:Glad someone's enjoying this.: Silar's voice sounded weaker than before.

She nudged him, sending a little shock of electricity through the link. There was no answering grumble. :Silar? Commander?:

Nothing.

:Hollis?:

"Set a timer," Rowena ordered the grounders. "We need six minutes for the drugs to work their way through his body. They have a fast absorption time, but that's to our advantage. In an hour there'll be no trace of this meeting."

Trace.

The word made Hollis tense.

"He'll tell us everything?" Bakker asked.

"Everything," Rowena promised.

:How should I feel?:

Rowena did a discreet search of her database, aware that Hollis was capable of sensing most of her thoughts. The longer she kept him tethered, the more information he'd gather.

Frustrated confusion filtered through the link.

"He'll feel relaxed," Rowena said for the grounders' benefit, "but every touch will be like fire on a raw nerve ending. The cocktail was originally used in lower doses as a party drug. Lower the inhibitions. Enhance the senses. Make every touch become almost too much. This dosage makes a gentle touch feel like your bones are being ripped apart. Very effective."

She looked down at Silar. :You should feel relaxed—:

:Not feeling it.: His jaw was tight with rage.

:—and talkative.:

:Not homicidal?:

:Alas, no. Save that for later. Just act stupid.: She twisted the knife in her hand and considered their options.

Hollis's thoughts grew darker; it felt like a storm was brewing at the edge of her brain.

:Patience, Commander.:

The fury snapped into focus. He really didn't like being called stupid, or listening to the same voice she'd used to pacify Baular commanders during the war.

She looked him in the eye.

:How are you not angry?: Hollis was an embodiment of rage, incandescent and luminescent in her telekyen-aided sight.

:Anger has only ever gotten me broken arms and broken jaws. Staying calm has gotten me everything else.:

He took a deep breath.

She could feel the cold air in his lungs. :We don't need anger right now.:

Hollis's eyes opened; his whole face looked relaxed. If she didn't know the power behind his small smile, she would have been fooled into thinking he was compliant.

"Time," Emerson said. "We should have twenty minutes."

"More than enough," Rowena assured them, resting her foot on the edge of the torture chair so she kept herself between Hollis and the grounders. "Ask away, I'll make sure you get your answers."

The two grounders consulted for a moment and then Bakker approached them. "Get the basics from him."

Rowena tapped Hollis's arm, nudging the needle out a little. "What is your name?"

He smiled up at her. "Hollis," he said, slurring slightly. "What's your name, beautiful?"

She glanced at the grounders.

"Tell him we're the Loyal Ones. Rightful Children of the Emperor."

"I'm a Rightful Child of the Emperor."

:What the crack does that mean?:

:I don't know, that's why we're here.:

"You're in line for the throne?" Hollis asked slowly, as if he was fighting the drugs to talk. "Never had a princess in my bed before. Bet you learn all sorts of fun things in a harem."

Emerson sniffed. "Uneducated savage."

For a strange second her thoughts aligned perfectly with Hollis's. *Idiot.*

"Ask the Lord about how many vassals he controls."

"Vessels?" Rowena asked.

Both grounders looked at her in disgust. "Vassals," the older one said. "Slaves."

Rowena looked down at Hollis. "How many people report to you?"

"At bedtime?" Hollis asked cheerfully.

"How many do you command?" Emerson cut in, stepping closer than Rowena liked.

"Twos and twenties." Hollis's grin widened.

Bakker shook his head. "The drug isn't working right."

Rowena made the knife dance between her knuckles. "He needs encouragement." She looked into Hollis's eye. :Think about Trace,: she ordered as she drew the dull edge of the knife across his arm.

There wasn't so much as a red scratch but Hollis screamed. It was a primal sound that tore through her, triggering every memory of Trace's death. Finding him dead in his cockpit, neck broken, crying until Mal pulled her away, Old Baular ordering a recording of his 'torture' so he could torment the remaining Silars.

With a thought, she choked the connection to Hollis. If he caught any of this, the operation would be over and they'd both be in danger.

She was supposed to smile now. Supposed to keep all those memories locked away before they got her killed.

Smile.

SMILE.

Rowena forced her lips to curve up as old wounds seeped poison into her mind and her heart beat against her ribs.

Hollis's lips curled into a snarl as he turned his attention to the grounder. "What do you want?"

"Tell us who you report to, and who reports to you," Rowena said. She pulled the dead torturer's phone from her pocket and showed him the message from the cryptically named Lady.

Bakker and Emerson peered over her shoulder.

"The Emperor's Lady contacted you directly?" Emerson's voice held a touch of awe.

Rowena nodded. "Tell me, Hollis. Tell me the names of your security detail."

There was tension on the connection; Hollis was pulling at it, trying savagely to reconnect.

Who had come up with this stupid idea?

Oh. Right. Me.

"Trace Silar," Hollis said, repayment for her pain. "Kiernan Silar." Another brother. "Lindel Caryll. Nevah Moren. Ashli Tejan. Vincent Mirtol." Names of the dead.

Hollis twisted the choke point on their connection.

It was an attack. He was going to bring out a silent assault in the middle of her op. Undermine everything and destroy her. She set her shields and braced herself. This was going to get ugly.

"Tell us the names of the ships you command."

"The *Victoria Guerin*, the *Ida Well*." Both easily checkable by the grounders. "The *Diana*." A Caryll ship she'd destroyed. "Hospital ship *Etain*."

:It was empty.: She growled silently at him. :The Carylls evacuated and turned it into a trap.: She'd gone because her choices were to go herself or to send Aronia. A tight internal shield kept Silar from touching her emotions, seeing the old war wounds ripping open.

"The *Errol*." A Baular ship. "The *Bassi* and the *Aryton*." Both Lee ships that Selena Caryll had taken out.

Let the thoughts bleed.

They were all names of ghosts anyway. People waiting in the Lost Fleet to settle the score. They could keep waiting. She wasn't planning on dying easily.

Bakker smiled. "This is good. Tell us how many people you can bring to the Emperor," Bakker said.

"Tell him about your plans," Rowena told the grounder. "Tell him why he needs to bow to you. He's completely malleable right now."

Bakker's face twisted in a sickening grin. "Our new emperor stands ready to take over. All we need is a few people in key positions who can twist the loyalty of those that follow them." He looked down at Hollis.

Rowena brought the blade close to Hollis's face. "You are the one from Enclave who everyone loves, aren't you?"

"Yes."

And I'm the one everyone hates. How many hours until Hollis got home and told everyone what she'd done? Maybe it was a good thing the investigation was going to keep her on the second continent for a bit.

"How many will follow you?" Bakker demanded. "How many will be loyal to you?"

"Thousands. Every ship in the fleet is loyal to the emperor," Hollis said still glaring at her.

"You will obey?" Bakker asked.

Only Rowena could see the way his jaw tightened and his eyes narrowed in fury.

"I always follow orders." His hand flexed, brushing against hers and reestablishing the connection. :What are you trying to hide, Lee?:

Everything. She stepped away from the chair, aware of Hollis with every synched heartbeat. Every nerve in her body screamed at her to run. There was no backup coming and enemies on every side.

:Rowena?: Hollis was responding to her panic.

She buried her instincts with her pride. There was a job in front of her. Nothing else mattered. :I need a plan from them. Something concrete.:

"What can I do to better serve the emperor?" Hollis asked his eyes never leaving her.

"Die," Emerson said.

Bakker held up a hand. "Save that for later. I want this one alive."

:I want that one dead.: It was Rowena's thought but Hollis was in complete agreement. The bond was settling, their breathing and thoughts falling into sync. It felt like tapping an endless reserve of energy and power.

All it would take to turn this building to ash was a thought.

The secret to golden Silar fire was at the tip of her fingertips, she could almost see the code. And then? A whisper was all it would take. Years of pain burnt away in the blink of an eye.

Hollis's sudden worry for her brought her back to the moment. :No destroying buildings. That causes paperwork.:

No, she was wrong. He was annoyed, not worried. :But it would be so easy.:

Memories of mountains of paperwork filled her mind along with Hollis's deep sense of loathing. Anything they did had to keep him away from that paperwork.

:I can make it look like an industrial accident.:

:And where were we at the time?:

:Mmmm.: Several ideas presented themselves for her approval. Not all of them were her ideas, but just now it didn't matter. Her stomach growled at the thought of food as Hollis tried to change her mind with a memory of a good meal.

"This isn't going to work unless this Fleet Lord can get access to what we need," Emerson said. "He'll promise us anything right now."

"Ask him," Bakker said. "Ask him if he can get to the control room."

Rowena nodded and turned back to Hollis who was looking at Emerson with a grin that promised bloody retribution. "You there, eyes up here."

Hollis focused on her.

"Do you know where the control room is?" Rowena asked.

:Which one?:

:Any one?:

"Sure." It wasn't a memory of confusion but a shared emotion that crossed the link. :What do they need from Enclave?:

Housing crisis.

Building material.

Seize Enclave. That's what Tyrling had said the grounders were trying to do. They were hungry for the hulls. Looking for a way to take away what made the fleet The Fleet. She hid the thought from Hollis. He couldn't know—no one could know—until she was certain. The threat of losing the ships would be enough to spark a war the grounders couldn't win.

"We need his loyalty," Emerson said. "When the rightful heir returns—"

Her thoughts flashed to Mal.

"—we need the spacers to fall in line."

:It's not Mal,: Hollis said, pulling her away from the past again. Whatever anger he'd felt toward her seemed to have burned away in her thoughts of fire.

:Same rhetoric.:

:Same rhetoric used by everyone since the Malik System was discovered. Stop thinking about it. Focus on me.:

She stared at Emerson as war memories threatened to drown her. Smoke from the wires of her fighter. The unbearable cold of a derelict she was raiding for food. A gnawing emptiness—

:Rowena Lee, look at me.:

Her thoughts were pulled forcefully away from the past. She could almost feel Hollis's arms around her, like they were grappling in the training gym. The phantom touch gentled, becoming far more ethereal and intimate, coaxing her back from the brink of battle madness.

It was so easy to forget what mattered.

:Rowena, I'm here. Stay with me a little longer.:

Slowly, she turned back to Hollis.

"Get the device," Bakker said.

Emerson stepped out of the room and brought in a box that nearly glowed with radiation.

:Crack my hull.: Hollis was running scans, same as her. :Poison?:

:Possibly.: She put a shield up against whatever was in it. :It's trackable at least, but I didn't see anything like it when I walked in.:

Emerson opened the box and pulled out a tiny glass egg with gold filigree and a sliver of orun suspended inside.

:Why does that look familiar?: Hollis asked.

:It was in the dead man's chest at the morgue.:

Emerson pulled a wide tube with a small trigger attached. "Here. You know how to work this."

"Of course." Rowena took it. "I love this." Shiny new tech to play with. It looked similar to the one in Jae's chest.

:I hate it.: Hollis glared at the tube.

"Don't mind me," she said out loud as she pressed the tube to Hollis's chest. "I'll be fine."

She teleported the egg out to the science labs on the *Persephone* with a note for Titan and pulled the trigger. The techs would have plenty to work with. Fingerprints, skin cells, even the tech itself would have clues as to where it was made.

There was a popping sound like a micro explosion, and when she pulled the tube away there was a red mark on Hollis's chest.

He looked down at it. "That wasn't fun."

Rowena handed the tube back to Emerson. "Three minutes left, anything else you need from him?"

"We need to make sure he won't talk about this," Bakker said.

"The drug will make his memory fuzzy, but we can stage a scene and fill in the blanks," Rowena said. "Call a car around, I have a hotel room."

Emerson frowned at first, and then his lips twisted into a smirk of understanding. "I hear they're all shriveled down there from not being in proper gravity. But you can try him if you want."

"Call the car," Bakker said, hitting Emerson's arm. "I'll go get him a clean shirt. The gear he was wearing—"

"I'll need it," Rowena said. "It needs to look like he stumbled back on his own. If he questions how he got there, he'll start digging."

"I'll get the clothes," Emerson said. "And I'll have the men outside disperse. How long until his vassals notice he's missing do you think?"

"A day or two," Bakker said. "He was supposed to be out with the Jhandarmi."

:Erach,: Hollis cut into the conversations. :A Jhandarmi agent that was with me. He might be in trouble.:

:I'll have Tyrling check on him.: She pulled the needle from Hollis's arm and started unlocking the restraints.

"Hurry up," she told Bakker. "We need to get him out of here before he's aware enough of his surroundings to remember this place."

Emerson brought Hollis's clothes back in and Rowena pulled the shirt over his head, hands brushing over his skin in a way that brought a shiver to both of them.

"Goodbye, gentlemen," Rowena said, pushing Hollis out of the room, along a dusty trail made by a wall and a section of roof, and into a waiting car. She had their faces now. In a few hours she'd have the Jhandarmi tracking them down.

A few minutes later, the driver pulled to a stop in front of an anonymous hotel around the corner from the hypertram station, another dreary brown building in a part of town made up of brown rectangles. "Room five-oh-four, miss."

"Out," Rowena ordered as she helped Hollis stumble up the back stairs to the room. It was midday in Tarrin and the halls were empty, the elevator waiting, and the room at least was clean. The walls were a dull, uninviting beige, the blanket on the bed a faded brown, but it was safe.

She scanned for listening devices, found none, and put up a shield anyway.

Hollis collapsed on the bed, trembling with delayed shock. His shields were spiking a distress signal and his implant was still below reasonable levels. The bruises were beginning to show now, large black splotches along his arms. There were probably more hidden under his clothes.

All the panic he'd pushed aside earlier had come to the fore.

Rowena cut the connection and stepped back, giving him room to breathe.

Hollis looked up in alarm.

"What?" Rowena pushed aside her own concerns. "What can I do to help? Do you need space? Food?" He'd been thinking of food earlier. "A shower?" She tried to think of what she needed after a bad day. "How do I help you ground yourself?"

"Touch?" His voice was broken. Hollis closed his eyes and sent her images of time with his family. Physical touch was what he used to calm himself.

Her stomach twisted. Touch meant bruises, pain, rejection. Touch meant getting hurt.

Hollis sensed her reluctance. :I'm fine.:

"And vacuum is breathable," she said with a snarl. Locking her own emotions away, she walked to the bed and pulled him close.

Hollis sagged into her, his head resting on her shoulder. His arms wrapped around her waist, holding on, but limp with fatigue.

"I'm sorry." She brushed her hand through his hair the way she'd seen others do. Dirt and leaves from the mountains fell away from the red strands. "I'm sorry I made you go through that."

She'd been right. This hurt worse than his anger. She was supposed to run the op and she'd been the one who needed help. She'd failed. Again.

18
HOLLIS

ROWENA'S HEARTBEAT PULSED IN his ear. The scent of her soap and the grease from engines surrounded him. Her fingers ran through his hair, comforting him even as he felt the tension in her body.

"I'm sorry," she whispered.

He smiled into her soft, black shirt. :It was the job I signed up for.:

Regret touched him through the thin thread of their connection she'd tried to sever. :I should have found another way. I feel...: There was a jumble of emotions. Shame. Anger at herself. Disappointment. Fury that someone had forced her into this situation. Regret. Concern for him. Worry.

Hollis rubbed her back and pulled himself away from the warmth of her body. "I'm fine."

"Liar." So beautifully calm, even when her tone was teasing and her own emotional turmoil was threatening to break her. So beautiful and so complex.

He smiled in acknowledgement. They were light-years from fine, circling the event horizon of disaster, and somehow still smiling.

"I think we can safely say bondage is not my kink." He tried to make it a joke, but the words broke in his mouth. Nothing could be worse than being that helpless.

The look on Rowena's face was undefinable. Concern mixed with something he didn't have a word for. He'd felt how close she was to breaking before, how much of her past she'd tried to forget, and still she was concerned for him. This was the Rowena no one else saw. Generous and caring.

Almost… loving.

Rowena touched his face, brushing away his hair and coming closer than she ever had outside of training. "I don't like seeing you like this. This broken. This injured." Her lips pressed into a worried frown.

Catching her hand, Hollis kissed her palm. Ran his thumb along her wrist as he looked her in her eyes. It was enough of novelty that it centered her here in the moment with him. "You've seen me worse."

"Yes, when I was trying to kill you." Guilt weighted her words.

"And I was trying to kill you. Glad I didn't though. Who would have rescued me today if you weren't around?" He smiled up at her, inviting her to smile back.

The frown stayed in place. "Someone who would have gotten you out of there and directly to the medical bay." Her knees were on the edge of the bed, her body angled over his.

This warmth he knew, the lust and the hunger, the desire to bury his problems in the distractions of a moment's pleasure. He let go of Rowena's hand and pushed away before he could give in to the urge to flip her on the bed and pull her even closer.

Her frown deepened as she made a decision. "Take your shirt off."

"What?" Hope and alarm both spiked, demanding attention. "I mean, the idea is wonderful, but I'm not sure this is the best time..."

She put a hand on his shoulder and gave him a bored look. "Take your shirt off so I can see how badly you're injured."

"Oh." He breathed.

"Ancestors above! Do you think I'd torture you even more today?"

Some of the chill wore off as he laughed. "What I was thinking of would not be classified as torture."

"Because everyone wants an inexperienced partner?" Rowena rolled her eyes at the idea.

He unbuttoned his shirt and tried not to think about how enjoyable discovery could be. "Stop tempting me." Falling onto his stomach, he left his back exposed to her.

Rowena sucked in air in a sharp wince. "What hit you?"

"A mountain. I'm certain I told you that." Every moment of the last hour was burned into his brain.

She leaned over to look him in the eye. "Hate to say it, Silar, but I think you lost this round."

"I'll get it next time," he promised.

Her hand was cool and gentle against his skin. There was a tickle of nanites moving as she ran a scan. "Nothing broken, which you should thank your ancestors for. That's a divine miracle."

"I need to contact Jhandarmi Agent Erach Dolus. He was with me when the mountain slide started. I kept him safe, shielded, but he'll be worried. Last I saw him he was going to get help."

There was an uncomfortable silence.

"Lee?"

No answer. He switched to direct contact. :Rowena? What are you thinking?:

She ran her hands along his back in a mechanical way, emotionless and distant, and she kept her thoughts to herself.

:What?:

The pressure on his back increased. :Lee-levels of paranoia. How did this group find you? It wasn't an accident. They'd arranged for their pet torturer to be here. They had everything set up. You were not a target of opportunity.:

He rolled on his side so he could see her expression. :So?:

A Rowena Lee forged in war looked back at him, all softness gone, or at least hidden. :So someone knew you were going to be alone and vulnerable today. You weren't supposed to be using your implant at all during the training week.:

:You think someone in the group helped them?: That was a disquieting thought. :That leaves us with a serious security breach. Who in the Jhandarmi do you trust?:

The look she gave him would have had him reaching for a knife most days. :Me? Trust?:

He knew his answering smile was feral. :So, here we are. Out in the cold. Possibly betrayed. This is not how I planned on spending my weekend. Just you and me.: Now that he said it, the idea had appeal. If only he could convince Rowena to see it too. :You trust me, don't you?:

:As far as I can throw you.:

:You can force teleport me out of orbit, so I'll take that as a compliment.:

"You're an idiot." Her words were softened by a smile he was certain few people would ever see.

"Your idiot, at the moment." He fell on his back, regretted it, and sighed. "I don't know if I want to hit someone, or just hit the showers and call this whole mess a wash. And I don't think I have energy for either."

"Emotions are draining like that. It's why I don't have any."

:Liar.:

Rowena stood in front of the room's mirror, tugging at her clothes. "It's almost over for you. After I leave, head for the tram station and go back to Enclave. I'll give your implant a boost so you can shield and start healing."

"Where are we, exactly?"

"At the northernmost waypoint for the hypertram that's still considered Tarrin's territory. I don't think they wanted to be seen by the border patrols. The good news is you can be home in thirty minutes."

There was too much emphasis on the word *You*. "Where are you going?"

"To meet with the rest of the group, get whatever else I can from them, and dump a corpse in a place where it won't be found for a few hours." She turned, clothes in minor disarray. "Do I look like I just took advantage of someone's drugged state?"

Hollis pressed his lips together and shook his head.

"How does one look after torturing someone, then—" She turned back to the mirror and untucked her shirt.

He could feel her abhorrence of the thought. "Raping them?"

Her shoulders hunched forward slightly, an instinctive response to the threat of horrific violence.

"In fleet, they look very, very dead, and for good reason." He kept his voice calm, unconcerned. They were two friends talking about nothing. Rowena was too fragile for anything else.

Through their lingering connection, he could feel her self-loathing.

Just what had Old Baular taught her? Lost Fleet burn his soul.

"Come here. Rowena."

:Ro.: He switched to the more intimate form of communication. :Come here.: He sat up, crossing his legs, and waited.

She stayed where was.

:That's an order from a guardian. Come here.:

Lee pivoted slowly, anger written in every line of her body.

:You're still my operative in the field. And you're upset. It's my job to help you do your job. Come. Here.:

:You're injured and off-duty.:

:I'm the only one here. I don't like seeing you like this.: He echoed her words from earlier.

"I'm fine," she said out loud, but she took a step toward the bed.

:You're not.: He caught her hand and pulled her closer, maintaining eye contact. :You're angry at yourself for this. Don't be. It's not you.:

She took a deep breath. "Isn't it?" Her dark eyes were filled with fear. :This is what I was groomed for. This is what I was meant to be. A sadistic torturer serving the Baulars. This is what I'm supposed to be good for. This is what I am.:

"No. Rowena, no." He pulled her down to the bed and into his arms, shielding her from everything else. Blocking the dingy room with his body so she was safe. Cradling her in his lap. She was too thin, too light… "This is not who you are. I'm fine, see? I'm not hurt. You didn't hurt me." He put her hand over his heart so she could feel the rhythm.

:Today.:

Drawing her head to his shoulder, he stroked her hair like she was a injured child. :All that matters is today.:

He could feel her fear: of reprisal and repercussions and judgement. She wanted to run, to lock everything away again. He couldn't let her. :Shhh. Calm down. I won't tell anyone about this. This is between us. Just us.:

A layer of fear peeled away.

:I hate what I'm good at. I hate... me.: Broken memories of training for torture, of envisioning a scenario much like today with him at her mercy, filtered through to him. :I've done so many awful things.:

"So have I," Hollis whispered in her ear. "We both have." :We're both monsters.:

:You're a hero.: The words came with a bitter taste of anger.

:If I'm one, you are too.:

:Heroes are the ones who win. Monsters are the ones who lose. I lost. I failed. I couldn't even die when I was supposed to.:

More memories...

Of Trace's death.

Of the end of the war.

Of being locked in a brig with no light and no contact after landing. So many times she should have died, but survived out of pure stubbornness. Because someone else needed her, never because she loved her life enough to fight for it.

Ancestors, how do I help her?

He held her tighter as a hot tear dropped on his chest. Rowena understood service, duty, survival. It would be enough for now. It would have to be.

:What would have happened if you had died before today?:

:Who knows?:

:We can guess,: Hollis said. :This situation today, no one else could have pulled it off. No one else has the skills needed to run this op. You were the best and only choice. And there's no one else I would have made the decision to stay with. No one else I would have felt safe running a counter interrogation with.:

:Carver. Marshall...: She started listing guardians and crew.

Hollis grabbed her chin and tilted it up so she was forced to look him in the eye. "No one else."

Her eyebrows bent together in a confused frown.

"This isn't the sort of thing you can fake. It required someone with the training you had, the skills you have, the temperament you have... Someone who can menace convincingly, control a room, and give no hint that you care."

"But—"

"I know you. I know when you're angry. I know when you're ready to kill. I know you put the mission first, and if your job was to save an enemy, you would without question or hesitation."

She looked unconvinced.

Hollis leaned in and rested his forehead on hers. :It's okay because it's us. I wouldn't have let any other team run an op like this. I wouldn't have let it play out like that with anyone else. I wouldn't have trusted anyone but you to handle it and get us both out alive."

There was a flicker of purple and green fire in her eyes.

:You did your job and you did it well. We're both safe.:

:I'm not done yet.: She pushed away and he let her go. :I have to clear a path for you.:

Cold swept over him, a healing draught after a moment of intense emotion. The space was good... If he ignored the sense of loss and emptiness, the space was good.

If he acknowledged how comfortable he felt with Rowena, it would all fall apart. He'd lose her because she'd never allow him that close.

Lee tugged at her clothes. "How do I look? Like the vilest form of human life? Like someone who just robbed someone of their free will so I could gain a momentary pleasure?"

Hollis leaned back, resting on his arms and stretching out his legs as he tried to divorce his emotions from the situation. "Rape is another form of torture. It's about power, abuse, and conquering someone."

She made a face. "My stomach's already turning. How could anyone do that?"

"By thinking of themselves and only of themselves. And by having no soul or redeeming qualities. There's a reason the punishment in fleet is an automatic death sentence." To be carried out by whoever found the rapist first. If someone attacked, the victim was allowed and encouraged to force teleport the attacker into vacuum.

If the victim couldn't do that, the first officer they saw afterwards would do it for them.

Rowena still looked upset.

"If it makes you feel better, you aren't actually doing anything to me. And even if you had, if the plan went the way our friends thought it would, I'd be walking out of here thinking everything was consensual."

"Torture is never consensual, by definition."

He forced a smile he couldn't quite feel with Rowena so worried. "Straighten your clothes. Put your chin up. Hair back."

She did.

"Think about the first battle you won. Your first kill."

There was an uneasy glance in his direction, and her lips puckered in a frown.

"Remember how you felt vindicated? Victorious? Untouchable? I do." Young and stupid, coming back to *Virginia Vallejo* after the first battle in war had left him drunk on an illusion of strength. It wasn't until he'd seen the cost of the battle that reality had cut into him like a knife.

Clearly all Rowena remembered of war was the price.

"Remember how you felt the first time you knocked me unconscious?"

This time her smile reached her dark brown eyes. "Ancestors, you deserved it. I'm not even apologizing. You were being such a dick, and giving Mal a hard time. You got exactly what you deserved."

:Perfect.: *So perfect.*

Rowena looked over at him in confusion.

"That look right now. That's the look you need when you walk out of here. Like you've won. Like you have everything you want."

:But... I don't.:

:Want to hit me again?:

She made a show of weighing the option, tilting her head with an exaggerated frown. Then wrinkling her nose and shaking her head. :I don't actually want to hit you right now.:

Hollis gasped in dramatic shock and put a hand to his chest. "Rowena Eden Lee! What would people say? I'm scandalized!"

Rowena pointed an admonitory finger at him. "If you tell anyone I thought that, I'll deny it. And then I'll prove that I'm happy to hit you."

:Your secret is safe with me. I wouldn't ever let anyone know that you have a soft side.: He winked.

She raised an eyebrow. :What soft side?:

He grinned. :Only I get to see this side of you. Training partner's privilege.:

"You're ridiculous," she said with a snort of amusement.

"You wouldn't trade me for anyone."

She spun around rather than answering, but he could feel the answer there regardless. She was happy because he was smiling.

That was enough for today.

"See you back at base?"

Rowena looked over her shoulder with a smug smile. :I'll be there. Stay safe going home. I'm not rescuing you twice in one day.:

Magnetic Storm Rowena, destroying her enemies and looking beautiful as ever. Ancestors above, but she was fun to watch.

The door closed and he felt an unpleasant chill. The room seemed darker without her, like she'd stolen the sunlight. He rubbed his chest where the grounders tracking device would have gone as he shook off the lingering sense of abandonment.

Just another day in the Starguard, protecting the Malik System and trying figure out what secret Lee was hiding from him. Nothing new here.

Nothing new at all.

19
MALCOLM

NARCISSISM SEEMED AN UNAVOIDABLE affliction in the rich, Malcolm mused as he broached the sanctity of the Lethe conference room.

It was more than vanity, it was a culture of self-idolization. There were hints everywhere, from the portraits framing the entryway to the mirrors on every door. This was a minor Lethe holding, a central office for the hypertram in Ryun, and they'd still managed to have a stage and framery for distinguished guests.

Sonya stood out, a sparkling queen beetle in a swarm of muted suits. Even the other women in attendance wouldn't risk outshining the sun around whom the audience orbited.

On a foot-high platform in the center of the room, the Lethes did not move; they stood still and permitted the supplicants come to them.

"Isn't it lovely?" Harringworth bubbled, standing on tip-toe to look around at the conference room, as if designing a box with an inordinate amount of stairs was somehow the greatest achievement of mankind. "It always put me in mind of a music box. You know, the fancy velvet-lined ones you give Grandma for Landing Day."

And you put me in mind of Mister Mischievous from the children's book, with sugar floss hair and oversized spectacles.

But he couldn't say that to his boss. "An elegant reminder that we're trinkets owned by wealthy men?" Malcolm asked, sipping his flat champagne and cursing everyone on the continent for thinking this was an acceptable alcohol.

The islands had ruined him for any drink that couldn't get you intoxicated off just the fumes. Who cared if the cheap ale they sold at the docks tasted like motor fuel and burned your throat? One drink and you'd forget every problem. Two and you'd forget how to breathe.

Maybe he could find the person who had marinated in a perfume of fermented strawberries, that would probably be toxic enough to make him forget his worries.

"We're not owned," Harringworth said. "Not yet. We're currently free men here to enjoy this, uh"—he lifted the pamphlet that had been sitting at the door to inspect it again—"celebration of cultural goodwill."

"Between us and a city-state that shares our exact same culture?"

"Yes!" Harringworth blinked. "No! Kytun and Ryun are very different. We, huh, we have more waterways than they do. They have the flowers. Quite different." He nodded as if reassuring himself.

Malcolm patted the man on his shoulder. "Keep saying that, sir. I'm sure you'll find a difference soon enough. You're from the same ship stock, speak the same language, cook from the same recipes, and share all the same suppliers. But I'm sure you do it all with as much uniqueness as is possible considering the circumstances."

"Islander," Harringworth muttered.

Malcolm smiled at the epitaph. He drifted into the crowd, waiting for someone to trip. Generally speaking conference rooms had nice, flat floors. This one, however, had winding daises. They weren't quite stairs, but the uneven floor meant the insecure were vying for attention by constantly trying to step above their peers, all the while remaining on a lower level than the Lethes.

He slunk along the middle level, trying to shake Harringworth and ignoring as much of the conversation as he could, but picking up enough of it to get the gist. Everyone here was in the design industry in some way, or else newly wealthy. They were hungry. They were eager. They were people who had tasted power and wanted more.

And Lethe stood in the middle of them like a puppetmaster.

The master of the Lethe transport empire looked suitably kingly, snow-white hair and a heavy brow like some ancient monarch in a holodrama. He had the same limpid blue eyes as his daughter, and the same sneering look of superiority, although his thick beard hid it well.

"Malcolm!"

It had really been too much to hope he'd go unnoticed. Malcolm turned to see Sonya artfully framed by an arching window and deep blue curtains that brought out the color in her eyes. "Miss Lethe."

"Please, Malcolm, this is a social gathering. Call me Sonya."

He pressed his lips together in a tight smile.

"Come meet Father." Sonya took his arm and tucked herself in close, the smell of rotting strawberries making his eyes water.

Father. Not 'My father' or 'Mister Lethe'. Malcolm hadn't come to a social gathering; he'd stepped into a cult meeting.

Several colorful curses ran through his mind as Sonya dragged him to the center island.

"Father!" Sonya pushed him up the stairs in front of her like an offering. "This is Malcolm Long, the one I told you about."

"Ah, the insightful young man from Ryun. Lethe. Virgil Lethe." He held out a hand with a large ring made of silver, some sort of crystal, and what looked like a sliver of orange lightning. It was a memorable design.

A small, static charge from the dry air zapped as Malcolm shook hands without hesitation because he knew how Kedic Winn the Fourth had looked after meeting the Lethes. Splattered across a public highway was not a good look. "You look just like your portrait outside the tram station." A thick head of well-groomed white hair on a long, face with a lantern jaw.

Virgil Lethe laughed. Loudly. "That was done decades ago, but I have aged well. Tell me, what do you do, young man?"

"I design engines," Malcolm said with a shrug. "Aeronautics is my field, and Bennu Industries pays my bills."

"Ah, the clever people of Bennu." Lethe nodded sagely. He smiled at Sonya as if they were sharing a secret. "Your CEO is an ambitious man. Reminds me of myself when I was younger."

"Indeed," Malcolm agreed.

If the CEO had been born into a wealthy family, guaranteed the best education the planet could provide, and had a name that ensured everyone would agree with anything he said, they'd be exactly the same.

So would have Malcolm, and everyone else, when it came to that.

Wealth bought power and power controlled *almost* everything.

Pity it didn't control the important things.

Malcolm's gaze went past Lethe to the narrow slit of a window, the city, and, on the far edge of the view, the spires of the Marshall holdings burning fiery orange in the sunset.

Virgil Lethe slapped his shoulder, bringing him back to the moment. "Have you ever worked on city transport, my boy?"

"No," Malcolm said coolly, brushing off the unwanted 'My boy'. "The cities seem to all have them running well enough."

"The current cities." The elder Lethe's eyes sparkled with delight. "Only the current cities."

Sonya stepped forward, retrieving Malcolm's hand so he was trapped between the two. "Everyone here is discussing the current housing problem. Too many people, not enough houses, not enough jobs."

"If people weren't working two or three jobs to feed themselves, I imagine there'd be plenty of work to go around." Imagination could drown in the briny sea; Malcolm had done the math. "All it would take is a reallocation of some resources, a raise in standard wages, and permitting the working class to have the freedom of time and education that the rich enjoy." He smiled sardonically.

Sonya's blonde hair danced as she laughed and shook her head. "Oh, how droll, Malcolm. Dearest." She gave her head a tiny shake, accompanied with a small frown. "He is a laugh, isn't he, Father?"

The elder Lethe laughed along with her, head tilting back in a roar of amusement. "Reallocations and standard wages? Don't tell me you fell for that old song, Long. You're an educated man after all. You know the true order of the universe."

A half-forgotten memory of his childhood schooling came back. "True Order? The Imperial theory of history that proves that all human cultures eventually fall into some form of stratification?" Malcolm had written a paper calling the idea the dirge of civilizations, and still had the scars from the beating his grandfather had given him for it.

"Yes." Virgil Lethe smiled, eyes gleaming with mirth—and greed. "Order is what keeps the rising man from becoming the craven coward. It elevates us all. Allows even the weakest among us to have a place and purpose. We need that order, or we will become like those barbarians Icedell took in. Wild-eyed savages who drink each other's blood and kill the young."

Malcolm swallowed a cough. "I think... I'd *heard*," he corrected, "that several of those savages can trace their lines back to the Imperial throne." Which was more than Lethe could claim.

"Oh, I'm sure they say that." Lethe chuckled. "Some sort of oral history. They say they have it all stored in their heads."

Sonya laughed again and pinched Malcolm's arm.

He looked down at her.

Laugh. She mouthed the word with a threatening glare.

Malcolm dredged up a smile.

"You're too much, Malcolm." Sonya squeezed his arm harder. "Everyone on this planet will tell you they have imperial relations, but only one has the Grant of Patronage."

"Two," the senior Lethe corrected. "The Marshalls still have theirs and they're strong enough to hold it if challenged."

"I heard they had Imperial blood too," Malcolm said, just to be contrary.

Lethe Senior sniffed in disdain. "A second son from a third wife from an Emperor who isn't alive anymore. At best, they were still thirty or forty people from the throne, and that was at their height. But, a Grant of Patronage? Why, if the wormhole opened today and the Emperor returned, my Sonya would be his wife. The Empress of the greatest empire ever known."

An empress, singular, he thought to himself. The Emperors had always kept large harems. But he had the good sense not to say that out loud. He smiled at Sonya. "You're waiting for an Emperor? No wonder everyone here looks so forlorn."

Sonya preened. "My father dreams of a returning Emperor. I"—she leaned against his arm—"am a little more realistic. But that's not why I absconded with you." Her whole demeanor slipped from flirtatious to business in a second. "My father and I were discussing an ideal city, and since you come from such a small town, I thought you might have some insight on how many people you would need to run a city."

"Run to what purpose?" The idea was just intriguing enough and it wasn't like Sonya was going to let him leave. If he was pinned down here, at least he could keep them on a topic that he had some experience with; his family had always taken leadership positions before the move to Descent. "If you want a political rival to the great city-states you ne—"

"Oh no!" The senior Lethe shook his head. "Not a rival. A self-sufficient city-state. Nothing more."

"For how long?"

Sonya and her father shared a puzzled look. "Does it matter?"

Malcolm shrugged. "If you want it to run for a few years, no. If you want longer than a few generations though, you need to consider genetic diversity. There's all sorts of math formulas applied to the topic. Especially when people discuss settling Malik III. I know it's come up in conversation at the university several times since the fleet landed in Icedell. The quickest way to ease the housing problems would be to move people off planet."

"A useless dream," Sonya said with a dismissive gesture of her glass. "The only space-worthy fleet is nothing but scrap metal. They can't get airborne. They certainly can't go between planets."

"With a new fuel source—"

Sonya cut him off, her smile tight. "Those ships will have their uses, but not as transport. They'll be handing them over to the authorities in a few weeks. You'll see."

That sounded like a very fanciful dream. In his experience, people were loath to give up their homes just because some wealthy stranger demanded it.

"Building material," the elder Lethe said, seeing Malcolm's frown. "Thousands of tons of metal and material, ready to be harvested."

Malcolm took a glass from a passing waiter and kept his expression politely neutral. "I doubt they'll hand over the metal. Those are their homes." Numbers ran through his mind: the cost of moving the material away from Icedell, the impact of rehoming nearly a million people, the political impact of both costs... It wasn't worth it.

The Lethes had to know that.

"They will hand over whatever we ask for," Sonya said again, this time with a smile. "They're very persuadable people, if you talk to them correctly. And if they don't feel persuaded?" She shrugged, eyes glinting cold over the smile. "Wars happen. Everyone knows that. Especially between savages. Everyone heard of what happened last year, and that was just a silly tiff over a boy!"

"I'd heard it was a little more than that," Malcolm said carefully. Attempted murder, if he'd understood the news reports correctly. Over the islands, they said it looked like the sky was full of falling stars day and night in the end. Each bright light another life lost.

He threw back the rest of his drink and looked around for another one. The waitstaff seemed to have abandoned him. *Does anyone in this crowd have a flask?*

"A tiny thing," Sonya assured him, pulling the focus back to her. "Another fight would be easy to start. Especially when we already know where the tipping point will be, don't we, father?"

Lethe smiled at his daughter. "It's an educated guess at the moment. Fed off rumors and little else. They're a quiet people, you know, and not given to reading or writing."

Malcolm felt his teeth grind together. "My grandfather used to say the same thing about the islanders before he went there. So primitive. Living in huts. Catching fish only to eat them hours later. No long term planning or strategy." All biases built with a complete lack of understanding of the islands. Malcolm had spent enough of his life there to know the difference now.

"Your grandfather has a point," Virgil Lethe said.

"The islands aren't so bad," Sonya said. "They're not as well organized as the city-states, perhaps, but they don't need to be. They're small. No one depends on them for leadership or insight."

A tray passed just out of reach.

Next time someone dragged him to one of these events, he was coming prepared.

Where was Harringworth anyway? Malcolm searched the crowd for Harringworth, or any other excuse to get away.

"All unimportant," Lethe said. "What matters now is the future, yes? A better, brighter future. Controlled and organized and arranged so it will run seamlessly."

"As an engineer, sir," Malcolm replied, eyes still roving the crowd, "let me assure you that there is no such thing as perfection when you are dealing with humans. They always find ways to ruin things."

Sonya chuckled. "Only if you let them run uncontrolled." She tugged at his arm. "Father, if you'll excuse us, there's one last thing I need to discuss with Doctor Long before he leaves."

Lethe Senior raised his glass in his daughter's direction. "Naturally, naturally. Take your time, my dear. Long"—he nodded generously—"good to meet you, I'm sure we'll have occasion to cross paths again."

Malcolm shook his hand and dipped his head politely.

Sonya dragged him through the crowd and into a dark corner.

There didn't seem to be any reason for their sudden departure, but a uniformed security guard shut the door, leaving them in the dusty gloom alone.

"Is everything all right, Miss Lethe? I hope I didn't upset your father..." ... *enough that he'll want to kill me.*

"Nothing like that," Sonya said, pulling a pin from her hair. "Father probably thinks we've stepped outside for an illicit rendezvous." She twisted the pin, releasing a tightly coiled string of paper. "Names to help you rebuild the information I need."

He unrolled the paper. *Trace Silar. Kiernan.* "The *Bassi*?" He looked up at Sonya.

"A sailing vessel that's involved with smuggling. The names belong to people we think stole some data from one of our regional offices. They're low level trouble at best."

"The name Silar sounds familiar," he said carefully, hoping Sonya wouldn't question why.

She shook her head, dismissing the thought without consequence. "Perhaps you heard it in passing. They're low level ruffians in a gang in Icedell."

"And this is current information?" He glanced at her. "People who would be listed on what I'm decoding?"

She nodded, eagerness slipping through her crafted façade. "I'm certain of it. Our informant gave us the names only hours ago."

Malcolm gave a single, decisive nod in reply, and pocketed the paper. "Then I'll apply them directly. If there's any way of restoring the data, I'll find it." Unlike Sonya, he was a very good liar: The smile he flashed her was charming, his body language signaling loyalty and affection—and Sonya believed him.

20

ROWENA

ROWENA ARRIVED AT KORE Technology, Selena and Titan's rebranded and expanded groundside enterprise, as soon as she was able to break away from helping the Jhandarmi drop the body of Hollis's would-be torturer outside Tarrin. She'd taken a few minutes to shower, change, grab a ration bar, and set the codes to start regrowing her hair. It itched, but she'd put on two inches in the past hour and almost looked like herself again.

The offices of Selena Caryll's groundside operation were discreetly tucked away in a middle floor of a tall tower overlooking a public space and fountain. The waiting area looked distinctly Tarrin: a low, wide couch with off-white fabric and muted blue-gray walls. Visitors could sit uncomfortably and stare at a painting of pink roses framing a white fountain.

It was all a form of tedious torture, unless you knew how Selena's mind went—and then it was hard not to snicker. Caryll seemed so innocent, but her mind had a twist in it that Rowena had learned to appreciate. It was that or lose her own mind every time she wanted to see Titan.

Yonic roses and a couch only suitable for laying down on. A Caryll classic.

Rowena ran a scan of the building and bumped up against the shields that kept casual visitors from coming near the labs.

Titan flashed a signal back at her a picosecond before teleporting into the waiting room. Tall, lithe, and lethal. His skin was black as the night between stars and his eyes glowed a striking emerald green. When he wasn't smiling, Titan looked like he was plotting to slowly kill someone.

All Rowena saw was her childhood friend. Someone who she'd played with as child. Who'd supported her even when the rest of the fleet abandoned her. Someone who loved her when she wasn't lovable.

"Are you early or did you change the meeting time?" he said, walking towards her. He wouldn't hug her, because he knew she didn't like being touched, but he'd be close. For them, that was enough.

"Early." She smiled. Being near Titan made her feel safer than she had in weeks. This whole grounder mess and relying on Hollis had left her off kilter.

"Good." He put a datpad down on the empty reception desk and narrowed his green eyes into a glare.

Rowena mimicked his look.

Titan's glare grew comical and he laughed. :How are you?: A quiet voice in her head filled with a soothing sense of belonging.

:Fine.:

As long as she let the daylight wash away all her worries. She wasn't going to drag Titan down into the muck she was drowning in.

"Really?" Titan's voice was deep and unsettling in its coldness.

She raised her eyebrows in question and nodded. "Is there a reason I shouldn't be?"

"Rumor fuels the fleet, as do reports. I just finished reading Silar's writeup of this morning."

What the crack had Silar written in that report? She scanned the file Titan shared with her, jaw tightening as she braced herself against a rebellious resurgence of the emotions the interrogation had drawn out of her. The worst part of the afternoon had been summed up in a single sentence: Drill Instructor Lee escorted Guardian Silar to a nearby hospice, ran a medical scan to ensure his health, and left to continue her mission.

No mention of her tears.

No mention of her breakdown.

No mention of curling into his arms.

Her teeth ground together. Of course there was no mention of it. To Silar it probably didn't even matter. People threw themselves into his arms all the time. Not that she wanted anyone to know how vulnerable she'd been, or that she'd let Hollis Silar comfort her, of all people. It was better this way. They could all forget it. Move on.

With a thought, she mentally burned the report out of her implant's memory and looked at Titan, arms crossed. "So?"

"You're running ops with Silar now?" Titan's tone was filled with doubt.

Rowena pushed the unpleasant memories aside. "Not intentionally. We had to work with what we had. The Jhandarmi found the interrogator but she had a suicide capsule on her. All we got out of her before she died was that the target was fleet. I searched for a fleet signature near the kind of tech needed for that kind of operation and got lucky." Really lucky.

Tryling was still flying on the belief that her scans had found the grounders.

"Once I found Silar, we agreed running an interrogation there was better than trying to search the place for information. We both had the training, and it wasn't like the grounders were going to give us another opportunity."

Titan looked skeptical. "A scan took you to the workshop? I read the report, Rowena, there's no way you could have found the place easily. Where'd you get that information?"

She sighed, mentally cursing every last Silar in existence. If that self-important yaldson was going to falsify official documents, he could at least do it competently. "Silar sent an OID signal on one of the tight channels I used to talk to Mal on."

"How'd he get that?" Titan's voice was sharp with the promise of violence.

"Who knows? It's Silar. He pokes at things until they make sense, takes them apart, plays with data. He's always been like that." Although she hadn't realized quite how much he knew until today. As soon as she could spare a moment, she needed to sit and think about what had happened.

"When were you going to tell me about this?"

Rowena blinked. "About what? Working with the Jhandarmi? You arranged this."

Green eyes narrowed in true frustration. "You nearly died in a Tarrin morgue last week. Didn't tell me. I asked Nia about it and she didn't know you'd left Enclave."

She shrugged. "Nia doesn't care what I do." Most people in fleet didn't.

"I do!" Titan said.

"And I would tell if you if it became relevant," she said levelly. "But I don't report to you. Never have." And she wasn't going to start now. Titan had a good life—a happy life—she wasn't going to let her battle damage pull him down.

The old color code for annoyance and a fight flashed across her implant. Titan wasn't happy. "You could have mentioned something casually. 'By the way, I was in some random city-state no one has ever heard of this week' sort of thing."

Rowena shrugged again. "Kydell is boring, humid, and unremarkable. There. That's all you missed."

"You know that thing where you'd back me up for anything because you're my friend?" Titan asked. "That's supposed to be a reciprocal thing. I'm supposed to help you when you have problems."

"When I have a problem, I will let you help," Rowena said, projecting genuine calm and confidence. Titan had spent most of the war in the infirmary, not standing next to the worst monster the fleet had ever created, lying with a smile. He was no match for her level of duplicity.

"What about the thing with Silar?" He sounded genuinely concerned. "Mal would have cracked a hull before he let you go into a situation like that. He knew—we knew—how much you hated what Old Baular wanted you to do. If you'd pinged me, I could have gone in for you." Old memories touched the edge of her shield, concerned looks between Titan and Mal. The very real fear that they'd lose her to Old Baular's plans before Mal could fix things.

She brushed the fears aside, projecting strength and confidence. Titan could never know she was worried. "There wasn't enough time, Titan, and the woman was my height. I was the best option."

Titan reached for her shoulder and she stepped back instinctively. He dropped his hand. "Were you hurt?"

"No." Not in the way he meant. "The grounders didn't suspect a thing."

"Nightmares? Feelings of despair? Anything like that? I know it's only been a few hours, but..." Titan raised his eyebrows as he searched for a reaction.

She uncrossed her arms. "I'm fine."

"You ran a field op with Silar, which is as far from fine as you can get without crossing the event horizon of a black hole." Titan's battle shield flickered to life, expanding and filling the lobby. "He has no clue what your history is, no way of providing the emotional support you need after a situation like that. I know he has a temper, and he probably lashed out the minute you two were alone."

Rowena bumped Titan's shield hard enough to sting, a quick rebuke for switching to battle mode. It was fine that he was upset, but she didn't need another fleet war because of a stupid misunderstanding. "Hollis only has a temper off-duty. He's a good field officer, and he lived up to that reputation."

Titan eyebrows went higher. "Hollis? He's Hollis now?"

"Ancestors keep me! There's Silars everywhere. I have two in my class, there's—what now—eleven Guardian Silars running loose? I have to differentiate between them some-how."

Titan made a non-committal noise as his expression neutralized. "Speaking of classes..."

Thank the Ancestors he was changing topics. "The Sciarra fleetlings are doing fine. I keep an eye on them."

"They keep an eye on you too."

"What's that supposed to mean?" She'd been eating, sleeping at least a couple nights a week, and keeping out of fights when she could. What could they possibly have to report to Titan?

"Nothing," he said in a drawl that meant everything. "Although their reports say a certain Guardian keeps showing up at class."

Rowena rolled her eyes. "Not my fault. Or his. There's a six week rotation at the training house and the Guardians seem to all have excuses when it's their turn to supervise my class."

It was a very minor insult, not one she let herself dwell on.

"Besides, he's been my sparring partner since Mars is so busy and you have Selena."

Titan grimaced in apology. "He's not a bad match, as a partner. Normally I'd say he's too tall to be your training partner, but your fighting styles complement each other." She caught his thoughts on their matchup physically; they both favored brute force attacks and Titan seemed to like that. "It works, even if the physics says it shouldn't."

"It's not like I get the luxury of only fighting people as short as me." There had to be a way to get Titan off this topic. Hollis Silar was taking up too much mental space right now.

"Still, it's probably time to change it up. What about Kenzi?"

It took her a moment to place the name. "What, the one who's a cousin a couple generations back on your mother's side?" Kenzi was a bit shorter than Titan, a little more muscular, and left-handed, her implant reminded her. It was a useful thing to know in a knife fight, but it didn't help now.

"That's right." Data from Titan streamed toward her. "He graduated the Academy the year before the war and ran a Sciarra hospital ship for most of it. Good pilot. Excellent officer." There was a hook in Titan's voice. "He has two warships in his dowry. He'll be a sub-captain with his spouse as XO."

Kenzi Sciarra, a perfectly average officer, nice and safe. Perfect spouse for someone, although she couldn't imagine who Titan thought she should match him with. Nia was already married and Yunjin was too young. Rowena let the confusion show on her face. "You think I should train with him?"

"It wouldn't be a bad idea. He never tested as Elite, but he's strong. He'll learn to keep up with you in a few months."

"I'm already training fleetlings. I don't want to break in a new sparring partner!" she said in exasperation.

"It would be better than keeping Hollis Silar around!"

Rowena tried to wrap her head around the idea of Hollis not being there to fight with her. There wasn't a decision tree for that kind of event.

Titan raised an eyebrow. "Wouldn't it?"

"I suppose." She shrugged off the chill of the thought. "I don't know. He's a good sparring partner."

The sound of voices coming out of the lift saved her from further interrogation. Hollis was a good sparring partner. There was no reason to replace him. And no reason to think about why she wanted to keep him either.

"If you want to keep him around... Have you talked to him?" Titan asked as Tyrling's voice echoed in the hall outside. "Did you check on him?"

"He's on quarters for recovery," Rowena said. "The medic said the mountain did minimal damage dropping on him. He got his shield up in time."

"You need to talk to him," Titan insisted. "Silence is where worry breeds. If you want whatever is between you two to work, he needs to know you were thinking about him."

Rowena shot him a death glare as the door opened. There was nothing between her and Hollis except animosity and atmosphere. Not wanting to break in a new training partner wasn't the same as wanting to keep Hollis around.

Titan was reading too much into the situation.

Selena Caryll, effortlessly beautiful and pale as the stars, walked in with Tyrling and Doctor Keen.

"Hello." Selena reached for Titan's hand, a moonbeam across the vast blackness of space, and kissed his cheek in one practiced movement. "Lee." A nod.

"Captain Caryll." Rowena nodded back. "Director. Doctor. How are you?"

"I'm well, thank you," the doctor said. Keen had kept her bland, brown clothes, this time a taupe sweater paired with darker brown pants.

Tyrling nodded to her, the lights of the lobby reflecting off his bald head. He shrugged in his coat. "Lee, good to see you out and about. Titan, good to be back at Kore."

"We love having visitors at Kore Technology," Titan said, "especially when you bring us interesting technical challenges."

Off to the side Rowena caught the eye-glow of fast communication between Titan and Selena, and the data sloshing over. Selena was catching her husband up on the latest information.

In return, he was filling her in on Rowena's activities.

Selena sent her a worried look followed by a ping filled with concern.

Rowena responded with a flash code for safe and smiled at the grounders.

"Let's get started," Tyrling said. "The conference room or the labs?"

"Labs," Selena said, taking over. "Lee sent the device to the containment room on the *Persephone* first, but we were able to transport it down here for you to view."

"Have you figured out what it is?" Keen asked.

:Have we?: Selena asked.

Rowena nodded as she unlocked the door to the lab. "More or less. I know where it came from and how it works. I just don't know how it was made."

"Is that relevant?" Keen asked as she stepped in and surveyed the lab.

Deep blue-gray metal benches and low lighting made the space seem to contain depths and distance that weren't possible. It was a Caryll aesthetic found on several of their ships, and it was growing on Rowena.

The device she'd kept out of Hollis's chest hung in a beam of light, suspended above an anti-gravity column and surrounded by several layers of shields.

Titan flipped the shields to visible so the grounders could see them.

"Intricate work," Rowena said. "You've added a new technique." She made a mental note to figure out how later.

"Thank you," Titan said. "Doctor Keen, can you confirm that this device is similar to the one you pulled from Brinceno's chest?"

The doctor nodded. "It looks the same to me."

"Only similar," Rowena said, she pulled up the image of the original egg. "The one you found during the autopsy, and that self-destructed a few hours later, was slightly smaller and had less metal caging around it. The orun sliver was also noticeably larger."

"Relevance?" Tyrling asked.

Rowena shook her head. "Hard to say. I don't think the design is integral to the function."

"She means it could be shaped like anything," Selena said. "It would fulfill the same function even if it were smaller and didn't have the golden filigree."

"Did you figure out how it was working?" Keen asked.

"Electric impulses for the most part," Rowena said. "The device doesn't need to be near the heart, that seems to be a stylistic choice on the part of the user. All this requires is physical contact with the victim and it can work as long as the contact is maintained. It's cell-level technology that interferes with the nervous system. It sends false messages and rewrites the brain chemistry."

Doctor Keen raised her eyebrows. "It would be fascinating to see it in use."

"I have," Rowena said. "While I was in Kydell I ran into at least two people who had devices like this implanted in their bodies. The one I was able to talk to had no knowledge of its presence."

"Any symptoms?" Keen asked as she took out a note pad. "Chest pains? Swelling? Anything like that?"

"He rubbed his chest several times, but the device was accelerating his heartrate. He was acting like an addict, obsessing over doing what he was guided to do."

Tyrling frowned. "Would they all act like that?"

"Probably not," Selena said. "I've reviewed the data Lee collected and, politically, it wouldn't suit the user's needs to have all the victims acting that way. The ones Lee interacted with were lower on the social scale and were being abused."

"They were test subjects," Titan translated.

Rowena nodded. "Both of them were rowdies in Kydell. They're disliked by the ruling class and both of the ones I saw were being used in fixed fights."

"Both dead, I presume?" Keen asked, pen at the ready.

"One dead. One survived."

The doctor looked up questioningly. "Forced to fight while unfocused and not fully in control of their faculties? That's a very strong individual."

"I may have given him a little help," Rowena said. "The signal from the device can be jammed momentarily."

"And it can be intercepted," Selena said. "That's why we actually called you here." She held out a palm-sized datpad to Tyrling. "It's a rolling encryption but we were able to break it last night. This is the signal the device is sending out now."

Tyrling looked over the readout. "Is it in words like this?"

"No," Rowena said, "the original code would send electric impulses to the brain to trigger these responses."

"Is it receiving anything from the victim?" Keen asked.

"Not that we're aware of," Rowena said. "At most, it would be able to create a passive signal of some form so the operator could track the victim. Since the device seems to need a steady electrical field to prevent destruction, it would need to stay on a body, or in a set up like this, to keep working."

Titan stepped forward. "It's almost a living thing. A metallic parasite."

"What about the transport technology they were using to put it in the guardian's chest?" Tyrling said. "Did you track that down? It's fleet, isn't it?"

"No," Titan said. "Rowena gave me the full schematics and we both searched every available fleet file. The system is markedly different from the one we use."

Rowena pulled up the schematic of the implant gun. "This configuration here is similar to something *Eden* was using to load cargo prior to isolation."

"Eden?" Keen looked around in confusion. "Who is that?"

"Space Station Eden," Tyrling said.

Rowena took over because the doctor still looked confused. "The *Eden* was supposed to be the transport bridge between Malik IV and Malik III during the later stages of settlement. After the wormhole closed, it served as an orbital station and meeting point for fleet and colonists."

"The silver moon?" Keen asked. "I've heard the stories about it, but I didn't realize they were true."

"The *Eden* wasn't larger than Malik IV's moon," Selena said, "but it did orbit closer and so looked larger when it was in orbit."

"So, this device might be from the space station?" Keen nodded.

Rowena shook her head vehemently. "Not possible. The *Eden* went missing in the days before isolation. The entire station was emptied, fleet and grounders, and the theory is there was an engine collapse that fogged it."

"Fogged?" Tyrling raised his eyebrows. "Is there a translation for those of us who don't speak Lee?"

"With a large enough explosion, a ship can be reduced to particles," Titan said. "It looks a little like the weather event fog that you see on the ground."

The grounders looked concerned.

"*Eden* probably didn't explode," Selena said. "An event like that would have registered on someone's scans. But it is missing."

"Probably crumpled," Rowena muttered, shooting Selena an amused look.

Selena pinged her with a memory of an exaggerated eye roll. "Crumpling a space station the way I did a spaceship probably wasn't an option. At the time *Eden* went missing, the tech was limited to command gauntlets and near-useless teleport devices. The one Rowena found has a range of only a few meters. Great for party tricks, but it won't do anything more."

"How does it work?" Keen asked.

"How much do you know about time corridors, quantum entanglement, and einselection?" Rowena asked.

Tyrling's face paled. "I think, for the time being, we can skip the technical lecture."

"Probably best," Keen muttered.

"Titan," Tyrling nodded to him, "did you follow up on the report we had from Marshall?"

"I did, sir." Titan took over the display screen and pulled up the view of a city dominated by a step pyramid. "Kytun, home of the Lethe corporate empire. Also home to repeated time corridor signatures. Which, for those of you who never sat through Lieutenant Graveri's lectures on physics, means the tech signature for the teleport is found here."

Keen pursed her lips in a thoughtful frown. "The Lethes have been talking about expanding their assets for some time now. Teleportation could easily make the hypertrams and planes obsolete. Not to mention personal motor vehicles."

Rowena shivered at the thought.

"Not with this kind of teleportation," Titan said. "The fleet doesn't use them because the result of two teleportation events of this type crossing results in explosions. It would be a very dramatic way to turn your favorite city-state into a sink hole. The only reason the Lethes haven't had problems yet is that they're not doing large enough jumps. Yet."

"Yet." Tyrling sighed. "There are a lot of people in that city-state."

"I know, sir."

Selena tapped her fingers on the edge of the bench. "I don't suppose there's a way for the Jhandarmi to have a quiet word with Lethe?"

Tyrling shook his head. "Lord Lethe is not the sort of man to see reason. Not when it comes to transport. He's very driven, and it's gotten worse over the past year. If I didn't think the Lethe's lawyers would magically appear to sue me, I'd say he's suffering from the early stages of dementia." He clicked his tongue. "That's the problem I have with this. Virgil Lethe isn't the type to experiment on people or risk his reputation. He's a business man. His family had made a fortune by being careful."

"It wouldn't need to be orders from the top," Rowena said, from experience. "An underling in the right position, and with little oversight, can do a lot of damage. All they would need from Lethe would be his trust."

That's all she and Mal had needed from Old Baular to end the war. Trust... and a reason to stop fighting the Allied Fleet. Mal had found a reason, and she'd gone along for Mal's sake.

Titan sent her a flash of condolence. He knew what had happened and what she'd lost.

She sent him back the memory of a smile. :It's fine. Old news.:

Just not old enough.

"There are a few people working with Lethe who have the right mindset for an operation like this," Selena said.

"Sonya?" Tyrling guessed. "She's always been more ambitious than her father, as she proved last year."

"Is she still saying she was impersonated?" Selena asked.

Tyrling nodded.

Rowena picked up a quick, curse-filled exchange between Selena and Titan. Sonya Lethe had no friends here.

"What Sonya doesn't have is technical knowledge," Titan said. "And I doubt her engineers are good enough to do this on their own."

"I doubt they did," Tyrling said. He pulled a printed image of handsome man from his pocket.

Rowena looked at the black and white likeness: fair hair, stormy eyes, and a squared jaw. Mal would have looked a lot like that if he'd lived long enough.

"Who is it?" Keen asked.

"Doctor Malcolm Long of Bennu Industries. His family is from Seahome originally, at least on his father's side. His mother is an Amherst from the city-state of Northland."

His tone of voice made Rowena look up. "Is that important?"

"The Amhersts are titled family. Not as wealthy as the Marshalls or Lethes, but they were one of the first five hundred bloodlines on the planet. In Descent's social structure, that's significant. It's what got Long into the university there. He has multiple degrees in mathematics, engineering, and aeronautics. He published a paper on the Lyrorilna Equation three years ago."

Rowena, Titan, and Selena groaned in unison.

Doctor Keen raised her hand. "Explain, please."

"It's a quantum physics equation that was considered almost unsolvable," Titan said. "The Academy instructors used to give it to cadets to see if anyone could crack it."

"Mal came close," Rowena said. "Ancestors keep him."

Selena nodded. "Hermione too. They made it something of a competition."

"Well, Long beat them," Tyrling said. "He also dabbles in decryption as a side hobby."

"What a fun little genius," Selena said in a stretched tone. "It's amazing no one has tried to kill him for his own good."

"Who is Bennu?" Titan asked. "I've never heard of them, and I know all the serious competition for Kore." Selena and Titan guarded their company better than some crews guarded their ships. In the past year they'd seen rapid growth, developing software for several major city-states and strengthening alliances for the fleet.

Tyrling changed the screen on his device. "Bennu Industries is a very small research firm that usually takes contracts from the airline companies. They specialize in wing design and engines. Nothing you or Kore Technologies would be involved with. Your research is mostly medical, isn't it?"

"Medical and security," Selena said with a nod.

"No reason for you to know Bennu then," Tyrling said, one shoulder shrugging. "Long wasn't even on our radar until six weeks ago when he broke his pattern and went to meet Sonya Lethe in a private conference."

"Could be a marriage meeting," Keen said.

Everyone looked at her and she shrugged.

"He is a titled doctor from a bloodline that is likely to be very distant from the Lethes. They need some new genes in the mix and Sonya is famous for avoiding serious relationships, but she's been seen twice—in public—with the same blond man." The doctor looked up at them. "What? Don't you read the gossip?"

"Not as much as you, perhaps," Tyrling said.

The doctor shrugged again. "I spend all my day with corpses and reality. When I relax, I like flights of fancy and speculation about strangers. It's like a social life without the uncomfortable requirements of doing my hair or leaving my house."

Rowena chuckled. "I like you."

"You never do your hair," Titan said.

"I pull it back!" Rowena scratched her head. It'd be morning before she had the full length grown back. Stupid short-haired assassins.

Tyrling cleared his throat. "Looking at his body of research, do you think Malcolm Long might be capable of this?"

"He has the technical expertise," Rowena said, studying the picture. "The broker in Kydell, Nolotitus, he was selling information on a man who looked like that. It could be him."

"Doesn't mean he has the temperament," Selena said. "Whoever is doing this is cruel. Implanted parasites. Taking control of someone's body and mind. The casualty rates. All of it suggests someone with a complete disregard for other people."

Doctor Keen tapped her pen on her notepad. "Could be a sociopath."

"Or someone who believes that the people they're victimizing aren't really people," Titan said.

Old Baular had been like that. Anyone who allied with Carver wasn't really fleet. They weren't really people, so it didn't matter how many died.

"How do we want to run this?" Tyrling asked.

"We can't risk a full scale attack on Lethe," Selena said. "There's not enough reason for the Jhandarmi to go in. But we could work the Long angle. Get close to him. See if he lets anything drop."

Titan nodded. "People who feel superior like to brag. Selena and I can go make contact at Bennu, get him talking, see what we can find."

Tyrling nodded. "Doctor Keen?"

"Now that I have the schematics, I'd like to look at finding a way to remove the devices. Agent Lee, you said you knew someone who was alive who still had one of these actively implanted?"

"If he's still alive, yes, there was one in Kydell."

"Could you make contact with him again?" Keen asked.

Rowena nodded. "It shouldn't be hard."

"Then I'd like to pursue the medical angle," Keen said. "See if I can treat this parasite."

Tyrling looked over at Rowena. "That means you'll need to establish a base there. Can you do that?"

"It won't be a problem. There are several places I can safely teleport in."

"We'll look into getting you an apartment there if this looks like it will be long term," Tyrling said. "But make contact first. See if the situation there requires anything. And then there's this." He nodded at the device suspended in front of them. "What do we want to do with the device we have?"

Rowena frowned. "We'll monitor it. Right now, if it was implanted the device would do nothing more than encourage Silar to forget about what happened. If the directions change, we'll decide how to react."

"Good enough," Tyrling said. "Rolling updates, if you please. I want to know what's going on as it happens, not at the end of the week. I'll speak to Marshall, see if she can get close enough to Sonya to monitor her for a bit. Doctor Keen, loop in Lee. She'll be your boots on the ground."

"Of course." Keen stood up. "I look forward to working with all of you. After our little misadventure in the morgue a few days away from my normal duties will be refreshing."

"I'll show you out," Selena said. She gave Titan's hand a squeeze and left with the grounders.

Titan turned to Rowena. "You know what this means?"

"Hoshi's going to lose an engine when I tell him I'm working extra hours for the Jhandarmi?"

"No, it means someone has to fill Silar in on what's happening. You just volunteered him for this mission."

Had she? The meeting replayed in her head and winced. She had.

"Want me to tell him?" Titan asked. "This is going to come up at the staff meeting anyway."

"I'll do it," Rowena said. "I'm sending him reports anyways."

Titan's eyebrows went up in surprise.

"Don't look at me like that. I have my reasons."

He held up his hands in a protest of innocence. "You need to talk to him anyway. Let me know if you need back-up afterward."

Rowena grimaced. Maybe she should go back to the morgue and see if there was another walking corpse. Or to Kydell. That was a safe location to send this report from. An ocean and several time zones felt like the right amount of space to put between her and her problems right now.

Maybe it would be enough space and time to sort out what she was feeling.

If not, at least it wouldn't be easy for Hollis to track her down and ask questions she wasn't ready to answer.

She checked her implant. Six hours until her class started, and she hadn't finished coding the assignment for the day. Good thing she didn't want to sleep.

21
HOLLIS

HOLLIS SAT AT HIS WORK STATION on the battle-scarred command deck of the *Veronica Guerin* with the lights dimmed. It was night, and only a skeleton crew was up running errands. The captain's seat was empty; around it in half-moon rings were the other duty stations. Nav was a slag heap; the smell of burnt wires and plastic from a power surge during the *Veronica's* final battle were still sharp in his mind.

The weapons station had been broken down for parts to repair the environmental system after Landing. The chairs all needed new padding.

Another thing to add to the never-ending list.

For now, though, Hollis was alone with his thoughts, a place he would be first to admit was not a good place to be. Perrin probably wasn't trying to punish him by confining him to quarters for recovery, but it sure felt like a torment.

His ribs were bruised; his brain was fine, and stuck on things it shouldn't be.

Grumbling under his breath, he sorted through the information needed to keep a grounded warship operating. Crew assignments, food rations, water rations, laundry rota. Oh, and someone had broken the training shuttle again.

Maybe Rowena could—

He cut the thought off and burned it out of his head. Rowena was not coming on board the *Veronica*. Rowena probably wasn't going to talk to him again. Rowena was—

His implant pinged with a backchannel code he didn't know. :Silar.: He put up his sun and desert and waited.

Titan's face floated like a phantom. It was hellishly disconcerting. :How are you?:

:Drowning in ship work and wishing the mountain had killed me. You?:

:Playing dress-up on Descent while we track down a lead. Remember way back when we were stuck in the Integrated Tech class together?:

Hollis dredged up a memory of an aging woman from a minor crew who had lectured in monotone about relic technology. :Vaguely. I dumped most the files into permanent storage. Why?:

Titan sent him an image of a crystal egg with gold swirls and orun. :Look familiar?:

:Is that the thing the grounder tried to kill me with?:

:Yes, and it looks like something that came as a curiosity on the *Qīnglóng*.:

A droning voice echoed in Hollis's head as he sorted through the memories from school. The *Qīnglóng* had been a Baular ship at one point, but it had been reduced to scrap centuries ago. A passage from his text book caught. :Metallic trees. Something they were experimenting with for purifying the water on Malik III?:

Titan gave him an annoyed look. :That's all you remember? What were you doing during that class?:

:Flirting.: With everyone. It had been their first term at the Academy and Hermione hadn't dominated his thoughts yet. :What were you doing?:

:Sleeping.:

:Fair enough.:

Annoyance pinged off him. It wasn't like Titan to talk without all the facts, which meant the egg wasn't the reason Titan was reaching out to him.

:Why'd you really contact me?:

Titan scrunched his eyes shut and opened them into a glare. :I need you to promise to be gentle with Rowena.:

Hollis didn't try to hide his surprise. :I've been locked in this hull for under fourteen hours. What did I miss?:

:You don't know what Old Baular had her do.:

He did, but he didn't interrupt.

:Rowena was never suited to that level of viciousness. She says she's fine, but I read the report and I know she can't be. I want you to give her some space.:

:Space?: He kept his tone neutral.

:You're recovering,: Titan said. :Let someone else work as her training partner as a bit. I've asked Lieutenant Commander Kenzi off the *Julia Cattoni* to step in as her training partner for the next few weeks.:

Kenzi wasn't a bad man. A Sciarra, and one of the quieter ones, but well-trained. Good looking enough. Nice smile. Mellow temperament.

But a Sciarra officer spending time with Rowena? That wasn't going to happen.

:He doesn't need to do that.:

:You're hardly up for any serious training,: Titan said.

:Bumps and bruises. And the class is about to take a two-week break.:

Titan's eyes narrowed. :Silar, I swear on the ships of my ancestors, if you start playing with Rowena and hurt her, they will never, ever find all your pieces.:

:Aren't we allies now?:

:Only as long as you don't hurt one of mine.:

Hollis sent an image of himself holding up his hands in surrender. :I'll be good.: Let Titan chew on that double meaning.

:I mean it. Rowena already has too much going on. I don't want her hurt.:

:Neither do I.:

With another warning glare, Titan dropped the connection.

Rowena.

Hollis rocked his chair back and thought about her.

She'd changed in the past year or so. A year ago she would have spat in a grounder's eye and let them die, but she'd saved the doctor, and she seemed comfortable working with the Jhandarmi.

She handled the cadets well.

He ran a hand through his hair and ran a scan for her to ease the worry tightening his chest.

Not knowing where Rowena was at was like losing gravity, or the moon falling out of orbit.

Some things were meant to be there, and Rowena should show up when he ran a scan. He'd been doing it for how long now?

It had started just after her trial, while she was in the brig of the *Danielle Nicole.* He'd woken in a cold sweat from dreaming she was on the *Veronica,* coming to kill the babies. An irrational fear, Rowena would never hurt a child, but he couldn't shake it. Without knowing she was far away, he couldn't sleep. Hermione had left him by then, so he found his own way to get past the Lee shields. There was no way to hurt her, but he could track her, make sure she was nowhere near his crew.

The scan ran almost automatically for years. Now it found her in the gym, probably prepping for her early morning class.

It also pinged off someone standing outside his door, trying to hide.

"Come in or go to sleep," he said.

"I have a question, sir. Permission to enter?" It was Alcyn.

"Permission granted." Hollis sat back and eyed the younger boy as he entered with his red hair shaved short for training and his teenage body lanky. Almost a man but still growing. He'd been doing well in Rowena's training classes and had potential. There'd been nothing to suggest he was struggling enough to seek out the acting CO's help. "What's on your mind?"

"How can you treat Lee like that?" Alcyn asked without preamble.

Hollis raised an eyebrow.

Alcyn cleared his throat. "I meant how can you treat Drill Instructor Lee like you do, sir?"

"Forget the honorifics; what do you meant by treat her like that? What are we referring to?" He'd been confined to quarters for less than a day. There was no way he would have missed rumors about him and Lee swirling around the fleet.

There was no way a cadet would know the memories that crowded out every other thought.

Of the way he'd held Rowena.

Of the *almosts* that filled the space between breaths.

"I see you two during training, sharing smiles, acting like friends." Alcyn made a face of disgust. "She'll knock you down and you'll smile. She leaves an opening where you could hurt her, and you don't. I don't understand why, or how. How can you treat any Lee like that? How can you stand being near her and seeing her happy after everything her crew did to us?"

Hollis ran a hand through his hair again as he thought over the possible answers. That was a good question. When had he stopped seeing her as the enemy?

The day I first saw her smile.

Too far back.

The day she asked for help and took my knife.

That was it.

"You have to understand that Rowena and I were friends before we were enemies," he said, letting the memories resurface. "Our first year at the Academy, we were on the flight team together. The battle lines weren't drawn yet. We weren't allies, but we worked together, trained together, flew together, and we were good together."

Not as good as they were now, true, but he and Rowena had always found a rhythm.

"Then, you have to know we've tried to kill each other. Throughout the war we fought multiple times." All he had to do was close his eyes and he could see the shot he'd taken that cracked the canopy of her fighter. That had felt so satisfying at the time, but now the memory was tinged with a strange, sour fear.

"I know what Rowena Lee looks like when she's planning to send you to the Lost Fleet, and the trainer you see in the gym every day isn't that woman. We went toe-to-toe in close quarters combat for eighteen hours one time. Implants drained." He still had thin, white scars along his hip where the initial damage hadn't healed even after he got his nanites back. "Stranded on a ship we were both trying to raid for fuel and food. Injured teams to guard. Eighteen hours. Do you know what that means?"

Alcyn shook his head.

"Battles in war are fought fast. At the speed a spaceship can move, you might have only seconds where your enemy is in range of your weapons. A sustained bombardment rarely lasted more than a quarter hour. An hour of battle was a full siege.

"Eighteen hours is nearly impossible. For almost anyone else, it would have been. But that's why we're ranked Elite. It's not just brute force and better tech, an Elite is the kind of person who—when pushed back into a wall—still won't surrender. Most people will run when injured, it's survival instinct. Even a good fighter will admit defeat when they meet a stronger opponent. But Elites? Even if we are beaten, we won't let it last."

Alcyn perched on the end of navigator's melted station. "Captain once said Elite meant stupid."

"Garius is a good captain, but he doesn't understand my cohort. We were born at the end of one war and became adults as a new war started. Most of us were fighting for our lives since day one. That's why there were so many over-powered people in my cohort.

"When Carver and Baular came to the blows, the loser went home and practiced, trained on their own, got better. They'd clash again, and the cycle would repeat, dragging everyone in their inner circle in with them."

"The war's over," Alcyn said. "There's not an inner circle, there's the winners and losers."

Heroes and monsters.

Hollis exhaled. "When I look at Rowena at training, I know she's not trying to hurt me," he said. "If she was, she'd lure me to an isolated position, trap me, and then go after you and the rest of our family. She knows I'd do the same. If I wanted to take out Lee, I'd neutralize the support from the Sciarras and Carylls first, then weaken her crew, and then take out Aronia Lee. Rowena would be destroyed without me needing to touch her."

Alcyn's brow furrowed in frustration. "You know how to take her out?"

"Yes."

"Then why haven't you? Why didn't you once we landed? How can you be so nice to her?"

"Nice?" The laugh tasted bitter on his tongue. "I'm not nice to Rowena. I've heaped abuse on her and she's sucked it up like black hole. I know I've said things to hurt her. Intentionally, usually. I know she goes home bruised, and sore, and tired after dealing with me. You'll never see her cry or complain, but she'd never call me nice."

Alcyn shook his head. "You let her live."

I'm glad she lived.

I need her to live.

But he couldn't tell Alcyn that. The cadet wasn't ready.

Neither was Hollis. The emotions were too new, the thoughts too dangerous. If he thought about how much Rowena's touch in the hotel room did to him, if he thought about how much he wanted to hear her voice, he was going to lose his mind before his medical quarantine was up.

His implant linked the memory to an older time, a darker one, when he was confined to quarters for another reason.

"Letting Rowena live was the price of war. Near the end, after Hermione was rescued from the Baulars, she called Carver's cadre in and asked us whether we wanted revenge, or if we wanted the fleet we'd all believed in when we were young. Did we want our enemies dead, or our future to live? One was easily achieved. The other would cost more, in time and emotions, and would be a much harder battle."

"What did you choose?"

"Revenge," Hollis said quietly. "I promised her I'd follow any order if she'd give me Baular and Lee's deaths. It was all

I wanted. More than I wanted Hermione's love. More than I wanted my own safety. More than I wanted a future for our crew."

Alcyn's posture relaxed. "That was a good choice."

"No, it wasn't," he said, fighting hard to keep the anger from his voice. "It was a selfish choice. It was the easy, lazy, stupid choice. And Carver had to keep me off the flight lines for over a week before I was willing to listen. Hermione came back and asked me what I would give up to ensure the safety of my crew and the fleet. I told her I'd give anything. Everything."

Alcyn nodded in agreement.

"Marshall asked me to give up revenge." Hollis shook his head as the burning sorrow he'd felt at Trace's death rushed over him. "I hurt so much. I couldn't."

"What happened?"

The feeling of hopeless rage was imprinted on his memory forever. He'd felt so helpless. Adrift. Cheated.

"Carver came later. He said he understood, he wanted revenge too, but more than that he wanted a future for his children. He asked if, for Gen, I'd be willing to let Baular and Lee live. If that kept my baby sister alive and happy, would I let them live?"

Hollis sighed, letting the old rage wash away. In his mind, he replayed Rowena's confession. Trace had been dead on impact. He hadn't suffered.

"It was one of the hardest days of my life. Easily the hardest decision I ever made. Because Carver was asking me to forgive when I didn't know why. They'd never apologized. They weren't surrendering. The only thing that I could change was myself, and it was hard."

He smiled sardonically. "You know what? During Rowena's trial it came out that she'd been asked the same thing. She wouldn't give up for herself, or her crew, or the greater good. But when she was asked to do something to protect her sister? She did it. She'd do absolutely anything for Aronia. It's how Hoshi kept her in line. It's why she let Carver's fighters through in the final battle. It was something we had in common."

"But... she's still awful," Alcyn said. "She still killed our family. Your brother. My mom. She shot them down."

Hollis nodded. "I know. She knows."

"She probably likes it." Alcyn crossed her arms. "I can see her gloating when we're at training."

"No," Hollis said.

Everything he'd been ignoring for the past forty-eight hours rushed back. Rowena near tears in his arms with her grief and regret pummeling him.

"You've never seen her gloat. You've never seen her happy about a kill, because she never is. For all her threats, the key to understanding Rowena is that she's not a conqueror. She's a protector. You give Rowena Lee someone to protect, and she will, in this life and the next."

Alcyn frowned. "I don't like her." His voice vibrated with anger. "I won't. Nothing she does will ever bring the dead back."

"No," Hollis said gently. "But we're not dead. Which means we need to change. We need to grow. We need to let the past stay in the past, or we'll have another war and bring all this pain to a new generation."

"Still don't like her," Alcyn muttered, scratching at a flaking curl of paint.

"You don't need to. All the crew is asking is that you learn from her. She's one of the best officers in the fleet. She's a good instructor. If you are a fraction as good as she is, you'll make a fine senior officer one day."

"What if I were as good as she is?"

"You'd make captain." Hollis smiled.

Ancestors, who wouldn't he kill to have a captain like Rowena? Someone who put the crew before themselves, unlike Garius, who was sulking in his quarters, where he'd been hiding since Landing.

The Lees didn't know how lucky they were.

Hollis glanced back at Alcyn. "Doesn't your class start soon?"

"In ten minutes, sir."

He stood, stretching his sore back. "I'll go with you. There's a couple things I need to check on." He patted the cadet's shoulder with a smile.

"Weren't you supposed to stay on bedrest, sir?"

"I'm rested enough," Hollis said as he herded the cadet towards the exit ramp. The gym was close by and he needed to stretch his legs.

Alcyn's frown softened. "Do you really think I could be as good as Lee?"

Hollis looked at the cadet and shrugged. "Probably, although I recommend taking an easier route to excellence than the one she took. You shouldn't need a war to hone your skills. Practice on your own time. Challenge yourself. Learn to keep trying after you fail. Keep it up, and in another decade you could make Elite ranking."

"And then, could I take out Drill Instructor Lee?"

He bit back a snort of amusement. "I can't kill her at my best. Carver couldn't. Neither could Marshall or Caryll. I cracked her fighter's hull once and she still didn't breathe vacuum. So, my guess? No. The only thing that will send Rowena Lee to the Lost Fleet is Death herself, and, even then, I'd except there to be a fight."

Chuckling at the thought, he licked his lips. Oh, ancestors, Rowena Lee fighting. That was always fun to watch. His implant flashed to the memory of Rowena under him with a knife at her throat, then to Rowena beside him, ready to burn through the grounders to keep him safe.

They were perfectly safe when they were together. His smile faltered. Rowena was out there alone right now and he was stuck inside a dead ship.

He flipped to his implant and started searching for reasons to place an officer on medical rest or leave. If he wasn't allowed to fight, then Rowena should be taking some well-deserved downtime too.

22

ROWENA

A KISS ON HER PALM, HER WRIST. A silent question. A rush of pleasure.

Rowena sat in the training gym and reviewed the whole scene again, breaking down every second for inspection.

The pleasure bothered her. Oh, yes, touching was annoying, but every other time someone had touched her, she knew how her body would react.

Silar had managed to surprise her. And not knowing how he'd done it was frustrating her.

There was no code in the kiss. No electric charge. Nothing that should elicit a response.

She closed her eyes, visualizing it again, examining every detail.

Cold air.

The cold air of the hotel room and the heat of their bodies. He'd held her hand and looked into her eyes. There's been a contrast between the heat of his touch and the chill that slid across her when he let go.

Good. One factor sorted.

She ran the memory of contrast between touch and air temperature through her implant, looking for similar memories. Most of them were of cold hands in warm environments. The majority of them were casual touches, accidents. A few were attached to memories of cruelty. None had brought pleasure.

Frowning, she searched for memories of kisses. Kisses on her cheeks from her sister and parents. Mal kissing her temple as he glared at someone. That had been a lifeless, meaningless kiss. A display of dominance rather than affection. Her grandmother's formal kiss on her forehead before she left for the Academy, chilly and distant.

Affection could be ruled out. Hollis Silar had been working, not flirting.

Hadn't he?

She played with her shield, running it through various battle modes while she thought.

Maybe the kiss and the pleasure were two separate variables, rather than an action and response?

Hollis had been trying to distract, trying to protect her. Maybe that's all she'd responded to.

She tugged at that strand of thought.

Things had been different. They weren't just working together, and they weren't fighting, they were... A list of possible options ran across her mind's eye.

Working together.

Balanced.

That was another factor, then. In every other situation, there had been a power imbalance. She'd been beholden to the person touching her, in one way or another. But not Hollis. Neither of them had taken charge of the op. They'd run it together. Worked together. Shared information at the speed of thought and worked as a unit.

So, balance, contrast, and what else?

Trust.

Even though she'd been in her enemy's arms, she'd been relaxed. None of it had felt threatening or made her reach for a weapon.

When the battle memories threatened, she'd reached for him.

I reached for Hollis. I wanted a connection to him.

That was terrifying.

There was a tap at her shield.

Dropping several layers, she looked up to see Hollis in his all-black Guardian uniform. "What are you doing here?"

"I came by to help."

She tucked her internal debate behind several layers of mental shields. "Why? I told the guardian on duty that I didn't need a partner today." Her voice came out perfectly emotionless. Good. Silar didn't need any more ammo to shoot her down with. "And you're supposed to be resting." Somewhere far away from the storm of confusion she was fighting her way through.

"I walked Alcyn to class and the fleetlings asked if I would intervene since I was here."

Rowena looked around the empty gym in confusion.

"They're huddled outside trying to figure out why their drill instructor has her war shield up."

She shrugged. "Just playing."

"Uh-huh." Silar looked every inch a guardian, and very much like he wasn't inclined to believe her. "Are you all right after yesterday?"

"Perfectly fine." She lied while maintaining eye contact and smiling.

:You sure?:

:Yes.:

He sighed. "Are you running a class today?"

"The last one before the break. You can stay if you want, but it's going to be dull. I'm giving them one last exercise, and then partner work for the break." There, the perfect excuse for him to leave.

Hollis kept his smile perfectly polite. "If it isn't a bother, I'll stick around. It'll keep the fleetlings from worrying."

"Suit yourself." She sent a summons to the children hiding outside the gym.

They reluctantly came in, huddled in groups and watching her warily.

Hollis's presence seemed to reassure them that no one was going to get broken today. The poor fools.

If she had to suffer, so did everyone else.

"Take a seat on the mats," she said, gesturing to the open space outside the main combat ring.

The fleetlings sat in various postures of attentiveness in a semi-circle. They were cautious, but relaxed.

Hollis stood at-ease slightly behind them.

She kept a light shield up, just to be safe, and smiled in a way that made the fleetlings all have a sudden interest in inspecting the ground. "This is our last day of full instruction before you have two weeks to relax and heal broken bones."

Several of the smarter cadets looked up in alarm.

"Who here has someone here they'd like to punch?" Rowena asked.

Lights bloomed over every head, little globes indicating affirmatives of varying enthusiasm.

"Excellent. Today we're going to do a little exercise that's going to leave several of you broken and in tears. Like every good drill instructor, I'm looking forward to this more than you are. So, everyone up. Find the person you want to kill."

The cadets started making eye contact as their shields fell into place. Blood was racing. They were ready to fight.

Rowena's grin widened. "When you pair off, put up a visual shield. I'll need deniability in case you do actual damage."

A light went off over Cadet Moren's head.

"Yes?"

"Can we do damage?" he asked.

Rowena shrugged. "I don't know. Can you? Have you learned enough these past ten weeks to fight?"

His smile was sharp as a knife.

She nodded and sent them coded packets of information. "Once you are paired off and your visual shield is up, decrypt the task packet, and get to work. You have thirty minutes."

The fleetlings moved with a war-fed speed.

Stellan Moren faced off against Yunjin. She'd stepped to the side and Moren had followed. He was looking for revenge.

:Be careful,: Rowena told her cousin.

Yunjin sent her back a flash of acknowledgment. :I can handle it.:

:Force teleport him to the black if he gives you trouble.:

Hollis raised an eyebrow. The link they'd established the day before wasn't as dead as she would've liked it to be.

"They'll all live. Probably," Rowena muttered as she looked over the other pairings. There was plenty of enmity to go around. She nodded. "Begin."

Gray domes of visual shields went up with audible crackles.

"They do realize you can break those shields if you need to, right?" Hollis asked, his voice warm and amused.

"I doubt any of them thought about that. Right now, all they're thinking about is their wounded pride and a chance at vengeance." She kicked off her boots and sat down.

Hollis sat beside her. "Do I get a packet?"

She sent it to him without the encryption.

"AAR?" He laughed. She could see the gold fire in his eyes as he looked over the action plan. "Post-op care, recovery, and after-action reports? You're making them do this with the people they hate most?"

"Yup." She poked a toe at him. "Are you my partner or are you going to skip out?"

The look he gave her could be an invitation to a fight, or to bed. He sat down beside her and lifted her foot into his lap, thumbs finding the tender spots. "You are a cruel, cruel woman."

"They want to be fleet officers. That means, eventually, they'll have to depend on someone they hate. If they're good officers, they'll also have to care for the physical and emotional well-being of the people they hate. This is a good lesson for them to learn."

"How long until we get the first protest?"

Rowena considered it. The encryption wasn't that hard, so... "Ten seconds?"

"Wanna place bets on who breaks out first?"

"No bets. Moren and Yunjin have been fighting nonstop the past few months."

There was a sizzling sound as a shield behind her dropped. She didn't even look over her shoulder.

:Told you so.:

Hollis grinned in response.

"Ma'am?" That was Yunjin at her politest. At least she hadn't tried to go around the system and appealed to Rowena on a family level. "There seems to be something wrong with the assignment you sent us. It seems to be the wrong one."

Rowena looked lazily over her shoulder, watching the slim Lee girl, her fists clenched in fury. "How so?"

"We weren't given a battle sequence," Moren said. He was taller than Yunjin, broad shouldered but not as quick. His whole crew favored brute force when they could, and he had the makings of an Elite warrior. But what Rowena noticed was the confusion on his face. The anger.

The betrayal.

She smiled. "This is part of a battle sequence. This is what you do after you make it home alive."

"But... we're enemies." Yunjin looked at her pleadingly. "What situation would we ever be in where we'd need to do this for each other?"

Rowena looked pointedly at Hollis massaging her ankle.

Hollis looked up at her. "There's a knot here. Did you twist your leg?"

Rowena nodded, letting the cadets watch.

"When?"

"Yesterday, at some point between hitting the betting ring and doing Jhandarmi field work."

"Ah." Hollis ran a soothing hand along her tight calf. He squeezed a pressure point, releasing the muscle.

Rowena sighed happily then looked over at Yunjin and Moren. "Well? Are you going to get to work?"

"It's just..." Moren looked at Yunjin. "Well, we're... Our crews don't work together. This is a bad pairing."

"Lees and Silars don't work together," Rowena said. "That doesn't mean anything. If you want to be a fleet officer, you belong to the fleet. That means giving aid to anyone, friend or not. Ally or not. If you can't do this, you aren't fit to be a fleet officer."

"Guardian Silar?" Moren turned to Hollis in a last ditch effort to escape.

Hollis shook his head. "Your drill instructor is right. If you can't do this, walk out. You aren't officer material." He tapped Rowena's knee. "Other foot."

A shield popped over the grumbling pair.

Rowena watched it. "Now, the question is if they'll kill each other against orders, or actually follow through." Either way, it'd be a good test.

"Want to see?" Hollis asked.

"I want them to think they have privacy."

"They don't have a Guardian Veil." His eyes turned gold, and suddenly she had double vision.

She was seeing with his eyes, through a complex code that turned all the shields around them into gauzy laceries. When Hollis turned his head, she could see each of the pairings.

Yunjin had sat down and taken off her boots.

Stellan Moren was rubbing Yunjin's foot as he asked the questions Rowena had given them.

"They look calm enough," Hollis said.

"For now."

Hollis looked around at the rest.

Like she'd predicted, someone was crying. Knees curled to his chest, his partner's arm around his shoulder. It was a healthy cry, though. Pent up frustrations and concerns finally spilling out in a safe place. Others were talking, teasing, a few were laughing.

"Cadet Daunfar figured out how to make this exercise work," Hollis said.

Rowena looked through his eyes and saw Makbi Daunfar with his hand up Jila Silar's shirt. She broke their shield and glared at them. "This is a platonic exercise, thank you. If you want to get naked you can do it after class."

Jila Silar's cheeks turned bright red as she looked at her commander. But she smiled and put the shield back up without apology.

"Cheeky rascal." Hollis laughed as his hands worked on Rowena's leg. "I don't think those two took the offer to kill anyone seriously."

"Not everyone can fight like we do."

He caught her eye, smiled, winked. "No. They can't."

Rowena closed her eyes and fell back into the mat, enjoying the sensation of not doing anything for a moment. Pleasure. Peace. Happiness.

Hollis tugged at her leg, pulling towards him.

She opened her eyes and he was peering down at her. "What?"

"Remember in the Academy when someone found the tests that matched animals to personalities?"

"Yes?" A cadet two years older than them had introduced everyone to an old file on based on animals of the Empire.

"Remember what you were?" Hollis asked. His hands were warm, gentle, and working miracles on her aching legs.

Rowena dipped into her implant's memory. "Let's see. Mal and Titan were both panthers, solitary hunters. You were a tiger. Carver was a sunwolf. Marshal was a winged lion?" She frowned. That didn't sound right.

"Native of the Kelsot System, very intelligent and very lethal," Hollis said. "It fits her beautifully." He was proud of Hermione, his former lover. He pushed Rowena's pant leg above her knee to touch her thigh. "You were a dire bear." Pride mixed with pleasure.

"I remember the bear, but I never looked up the species."

"I did."

That didn't surprise her.

"The dire bear, three meters tall, angry, and territorial. They're nearly impossible to kill. There was footage of a squadron of Imperial ground troops fighting one. They took half the bear's head off and they still couldn't bring it down."

Rowena laughed. "I'll take that compliment."

"You should. But there was other footage. Someone managed to get a silent drone into the bear's territory, and there's this image in my head of a giant, dangerous beast lying in a meadow of flowers looking perfectly content. That's what you remind me of. A fat, happy, lazy, grumpy bear."

She opened an eye to half-heartedly glare at him. "What's that make you? A smug tiger?"

"A smug tiger who caught a dangerous bear." He pulled her pant leg down to her ankle. "My turn?"

She nodded.

Hollis stripped off his jacket and shirt in record time and fell to the mats face down.

The bruises along his back had healed quickly thanks to the nanites, but there were still places where the skin looked too new. "How do you feel?"

"Healed, but tender. Everything feels too tight."

She pressed her palm into his back and felt the knots. "Holding onto some stress?"

"Mmmm."

"Relax."

"Give me something else to hold and I will." He sent her the memory of a wink.

She leaned over so her regrown hair brushed against his bare skin. "Behave. There's children watching."

"They have to learn to flirt eventually."

Sighing, she focused on the knot between his shoulder blade. "How are they doing?"

He sent her an image of Moren holding Yunjin's foot, watching her. :See that look?: Hollis asked. :See how he keeps dropping his gaze from her eyes to her lips? He's going to lick his lips in three… two…:

Stellan Moren licked his lips and his shoulders moved in a sigh.

:Poor thing. He's smitten.: Hollis seemed happy about the idea.

:What about Yunjin?: Rowena had trouble reading her expressions.

:Look at her shoulders, her eyes. She's relaxed. She'd fight Stellan if that's what he wanted, but she's ready to make peace if he will.:

Yunjin moved, pulling her foot away and gesturing for Stellan to pick a sore spot. He gave her his hand.

:Good,: Rowena said. :They deserve a better future than we had.:

:I vote we do this for the next war,: Hollis said as he closed his eyes. :Instead of trying to kill each other, we have to sit down, give each other backrubs, and listen to each other's problems.:

:You have problems I need to know about?: Rowena teased as she warmed her hands and went to work on his other shoulder, feeling him relax under her touch. :Your current lover not giving you enough attention?:

He sighed contentedly. :Don't have a current lover.:

:Did they get bored?:

:No, I did. Months ago.: He opened his eyes and looked at her. :You?:

:Same as always.: Single and uninterested in changing her status.

Hollis smiled. :Excellent. That means I don't have to share your massage skills with anyone.: There was a flash of intense satisfaction through their shared channel. :Hmm…:

:Hmm what?:

:I'm drafting a Declaration of Courtship and trying to figure out how I can negotiate for daily massages. Do you want a trio of fighters or a small gun ship?:

Rowena laughed at his ridiculousness.

"You think I'm joking?" he asked out loud.

It felt sincere.

"Think of all the trouble," Rowena said. "Draft the declaration, make the declaration, get the courtship accepted, actually court someone. You'll never have the time."

Hollis rolled under her hands, flipping to his back and catching her hands so their fingers intertwined. "I love where your mind is, and, yes, that's the right answer, but only if I'm asking. Normally, it's 'make the declaration, get the declaration accepted'. The declaration goes first. If the courtship is accepted, the couple is listed on the fleet records as spouses. That's an important detail for you to remember."

"Because we think someone would honestly make a Declaration of Courtship to a Lee?" She laughed but couldn't force herself to pull away. In this stolen moment, she was happy.

"If anyone ever finds out how good you are with your hands, I'm going to wind up fighting most of the fleet just to keep you as my sparring partner."

Rowena pulled one hand free and ran it through his hair thick, red hair. "Poor Hollis. So neglected. So unloved! Who is going to break your ribs and rescue you from grounders when I find true love?"

He brought her other hand to his lips and pressed a kiss to her wrist. "You can decide I'm your true love and keep rescuing me." He nodded for emphasis.

Rowena wrinkled her nose and shook her head.

"No? Oh, come on. Don't tell me you found a better officer. You know you couldn't."

That much was true. Unless she wanted Hermione Marshall as a spouse, there wasn't another available Elite-level officer in the fleet. But she couldn't let Hollis win that easily. "Maybe I want to wait until Mars Sciarra gets a little older. Everyone knows Sciarras are sexy." Mars was a younger, gentler, version of Titan. Equally lethal, but more likely to laugh.

"Oh. No, no. No, no, no." Hollis sat up. "You are not telling me that a teenage Sciarra is a better officer than me."

"Probably not a better officer. Yet. But he does have an amazing smile," Rowena teased.

"Amazing, huh?" Hollis closed the space between them so his nose almost touched hers. "You're not the one attracted to beautiful smiles."

"I'm not?" she asked with breathless innocence.

"No. That's me. I like beautiful smiles. Especially yours."

A timer went off in her mind and she pulled away. "Time to get the fleetlings out."

"Leave them in their bubbles," Hollis said catching her hand. "It's been years since you've flirted with me."

Obviously Hollis had a different definition of flirting than she did. "This is playing, not flirting."

"There's a difference?" He looked surprised as he released her hand.

"Flirting implies an intent to follow through." She sent a ping to the cadets telling them to wrap up as she stood and stretched.

Hollis stood up too. "Are you suggesting I wouldn't follow through?" There was a hint of fight in his eyes.

She gave him a dismissive look. "I'm sure you would, and I might even enjoy it, but then you'd get bored and move on to someone else. You're like this with everybody, at least when you're in a good mood."

"Do you see me flirting with anyone else right now?"

"We're the only adults in the room."

Hollis scowled.

"Put your shirt on so the children don't drool."

:We're finishing this discussion later.:

:If you're interested later, maybe.: But she wasn't getting her hopes up.

Shields dropped around the room and the cadets sat there looking shell-shocked. Confident bravado was gone. Angry smiles and exaggerated scowls were absent. For the first time since training started, the fleetlings looked like what they really were—children who had survived a war.

"No blood?" Rowena asked.

Everyone shook their heads. No one looked up.

"Any questions?" Silence. "Good. That's your final training exercise before your break. You'll have two weeks without my charming presence. And I'll have two weeks of not worrying about one of you putting a knife in my back. We'll all be happy."

A few of the cadets looked uneasy. Nice to see she wasn't wrong about a few of them still wanting her dead.

"While you are free from scheduled classes, you'll need to maintain your own training schedule. Your accountability partner is the person you were paired with today."

Twenty-four sets of anxious eyes looked up at her with sudden fear.

Hollis sent her a memory of laughing hysterically, although he looked suitably sober on the outside. :You are mean.:

:You knew that.:

:I love it.:

She smiled. "At the end of the two week period you will each turn in a report about how your personal training went."

Pings of alarm burned through the air.

"In this scenario, you are the ship's training officer. Prep your report as you would for your captain."

A sphere of light appeared over Cadet Ukoroh's head. "Ma'am, what does that mean?"

"I mean I want a report from a training officer."

Nalan Ukoroh blinked. "What goes on that kind of report?"

"Ask your ship's training officer," Rowena advised.

"But what if it's different than Lee reports?"

Rowena shrugged. "Ask my ship's training officer? I'm your drill instructor, not your language teacher. Figure it out."

Yunjin lit a globe.

"Yes?"

Her eyes darted to Stellan quickly then back to Rowena. "Ma'am, do you expect a report on the emotional—I mean, the psychological fitness of the crew we're training?"

"Would your captain need that information?"

"Yes, ma'am."

"Then what do you think?"

Expressions turned pensive.

Alcyn Silar set a light over his head. "Ma'am, that is confidential information. With all due respect, not everyone here is allied with your crew. Do you expect us to turn over critical data like that?"

"Only if you think your captain would need it," Rowena repeated.

"My captain would," Alcyn argued, "but I trust my captain."

:Idiot.: Hollis's thoughts mirrored her own. Garius was hardly fit to be called captain.

"Must be nice," Rowena said out loud. "Not everyone has that luxury. You won't always have that luxury, unless you think you'll like every Silar captain for every ship in your armada. Or every Starguard commander. Or every OIA officer." She walked around the ring of cadets, letting their worst fears fill in the silence. "You will not always have a senior officer that likes you, or wants to protect you, or gives you good orders. You won't always like what your crew is doing."

Yunjin met her eyes and looked away in shame.

"That doesn't mean we should trust a Lee," Alcyn argued.

Rowena squatted down so she could look him in the eye. "If you trusted me implicitly, I'd fail you. I'm your instructor, not your ally." She stood up again. "I'm not your mother. I'm not your aunt. I'm certainly not your friend. All I am is the person the fleet trusts to see you become good officers. Do you know what a good officer is?"

There was a mix of responses.

"A good officer is someone who thinks fast. Who thinks of the fleet before themselves. Who can put their pride aside and work with anyone if it means survival. A good officer asks questions. A good officer listens. A good officer knows when to refuse a bad order."

Someone muttered, "Then you weren't a good officer."

She had a guess who it was, but it was there. And most of the fleet thought it already. "You're right."

"You're wrong," Hollis argued.

She frowned at him. :Hollis…:

He ignored her. "Drill Instructor Lee was a cadet when the war started. She went into war with bad officers, bad leaders, and bad instructions. Somehow, with all that working against her, she managed to be an exemplary officer. If you're smart enough to learn from her, you might become half as good."

Alcyn scowled rebelliously. "If you think she's that good, why not recruit her for us?"

"He tried," Rowena said, enjoying the ripple of shock. "But the guardian isn't as persuasive as he thinks."

:You could try making me a Lee,: Hollis suggested on a tight channel.

Hoshi would lose his mind.

Rowena smiled at the class. "It's simple. Go on break. Keep your training up. Turn in your reports in two weeks."

"And you'll determine whether we move to the next phase of lessons based on that report?" Anak Black was one of the quicker ones.

She nodded at him.

"Not a test?" There was a hint of alarm in his voice.

"This is the test," Rowena said. "You're being given an officer's task. Let's see if you can do it. Class dismissed." She watched them go.

A few teleported away, eager to escape. Yunjin and Stellan walked side by side, talking in short sentences. Jila Silar was holding Makbi Daunfar's hands in a proprietary way.

"Looks like those two are headed to Cargo Blue for lunch," Hollis said, coming up close behind her. "Want to go chaperone?"

"Not my crew, not my problem. And I have other things to do today. Errands to run for the Jhandarmi."

:Arm/shoulder.: He wrapped an arm around her, settling her shoulder in the crook of his elbow and pulling her close. "I meant what I said. You're a good officer. A good person. The fleet is lucky to have you, even if most of them don't know that."

Rowena lingered in his friendly embrace. *Trust. Balance. Contrast.* This was a different kind of pleasure. Something relaxing and calming, rather than sensual.

"Want to go for another rounds on the mats?"

Rowena put her elbow in his stomach, hit a shield, and teleported out of his reach. "Go find someone else to play with. I have to get to work."

From across the gym, he winked at her. :When do I see you again?:

:Depends on the Jhandarmi schedule.:

:Reports?:

:You'll have them.: She found herself stepping closer to him. Again.

"Is there something else?"

"I..." She looked up to the ceiling and hoped this wasn't going to ruin everything. "I broke a rule."

Hollis quirked an eyebrow up in question.

"I volunteered you for something."

Both eyebrows went up. "Volunteered? Is this your safe word? A distress code?"

"I told Tyrling that if the device the grounders tried to put in your chest goes off, you'll respond as if it's working."

"You like rescuing me from danger, don't you?" His hand touched her hip and pulled her closer. "Or are you coming as backup again?"

"I'll be there." She rested her hands on his chest, not pushing him away but keeping a distance between them. "But right now I need to go find some grounder clothes and go to Kydell."

Hollis grimaced. "Again?"

"I need to find the rowdy who had a device in his—" She stopped and closed her eyes. "I need to send you a report and then go to Kydell for a quick visit during my lunch break."

"A report would be nice. I feel like I missed weeks, not hours."

"And Hoshi has a list of chores for me on the *Danielle Nicole*. I don't have a class, which means I have extra free time to go repair everyone's environmental systems."

He laughed. "Aren't there other engineers in this fleet?"

"That's the rumor, but no one's ever seen one." She gave him a lazy salute and teleported home. Her shields went up automatically as she landed in the *Danielle Nicole's* engine room.

Shields down near a Silar and up when she was on her flagship. The universe was upside down. For a long moment, she let her thoughts linger on the memory of Hollis's praise, his gentle touch, the soft look in his golden brown eyes.

And then she locked it mercilessly away.

There was a job in front of her and the most important part of it was keeping the fleet safe from the grounders plotting to destroy them. Hollis was too important to get caught in the crossfire. Titan, Selena, Mars, Nia... they were all too important.

She'd handle it alone.

23
HOLLIS

:WHEN DO I SEE YOU AGAIN?:

:Depends on the Jhandarmi schedule.:

It had been supposed to be days that Rowena was in Kydell for. Hours, preferably. Instead, it had been over a week. Hollis ran a scan of Enclave and Tarrin, looking for Rowena's signature somewhere nearby. Nothing.

He checked the time in Kydell. Past midnight.

It was late in Enclave too, so wherever she was, she should be asleep, probably tucked under a heavy shield or with her implant off. The Kydellians had put up a new shield two days ago and Rowena's report said she wasn't sure what it would catch. She was testing it slowly, figuring out the how and why of the politicians as she waited for the man with the orun in his chest to resurface.

Soft, yellow lights from the empty bullpen twined with the green lights of security readouts and danced along the smoked glass of the window between his office and the outer rooms. How long had it been since he'd slept? It was all a bit of a blur, and his implant was advising against teleporting. He needed to recharge at some point.

Resting while Rowena was in the field made him uneasy in a way he couldn't quite articulate. Sure, Titan was up on the *Persephone* busily trying to dissect the metal egg the Jhandarmi had captured, but that meant he was busy. He might miss a distress signal from Kydell.

:Guardian Silar we have an emergency!: Demberli Vaneer's desperate voice jolted Hollis to his feet.

He overrode the safety function and teleported to the front desk where two very junior guardians were cowering behind the desk in the otherwise empty dome. Moonlight spilled through the stained glass overhead, drenching the scene in colored shadows.

Vaneer pointed at Rowena, dressed for engineering work, standing in front of the desk, arms folded, eyes closed, shields down.

"You all right?" Hollis asked Rowena. Her shields shouldn't have been down. Ever.

She opened her eyes and there was a flash of green. "Let's talk."

:Hello to you too. If you want a fight, we need to table it until morning. I'm too tired for this.:

:Same.: Her implant connected with his and he saw the readout. She was below ten percent power.

With a forced smile for the young guardians, he led Rowena down the steps to an empty office. "Why are you here?"

"I need you to arrest me." She put her hands behind her back and took an at-ease stance. Anticipating censure.

"Arrest you?" He waited for an explanation but Rowena stared straight ahead. "For what?"

"Pre-emptive arrest so I don't murder Hoshi Lee."

He leaned against the wall because he was too tired to keep standing. "That's crew business. Fill out a form and you can teleport Hoshi to the black for all I care. No one will miss him."

Rowena narrowed her eyes in annoyance.

"Well, I wouldn't."

"I do not have the energy to fight Hoshi and his half of the crew right now. He's pushing me, won't leave me alone, won't let me recharge, won't let me sleep. I'm running sixteen hour days in Kydell for the Jhandarmi and then coming back here to do repairs. Today he *accidentally* broke a power link on the *Danielle Nicole*," She put a full volley of venom into the word 'accidentally'. "If he keeps it up, I'm going to snap, there will be a bloodbath, and I'm not going to come out of it alive. If you arrest me, I can sleep."

And live.

Hollis shook his head. "I can't." She opened her mouth to protest. "Legally I can't. The Captain's Council would have my rank in an hour. Hoshi would protest it. I can't put you in the brig without cause."

She slumped ever so slightly, wilting with defeat.

"Did you try going to Selena and Titan?"

"They're busy decrypting the thing we picked up in Seahome and running a trace on the grounder I'm tracking. I tried sleeping on the *Persephone*, but it's a noisy ship right now."

"Selena's apartment?"

"Staging ground for Tyrling since he doesn't trust anyone in his office right now. The whole incident with you going off the cliff has him paranoid." Frustration and defeat turned her words to a snarl. "And I can't move into the apartment in Kydell for a few more days."

Hollis sighed. "There's one option I know of."

Rowena looked up, eyes wide and tired.

"You'll probably hate it."

"Not as much as I'd hate dying. Will I be left alone there?"

"Utterly. No one goes in or out without my say so. The shields are thick. You won't hear a thing, no one will raise you on coms, no one will be able to track you."

"I'm in. Give me the coordinates."

He hesitated. "This is a secure location. I can't just let you teleport yourself in. If you trip any alarms we'll have a war on our hands."

"Where are you taking me?" she asked as she held out her arm, ready for a joint teleport.

"The *Veronica*." Hollis took her hand, pulled her close, and teleported her to the one place he knew she'd be safe.

For a moment he held her in the darkness, unsure of his decision, then sent the mental command to turn on the light.

Rowena stepped away from him slowly, looking around, cataloging the sloped ceiling, the narrow dimensions of the room, the metal locker welded to the wall, the folded desk secured behind the door, the shields that made the quarters an impenetrable cocoon of safety and silence.

She pressed her lips together. "Your quarters?"

"No one will look for you here."

A slow nod of agreement. No one in their right mind would ever suspect a Lee of hiding on a Silar ship.

"You bring your lovers here?" She sounded skeptical.

"I don't allow anyone in here except Gen, and even then she's under orders not to enter unless she thinks I'm dead. Most days I don't even sleep here. I made Perrin give me an office so I could sleep on the couch."

This was such a bad idea. It was barely a room. This was embarrassing.

"There's, um, clothes if you want to change." He tried to think of what he could offer. "And a shower. I haven't used my water rations in Ancestors only know how long. You can clean up, or whatever." He fumbled with the door to his locker to find her a clean blanket. Everything smelled of neglect, the faded scent of soap mixed with dust.

Rowena peered into the closet. "Do you have anything that isn't Hollis-sized?"

He looked at the neatly folded stacks of uniforms he'd shoved in there the last time he'd grabbed his laundry from the ship's washroom. "Um..." It wasn't like any of his former lovers had left things; they'd never even been here. He pulled out an old, black shirt he'd worn from training when he'd been younger and skinnier. "This is the smallest thing I have."

Rowena nodded stoically. "Thank you."

"I'll get going so you can sleep."

"Are you sure you shouldn't take a few hours for yourself?"

He shrugged. "I'll be fine. And I'll be back in about"—he checked his internal clock—"ten hours to teleport you out of here."

"That works. There's a ship arriving mid-afternoon in Kydell and I'm hoping Jae will be there to unload. If he's not, I've run out of leads to track him down." She eyed the metal door dividing Hollis's quarters from the rest of the ship. "You're certain no one will notice me?"

"Not unless you try to go out the door or teleport. If you're hungry, there's probably a ration bar or two stuffed in the cubby next to the bed. There should be a cup too."

Rowena shook her head. "I sleep in a corner of the engine room and I have more stuff than you. How do you live like this?"

"By not living here most the time." He smiled apologetically. "I'm the acting fleet captain for the Silar armada, the commander of the *Veronica*, Carver's second-in-command for the Starguard, an OIA liaison, on the Academy committee, and I oversee the instructors at the training house. It's not like I have copious amounts of free time to linger here."

"We either need to figure out cloning or hire more people, that's too many jobs."

"Says the woman who's an Academy instructor, an OIA rep, a Jhandarmi agent, the fleet's chief engineer, and who still has crew duties?"

That won him a small smile. "If we both quit, would the fleet fall apart?"

"Probably not, but there'd be a lot of cranky people trying to fill our shoes." He brushed his hand over her arm because he wanted to touch her and knew she wouldn't accept a kiss. "Get some sleep."

Rowena nodded agreement. "Good night."

He teleported back to the bullpen and collapsed into his chair. Now he'd acknowledged that sleep was an option, his body was trying to cash in on what it was owed. His eyes burned. His legs felt like jelly.

Stimulants and implants could only take a human body so far. Implants were designed to need periods of self-maintenance, conducted while the wearer was sleeping. The recharge cycle forced normal sleep habits, theoretically.

Somewhere in the office was a recharge cube that Perrin kept hidden from the guardians, but on stand-by for emergencies. During war, there wasn't always time for sleep.

Hollis pushed himself to his feet and ran a scan for an energy source. His implant pinged off the cube at the same time the Enclave shield registered Perrin and Gen's incoming signatures.

His sister appeared at the entrance to Perrin's office dressed for a date in a butter-yellow dress, her red hair in loose curls. "Hollis! I didn't know you were on duty to-night."

He shrugged. "The Carylls were working on the data the Jhandarmi brought in, so I told Titan I'd watch the office."

Gen tilted her head. "You look like someone who forgot what his bunk looks like."

"Not true. I saw it not five minutes ago." Fifteen, accor-ding to his implant. He must have sat in the chair longer than he thought.

"Gen, love, I've got—" Perrin turned the corner at his usual near-run and skidded to a stop, dark brown hair fall-ing across his eyes. "Oh, you found him already. Hollis, why are you on duty?"

"Titan is working off-site."

"There are more than three guardians in this office," Perrin said. "I know that for a fact. I have a roster of every-one under my command. There's nearly four hundred of us."

"A lot of them are junior officers."

"So?" Perrin looked baffled. "Unless the office is on alert, we can have a lieutenant watch the com line at night. I know that's a rule. I wrote it. And there are two lieutenants upstairs right now."

Hollis ran a hand through his hair. "Fine, I'll just go crash in my office. It's fine. I'm fine."

Gen gave Perrin a worried look.

"Don't you have quarters somewhere?" Perrin asked.

"He said he went there. Probably long enough to change clothes." His sister folded her arms. "What did you used to tell me? Something about working too hard and burning out and recipes for depression?"

"I'm not depressed!" Hollis protested. "I'm just a little tired is all."

"Then go to your quarters!" Perrin looked exasperated.

"I—"

"That's an order! Eight hours, confined to quarters, or so help me I will find someone else to do your job!"

Hollis diverted some mental energy to visualizing a life without Perrin dumping stacks of reports on his desk. "When you put it like that..."

"You offer him an escape hatch and he'll use it," Gen said. "Hollis, you can't quit until you train a replacement." She grabbed his arm. "Come on, let's get you home. Love," she said to Perrin, "I'll be back in a few minutes."

Teleporting with Gen was disorienting. He felt his skin fizzle and then they were back in the partial gloom of his quarters.

"Come on," Gen said. "Boots off, shirt off, into bed." She grabbed at the hem of his shirt.

Hollis clutched at it tightly. "I can keep my shirt on. You don't need to undress me."

"You always sleep with your shirt off. When did that change?"

"I... It's nothing. Just..."

The lighting was set at twelve percent, turning the room into a contrast of shadows and muted colors. Rowena was on the bed, black hair flowing like a river of ink across the white pillows, oversized shirt slipping off her shoulder and bunched around her waist so he could see the tiny black shorts and the hint of long, tan leg.

"I can take care of myself, Gen."

His sister stepped back, frowned, and lit her hand up with a soft white glow. Frown deepening, she turned towards the bed. "Is that..." :Lee?:

:Yes.: He overrode Gen's controls and shut off her light. :Out.:

:Are you going to explain?:

:Having a woman in my bed? No.:

:You never let anyone in your quarters!:

:I made an exception.: He grabbed Gen's shoulders and maneuvered her toward the door. :Out.:

:Who else knows about this?:

:What 'this'? She was tired and Hoshi wouldn't let her sleep, so she's crashing here. It's no different than falling asleep on the mats after working out in the gym.:

:It's Rowena Lee in your bed!: Gen's thoughts were filled with confusion, elation, and curiosity.

:It's platonic.:

She snickered. :That's what I said when I crawled into Perrin's bed the first time. Strictly platonic. I just wanted someone to cuddle.:

Perrin's defenses had fallen without a fight.

:I can't see Lee using that strategy.: Hollis hit the door panel and shoved his sister into the hall. "Goodnight, Gen." :Tell anyone about this and I kill you.:

Gen smiled radiantly. "You wouldn't kill your baby sister."

"But I'll think about it." He closed the door.

It could have been worse. His captain could have called a surprise inspection. The universe could have collapsed. He could wake up and find out this was all a sick dream and he was back in the Academy with Mal Baular alive and Rowena out of his life.

He shook his head, knocking loose the fatigue-fed fears, and opened his locker to search for a spare pillow. The supply clerk issued new pillows every two years, so there had to be one in here somewhere with the rest of random things supply thought he needed. Where was the inventory he'd done?

There. Bottom right corner. He shut down his implants and dropped his shields as he grabbed a blanket and pillow. A makeshift bed on the floor would be fine.

:There's room on the bed.: It was a soft, sleepy whisper in his mind.

Hollis turned.

Rowena stretched and rolled over to face him. :Floors aren't comfortable at our age. The bed's big enough for two.:

:You sure?:

She sent an affirmative as she yawned and her eyes drifted closed again.

No shields. Barely any clothes. If either of them had energy, this would have been dangerous—or very, very fun.

"You think too loud," Rowena murmured.

He lifted the blanket and fell into the warm bed beside her. The scent of soap had been replaced by a wild scent of flowers and spice that didn't belong to any Silar ship. It was strange, but intimately familiar, a smell he knew from training and countless bar fights.

His hand reached out until he found Rowena's fingers, and rested there, hands back to back. It was enough.

:Sweet dreams.:

A picture of dreaming moon over a forest of flowering trees appeared in his mind. In the midst of the chaos of life, they'd found a moment to dream.

24
MALCOLM

"KYDELL," SONYA SAID WITH A sweeping gesture over the city of domed buildings half-devoured by the encroaching jungle. "Such an adorable little trinket." She turned to Malcolm, back arching and blonde hair falling in loose waves so the sinking sun gave her an ethereal glow.

Malcolm faked a smile and tried to keep himself from turning back to the private plane they'd arrived in. That was more interesting than the rooftop Sonya was enthusing over. The forward-swept wing design looked like it added to the drag, but the plane flew particularly well over the turbulent seas. Sonya had kept him from interrogating the pilot, but he'd sketched enough of the design to model it when he got home.

And home was where he desperately hoped he would be in a few hours. There was nothing appealing about Kydell. It was a typical Seahome port city: old buildings built from scraps of the colonial ships, narrow roads made of whatever local rock or shell was available, ruled by a class of people who knew the names of their sixteenth great-grandfather, but actually functioning because someone who didn't even remember his mother's name worked eighteen hours a day for enough money to buy dinner.

It was tasteless. Or, rather, he wished it were. The humid air smelled of rotten fish and he was deeply concerned it was going to be the only thing he'd be able to taste all week.

"What are you looking at?" Sonya asked. She stepped closer than he liked and peered around the plane to the jungles. "The plane? The plants? There's not much to see that way. Banfur was there a century or so ago, but one of the typhoons destroyed it. There was no point in rebuilding."

"Even in a housing crisis?"

She shrugged the concern away. "My grandparents visited it once before it was destroyed. Grandmother said it was a particularly smelly city, which isn't hard to believe in Seahome. The whole place smells tannic. Never eat the fish here, they taste muddy." She shivered in a way she probably thought was delicate and cute, but was as calculated as all her other gestures.

Not much different than Kydell, then. "I'll consider myself forewarned." At least there was a sea breeze off the port bringing in cool air to refresh the evening. Kydell wasn't a large city, but the hill leading down to the port was steep and if Sonya wanted to traipse down there it meant— eventually—they'd have to walk back up that hill.

Sonya grabbed his arm and caught his elbow in hers. "That's all right, we won't stay here long. There is a darling little bakery near the main forum that does excellent cream puffs, but that isn't why I dragged you here. It's not exactly a date." Her ashy-blonde eyelashes fluttered like the blink of a snake.

"I see. Why am I here, in that case?" He let Sonya drag him towards the wide stairs that wound down the side of the building. "And where is here, exactly?"

"This is the capital building," Sonya said without slowing. Her familiarity with government buildings was becoming a theme. Twice now she'd invited him to a remote location, as a representative of Bennu Industries, and walked around as though she owned everything.

Virgil Lethe was an elected leader in Kytan, but Sonya acted as if she owned the planet.

"You'll see," Sonya teased with a wide smile.

Malcolm made a noncommittal sound and cataloged his surroundings. Kydell was a small city-state, little more than a port and a cluster of government buildings on a hill with a fringe of respectable housing for the better class of citizens. Ornate columns carved of a pink-and-white stone held up porticos of houses with blue-tiled roofs. The older part of the city was paved with crushed white shells and lapis blue stones.

"Isn't it beautiful?" Sonya sighed happily as she looked over the verdant garden of the governor's estate. "Antiquated, certainly, but the rulers here can trace their lineage to the first ships to come to Malik, and they brought the gardens of the Empire with them. For centuries Kydell was considered one of the most luxurious retreats. A tropical paradise where it was always summer, where there was always a party. It was considered quite romantic too, once upon a time," she added with a little coo and a meaningful look.

"What happened?"

"Greed, for the most part."

He nodded. "It would be easy to be greedy if you were the playground of the rich. Did the locals ask for too much?"

"No," Sonya pushed away from the stairs and stepped onto the shell pathway. "The servants did. The original ones were indentured. They worked for generations to pay off their passage. After they died out, outsiders were hired. But they wanted higher wages, fewer working hours."

"How did whole family lines die off?"

"Most never had families," Sonya said. "That's the real tragedy. They owed the founders a great debt, seventy-two years of service, and in a lifetime a person might work only forty or fifty years total, once you account for time away from work or money spent on them. Each of the servants should have had progeny that stayed in service for another two or three generations.

"Naturally, as they were given food and housing, the costs would add up. In Kytun, the last indentured families didn't pay off their debts until only a few years ago.

"It's excellent having indentured peoples. But someone thought they were clever and passed out contraceptives to the servants." She sighed as if disappointed by the long-dead abolitionist. "No children. No new servants. The founders had to hire others who wanted exorbitant wages."

"Probably enough to keep them alive," Malcolm guessed. "It wasn't like there was cheap housing available, I imagine."

Sonya nodded, completely missing his tone of voice. "Yes. Cost of living and such." She shook her head with a little huff of annoyance. "They should have offered indenture instead. That's what my father does when he hires personal servants. It keeps them loyal."

Malcolm studied his shoes intently.

"Oh! Don't be like that!" Sonya stole his arm again. "I would never ask that of you. Your family is titled. I hope you know I value that."

"I'm well aware." It was the only thing she valued.

"You're so much more than a servant to me, Malcolm. I think of you as a friend. A co-conspirator."

He raised an eyebrow. "What are we conspiring on?"

Her grin turned impish. "Do you really want to know?"

"Of course." If only so he could avoid future trouble. The only advantage to Sonya's attentions was that there was no possible way his parents would approve of him dating a genocidal maniac, or stepping into the power politics of Descent by snubbing her. She gave him a nice pocket of freedom as long as he balanced her worst tendencies out with careful guidance. It was like steering a particularly angry toddler, but it could be done.

Sonya led him past an arched gateway that divided the hill crest from the poorer part of the city. The street turned to a cobblestone made of smoothed sea rock and there were the small cars popular in overcrowded coastal towns. The buildings had less metal, more wood.

It was unusually quiet for midday. Most cities would be filled with workers, but Kydell felt abandoned. Storefronts were closed. Windows were dark. Cars had dust on them.

This was a forgotten closet of a city, a place where the unwanted things were dropped until needed.

It wasn't a terribly reassuring thing to consider while Sonya dragged him down the hill toward the smell of fish and saltwater.

"I knew you'd be interested in my plan. You don't mind getting a little dirty, do you?" she asked as they stepped over a puddle of muddy rain water.

"Dirty?" He looked down at the dull, gray suit he'd chosen. It wasn't fashionable, flattering, or remotely attractive. He'd chosen the suit for exactly that reason after the salesperson informed him it made him look sallow and unsexy. Sonya wasn't as repelled as he'd hoped.

She patted his arm. "You'll be fine. All I meant is we'll be walking in the seamier side of the city. It's not all picnic benches and roses, you know. There's a port, and that's where the rowdies are found."

He dug through his memory for a reference. "Rowdies are the non-native citizens?"

"Residents Of Wandering Descent," Sonya said. "I always liked the term. We can't use it in Kytan, naturally, there was too much blending between houses in the early days of settlement. Even I wasn't born there, but only because my mother insisted on having an elegant view when she was in labor, so I was born at a resort in Northland. But I'd still love to be able to differentiate. Wouldn't you?"

"Since I would be a rowdy, I'm not sure I can say I'm passionate about the idea of being labeled without my consent." Although, from everything he'd heard, the rowdies sounded a lot more fun than the Lethe clan. "What are you hoping to do with them?"

"Watch, for now. They're part of a shared experiment."

The hairs on the back of his neck stood up. "What kind of experiment?"

"My father and I have a bit of a wager going on," Sonya said as if she were confessing to something sordid. "He believes that all you need to do to achieve lasting change is influence key points in the social structure."

"Social Node Theory?" He scraped through his memories for the lecture. "In any social network there are key influencers, most are visible but some are not. What are they called?"

The city center broke into tributaries, the wide avenue turning into multiple smaller roads as the houses grew closer together and the smell of briny sea rose with each step. Overhead a gull screamed.

"Second Level Influencers," Sonya said. "People who directly control the visible influencers. In fashion it's the dresser who picks clothes for the six most influential women. Society sees the six women as influencers, but all of them had their decisions made by the person society doesn't see. In politics you look not at the orators in the forums, but at the advisors who sit on multiple city-state panels, or in the budget committee, or in the brothel where the leaders love to meet."

Malcolm nodded in understanding.

"My father thinks that controlling the second-level influencers is enough."

He shook his head. "Can't be done. Not easily. Those people are in those positions because they don't change their minds. They make a decision and it's the one they'll keep to for life. It doesn't matter how catastrophic it is in the long run." His father was like that.

Sonya took his arm. "Why wouldn't we be able to control them?"

"What could you offer to change their minds?"

"That is my little secret for now. But, play along, what would happen if we could reliably control all of them?"

"Worldwide?"

"Worldwide."

Nothing good. Which wasn't the answer Sonya would want. "I wouldn't trust that system. There's too many moving pieces. Too many chances for things to fall apart or for the system to be abused. You don't wind up in a situation where everyone in the room has turned against you because you trusted the system and they didn't."

She laughed. "I can't imagine that happening."

Why was he not surprised? Sonya had probably never been in a situation where things didn't go her way.

"Still, there's some truth to that. Influencers are good to control, but they never outnumber the common person."

"The common people." He knew which side he'd fall on. "The problem is you can never convince mobs to agree on anything. Everyone is pulling in different directions."

Sonya tipped her head. "Only when there's peace. In times of tragedy there's a unifying fear."

Malcolm schooled his expression. "You'll have to find something else. The only current crisis is the housing issue and that's artificial at best. There's plenty of land and resources. The governments just have to allow them to be used."

Sonya laughed. "Oh. It's cute how naïve you can be some days. The wealthy don't wait for the right moment, we create it."

She steered them to the left and down a low slope to the docks.

The wharf smelled of dead fish, sweaty humans, and briny sea air. It wasn't unpleasant compared the crowded boardrooms that smelled of cologne, avarice, and unremarked flatulence. At least here there was a breeze.

Malcolm looked around at the crowd. He stood out because of his suit, but there was a good range of phenotypes on display—all skin tones, heights, and body types readily visible—and a universal expression of hard-won distrust.

Groups of private security stood out like warning buoys in the crowd, their driftwood-brown single-piece uniforms marked with three orange arm bands. Whoever hired them had been going for a Look. Without fail, they were each over two meters tall with large builds that suggested steroid use rather than weight training, all with shaved heads and pale skin.

Lethe guards then.

Malcolm frowned at the setup in general. It wasn't his problem, but it was hard not to roll up his sleeves and walk over to help unload the ship. He'd been taught to work.

The native Kydellians lounged on the upper decks of the ship while the work was done and it made his fists itch. Laziness was nearly as bad as treason, maybe worse. At least treason could be forgiven, if one survived the uprising.

He forced himself to turn away and study the menu taped to the window of a dock-side bar with interest as Sonya finished complimenting herself.

The sooner they could get away, the better.

A movement, or lack of movement, caught his attention. There was a woman reflected in the glass who drew his attention. Black hair tied back in three rosettes along the nape of her neck, and the working clothes of a dockside rowdy, but she stood like a battle commander. Shoulders back, chin up, eyes narrowed, lips pressed into a look of grim frustration. Her gaze swept across the piers as she searched for someone.

Malcolm ducked his head, praying to whatever ancestors might be listening that he went unnoticed. She couldn't be searching for him. No one knew he was on Seahome except Sonya, and Sonya wouldn't tell anyone from his past that he was in Kydell.

There were certain things that couldn't be said.

Not here at least.

Not if he wanted to live.

Thunder grumbled across the sky and the angry black clouds pressing across the bay threatened a tropical downpour.

"Shall we get going?" Malcolm asked Sonya, knowing better than to demand they leave, no matter how much he wanted to run. Something was wrong on the docks. The hair on the back of his neck was standing up and the air felt heavy with more than just humidity.

Sonya's bright smile dimmed. "Now? The fun hasn't even started."

"F—" He bit off an angry curse. "Fun?"

If Sonya had the social awareness of a louse, she would have picked up the undertone in his voice, but she was oblivious. "One of the toys is ready for testing." She ran her hand across his bicep. "It's time to make the changes we want to see."

"Sonya, this isn't the place to start a fight."

Her hug was sudden and insincere. "Your worry for me is touching. We won't have to do anything though. There are people in this crowd already primed to take action. We'll be innocent bystanders."

Across the dock, the black-haired woman made eye contact. She dismissed him with a small sneer and focused grimly on Sonya.

"Will anyone be hurt?"

"It's all for a higher cause, Malcolm." She patted his arm condescendingly. "Don't be so prudish. Sacrifices have to be made for the greater good."

Malcolm watched the black-haired woman moving through the crowds like a shark on the hunt. "What did you have in mind for the demonstration? Can you put them to sleep or make them all leave?"

"I'm going to make them fight," Sonya said. "One of them might even die." She giggled.

The words 'over your dead body' burned the tip of his tongue.

"What's wrong?"

Malcolm looked at the black-haired woman and back at the sociopath smiling up at him. "Why not wait a few days?"

"Why ever for? This is perfect!"

"Except we're here." Malcolm took the control device from her hand and tucked it in his pocket. "And to keep the contracts I have at Bennu, I need plausible deniability."

Sonya pouted.

"Why not next week?" he asked. "While we're at the opera you've told me so much about?"

The lights of vanity glittered in her eyes. "Are you asking me on a date, Doctor Long?"

"I do believe I am, Lady Lethe," he said with a sincerity cultivated from a lifetime of surviving abusive narcissists. "If you think I'm worthy of you."

"You are very nearly there," she said, "but we'll have to do something about this awful suit. What would you say to a shopping trip?"

"I'd do anything to keep you happy."

Sonya smiled prettily. "How could I possibly refuse if my happiness brings you happiness?" She took his arm. "It wasn't my original plan, but it will work. The men here are, regrettably, very loyal to my father. It will become a problem in time. There will still be a fight, but it won't kill all the rowdies."

"Could you have done that?" It was a miracle she didn't hear the terror in his voice.

"Probably. My experiment can wait though." She patted the device in his pocket. "We'll play with it later, won't we?"

"Would having all the control make you happy?"

She giggled again. "That's a very personal question to ask before our first date."

"I'm an engineer. I plan ahead, and I'm... thorough." He put the right spin on the word, suggestive with just a hint of leer. And over her head he made eye contact with the black-haired woman.

The woman looked at him and then turned away, vanishing into the crowd.

Not the reaction he'd expected. Perhaps it wasn't his friend. It was better if it wasn't.

Safer, for his future and for the ones he'd left behind.

All he'd ever wanted was to keep his friends safe. Keep them safe long enough that they could dig themselves out of the mess they'd been born into. If it meant being Sonya's arm candy, so be it. With enough charm, maybe he'd be able to turn her away from the idea of genocide.

Whatever he needed to do, it would be worth it in the end.

25

ROWENA

CRACK THE HULL AND FOG THE engine, there was no way Lethe's being in Kydell was not related to her search for Jae. And the man who had been with Lethe had been uncomfortably familiar.

Rowena ducked into a fetid, narrow alley away from the noise of the docks and ran the face through her implant to verify her suspicion.

It pinged off the name Dr. Malcolm Long of Descent. Sonya's pet engineer and boytoy.

"Three guesses why they were here," she muttered to herself. If there was any doubt that the Lethes were up to their armpits in this mess, it was gone now. At least in Rowena's mind.

Somehow she doubted the lawyers in Tarrin would accept, "I saw Sonya Lethe near a place the murdered man had been three weeks ago," as conclusive evidence of a crime. This wasn't enough to tie Sonya to Briceno's murder or to the deaths of the rowdies in the fighting ring.

The evening air was thick with humidity, as if the rain were falling from the gray sky only to evaporate before it hit the ground. As the sun sank over the jungle swamps, sitting between the heavy clouds and canopy, the air became clammy and grasping. It soaked through the rough fabric of Rowena's clothes and made her shiver.

At least she'd had a good night's sleep and Hollis had sent her off after a real breakfast when she promised to report in if she needed help.

Sonya Lethe qualified as trouble, but she was out of the Starguard's jurisdiction.

And getting in touch with the fleet would mean physically walking outside the shield perimeter the governor had put in place, since Rowena's implant was as close to null as she was willing to risk just to keep the scans from picking up her tech.

The sensible choice was to run. Sonya's man had made her.

She needed to report to Tyrling and get another Jhandarmi operative here. Except... Long shouldn't know she was Jhandarmi.

Rowena's pace slowed as she considered the implications. Her face wasn't in the files Lethe had stolen last year. She wasn't on any of the official databases.

Why else would he stare that intently though?

She turned and saw another man studying her with acute interest.

At least this one, tall with curling black hair, was one she wanted to talk to.

Jae narrowed dark eyes and nodded to her in recognition.

Rowena jerked her chin toward a wall of wooden crates that offered the only illusion of privacy on the crush of the dock where the ships were unloading cargo.

"I know you," Jae said as he walked up to her. "Can't remember how, but I know your face." He grabbed the edge of the vest she was wearing and looked at the black t-shirt, the one Hollis had given her. "Ride a pilot?" He frowned.

"It's a shirt. Doesn't mean anything." Except that the Starguard closet didn't have anything suitably grubby for dock work and she'd had to scrounge. The shirt was loose and surprisingly comfy. She still hadn't decided if that was something to tell Hollis or not.

Right now it didn't matter. "We met at a fight last week."

Jae's face scrunched as he tried to remember. "One of the rowdies introduced us?"

"No, I was there hiring a bruiser."

He looked down at her worn boots, the many-pocketed workpants fraying at the hem, and the shirt with a stained dock worker's vest over it. "You're not a Pure Water, or a fine lady."

"But I dress like one sometimes."

His hand brushed against something concealed in his pocket. A knife or a cosh by the look of it.

"You're a good fighter, Jae, but so am I. Let's keep this civil."

"I prefer to keep it simple."

"You're hurt. There's something in your chest that's causing your problems. Sometimes it feels like you're losing control of your body. Sometimes it feels like your own brain is attacking you."

The panic in his eyes was unmistakable.

"I might have a way to fix it so it doesn't hurt you anymore."

"What's the price?"

Saying there wasn't a price wouldn't work. Freedom meant something different to the rowdies than it did in fleet. A debt was like death. They traded favors and helped each other, but hated owing anyone. "For now the price is trust. I don't know if this works, but if it does, you'll be healthy again."

"Rather take cash, thanks." He stuck his hands in his pockets. "You've got a pretty accent for a dirty girl. I don't trust pretty."

"It's your life," Rowena said.

"That's what I'm counting on."

There was a shout in the crowd and a scream of pain.

Jae moved reflexively, standing tall and looking for trouble. "Bera!" He ran towards the fight.

Rowena charged after him.

The crowd was surging, breaking into battle lines, but only one side had weapons. There were onlookers at the rooftop restaurant where Sonya Lethe had been. Armed guards and police.

"It's a trap." She grabbed Jae's shoulder and spun him around. "This is going to be a massacre."

His eyes were wide with uncontrolled rage.

"You have to calm down. The rowdies need to get out." She kept her voice level, soothing.

A guard said something too low for Rowena to hear and kicked a woman with tangled brown curls and an olive-green dockside uniform lying on the ground.

Jae tried to pull away but Rowena pulled him back. "I've got this."

She fought her way through the crowd and stepped between the city guard and the woman. "Back off."

"She's a thief." The man wore the city security uniform with bright orange stripes on the arm. Private security hired by wealthy families or businesses and then turned loose to harass the poor. He was as tall as Hollis and just as heavily muscled.

Rowena lifted her chin up. "Then you arrest her, you petty coward. You don't beat her to death in the street like some common thug."

Cheeks turning bright red with anger, the man raised his hand to hit her.

Rowena side stepped. Grounders were stupidly slow sometimes. "Ooo. Big man. Beating little women," she taunted. "We're all so impressed."

He stumbled backwards in confusion as Rowena stepped forward.

"What are you going to do now? Try to hit me again? Scream for help? Do you think they'll get here in time, or do you think they'll watch while I kill you?"

In the Academy they'd called it command presence, the ability to keep every eye on you. The skill to make everyone listen in silence. It was the measured cadence of the words, the tone, the steady rhythm that had them all anticipating every move.

She didn't break eye contact as she crouched down and pulled Bera up by her arms. "You are done here. We are leaving. Everyone is done here."

It worked for longer than she'd hoped. They were out of arm's reach before the guard yelled in protest.

The crowd erupted into shouts of anger.

Rowena threw Bera towards Jae, spun into a drop kick, and scythed the guard's feet out from under him. "Run!" she ordered the stunned onlookers.

The rowdies tore off in every direction. There were shouts from the police and yells behind her, but it didn't matter.

She grabbed Jae's arm and scooped Bera up, putting the lighter woman over her shoulders. "Keep running."

Jae was breathing hard, sweating when he shouldn't have been.

There was a groan and Bera tried to move.

"Stay put."

"I can walk. I'm dizzy, but I can walk."

Rowena put her down.

They both looked at Jae.

"Pretend you don't see this." Rowena slapped Jae and released a concentrated burst of energy.

He froze and toppled over.

"It's fine," Rowena assured Bera. "Nothing wrong here. He's going to be fine. How do we get out of here?"

She slung Jae over her shoulder and wished she hadn't. He wasn't as light as Bera.

The other woman looked scared. "There's a rally point on the edge of the city. If we can get there, we can get out."

"Lead," Rowena said. "I'll follow."

Bera ran, weaving through the crowds and leading her along the docks until there was a break in the mob. They dodged inland, going past fish stalls and small shops whose owners were already pulling their wares inside in anticipation of the security forces attacking.

The crowds thinned the further uphill they went.

"Here." Berra directed her into a narrow alley between two crumbling buildings.

Rowena rolled Jae off her shoulders and stretched. How did grounders survive without nanites rejuvenating their muscles constantly? Every muscle in her back ached, her legs were wobbly with fatigue, and she was sweating from the humidity and exertion.

Bera licked her lips. "They'll keep coming. Start knocking on doors. Going into the apartments."

"Is there a backup plan?" Rowena asked. "A safe place for the rowdies?"

"The swamps for a day or two." Bera didn't look too happy about the idea. "With the rain it will flood enough they can get boats out there. But we know it well."

"How do you agree to go?"

"Someone we trust tells us to run." Bera's eyes fell on Jae, giving away who the rowdies trusted.

Briceno had been a mid-level manager. Someone with just enough influence. Jae, it seemed, was in the same social position.

"Go tell everyone Jae said to run."

Bera gasped in shock. "Without him?"

"Yes. He'll be there soon. I promise. I'll get him out of the city safely."

There was a shout and heavy boot steps from the street.

"Go," Rowena ordered.

"But, they'll be so many—"

"Go! If I can't handle this then it's on my head, not yours." Tyrling was going to hate this report. Hollis was... She didn't want to think about Hollis right now. There were too many undecided feelings tangled up with him. She stripped the vest off—it gave an attacker too good a hand-hold—and pulled out her knife. The last time she'd brawled with no tech had been during the war.

Oddly, that was a comforting thought. This was a war. She had clear orders to keep Jae alive. So that's what she was going to do.

Six men turned the corner wearing the city security uniforms. Flecks of fresh blood speckled the orange stripes. Gentle wasn't in their vocabulary.

Forgiveness wasn't in hers. That man had been ready to kill Bera, and for that he earned no mercy. "Afternoon, gentlemen."

The leader was twice her size, with a nice long reach, and a heavy truncheon. "Put your knife down and give us the rowdy."

"No, that's not how this works. You see me?" She squared her shoulders, ready to fight. "My name's Rowena. This your warning. Anyone who wants to back off now can go home, safe and sound, no grudges. You keep walking forward and we're going to have a fight. You ever killed anyone?"

The leader looked puzzled.

"I'll take that as a no. I have."

Someone whispered, "Murderer."

"Wrong. Again. I'm a hired fighter. Currently being paid"—sort of—"to keep a certain individual alive. If you want to take that up with my employer, I'll give you the contact information. But you need to know I'm allowed to use lethal force. What's your name?"

"Mitch."

"Good. Now we know what name to put on your toe tag."

One of the other men chuckled. "You think we're scared of you?"

"It would be the smart reaction," Rowena said. "So, no, probably not. You aren't that bright."

Mitch's truncheon swung her way.

Rowena side stepped, moving in closer, brought her boot to his ribs, and slammed the butt of the knife into the back of Mitch's skull as he fell. "One down. He'll live, regrettably, but notice he's down and I'm not. Why risk this? You're not getting paid enough."

Someone blew a shrill whistle, calling for back up as Chuckler rushed forward.

He threw out a low kick, swinging a big fist at her ear.

Rowena kept her hands high and countered, blocking until she could get in an uppercut that stunned him.

Another guard circled, truncheon up. He chopped at her legs, forcing her to dodge.

She ducked away, jumped, slid on the mud of the alley, pulled herself back to her feet. Twisting, she cut one across the thigh as she came back up. Put an elbow in his lowered jaw, and kicked him away.

Two down.

The alley was filling up faster than she'd hoped.

Circling, Rowena put herself between the majority of the attackers and Jae, who was barely coming to. With a low shield under her skin, she was going to get bruises. There were going to be so many questions she didn't want to answer.

She scanned the shield overhead again. There wasn't an opening nearby to force teleport these idiots to the middle of the ocean.

"Ready to surrender?" one of the guards asked.

"Haven't even broken a sweat yet," Rowena said with a taunting smile. "I thought you Kydellians were tough. You want a fight? When are you going to start trying?"

Come here, stupid man. Pay attention to the woman making you angry and not the man lying vulnerable on the ground.

Three of them rushed her at once.

She covered her face, took the hits, found her openings.

There. A telekyen-backed punch slammed past an attacker's defenses and bone crunched under her hand.

The man stumbled backward.

"Zeke!" A similar-looking man rushed to his side. A brother or cousin, and he didn't look happy—but the fight pivoted away from Jae.

Rowena shrugged and elbowed another man in the eye. "You can still run."

Knives came out.

"Really?" Rowena shook her head as she saw Jae struggle to stand. She tossed her own knife in the air, drawing attention away again. "Who's next?"

The cousin rushed her, knife held wrong.

She knocked it aside and kicked.

He punched, landing short but hitting her shoulder hard enough to numb it.

Rowena's uppercut found its way through his guard, striking her opponent's face.

The cousin continued to move forward. He kicked at her leg, trying to pull her down.

Rowena pounded his body with punches and kicks, keeping the knife held so it protected her wrist. The fewer dead bodies she left, the fewer reports she had to file.

A knife snicked past her guard, slicing her forearm.

Someone came up from behind, walloping her ear so her head spun.

"Fog it." That was enough being nice to the poor grounders. She brought her knife back hard, cutting into someone's gut. The reek of blood and intestines filled the area.

She broke away from the cousin and head butted the man who'd come up to her side, breaking his nose before her knife slashed at his arms, severing a tendon in the elbow.

Light on metal glinted in the corner of her eye and she turned in time to see Jae bringing a heavy rock down on the head of the man trying to stab her.

A hush fell over the dying and crying.

Rowena nodded. "Thanks."

Jae looked around at the carnage. "Why'd you do this?"

"To keep you safe. I promised Bera I would."

He staggered backward, clutching at his chest. "We—We have to go. I want to bash them all bloody."

"Very tempting," she agreed, kicking someone in the face as she tried to stand. "Know any good exits?"

Jae took her arm for support. "A quarter klick away, there's a gap in the city's security perimeter." He stared at the downed security forces with a vengeful hunger. He licked cracked lips and smiled. "I want to rip them apart. This isn't me, but I want it. I want blood."

"Blood later," Rowena promised.

She had to half drag him out of the alley, but once they were away, he regained some focus.

"If I punch you—"

"You won't," Rowena said. To him it might have sounded like encouragement, but she'd put a tight shield around Jae. He wasn't going to be able to lift his arm, let alone punch anyone.

He was swaying as he walked, but moving fast. "Can you make this stop?"

"Probably," Rowena said as he led her past the burnt-out ruins of an old apartment. "We haven't had a chance to test it yet."

Jae stopped in front of a broken door leading down to a cellar storage area. "No chance to test it, or no survivors?"

"Most the people who have one die quickly. Your friends in the fight rings were only a few." The Jhandarmi had found six more on the third continent alone. And there was the heir in Ryun who had a suspicious hole in his chest after jumping from a hypertram into a river in a case the local police were calling suicide.

Walking down the broken wooden steps, Jae nodded. "This way. The basement walls cracked along with the foundation of the city wall." Quietly, he led the way down the stairs and through a narrow passage mostly filled with broken boards and abandoned tarps used to cover cargo at the port.

The smelled of stagnant water and mold itched Rowena's nose. Water splashed at her ankles, then Jae turned and they were going uphill again, climbing a natural incline to the outer wall.

"I feel better here," he said, rubbing at his chest. "Calmer. Saner."

"It's probably the distance from the control device."

Kapok trees heavy with hanging moss drooped overhead. Fat drops of water fell to the soft ground underneath her feet. It was quieter here, cleaner, and without the shield overhead she finally could use her implant to connect with the fleet. A quick scan of all the channels told her Carver was calling a meeting in twenty minutes, and she'd been tasked with going as the training house rep.

This had to be quick.

Rowena licked her dry lips and tried to think of a way to broach what she was thinking.

Jae stopped walking. "Wow, that's not the look I was hoping for." A lopsided grin kept his words friendly. "I haven't even asked if there's a chance your rescuing me could lead to a long night talking together and already you're looking for a way out."

"It's not you, I just have to be somewhere soon. I need your decision. Can I try to take that thing out of your chest or not?"

Still smiling, Jae took a step closer. "If I say yes, will you come back to me tonight?" Before she opened her mouth to answer, he shook his head. "No. There's already someone keeping you close."

She wrinkled her nose. "You're good at reading people."

He raised his eyebrows in acknowledgment. "It's how I survive. I fight too, but not as well as you. How many men did you take down back there? My brain was a little..."—he waggled his hand by his ear—"…sizzled. You held your own, though."

"You helped," Rowena said. "Are you ready?"

"What's going to happen?" Jae asked.

"I'm going to try and remove the thing from your chest. You might die. It might be painful."

Jae rubbed a hand over his heart. "If it works, I won't hurt anyone? I came close today. I wanted to attack the man who knocked Bera down. If I had, others would have followed, it would have been a massacre. I can't let myself hurt them."

"If it works, you won't."

He nodded. "Good. Do it. I'd rather die than hurt my people."

Rowena looked around and pointed to a nearby stump. "Sit down. Close your eyes. I'll make this quick."

Jae sat and she put her hand a few inches from his chest. The coding was intricate. The whole goal was to do a force teleport on the device without severing any of the blood vessels. To do that, she had to transfer nanites in, block the device's connections, pull the device out, and then allow the nanites to splice the blood vessels back together.

"Is this a magic trick?" Jae asked.

Rowena wrinkled her nose at him and sent the code. It took nanoseconds but it seemed like a lifetime.

Jae was gasping for breath and the device was in her hand, slick with blood, and warm.

"How do you feel?" Rowena asked.

He pitched forward, clutching at his chest, his mouth gaping open in a scream.

"Don't die. Don't die." She grabbed his shoulder and tried to run a diagnostic.

"It feels like something is crawling inside my skin!"

"Nanites. That's normal. It'll stop in a minute."

He looked up at her in horror.

"You're going to live," Rowena said. She held the egg-shaped device out. "Do you want this?"

"No." He took a deep breath and sat up. "You're going to explain what you did."

"Sure." Her implant pinged a ten minute warning. "Eventually. I have to go."

Jae managed a smile. "Go? Where? Back to the city?"

"Something like that." She stepped away from him. "See you soon." She teleported out, leaving Jae to reconcile what he'd seen alone. Hopefully the next time they crossed paths, he'd put her vanishing act down to a bad memory caused by the trauma of the device.

Or at least forgive her for being fleet.

26
HOLLIS

PERRIN CARVER'S IDEA OF A meeting room was an old maintenance hangar for a small shuttle. Ancestors only knew why Carver had picked this room out of the warren of offices that ran underneath the old spaceport that fleet had taken and renamed Enclave. Maybe it was the lingering smell of fuel. Maybe it was the heavy shadows clinging to the walls. Maybe it was because the room was too far underground for most people to feel comfortable teleporting to, so Perrin's stash of treats was safe from the rest of the Starguard here.

Hollis picked out self-chilling bottle of mango juice and leaned against the rough wall. For a moment, it was just like the old days, with Hermione and Perrin arguing while he looked on. Except he didn't want to grab Hermione and calm her down by stripping her clothes off anymore.

As if she caught the thought, Hermione glanced at him. "This isn't entirely our decision anymore."

"It should be mine!" Perrin protested.

"We're not isolated any more. We've made agreements with the other political bodies on this planet. Let's get some more opinions."

Despite Perrin's disgruntled curse, Hollis felt the buzz against his shields as the message went out. Starguard debate over allocation of resources, sub-heading personnel missions. There were teleport coordinates attached, too.

A minute later, Titan and Selena Caryll teleported in, Titan in his all-blacks, Selena in her favorite—or possibly Titan's favorite—grounder outfit, a loose blue skirt and off-the-shoulder white sweater.

Genevieve bounced in, wearing a Silar uniform of copper and green, and gave him a sisterly nod before taking Perrin's hand.

"You know, people are starting to complain that the Elites are running everything," Hollis said. "This isn't going to help."

"Captain Sciarra asked me to keep her informed," Titan said. "She's handling contract negotiations with another crew."

"One of your cousins getting married?" Hollis guessed.

"We're trading an old fighter frame for some new organics in the ship's garden," Titan said, then corrected to, "they're getting." He smiled at Selena, who shook her head. A year in and sometimes Titan still slipped and acted like a Sciarra, not a Caryll.

Perrin knocked his knuckles on the table. "All right, this is a really quick and only semi-official meeting with representatives of the OIA, Starguard, and Captains' Council present."

"We should get someone from the training house," Hermione said.

"I put out the summons," Perrin said in an aggrieved voice. "If none of the trainers show up, they can't complain we left them out. Let's get on with this." He took a deep breath.

Hermione held up a hand to stop him from launching into a three-hour lecture. Perrin was good about talking around things when he didn't like the idea, or thought someone else wouldn't. "The situation is simple," she said. "Hollis was captured in the mountains—"

Everyone looked at him in alarm.

"I'm fine." More or less.

"He was taken to a location near Tarrin, where his captors intended to torture him and implant a control device," Perrin said.

"Slag them from orbit," Gen said.

Hollis nodded to his sister. :They didn't get a chance. I am fine.:

:Slag 'em anyway.:

"Hollis escaped without any real damage," Hermione said for everyone else's benefit.

True, if no one asked about the bruises from the rockslide or the lingering, empty sensation when Rowena wasn't around.

"But the captors did try to imprint him with the idea that he should attend a party in the city-state of Kydell on the second continent," Hermione said.

Kydell? Hollis looked up with interest.

Perrin growled.

With a roll of her eyes, Hermione continued. "Kydell is the port nearest Descent, and known for black market smuggling activity. The Jhandarmi presence is almost nonexistent and legal channels are…" Hermione paused as she searched for a word.

"Corrupt?" Selena suggested. "Kydell makes their money from multiple forms of illegal trade, from weapons smuggling to art theft to selling human skill sets. The government they have has an isolationist stance because they want to protect their monopoly on what other city-states view as illegal activity."

"Corrupt works," Hermione said as she sagged against the table. "The Marshalls of Descent have never been able to get a reliable operative in there. And the OIA has nothing."

"There's a Jhandarmi office," Selena said, "but not anyone I trust."

"We'd be sending Hollis in without any backup?" Titan shook his head. "No. I vote no. Remember last year when Selena went to a pool party undercover? She had a known alias and friends there, and she still almost got killed."

"And she left a crater in someone's yard." Gen grinned and Selena grinned back.

Hollis sighed. "Raise your hand if you ever went into a salvage situation alone during the war."

The group glared at him in unison.

"This isn't war," Hermione argued.

"Says the woman who got herself caught and tortured by the Baulars." And never really came home from it. Not all the way, at least. "It's a grounder city, I'll be able to shield and teleport. I'll be safe."

Hermione shook her head. "They have heavy blocks on the city to prevent electronic spying. It'll interfere with teleports and wreck your shield. The most you would have would be an advantage because you can probably microboost with telekyen. But it's too high risk and for all we know they just want you there to look pretty."

Perrin and Gen nodded.

"They killed someone," Hollis said. "They would have put their murder device in me if they could have. They are planning an attack against the fleet. That's Starguard territory, and I have an open invite to go find out more. We should use it."

"No," Titan said. "I still vote no."

"We vote no," Selena said.

"Silar is right." The voice in the shadows echoed slightly, warping it and making it seem like it was coming from light-years away.

Shields went up as everyone scrambled to identify the person who wasn't broadcasting anything.

Rowena stepped forward. She was wearing the black 'Ride A Pilot' shirt he'd bought her with tan cargo pants filthy with mud and blood, and her hair was frizzing from contact with humidity, although the Tarrin air was dry. There was a bruise on her cheek and a fresh bandage on her arm.

:What happened?: Hollis asked. He could feel other messages moving through the air; he wasn't the only one asking.

:Later: Rowena waved aside any questions. "Hollis is our best chance to get information on this group and their goals. Even if the fleet backs out, the Jhandarmi are in."

"I talked about this with Tyrling," Selena said. "The chance of losing an operative is too high. He can't ask someone to go in with those odds."

"He didn't," Rowena said. "Someone volunteered."

A cold certainty settled in Hollis's chest. "You volunteered?"

Rowena lifted a shoulder in a casual shrug, but she wasn't making eye contact, she wasn't moving into the circle or within reach of anyone. "I'm stationed in Kydell at the request of the Jhandarmi. It's part of the deal we made last year. Which means there's an operative there that Caryll can trust."

"You're going to back Silar?" Titan asked sounding bewildered. "Why?"

Finally Rowena looked up, lips twisted in a scowl of annoyance. "Sonya Lethe and her boytoy engineer were in Kydell today when someone tried to trigger a riot with the same kind of device the Rightful Children of the Empire tried to put in Hollis. Good money says Lethe will have a presence at that party, which means I'm going. We need to get a look at their control device. I can either sneak in, or I can walk in the front door with Hollis and his invitation. He's their new toy. Chances are high that they'll give him a new set of orders and release him back into the wilds of Enclave. Walk in. Get what we want. Walk out. No one will know there's a security breach."

"Ancestors above," Titan muttered. "We've... We've officially hit the end of our times and the heat death of the universe. Rowena and Hollis are agreeing on something. Let's call it a day and watch the sun go nova."

Selena smiled and squeezed his arm. "I don't think this is actually a sign that the world is ending."

"It's pretty near apocalyptic," Gen said with a huge grin. "I'm not sure my brother is still breathing."

"I'm fine!" Hollis protested. "And I agree with... Rowena." He felt like he'd jumped into vacuum without a hull. Everything was changing with a word.

:Yes! I knew it!: Gen's delight filled his mind.

Titan glared at him. :You are not supposed to do that.:

:Learn to love it,: Hollis advised.

Perrin shook his head in confusion. "You're going to trust Lee with your life?"

"I've done it before," Hollis said, keeping his face calm, his voice unaffected. He'd called her Rowena in front of their friends. In front of the only people who mattered to both of them. :We can do this, right?: He sent the message on a tight beam straight to her.

:Getting in was going to be the hard part. With an invite, this should be a stroll in a garden.:

Gen was muttering and glaring at Perrin, trying to get him to agree. :Can I tell him about last night?:

:No. Not without Rowena's permission.:

His sister frowned at him.

"This vote doesn't matter," Rowena said, blowing everyone's engines with a word. "I'm going, with or without backup. It'll be safer and more effective with two of us, but I can run this alone."

"No," Selena and Titan said in unison.

"Then send Hollis with me."

:You hurt her and I swear your sister will never find enough of you to mourn,: Titan said on a tight beam.

:What's Selena going to say to that?:

:She'll understand. Rowena is my best friend.:

Hollis smiled and finished his juice. "I'm going."

"There has got to be a better way," Perrin said.

"It could work," Hermione said slowly as she studied Rowena's blood-stained clothes. "With the right clothes and back story, it could work very well. The opportunity for gain here is something we shouldn't ignore. We need information from Kydell."

Gen shook her head. "What cover could they use? Selena has dozens of covers, sometimes multiple ones in the same city-state. How are Hollis and Lee going to go together? Is he supposed to introduce her as his annoying co-worker? The woman who wants him dead? His business rival?"

"She'll be my date." The words ran out of his mouth with all the oxygen in his lungs. *Ancestors, help me.*

The air in the room seemed too thin for anyone.

"Date?" Gen's voice had an odd squeak to it.

Everyone looked at Rowena, expecting her to reject.

She stared them down, eyes cold.

Titan rubbed his temples. "I regret ever telling you that we needed to find a common ground. I meant finding a favorite food you could share, not a mutual enemy."

"Your fault," Rowena said, obviously finishing a conversation that had been private. "You told me to work with the Silars."

Perrin grimaced. "How bad was the riot, Lee?"

"One of the hired guards pushed a dock worker down. Jae, the one who had a device in his chest, was ready to fight. I stepped in and calmed the situation down long enough for us to get away, but the rowdies are leaving Kydell tonight. They don't feel safe there."

Hermione pursed her lips together. "You're sure it was Doctor Long with Lethe?"

"Positive. Why?" Rowena asked.

"We were in school together on Descent after I came back from the war." Hermione's expression grew unreadable. "He's not someone I would expect to side with Lethe."

Rowena shook her head. "He was with her. It looked like he was willing."

"Did you scan him?" Hollis asked. "He may have had an implant."

Hermione's breathe caught. Hollis might have been the only one who noticed, but he saw it, the fear in her eyes. She wanted to protect the engineer.

There was a drawn out moment where he could feel Rowena thinking over her reply. She was watching Hermione too. "There was no orun on him," she answered Hollis. "I doubt he has an implant like the one Sonya tried to use on you. But I didn't scan for anything else."

Unspoken words formed an image in his head. :What kind of implant did he have?:

:Nothing that registered with a normal scan for fleet,: Rowena said, but there was a memory lurking behind her words. She met his eyes. :There are devices that were designed to not register. Mal had one when he died. I don't know if the OIA retrieved it or if it was buried with him. If it was buried with him, someone could have found it, I suppose.:

"It's still a complication," Hermione said. "Long is the only heir to a landed family in Descent. They're loosely allied with my family. If he's sided with Lethe, there will be problems. But if he hasn't, if he's unaware of the situation and merely flirting with Sonya—"

"—it shows he has exquisitely bad taste in women?" Rowena suggested.

To everyone's surprise, Hermione smiled. "It means that letting him get caught in the crossfire could endanger certain..." She paused to consider her words. "...Projects of mine."

"Can't you reach out to him?" Perrin asked. "You went to school together."

"We were never formally introduced," Hermione said. "I don't have an in there."

Selena and Titan shared a look.

"We've already scheduled a meeting at Bennu Industries," Selena said. "We'll be sure to meet with him. I'll run another scan, ask him about Sonya. Even if he says nothing, his reaction will be useful."

Perrin had a look in his eye that said he was seriously considering confining everyone to quarters for their own safety and his sanity. "This was so much easier when all we had to do was blow up ships." He looked over at Rowena, probably wishing he'd managed to take her out years ago.

Rowena nodded in sympathy. "Bigger target. Easier to hit. I can see why someone with your aim would miss that." The corner of her lips turned up in a teasing grin.

"Oh, you didn't." Gen's eyes widened. :You have been such a bad influence on her! She's teasing Perrin!:

:They were like that on the flight team,: Hollis said. :He'll live.:

"We're all friends here," Hermione said. "This is the price of peace. We have to solve things without punching anyone."

Rowena snorted in disbelief. "Suddenly I'm glad I'm not a senior officer any more. Lowly grunts still get to punch people. And, if Sonya Lethe gets near me, I will do more than punch her. I'm tired of her treating people like toys." She teleported out before anyone could argue or ask about the blood.

"Titan," Perrin drew the name out as he rubbed his hands across his face. "If she starts a war—"

"She won't," Titan promised. "Lethe hasn't threatened the Lees, and that's all Rowena will care about."

"Lethe threatened the rowdies and Kydell by going there," Hollis said. "The Jhandarmi have Rowena guarding them." Had no one else thought this through? "We need to have Tyrling pull Rowena from the area. She won't give ground if her commander tells her to guard it. She never has. After she goes to the party, her cover is going to be gone, whatever is left of it."

Hermione's eyes filled with nebulas and stars as she accessed her implant. "Her cover might be gone already. The Kydell security force is reporting multiple injuries and two dead after trying to apprehend a rowdy woman who started a fight on the docks. The description matches Rowena."

"Of course it does." Perrin glowered.

"The shields over Kydell didn't register any use of fleet tech," Hermione said as her lips pressed into a thin line of disapproval. "Perrin, she neutralized a squad of twenty-three men without using her implants."

Hollis tried to feel something. Anger that Rowena had been in danger. Concern that she'd become that lethal. But it felt inevitable. With her back against a wall, Rowena would do what she'd been trained to do, and she'd been trained to kill. Everything else she did, from helping the Jhandarmi to caring about the complaints of her cadets, was a choice.

And in defiance of everything she'd been taught, she was choosing to stand with him.

He wasn't going to forget that. Ever.

Perrin closed his eyes. "Did the Kydellians identify her?"

There was a pause and Hermione's eyes returned to their normal soft brown. "No positive ID. Her cover is safe."

"Let's keep it that way." Perrin looked at him. "You are certain you can run this op with Lee as backup?"

Hollis nodded. "It won't be a problem."

"We're in a precarious position," Perrin said. "We don't have enough allies on the ground. There are people getting nervous because we have voting rights in the continental senate. There are people looking for an excuse to take the fleet apart."

"Rowena won't give them a chance," Titan said quickly. "She's been working with the Jhandarmi for the better part of a year without a complaint."

:It's Rowena Lee,: Hollis told Perrin directly, letting his confidence in her show. :She'll die before she lets anyone hurt the fleet.:

It was his friend who met his eyes, not his commander. :Then your job is to keep her alive.:

:I will.:

27
ROWENA

IN THE FRAMELESS MIRROR, THE red silk sparkled and swirled. Even in the relative warmth of the Carylls' home in Tarrin, Rowena felt exposed. She tugged at the smooth fabric of the red gown, silently willing it to extend and cover her bare arm.

Selena Caryll swatted her hand away, blonde hair visible in the mirror as she fussed behind Rowena. "It's not meant to go that high."

"I'm naked." Showing more skin to the world than she ever had outside the medical bay.

"Not most of you, just the shoulder." Selena tugged the side zipper up. "There. It looks good on you."

Rowena looked in the mirror in Selena and Titan's guest bedroom and tried to ignore the uneasiness of having Selena 'I can crack hulls with a thought' Caryll standing behind her. There were days where the Reality That Should Have

Been and the Reality That Was were so dissimilar it felt like she was being tossed around in a solar storm.

The reflection of Selena in blue slacks and a shimmering white blouse smiled encouragingly. "You look good."

"Thanks," Rowena said. "I thought Nia would help me out, but, you know... the baby." It was a weak excuse.

"Classes at the university, a part-time job, and the baby?" Selena laughed. "I'm amazed she has time to sleep. If she had time for dress shopping, it would have been a miracle."

"Right." Rowena forced a smile. "Just that stage of life, I suppose." She smoothed the skirt and turned. The skirt fluttered up and settled against her legs. "This feels so cracking weird."

Selena nodded. "You sure about running this op with Silar? Titan and I can back you up if you want."

"Hollis has the in. And... we weren't always enemies."

"You were never friends either. I always thought Hollis was too loud for you. Not really the kind of person you'd spend time with."

"I used to be loud." And confident. And crazy. And loved. They'd been very alike when they were cadets. Life had just beaten it out of her. Forced her to keep her emotions in check. Bite her tongue. When she was around Hollis, it all came back, the arrogance and the confidence, the sensation that she could conquer the world.

The doorbell rang, interrupting her spiraling thoughts. It was just as well; the old Rowena was dead, lost to the war. Here and now, she needed to be the dutiful sailor who was willing to give up everything and take any face.

Selena teleported away and then Rowena heard, "Arwel! How are you?"

Walking out of the room to the bannister, Rowena saw a tall man with long blond hair pulled back in a chaotic knot on his head. Somehow Arwel had found the will to forgive Selena for bombing his backyard from orbit the previous summer.

"Ro, you know Arwel?"

"The man with the cooked pool?"

"I rebuilt it," Arwel said quickly. He looked at Selena. "This is the person you wanted the artwork for?"

Rowena walked down the stairs, holding her arms out for inspection. "I know my skin's darker than Selena's, but can you make it work?"

"You have fantastic skin!" Arwel rushed her, hand reached out.

Her stomach twisted in fear mixed with rage. Nausea built up and her shield bounced up with it.

Selena grabbed Arwel's hand. "Limited touching."

"Oh. Ah." Arwel snapped his hand away. "Sorry. I'm, I'm so used to people liking it when I touch them. Sorry. I didn't scare you, did I?"

"Of course not," Rowena said. It was strange when grounders reached for her; there was no shield to signal a touch. The wrongness of the touch being the first warning a person was there was something she couldn't explain to even Titan.

Selena slipped into the space between them. "Rowena does bodyguard work sometimes," Selena said, inventing as she went, "and the first touch is usually the first hint of a fight."

"Oh, rough line of work," Arwel said. "I'll be very careful. Just metallic paint you said, right?"

"Like the patterns people are wearing in Descent," Rowena said. "But simple. Like I'm trying to match but not quite getting it right." Tyrling had made her study the patterns and customs all morning so she could maintain the cover of aspiring socialite.

Arwel's face wrinkled in confusion. "But... I can get it right."

"I need to look like I'm a little st—"

"—uneducated," Selena cut in. "Like she's seen the fashion magazines but didn't have the money or resources to mimic the style exactly."

Arwel nodded. "One beautiful fraud coming up."

An hour later there was gold paint on the skin under her ribs that peeked through an opening of the dress, more gold paint on her legs, and a delicate lace of gold paint along the neckline.

Titan walked in at the last minute, stopped, blinked, and nodded. "Very shiny."

"She looks fantastic," Selena said, eyes sparking bright blue as she sent Titan a message on a tight channel.

Arwel looked at her legs with a pained expression. "I can do better any time you want."

"No need to defend your work. This is what I need tonight." Rowena checked the mirror again. The dress, the hair, the gold... It wasn't her... and it wouldn't be tonight. "Did you bring the mask?"

"Got it." Titan held up a slim, black roll. "Nanite mask good for fifteen hours. There's one for you and one for Silar in case you need to get him out without being noticed."

"Thanks."

"Not a problem. You sure you don't want us closer for backup?"

She really did, but Tyrling really didn't. "It's just a party," she said with a light smile. "We go in, we talk, we walk out. The absolute worst thing that could happen is someone throws a drink on my dress because they hate me. I think I can survive that."

Selena pinged her with a memory of one of their many fist fights.

"The hardest part is going to be picking up my date," Rowena said with a grin.

"I'm free!" Arwel raised his hand.

Rowena shook her head. "I already have someone."

"Lucky someone."

She tried not to smile. "Sometimes. I'm sure there are times he regrets knowing me."

Titan tilted his head. "I dunno, Ro..." The note of teasing in his voice made her roll her eyes.

"This is for work. We'll be too busy for anything else." Hollis flirted like it was part of his workout, but never on duty. Tonight they'd be two agents doing their job.

Rowena spun around and the skirt flew. It was nicely dramatic.

"Try not to ruin the dress," Selena said. "You should get a chance to wear it somewhere fun."

"Like a wedding celebration," Titan said. "As a completely random example and not a hint of any kind."

Rowena glared at him. "Selena, your husband needs sleep. He's delirious." She smiled at Arwel. "Thank you for your help."

"If it goes well, don't hesitate to recommend me to your friends."

"Will do. Good night."

It took a picosecond run a sweep for Silar's code and teleport to his location. Cargo Blue. It was like he wanted everyone to see them together.

She teleported into the shadows of the flight museum, staring at the bar in the distance. :This is the best place you could think to meet?: Cargo Blue was marginally better than meeting in, say, the *Veronica* under the Silar's shield, but only by decimal point fractions.

All this effort and there were going to be nishu books about this for years.

:I don't trust the grounders to feed us, but I'm almost done. Are you coming in?:

She sent him the memory of a glare and a flash of frustration. :I'm not walking into a bar looking like this.:

:You look beautiful.:

:You haven't seen my dress yet.: Unless Selena or Titan had sent him an image.

:I don't need to. You look beautiful. Now, come rescue me like you promised before Guardian Tejan tries to take my shirt off. Besides, you owe me.:

Rowena rolled her eyes. :Owe you?:

:If you'd kissed me in front of the fleetlings, no one would be chasing me tonight.:

She bit her lip to hide a laugh. :I'm not kissing you in Cargo Blue either.:

:Show up and smile at me. That'll be intimidating enough for most of them.:

Shaking her head, she walked across the gravel to the cement path running between the OIA building and the bar. It would be polite to let Silar know she was incoming—but where was the fun in that?

28
HOLLIS

"THIS WAS, WHAT, SECOND YEAR at the Academy?" Hollis asked Perrin as the crowd thickened in Cargo Blue. Condensation dripped off a glass of ice water, pooling on the recycled metal table-top next to a plate of forgotten fried potatoes as he smiled with his friends.

Tejan leaned over the back of the booth with a hungry look in her eyes.

Rowena needed to hurry up and rescue him before the pretty suit Hermione insisted on was ripped off him.

"End of the first year," Perrin said. "Remember, we had those awful one-piece uniforms with the bright green V on them?"

Everyone laughed. The jumpers were legend in the fleet.

Nodding, and ignoring Tejan, Hollis went on, "Right, the green things that itched and smelled like they hadn't been washed since the wormhole collapsed. Anyway, Perrin and I were late getting our report in—for very valid reasons, mind you—"

"—they forgot," Hermione translated for the crowd.

"You were distracting me! I would have done so much better in class if you weren't sitting in front of me." Hollis smiled up at her.

Hermione shook her head and sipped her drink.

A few years ago that would have been enough to make him spend the rest of the night dancing around her in the hope of winning her attention again. But the urge to chase Hermione felt like nothing more than a distant memory—treasured, but distant. "What I was saying... Did I get to the tunnel yet?"

Perrin shook his head. "The lift broke and we weren't allowed to teleport, so we took the tunnel, and—"

He was cut off by a long whistle from someone.

"Crystal fine," someone murmured a little louder than they probably intended.

"Ancestors be praised."

Hollis watched as several of the single officers broke away, craning their necks to get a better look at the entrance.

Shields popped up, not for battle, but for display. Scrolling information changed, offering everything from rank to age and offers for dinner to whomever was walking in.

Hollis chuckled and looked at Perrin. "Were we ever that desperate?"

"Yes," Hermione said.

Perrin held his hands up, acknowledging the truth. "It worked for me."

Hollis laughed and turned, trying to see who was causing the commotion.

The crowd parted to frame the silhouette of a woman in a tight-fitting red gown that pooled around her feet. Long,

dark hair fell to one side in loose waves. Her curves were...
familiar.

"Rowena?" Hollis stood up as she walked out of the
afternoon sunlight into the dimly lit bar.

The sunbeams chased her, bouncing off gold accents on
her skin.

"Rowena?" someone beside Hollis asked. "Rowena Lee?"
The disbelief rippled around the room.

She lifted her chin, but kept her shield low. "Ready to
go?"

Hollis licked his lips and tried to remember how to talk.
There was no probability matrix that could have predicted
this.

Ancestors. Even in his wildest, most erotic dreams he had
never imagined Rowena Lee looking like a mythological
goddess ready to take his soul.

"Silar?" Rowena lifted an eyebrow. :Say something.
Everyone is staring at me and I feel like an idiot.:

"You look beautiful," Hollis said. :I was right.:

She rolled her eyes for everyone to see. "Were you really
expecting something less?"

"No." The crowds weren't exactly parting for him, but he
moved forward all the same. Nudging people out of his way.

"I'd say you look good, but that might be redundant."
Rowena smiled but it didn't reach her eyes. She was tense.
Uncomfortable with the crowd surrounding them.

Several of the Warmonger officers were pinging Rowena. He could sense the communiques rattling against her
shield and falling away unnoticed. Even the Allied officers
who had sworn they'd never touch a Lee were recalculating.

He squeezed Rowena's hand. "You have the co-ordin-
ates?"

"Mm hmm."

Mars Sciarra stepped into view wearing a deep gray Sciarra uniform with the telltale vivid emerald green detailing. "Rowena Lee, you look gorgeous. Kiss for luck?" White teeth stood out against skin black as the expanse of space.

Rowena was right, the boy had a nice smile.

And Mars could keep smiling at Rowena over his very dead body.

"She has me. She doesn't need luck." Hollis ran a hand down Rowena's bare arm and skewered Mars with a glare. "Or a kiss from you."

The Sciarras could fantasize about having Rowena on their ships all they wanted, but while he was breathing that wasn't going to happen.

:It's hilarious that you're jealous of a lieutenant.: Rowena's voice was tinged with amusement.

:Not any lieutenant. Only the one you were flirting with.:

:Flirting implies intent.: Her eyes met his with a smile. :There was no intent.:

"Are you sure you want to take Silar?" Mars asked, looking skeptical. "You and I could have such a good time together."

She laughed as Sciarras in the crowd shouted reminders that she was welcome there.

"Sciarra green would look good on you," Mars said his voice pitched for seduction. "And I have four warships in my dowry."

Hollis's teeth ground together as he fought the urge to put up a war shield and make Mars back down. "Get moving, Sciarra. Lee isn't interested in your warships."

"You never know. I might be." She was smiling up at him. Playing with him.

Hollis took her hand and moved so he was behind her and she was tucked in beside him, his arm across her waist.

"You'd have more fun playing with me," he whispered in her ear.

Mars put his hands on his hips. "You two…" He tsked and then winked. "Have fun. Try not to break the guardian, Lee."

Rowena smirked. "We'll see. Guardian, the tram arrives at our station in five minutes."

Hollis gave a quick salute to the crowd. "That's my cue to hit the engines and get out of here. See you all later." The coordinates didn't ping his shield, but somehow slipped into his implant as if they'd always been there. :I need to learn that trick.:

:Good luck,: Rowena said with a sensation of smug superiority that said she didn't think he could.

:Let's go.: He teleported to the coordinates—and shivered.

The second continent was on the tail end of summer and at the altitude of the tram station they were taking to get to Kydell, the air was thin and cold. Far overhead, the dome of night was dusted with stars that bled into the dark horizon and the tiny, hillside towns. Small shrubs shivered in the cool breeze that whistled through the wooden frame of the tram station.

Rowena materialized beside him, looking alert and slightly angry.

:Relax. We have a good hour before we need to worry about anything.: They were alone again for the first time in weeks. Hollis wanted to stop time and savor the moment.

Running a hand along the red skirt, Rowena said, "Sorry for ruining your reputation back there. I know you'll catch shrapnel for this."

Hollis reached to take her hand as the tram pulled into the deserted station. "I'm not worried about it. The fleet will get used to seeing us together." He'd make sure of that.

The tram pulled up, a long, smooth tube of silver-white metal that had been splashed with mud on its journey through the countryside. They took a pair of empty seats in an empty carriage decorated in Lethe blue and gray, the lights dim and the moon outside bright.

He couldn't quite hear her thoughts, but he could sense a burst of activity. If he slipped the Guardian Veil over his eyes, he could see the thin, red thread of telekyen running between their implants swelling and then abruptly thinning as Rowena mentally shied away.

:What are you thinking?:

:We'll have to turn off our implants when we get there. No shields and no coms. Even if we get through this, we'll have the fallout in Enclave to deal with.: She leaned her head against the high-backed seat, face wan and shields tight.

Hollis tried to smile. :We can do this. It's us.:

:I feel...: Embarrassment leaked through.

:Naked?: he guessed.

Rowena shot him a look that promised a slow, painful death.

:So do I.:

:Everything is covered except your hands and face!: She sent him an image of the black suit he was wearing, with the ridiculously crossed-cut jacket and two rows of non-functional gold buttons. :I have a single strap on one shoulder, a bare back, and a slit in the skirt that shows more leg than anyone but my ship's medic should see!:

That was too much of an invitation to miss. Hollis exaggerated a lean forward to look her long, golden-brown legs, accented by more gold leaf patterns. "Looks like the same amount of leg I saw in training." And in his bed, but he kept that thought tucked away for when she was in a better mood.

"It's not the same with you."

He suppressed a smile, even though she'd just admitted he was allowed more skin privileges than the medics.

She shook her head. :You're reading too much into this.:

:What? You'd rather be with a Sciarra lieutenant and his warships?:

"Maybe," she said out loud, not looking at him.

He bumped her knee with his. "You don't mean that."

"Don't I?" Rowena smiled at him, eyes sparkling with amusement. "Maybe Mars is a little too young. He has a cousin who's older though. Kenzi has a decent dowry."

"We'll pick him up a nice girl from Kydell," Hollis said. "A souvenir date as a consolation prize."

Her laugh was beautiful. "Oh no. You know what we're becoming?"

"Friends?" *More.*

Rowena shook her head as she smiled. "We're becoming that old couple that tries to find a match for every single person we see. And we're not even a couple!"

"We could be."

Her smile vanished.

29
ROWENA

THIS WAS WHAT HEARTBREAK FELT like. It was having everything you ever wanted in front of you and knowing you could never touch it. It was watching everything you loved burn to ash as you approached.

Rowena looked out at the empty plains rushing by outside the tram window.

Warmth and happiness brushed along her mind as Hollis reached out across the link. "What did I say wrong?"

"Nothing."

Everything.

She had to stop it here. It had been fun to play, to flirt, to pretend that anything could happen, but it had to end here. With a thought, she put up a modified soundshield. Any recording, and anyone walking past, would hear an inane conversation about a popular holovid drama.

"Run that math, Hollis. Let's pretend, for a moment, that you'd lost your mind and fallen in love with someone short, prickly, and unlovable like me. Think of how it would work out."

Terribly.

"Beautifully," he said. Through the connection, she felt his thoughts. The surety that they'd work together, play together, run an armada together.

Rowena shook her head. "No. It would be torture."

"We work well together! We understand each other."

"What would you do when the Starguard who once respected you don't want to meet your eye anymore because your lover is a Warmonger? What will you do when your crew no longer speaks your name? Or calls you a traitor? What do you say when your beloved little sister won't let you see her baby because all she sees in you is an idiot whose lover killed her brother?"

He shook his head. "No. That wouldn't happen."

"It would." Rowena willed him to see reason. "It would. You're a war hero, the darling of the fleet. But even you can't make the fleet forgive a Warmonger."

"They forgave Titan."

Hollis made it sound so reasonable she wanted to tear her hair out.

"Titan didn't fight in the war and he has a first-class crew at his back. Elea is politically savvy and they have more Elite fighters than anyone else. If you wanted a Warmonger, you should have grabbed him before Selena did. He's the only one not carrying the taint of war on him. Choose anyone else, and you'll be branded a traitor." The truth was a savage weapon to use, but she had to make him see reason.

Shots fired and they glanced off Hollis's ego like a kinetic bombardment off his shields. "Then let them call me a traitor. I know how I feel. I want to be with you."

"I said that too."

Remembering felt like carving her heart out with a dull knife.

"Mal asked me if I wanted to go back to my crew or stand by him when war came. I made the same choice. Do you see what that choice won me? The Lees were never a first class crew. We were a B-level on our best days. I'm the only Elite the Lees have ever had. If I'd left him, maybe we would have been okay. Maybe I wouldn't be here, hated by everyone, shunned and scolded for living. But I told Mal I loved him no matter what."

Hollis's face grew cold. "You never loved Mal."

It was the truth and she didn't shy away from it. "Not the way most people would have, but as much as I could, I cared for him. I supported him."

Hollis's eyes glowed a molten gold as he ran the scenarios. He probably didn't need to, but he was thorough like that. "How do you think it would have turned out if you'd refused Mal? If you'd try to leave?"

"I would have died," Rowena said flatly. "Old Baular would have declared me a traitor and I would have died. Respected and loved, and dead at seventeen."

"What would have happened to your crew?"

She shrugged. "Who knows. Maybe Old Baular would have sacrificed them. Maybe they would have escaped. I don't know. I knew I had a chance of survival if I stayed, and none if I left. It was selfish."

"You were seventeen!" Anger heated the air between them. "You shouldn't have been making a choice like that!"

"No. I shouldn't have. But I did and now I'm living with it." She made herself cold, locking down every emotion. It made her angry too, and she couldn't indulge in that. "Death would be kinder."

Hollis opened his mouth to argue but she shook her head.

"Listen to me! I'm trying to keep you safe. I'm trying to tell you what I wish someone had told me. This isn't the life anyone wants. I'm the walking dead. Unregarded. Unwanted. Disrespected at every turn. I know I could have the respect, or at least the fear, of everyone. I could have a command again. But the price is too high."

"Rowena—"

"I won't go to war again. And I don't want to see you hurt. If they hurt you..." She snapped the connection and looked out the window at the passing night. If someone came after Hollis, she'd react the same as if he were Titan or Aronia: she'd kill them.

After a minute, Hollis changed seats so he was sitting beside her, body warming her bare shoulder. "Are you saying you'd go to war for me?" His voice was gentle, almost unsure.

"I didn't say that," she kept her voice perfectly calm.

"You implied it."

"Not the same thing."

He put an arm around her shoulder and pulled her back so her head was tucked under her chin. The reflection in the window showed him pressing a kiss to her head even though she couldn't feel it. "This is us, Rowena. We've had worse odds."

"Two against the fleet?"

"It's never going to be the two of us. Carver and Marshall will always back me. Most of my crew will accept it. The Sciarras will support you. Elea won't love it, but she'll support you if it means keeping you as an ally. The Carylls support you. We have all the Elites on our side."

Outside, the tram dipped down into the coastal plains, with Kydell a soft glow of lights under a thunderhead in the distance. Shrubbery grew thicker and taller as they passed the outer edge of the rowdy's jungle.

Rowena put her hand over his. "I don't know."

"Have you ever thought about it? About being in love? About letting yourself be happy and not just surviving every day?"

"No."

He rested his cheek on her head. "Then think about it. We have time. I don't want a day or two with you. I want forever. I want to see your smile when I walk into the room. I want to listen to you talk about your day. I want to see you make captain, pin on your rank, and run an armada with you."

She met his eyes in the reflection of the window. "Hollis! Most people start with light flirtation or sharing a meal!"

"We shared a meal. Ration bars after flight training." He pulled the memory up and shared it with her.

It'd had been a long day. They'd ached from being in the cockpit for hours on end and then she'd sat down beside him, knees touching, and offered him a ration bar before falling back on the mat and going to sleep. They hadn't even talked.

"When I was hurt and scared, you came to take care of me." He smoothed down a wayward hair escaping from the artful wave Selena had created.

"I'd do that for anyone," she said.

"You'd let anyone hold you?"

The thought made her gag. "I don't like being touched."

"Mm hmm. I know." The gentle arm wrapped around her squeezed into a tight hug for a second. "You like when I touch you though."

Rowena sighed, acknowledging defeat. "You have to do things the hard way, don't you?"

"Falling in love with you isn't hard at all. You left an opening so big I could have flown a squadron through it."

Impossible. "When did I give you an opening?"

"The night you told me Sciarra was missing and you took my knife. You trusted me enough to help, and to be there for you, and I knew if Titan was out of the picture I had a clear field."

"It's been nearly a year!" She sat up and looked at him. "You didn't say anything!" Searching her memory, she couldn't find a single thing that had singled her out. He'd come to training more often. Volunteered to spar with her. But nothing more.

"I didn't?" He raised his eyebrows and waited.

She settled back against his chest. "You're as bad as Titan." That was as much of a concession as she was willing to give.

"I'm taking that as a compliment." He kissed her cheek. "Time to drop the shields. We're coming up on the outer layer of Kydell and it does not look good." Through the guardian shield, he shared the view of the city. Wide ropes of yellow energy wrapped around the city like a fishing net. "What coding is that?"

"Not fleet."

"At the risk of sounding like an elitist xenophobe, I'm not happy with the idea of the grounders having that kind of tech."

Rowena turned her off her implant. "They don't. An isolated few do, that's why it's dangerous. Too much information in the hands of too few people is always wrong."

Only the heat from Hollis's body let her know he was there. She couldn't hear him. Couldn't feel his emotions. Her chest tightened with panic.

"I'm right here," Hollis whispered in her ear as he took her hand. There was a flash of thought, a red thread, and the words :Microburst communication.: "You realize you're advocating to put our tech out for their consumption?"

She looked up at him as the tram pulled into the station. "Do you object?"

Hollis looked mournfully at the dark city and sighed. "Only to being forced to pretend we barely know each other for the next few hours. Come on, let's get this over with and get home."

She almost asked whose quarters they were crashing in tonight, but the grim line of Hollis's mouth said that a question like that would get the mission called off. Hollis was here only for her.

For the first time ever, she smiled as she entered Kydell.

30
HOLLIS

HOLLIS STROKED THE BACK OF Rowena's hand with his thumb as they walked towards the vine-covered palazzo on the upper hill of Kydell. The path of crushed shells crunched under their feet and the sound echoed off the painted metal fence around the property. Patterns of leaves, flowers, and faces had been laser cut into the upper section to make the fencing more ornate, more elegant than the neighbor's fences.

Another little show of privilege and excess, in case someone had forgotten who owned the property.

A car drove past on the dirt road and Hollis reached to pull Rowena closer. :Hand/Back:

Tight muscles relaxed under his touch.

Ancestors, keep me strong. That was erotic. Hot as a solar flare and twice as dangerous.

"Quite the crowd," Rowena murmured as they entered through the gate.

Kydellians in bright yellow-and-orange single-shouldered wraps were mingling with wealthy visitors in suits like Hollis's in an ornate entry plaza lined with palm trees and imported marble. Long hair seemed to be preferred for women, and dresses of metallic gray and icy blues.

None of them captivated his imagination as much as Rowena.

"Of all the things we could do tonight…" Hollis tried not to think too much about it. Skin to skin contact allowed communication the grounders wouldn't be able to trace, but it meant Rowena was close to his thoughts. Still, the Jhandarmi could handle this without him, right?

:Wrong.: Rowena glanced over her shoulder, starlight glimmering on the golden accents. She probably wouldn't know a come-hither look if she saw it, but she knew how to give one. :You're expected at the party.:

"But think of all the fun things we could do with a night to ourselves," he whispered in her ear as they walked toward the courtyard strung with lights over carved pink stone and flowering bushes.

A fountain carved to look like a woman in a flowing cape burbled happily as they passed through the artificial oasis.

"I'm sure you have plans," Rowena said dryly.

"Mmmm." So many plans.

She smiled. "Do your plans get me information?"

"Maybe not the information you need for this project," he allowed, "but I think you'd enjoy them."

She put a hand to her face and turned. It wasn't Rowena looking at him anymore. The mask made her nose wider, her cheekbones sharper, her chin rounder and slightly dimpled. He stepped back as he assessed the changes.

:That bad?:

:It's not you.: He was staring at a stranger. Not an ugly one, certainly, but not Rowena. His hand dropped from her back.

:I still have a pretty smile.: She smiled, but it didn't touch her eyes.

:We might need to make note of this in our reports.:

:What?:

"A pretty smile isn't enough." He raised a shoulder in a shrug. :I feel nothing.: Except for the sting Rowena felt as he rejected her. :It's not your smile. I love your smile. But it's not you anymore:

If he hadn't known already, this would have been the final volley of a losing war. He was in love with Rowena Lee and only Rowena Lee. No one was ever going to replace her.

:Hand/Hand: He reached for Rowena in the darkness as they crossed the empty courtyard. :I'm sorry I don't like your mask.:

She sighed. "I hope my dress doesn't make me stand out too much."

He squeezed her hand. "Who cares if you upstage the locals? You look fantastic, and you're with me. That's all that matters."

The look she gave him would have had him reaching for a weapon a year ago. Now it was just a challenge. Or an invitation to play.

"What a lovely view." He could watch Rowena all day. Or night.

:A fortress on a cracking hill overlooking the city? How cliché is that?: She grabbed his hand, and as an afterthought sent, :Hand/Hand:

:Hand/Arm—It's not a fortress, it's a mansion. The outer wall was built using strips of a hull from one of the landing ships famous in this area. I researched it this morning.: With her hand tucked in the crook of his arm, they walked up the shallow incline. Up ahead there were bright lights and a dazzling crush of people exiting the long lines of waiting cars.

:That's not a real hull.: Rowena's disgust was a sour taste in his mouth. :Did you scan it? No radiation, carbon-scoring, or pit marks. If that's not recycled metal I'm a fogging Si—: Her eyes went wide.

Hollis smiled down at her. "Silar?"

A hint of Rowena's real smile peeked impishly through the mask. "I'm sure I meant it as a compliment."

"Liar."

An image of a scoreboard appeared in his mind with both their names, and one point to him.

He sent Rowena a revised vision of the scoreboard with their names together and the grounders on the opposing side. "What's your name tonight?"

"Rose Lauren, buyer of things for the rich and wealthy—or I'd like to be." She put on a bright smile that was so painfully fake, he had to smother another laugh. "Keep that up," she said, "and we won't get far tonight."

:Far? You keep leaving openings like that, Rowena, and I'm going to start taking them.:

:Focus!:

:I am.:

:On work.: She looked at him with a suppressed smile.

Hollis looked in her eyes. Tonight was going to be so much fun. "I—"

—*love you*. The words died unsaid as a burly man in a high-collared shirt stopped him.

"You in the picture line?" The man nodded to the main stairs under the lights.

Only if he had a gun pointed at him. "I think not. Hollis Silar and my Plus One." He pulled the invitation out of his pocket and held it out for inspection.

"Rose Lauren, the plus one!" Rowena actually managed a giggle. It was terrifying. :I'm trying.:

:To anyone who doesn't know you, I'm sure it's convincing.:

:And you?:

:I know you. The last time you giggled you were drunk-on-tired and flirting with Perrin.: The memory was clear as canon fire; he'd been jealous and not sure which of the pair he wanted paying attention to him.

:I wasn't flirting. He started a tickle fight. I can't remember how.:

The guard looked over the invite. "Everything's in order. If you don't want pictures you can take the side door." He pointed behind them to a small entrance on the side of the courtyard. "Go in, take a right. The elevator's on the left."

"Thank you so much." Hollis smiled and threw a flirtatious wink in for good measure. :When we have free time, remind me to sit you down and explain what the rest of humanity considers flirting.:

:I know you consider breathing to be flirting.: Her red skirt swirled as they stepped into the elevator.

Hollis helped her sweep it out of the way of the doors—and then the walls caught his attention. One wall was nothing but a mirror, and for the first time he saw himself standing with Rowena in his arms. Or almost-Rowena. "We look good together."

Rowena looked up. "We do."

"Red really is your color."

"Thank you." The door slid open with a soft shush, leaving them on a wide landing between a curving, marble staircase illuminated by soft blue lights. :Time to go to work. Divide and conquer?:

:Too obvious. Let's stick together and see who approaches me.: He ran a hand across his chest where the device would have been if Rowena hadn't intervened. :Up or down?:

:Down would lead to the formal garden out back. Up probably leads to the main party.:

:Up it is then.: They followed the staircase up into an open, high-ceilinged room filled with people. Mossy yellows and deep greens were the color of choice for most of the out-of-town dresses, but there were flashes of maroon and purple.

"I'm wearing the wrong color," Rowena murmured.

"You look perfect."

Waiters circulated around the curved room and its decorative pillars with platters of drinks Hollis didn't trust. He watched the ebb and flow of the crowd until he noticed the iceberg they were crashing against. A pair of blonds, a man and a woman, standing together. Her eyes were winter blue as she surveyed the room like a frozen queen. His eyes were a stormy gray.

"He has a very punchable face," Rowena murmured as she put her back to the pair. Her eyes were on Hollis as she put a piece of fruit in her mouth with a saucy wink.

"Who is he?" Hollis asked with a dazzling smile as if he were flirting with her, not gathering intel.

"The infamous Doctor Long. Looks enough like a Baular that I ran a bioscan on him yesterday. The vitals don't match Mal's records, but..." She shrugged.

He could see why she would. Mal had been underfed the last time Hollis had seen him, and there'd been hatred coloring his view. They'd barely been adults. But if Baular had lived, it was possible he would have grown to be like this man, taller and more muscular. Broader in the shoulder but with a fighter's light movements.

Rowena cleared her throat. "I am feeling forgotten down here."

Hollis looked down.

"He's handsome, isn't he?"

"He wouldn't fill out that dress as well as you," Hollis said with a wink. "Should we make an approach?"

"Might as well." Rowena finished the last grape in her hand. "I'm bored. Let's go bump their shields and see who shouts."

A few weeks ago, this would have been more fun. "You realize I might have to flirt with them?"

Rowena lifted her bare shoulder in a tempting shrug. "You smile and over half the people in the room usually fall in love. I didn't expect that to change just because you weren't planning to fall in love with them in return. Go be your combustible self and see if you can get some info from Sonya."

"And you?"

"Will be right there beside you." Her nose wrinkled. "Not punching them." Her eyes narrowed. "Probably."

Hollis rubbed his chest again, where a small lump of metal hidden under a synthaflesh patch mimicked the device he was supposed to have coming online. He reached out and brushed a hand through Rowena's loose hair, enjoying the sensation and sharing information at the same time.

:Orders to act gregarious, uninhibited, and social?: Her lips tightened as she suppressed a smile. :Wouldn't it be easier to tell you to be yourself?:

:Blonds were never my favorite.: He wrinkled his nose in a fair approximation of her favorite dismissive gesture and turned to get a better view. "Let's go make some new friends, my love."

They started walking in a long arc around the edge of the room.

"As I was saying," Rowena said as if they'd just dropped a conversation for a moment, "the price was outrageous.

Everyone thinks their family heirlooms are worth a fortune, but your dead auntie's necklace that was mass produced and worn by everyone on two continents doesn't make it a priceless treasure."

"It's Icedell though," Hollis picked up the fake argument. "It's rare there."

"Not the same thing. You can't buy good taste I suppose." Rowena looked over at Sonya Lethe in her glacier-blue gown with touches of silver and opal on her skin.

Hollis slowed, trying to get a read on the situation. It had been years since he felt such a stark lack of attraction. Mentally, he'd prepared for being angry with Sonya Lethe, or even annoyed, but this was something else. A complete absence of interest.

He snapped his fingers and turned to Rowena. "There's a phrase I'm thinking of, forget where I heard it, something about attraction limits? Attraction bias?"

Rowena frowned, looking genuinely puzzled.

"Artificial attractants? Maybe?"

"Oh!" Dark glee filled her eyes. "As part of advertising? It's a tactic where you stage something to be appealing even though it wouldn't incite any interest alone."

He nodded. "That's what I'm thinking of."

Rowena was smart enough to know why. She smiled. "As a marketing strategy, I don't find it has much to recommend it." She turned back to their quarry and started them moving again on an intercept course. The fly-by with cryptic insults was a classic Lee tactic that had started plenty of fights. "The problem with staging artificial interest is that it's so obvious to an educated audience. There's the framing technique."

She brushed against his shoulder and he saw a highlighted view of Sonya Lethe framed by a large, arching window.

"The cheap embellishments."

Fake pearls on the hem of Sonya's gown and the opaline paint on her skin.

"The complete lack of substance."

Their steps led them directly to Sonya.

Hollis laughed and made eye contact. He nodded, and turned back to Rowena, acting as if they were simply waiting for the other couple to meander past. "I can't believe anyone would fall for that."

Rowena shrugged nonchalantly. "For anyone with a decent education, it won't work. But you'd be amazed how many people will buy something just because it shines."

Sonya Lethe cleared her throat.

Hollis looked at her again, still smiling. "Is there a problem?"

"It's considered rude to have a conversation and not include everyone in the circle." Sonya's artificially perfect eyebrow went up in a look she probably thought was condemning.

Rowena sent him a memory of covering her eyes and sighing heavily as a cadet failed something basic.

"We weren't excluding anyone," Hollis said. "We were walking towards the balcony and waiting for you to move on." He gestured at the narrow space between him and Rowena. "Please, don't let us keep you."

:Friendly and outgoing,: Rowena reminded him.

:I don't like blonds.:

:Make like Marshall and fake it.:

Oh no... He looked at Rowena's impish grin. :You're wicked.:

There was the tiniest nod of acknowledgement.

:Marshall never had to fake it with me.:

Rowena covered a laugh with a cough.

She was so much more interesting than the rest of the room.

Reluctantly, Hollis turned back to Lethe with a huge fake smile. "Of course," he said out loud, "I've never been one to refuse a brace of blonds."

"They probably don't want to indulge in your fantasies," Rowena said, leaving a wide opening for Lethe to fall into.

Sonya laughed prettily, head tilted back, eyes wide, like she'd learned to laugh from one of the mock training vids the crew had passed around called How To Be A Grounder. "A fantasy?"

"A very erotic fantasy," Hollis said with a smile. Flirting with strangers was so boring. :You ruined me,: he told Rowena.

:You wouldn't have liked flirting with her anyway.:

"But we can put those plans on hold until I learn your names," he continued.

"Hollis!" Rowena said in mock shock. "Don't you recognize Sonya Lethe?"

"The?" He looked between the two women in surprise. "The Sonya Lethe? The one whose face is in every tram station?"

Sonya beamed, obviously delighted to be properly recognized. "I am that Sonya."

"How delightful." Hollis nodded to her. "I am Commander Hollis Silar from Enclave and this is Rose Lauren, a new friend of mine who I met in Tarrin, but... where are you from?" he asked Rowena, to establish her cover.

"All over, but Narrowley is where I rent an apartment," Rowena said referring to a city-state almost completely loyal to Lethe, with even less of a Jhandarmi presence than Kydell. "I'm a private buyer. Would you like my card?"

Sonya's smile turned chilly. "That won't be necessary." Her hand slid across Hollis's arm and he repressed an urge to shake the woman loose.

:Keep a smile on,: Rowena said.

:Can't escape. I've met boarding parties with less grip.: One of them being a Lee infiltration squad, now that he thought of it. He'd shaken them loose, but Lethe was sticking to him like a bad dream after dawn.

"A commander from Enclave?" Sonya sounded intrigued. "I've always been curious what happens there."

"Paperwork, mostly," Hollis said honestly as he kept his body loose; she'd probably notice the tension if he reacted. :I need a shower.:

Rowena's amusement at his suffering made it easier to smile.

Sonya shook her head. "I'm sure there's so much more you do. You should tell me all about it."

"Oh." Hollis cocked his head to the side as he frowned and brushed a hand against Sonya's face. Despite all expectation, she wasn't slimy. "My work is so boring. You, on the other hand, are absolutely fascinating. Running a business empire practically by yourself. Why don't you talk? I'm an excellent listener." He dropped his voice, playing at seduction.

Rowena started coughing again.

"Something wrong?" he asked.

She shook her head. "No, not at all." It was a wheeze hiding a laugh. "If you'll excuse me, I'll just step out onto the balcony. Get some fresh air."

Thoughts of Sonya Lethe being a pile of frogs painted as a human filled Hollis's mind when Rowena patted his hand.

:We're being terribly immature.:

:I won't tell if you won't.:

"A perfect idea," Sonya said. "Malcolm, darling, would you be so good as to wait with Miss Lauren? I'd hate for her to be alone."

Not as much as Hollis hated the idea of her being near the blond bastard.

"Rose…" There was no way to politely say anything and keep their cover. He looked at Dr. Long; the man looked too much like Baular for his comfort. "Keep her company, but if I come back and you say she's yours, I'll kill you. Do we understand each other?"

"Hollis!" Rowena glared at him.

Long's expression became guarded, jaw tightening in anger and eyes narrowing slightly. It wasn't the look of a man who hadn't considered whisking Rowena away.

"We'll all be happy with who we go home with tonight," Sonya said, patting his chest over where the implant should have been. "I'm certain of that."

:Ewww.: Rowena's disgust didn't touch her face, but he felt it all the same.

"I'll be perfectly polite," Long said through gritted teeth. "And I mislike the suggestion that I would do anything to hurt this woman."

"A minor prejudice," Rowena said as she stepped closer to Long. "Ignore him. He's only possessive on the first date."

"This is your first date?" Sonya sounded surprised.

"It is," Rowena said. "We just met at a club in Tarrin this week. Work's been exhausting and Hollis said he'd heard of a party from—"

"Some friend or another," Hollis quickly filled in.

Rowena nodded. "He promised me a free trip to Kydell and a night at the resort. We were both so excited we forgot it was monsoon season!"

They both laughed.

Sonya looked concerned.

Long looked disgusted.

Covering her mouth to hide another laughing cough, Rowena said, "Don't have too much fun while I'm away." She turned away from him, Long trailing behind her. :Get the info.:

Reluctantly, he looked down at Sonya Lethe. Why'd it have to be a blonde?

31
MALCOLM

AN EVENING BREEZE BLEW OFF the coast, bringing the smell of the sea and the rowdies' night market to the balcony. Malcolm looked out at the sea of yellow lanterns that surrounded the stalls in the distance filled with grilled meat and the seductive aroma of sizzling onions. One of the great mysteries of life was why the wealthy insisted on serving bland food when the local street food of any given city-state was delicious.

Rose Lauren walked up beside him and leaned out over the ornate stone balustrade to look at the decorated gardens below.

Taking a safe spot with his back to the doorframe where he could watch both the luckless woman and the room where Sonya had run off with the redhead, Malcolm tried to tamp down on his annoyance. Sonya pushing him over for Silar wasn't the problem. It was the man's attention to Rose that was biting at his nerves.

It was an irrational response, and uncontrollable. The sultry sea air combined with an almost-familiar face made the strange woman seem too much like someone he had known before he moved to Descent. Someone he'd never see again, unless life dealt him another cruel twist of fate.

And still he found his gaze tracing her face, desperately looking for a familiar shine in a stranger's eyes.

The focus of his attention turned, elegant red dress swirling around her, gold paintwork on her body catching the light. "Thank you for staying with me. I don't know anyone in the area."

"I'd say my pleasure, but your lover might object." Malcolm tried to keep the sardonic bite out of his tone, but wasn't sure he succeeded.

"He's not my lover," she said with an easy smile.

Malcolm looked back at the closed door where Sonya had hidden her newest boytoy. "That's for the best. Sonya isn't very good at sharing."

"And you are?" Miss Lauren moved so she was closer, but still out of reach.

"Sonya and I are work associates." *Miss.* He focused on that. She was a stranger. An unknown quantity. Not a friend. Not a confidant. Not someone he should be drawn to at all.

Miss Lauren raised a dark eyebrow in question. "I'm surprised. I know her reputation and I could see her keeping a lover that hated her, but not a business associate. She must want something you have desperately."

He tensed in alarm. There was no way that woman could know how he felt about Sonya. "I'm sure you're mistaken."

"Really?" Miss Lauren pushed herself up and sat on the railing, feet dangling and skirt sliding so the slit showed a long stretch of smooth, tanned skin flecked with gold embellishments. "I make a living off knowing how much people are invested in something. Antiques and information are only worth as much as someone is willing to pay. A hint of disgust or lust makes all the difference. And you look at Sonya Lethe like she's some bug you found at the bottom of your soup bowl."

"I'm sure I don't." No one could read his face, and there was no such thing as mind readers, no matter what mad conspiracy theories about the spacers in Enclave said.

Rose Lauren chuckled. "You do though. Your lip jumps up in a sneer every time she poses. Your eyes tighten when she talks. You tense when she reaches for you. Has no one else noticed?"

"No." His teeth ground together.

"Then I'll keep your secret."

Malcolm frowned at her. "For what price?"

"Oh, we're friends. Why be crass and discuss things like money?" Her smile was playful.

"We're not friends. And your lover sounded intent on keeping it that way." He'd seen them as they walked in, eyes on each other. They'd laughed and touched, leaned in together and divided the universe in two parts: them and everyone else. If all of that was the result of a few hours together and chemistry, he was envious.

The woman moved, looking out over the city, caught in the moonlight. After a day spent with Sonya, the lack of pretense was endearing, if not encouraging.

"What do you want?" Malcolm asked again.

"What does everyone want?"

"Power."

She laughed, a genuine chortle as if that was the most ridiculous thing she'd ever heard. "Oh, see, now I know you really are from Descent. The accent isn't pure, but the ava-rice is. I swear it's something in the genes. Show a person from Descent a group, and their first thought is always: how can I be in charge?"

"Why shouldn't I?" Malcolm asked, walking over to stand by the railing close to her.

She gave him a speculating look, leaning back a little so the drop to the ground yawned at her back. "With power comes responsibility and paperwork. It means never having a free day again."

"It also means the power to protect the people you love."

Something terrible crossed her eyes, changing her from a beautiful dreamer to a dark dream. "What a beautiful illusion you enjoy," she said, speculation dropping from her voice. "Power doesn't protect anything. At best, it's an agreement between two enemies to not hit as hard as you could. At its worst, it's a poison. It will take everything good in your life and turn it to ash."

"Is that the voice of experience, or a threat?"

"Neither." The moment passed and she straightened on the rail, smiling and becoming again a simple socialite. "I'm just very good at noticing little things."

Just. It was a filler word uncommon off the third continent, and even then it hadn't been common until the spacers settled in Enclave.

"Where did you say you were from?"

"Where does it sound like I'm from?" She didn't exaggerate her accent to help him out.

Malcolm narrowed his eyes. "Coastal Descent, but you've spent a lot of time on the third continent."

She smiled. "And your accent says born on the islands, educated in Descent, and you work there, but someone close to you hasn't adopted the local pronunciations."

His parents. "That's a lot to pick up from an accent."

Another smile, this one bordering on rueful. "You have been in public with Sonya Lethe a lot recently. The Lethes have deep pockets and lots of buyers."

Everything fell into place. "So, you're here hoping to make friends with Sonya through me?"

Rose lifted a shoulder in a shrug. "I brought a gift for her."

"The redhead?" *Silar.* The same name had been on the list Sonya had given him. It was hard to imagine that was coincidence.

"He has a reputation in Tarrin. A lover on every street, and a thing for brunettes. It wasn't hard to get his attention. He keeps things casual, never lets his relationships get serious, never says no to someone interested." There was a little hitch in her voice.

Malcolm latched on to the opening. "You're close to him?"

"We just met."

True. "You don't care for him?"

"Not more than I'd care for anyone else I suppose. I know he's playing for fun."

Lie. But what part of it was a lie?

"What are you getting from Lethe?" she asked. "Money? Information? Attention?"

"If I tell you what I get, will you make a counter-offer?"

She shrugged again. "Maybe. You aren't quite the antiques I usually deal in, but that doesn't mean there isn't interest. You're a well-educated man working for a very small company. Lethe wants you, and that means others have taken an interest."

"I'm not on the open market."

"Is that what your mother says?" Rose seemed more interested in the shadows visible in the garden under the strings of lights than in an answers.

Malcolm took a moment to think. "My mother?"

"Just a rumor," Rose said, skirt fluttering between the columns of the balustrade like a flag. "You're an unattached heir with land and a minor title. If you don't pick someone for yourself, eventually a broker will be called. Is that what Lethe is to you?" She turned back to him with fierce interest. "A way of putting off your family duties?"

"I've never heard it described as a family duty," he said, throat tightening. "What an alien way of looking at the world." Rose Lauren had figured out more about him than anyone in nearly five years. He wished it meant something more than it did.

Her face gave nothing away. He was certain he didn't know her, but the way she spoke, the timbre of her voice, her word choice...

He was reading into the situation. Wanting to see a friend where there was none. Desperately dreaming of a brief return to a time when he wasn't alone, drifting aimlessly as he tried to stay alive.

"We're all very different people." Static sparked between them as she touched his arm and dropped herself to the ground. "Won't you excuse me, I'm just going to step into the garden for a moment."

"I'll come with you."

The look on her face was one of suffused shock and frustration.

"Sonya said I should keep you company." And he wanted to see what had caught her attention.

Her hand moved, brushing across her thigh as if she were reaching for something that wasn't there. He'd seen the move on Descent in the training gyms and in the few street battles between rival corporations when things went wrong in public. Someone had trained her to use a weapon.

Interesting.

"You haven't given me your sales pitch yet," Malcolm said, using tactics he'd nearly forgotten. Everyone at Bennu tended to go along with what he suggested; even Sonya agreed with him.

But Rose Lauren was actively trying to shake him.

She sighed and the multi-colored lights of the party sparkled in her eyes. "Fine. Why not?" Gathering the skirt of her gown, she swept past him, back into the main room.

Malcolm fell into her wake, appreciating the crowd parting for her in a way they wouldn't move for Sonya.

Rose looked like a woman out of someone's dream—possibly a good dream, possibly a nightmare—but she moved with the sure confidence that everything was going to go her way.

Dropping his drink on a tray, he followed her down the stairs, the silk train of her dress flowing like blood on the marble, and into the beautifully lit garden.

Rose stopped and scanned the shadows between the trees.

"See anything?"

"A rare butterfly," she said in an obvious lie.

He chuckled and followed her across the grass.

Instead of heading to the table filled with delicate snacks like most of the guests, she moved purposefully towards the darkness beyond.

"What are you looking for?"

"Something that's not here," she said as the trees devoured the light.

"Sounds impossible to find."

She stopped. "No, actually, it's quite easy." She was looking at something hidden by the gloom. "Doctor Long, do you have a phone with you?"

"Of course." He pulled his out and switched it on to provide a light.

A guard lay prone on the ground, head titled at an uncomfortable angle.

Rose dropped to a crouch and pressed two fingers to his neck in a professional fashion.

"Antiquities dealer, information merchant, marriage broker, and medical doctor? You are a woman of diverse talents, Miss Rose."

"It's basic first aid training." She stood up and scanned the darker shadows.

Probably. But looking for trouble and keeping calm while doing it weren't.

"Care to tell me what I've wandered into?" Malcolm asked.

"No." Miss Lauren's skirt flared around her legs like living fire as she turned. "I invited you to stay upstairs. This isn't your concern."

"How is it yours?"

For a moment the expression on her face was frozen, as if she'd forgotten she wasn't supposed to be running someone's security, and then a smile bloomed on her face. "You really aren't an art aficionado, are you? This party tonight has a wealth of rare paintings on display. They are magnificent, and if I can convince the owner to sell, my commission will be enough that I'd never need to consider working for Lethe or any other powerful family again. If those paintings wind up on the black market, however, I don't get a commission. I don't deal with illegal or stolen goods, and I don't like people who do."

Malcolm stepped back with a nod. "I'm sorry. I misread the situation. Is there anything I can do to help?"

"Do you know anyone here?" she asked.

"Not as such."

"Can you name the host? Any of the prominent guests? Do you know who is here as private security?"

"I—"

"—don't," she finished for him. "Which means you'd go around making a fuss and worrying the guests. I'll go find the appropriate people and then meet you upstairs. By the time Lethe is done with Silar"—she spat the name like a curse—"I'll be back on the balcony chatting about the price of gemstones or whatever it is your family collects. Your reputation with Sonya will be safe and my future secure. We'll all be happy. Except those thieves." She tossed her black hair behind her and strode off like a fairytale warrior going to slay a giant.

He looked down at the fallen guard and flipped his phone in thought.

"That woman is very passionate about art, or very good at lying," he murmured.

Part of him wanted to chase after her, for the adrenaline rush if nothing else. No wonder the stupid redhead was acting possessive; twenty minutes with her was more exciting than anything he'd done in years.

But he'd chased that impulse before.

Nearly gotten himself killed falling in love with the wrong woman, and he'd lost her in the end anyway. It was a tempting path full of racing hearts and breathless wonder, but he wasn't going to run down it again.

Malcolm went to the desert table, selected the most recognizable foods, and went back upstairs to let trouble happen without him.

32
ROWENA

:PROBLEMS?: HOLLIS'S VOICE WAS a soft brush against her mind as she rushed through the darkness, following the faintest trail of warm footprints through the orchards.

:Plenty. That man reminds me too much of Mal, there's a security guard down, and someone here has an explosive.: She felt Hollis come on high alert. :How are you contacting me?:

:Look down.:

It took her a moment, but she finally saw the telekyen thread glowing red in her augmented vision, snaking down the side of the building and running through the grass to her. :Clever.:

:I thought so. Especially since I checked the room I left you in first. You wandered.: There was a hint of censure from the Guardian. A warning shot.

Time for a feint. :How are things going with Lethe?:

:She came at him like a warship on its final run,: Hollis said, quoting something. The image of nishu book with hearts drawn in the margins passed between them.

Rowena rolled her eyes. :There are books out there that aren't written in crayon by concussed cadets. You should try one.: She turned down the outside of the building where the gardener's shed blocked the way except for a narrow space.

:Ro...: Hollis was picking up enough of the situation to object.

:Where are you exactly?:

:Top floor on the half roof overlooking the city. Gorgeous view, except you're about to walk out of my line of sight.:

Rowena looked up and saw him silhouetted against stormy clouds that reflected the city lights. :You can't play sniper from up there anyway. Not with Lethe nearby.:

:Want to bet?:

:No. What is she doing anyway?:

There was a flash memory of Sonya talking about the importance of shoes in politics. :She's stalling. The device is supposed to make me feel protective, admiring, and smitten, or something like that. I'm bored.:

:So sorry.: Rowena stepped around the shed, carefully keeping her skirt off the ground and away from protruding nails.

:She's asking my opinion on Descent politics.:

:Give her a glowing review of Marshall and see if she kills you.:

The memory of Hollis stumbling back after a solid kick to his midsection came to her. :I thought you loved me.:

Rowena ignored him as she approached a group of grounders dressed in rowdy clothes. Plain cloth and the smell of the sea was a good giveaway, but Jae's voice was all she needed to confirm it.

"We go in here, I'll handle it," he was saying.

"We should all be there," someone who sounded younger argued.

Slipping off the nanite mask and tucking it out of sight, Rowena cleared her throat.

They moved as a group, turning to her and stepping into a close huddle.

"Hi, Jae." She waved. "Remember me?"

He frowned and then stepped forward holding a small handlight. "What are you doing here?"

"Intelligence gathering. You?"

The light swept over her and there was a murmur of approval from the men behind him. Jae waved a hand for silence. "Who are you with?"

"Someone who wants to see Kydell safe."

He looked up at the building. "Sonya Lethe is here stirring up people with her Imperial Heritage propaganda."

"She's on the top roof waiting for a show and looking downtown," Rowena said. "Why is that, do you think?"

There was another murmur from the mob, this one unhappy.

One of the men leaned forward and whispered something in Jae's ear.

Jae shook his head. "We're friends, aren't we?"

Rowena nodded.

"I'll handle it from here, then." Jae held out a hand and took something from a large man, then let the others fade into the night.

"You left the guard alive," Rowena said, "so I don't think you're planning on getting revenge. So what is this? Petty mischief?"

Jae held up the package. "Our boy Braun, the tall one, someone bought him a few rounds of beer and started talking about how this is all the Jhandarmi's fault. Handed him this as soon as he agreed."

"A bomb for the Jhandarmi office?" The political fallout would be significant, especially since the Jhandarmi was allied with the fleet. :Get Sonya to talk about the Jhandarmi.:

:Why?:

She let Hollis see what she was looking at as Jae watched her. "Why didn't you go there?"

He shrugged. "Jhandarmi have never been a problem for us. They aren't the dockside brutes and they don't give us trouble when we travel. Lethe's security does."

The package was an explosive, she was certain of it.

:Sonya says she's indebted to the Jhandarmi,: Hollis reported. :So very fond of them. They try so hard and she wishes she could support them better. She's about as sincere as Carver when he says he's sorry I'm filing the reports while he goes home early.:

:Not even trying to fake it?:

:I think she trusts the device.:

:Has she scanned for it yet?:

:When we came to the roof someone gave her a nod. That was probably it.:

Jae cocked his head to the side. "You thinking about screaming?"

"No, just checking with someone." She tapped her ear. "I have a comm set."

"I didn't hear you say anything."

"Didn't need to, they were feeding me information. I—" She stopped as thunder rolled across the sky. It didn't feel like thunder. It felt like—

:Rowena, did you touch the shield?:

:No.: She ran a full scan. :That's not fleet tech. That was a mass teleport. Lethe is here in force.:

Several of the more imaginative Silar curses ran through her mind. :What happens if she accidentally falls off the roof at high velocity?:

Rowena smirked.

"What?" Jase asked.

"I know what was planned. Braun, how smart is he?"

Jae's expression grew stony. "He's good at what he does."

"But he wouldn't question a friend. Wouldn't find it odd for a stranger to hand him something, and wouldn't blame that stranger if he got caught, would he?" That's why Jae was here. He was protecting the other fools.

"He's a bit trusting," Jae said. He lifted the bag up. "This is meant for a bit of fun. A way to remind people we're angry. They're cutting our wages, refusing to pay for hours worked, and then rounding up people who don't take dock jobs. Anywhere else it'd be called slavery, but here the Pure Waters allow it. They'll let Lethe come here and party, even though her family was never on the ship to Kydell. She's got money. That's all they care about. Meantime we have kids going hungry and getting sick 'cause they're living in the swamp during flood season."

That scanned. "Lethe just brought in more troops. Think. What would happen if you went to the Jhandarmi offices tonight?"

Jae sucked in his cheeks as he glared angrily at the building. "I knew it was a trap. We didn't go there for a reason. I'm not stupid."

"You're not cruel either. All these people are looking for is an excuse," she said taking a step forward. "Any reason to attack."

:Sonya's mentioned clearing the streets of vermin twice,: Hollis reported. :I can see troops in staging areas. They teleported at least a hundred soldiers in.:

"If you do this, all the rowdies are in danger."

"And if I don't?" Jae asked. "You think it'll get better if I stand here and let this happen?"

Rowena hesitated, her implant running calculations. There wasn't room in Enclave for another hundred thousand people, or even another five hundred. "There's a way around this. There always is."

"I don't see one."

"I don't either, but that's why I'm here wearing a stupid dress and smiling at people I want to stab in the eye." She took a deep breath. "I usually don't have backup wherever I am, but you came and rescued me before I got a knife in my back. I'll remember that."

:WHAT?: Hollis turned his full attention to her. :You didn't mention that.:

She gave him a mental shove. "I can help you, the rowdies, everyone if you let me. I need just a little more time. I'll find you food, clothes, medicine. I have contacts who develop medications."

"They'll deliver to the swamps?" Jae laughed.

"They'll deliver anywhere in the twelve planets in this solar system."

Jae's smile froze and fell. Slowly the light of understanding dawned. He looked up the stars obscured by clouds. "I've heard rumors. Never thought to see one of your kind. Is that how you vanished earlier?"

"Teleport," Rowena said. "It's a tech-assisted form of transit, and we're not the only ones who use it."

He opened his mouth and was interrupted by a shout. The huddle of men was rushing back to them.

"Jae, there's guards on the streets wearing Lethe colors. It's going to be a brawl." The speaker looked at her. "Who's she?"

"A friend," Jae said.

At the edge of hearing there was a shout of command and the sound of cobblestones cracking under the weight of a troop transport.

"How many rowdies are in the city proper?" Rowena asked.

"Only us," Jae said. "After this morning I told everyone to keep to the trees, but there's no quick way out of here now."

Someone moaned in despair. There were whispers of fear, doubt, anger.

:I'm teleporting the rowdies out.:

:What?: Hollis's frustration was cut with a commander's pure battle evaluation. :Can you get them all out safely?:

:Yes, but I'll need you to hold an opening for me if the shield starts to close.:

:Done. Be safe.:

:Promise.:

Rowena looked at Jae with her best smile, the one that made her cadets cry. "Why don't I walk you boys home?"

"What, you think they'll let you through because you have a pretty dress?" one of the men asked. "Lethe won't care about that."

"She can fight," Jae said. "Nearly as good as me."

Better, when augmented, but there wasn't a need to undermine him. "I know a short cut. Is that tree where we were this morning a good location?"

Jae frowned and shook his head. "Too well known."

"What about the islands in the inland river? You have settlements there, right?"

"How'd you know?" a voice asked.

"Yes or no?" Rowena demanded as Hollis sent her an image of Lethe troops nearing the palazzo.

Jae nodded. "Can you take all—"

The ground shifted and they started to sink in the island's muddy shore.

"—at once." Jae stopped and looked around. "Everyone's here?"

An insect chirped in the sudden cessation of sound. All the chatter of the party and music was replaced by the quiet nighttime whispers of the jungle.

"Everyone that was standing nearby," Rowena said. "You can do a headcount."

Jae took a steadying breath and surveyed his men. "Yeah..."

"What'd she do?" The loudest speaker stepped forward, finding a rock to stand on. "How'd you do that?"

"Practice and really good technology. I'll look for you here in a few days."

Jae grabbed her arm. "Where you going?"

"Back to Kydell."

"Why? There's nothing but a fight back there."

"And my team," she said. "I left someone watching Lethe and gathering intel. I need to get him out safe." And the shield was settling back over the city.

Jae let go. "You can come back if you need a safe place tonight. We've got some buildings up in the trees. Smells a bit at low tide, but you'll be safe here so you can rest or whatever."

"Thank you, that's a very kind offer. I'll remember it."

Hollis tugged at her. :Sonya is going downstairs to look for you and Long.:

"I'll see you soon," she promised the rowdies as she teleported.

There was an opening in the corner of a hall with lax security. Rowena landed, force teleported the mud off her shoes, checked her implant's charge, and dropped everything back to null as the security came back on.

She hurried up the curving staircase, rounded the corner of a narrow landing, and almost walked straight into Dr. Long.

"Ah, there you are." He held up a champagne glass as he tucked a scrap of paper into his jacket pocket. His gaze traced the contours of her face as if seeing her for the first time and trying to remember the details. "Was everything settled to your satisfaction?"

"Oh, yes." She took the proffered glass. "Someone else had already noticed the problem so there wasn't much for me to do. I hope you'll excuse my behavior. I get very wrapped up in work."

He smiled as if they were sharing a joke. "I do the same."

:Incoming,: Hollis said. :Get your game face on.:

Rowena stiffened. She'd forgotten about the face mask.

Coughing, she turned away and fixed it in place. When she turned back, Long was watching her with the same solicitous smile. Either he hadn't noticed the changes in the dim lighting under the shadows of the stairs, or he was one of those people who had trouble recognizing faces. It was a gift, whichever it was.

"Feeling well?"

"A tickle in my throat." She forced a smile.

Sonya Lethe's artificial laugh drifted down from above.

Long's face shifted through resentment, frustration, and a touch of anger. He looked at her and raised an eyebrow. "Do you want to go home with him tonight?"

"Who? Hollis?"

Long paused for a second, as if he were surprised by the name, then nodded.

"I wouldn't have come with him if I planned to leave him here, but..." She shrugged it off. There wasn't a firm extraction plan. There hadn't been time for one. Bad dates in the fleet tended to end with an abrupt goodbye and teleporting home. "Would you like to take Sonya home?" she asked.

The look Long gave her was almost pitying. "One of us should go home happy, don't you think?"

"You think you can pry Sonya away from her new toy?" Rowena motioned for him to proceed. "If you manage that, I'll buy you dinner next time we meet." Or toss him a ration bar when he was stuck in some Jhandarmi prison. She found herself smiling despite her reservations. Anyone who disliked Sonya Lethe couldn't be all bad.

"It's so sad," Sonya's voice cut in, a dull blade against the ears.

Rowena could hear Hollis saying something in a placating tone as he and Sonya drew nearer.

Long leaned in close as they came into view. "You're going to owe me dinner."

He was uncomfortably close. Acting unaccountably familiar. Maybe it was a grounder thing, or maybe Long didn't understand personal space, but they were rapidly closing the distance between Acquaintance and Intimate.

"Maybe. We'll see how good you are." Rowena stepped back, aware that she was in a precarious position on the edge of the steps with no graceful retreat available.

:What's happening?" Hollis asked as he caught her unease.

:Long wants Sonya back.: And I want him gone.

Hollis's smile appeared like the sun after a typhoon. "My friends! How are you? Were you terribly bored, dear?" He dropped Sonya's arm and swept past Long to come to Rowena's side. There was no mistaking the intentional maneuver that put Hollis between Rowena and the grounder.

Sonya's face turned several shades redder in jealousy.

For a long moment Long looked at her as if he was going to say something, then he turned, a forced smile on his face. "Sonya, did you get everything you needed?"

"Oh, it was a good conversation." The chill in Sonya's voice could have frozen an engine.

"I was telling her about my dear friend and commander," Hollis said, sounding for all the world like he was delighted with everything going on. :Hand/Waist.:

:How much am I going to hate what comes next?: Rowena asked as Hollis's arm settled around her.

:Not much.:

There was a tick in Long's jaw, the hint of frustration. "Anyone I've heard of?"

"Only if you know the best fleet commander," Hollis said. "He's a legend in Enclave, Mal Baular."

That was a name Long knew. His face grew still and distant as the stars. "Baular?"

"We've heard the name," Sonya said a like a lost cadet trying to prove they were keeping up with the conversation. "Someone mentioned it in passing once. I'd love to meet him."

"I'd love to introduce you." Hollis's smile was sharp as a knife.

:Subtle death threats now?: Rowena smiled up at him. "Wouldn't that be fun?"

"Unfortunately, he runs a very tight ship. If I snuck anyone onto Enclave, even someone as beautiful as any of you, I'd lose my rank." With a little shrug Hollis dismissed the idea.

"Can't have that." Long pulled the paper from his jacket. "Lady Lethe, if I could tear you away from these two for a moment? I have some news you might find interesting. A friend of yours stopped me and asked me to pass this along."

Sonya's lips pursed into a frown, eyes flicking from the paper to Long to Hollis. "Can it wait?"

"The worlds would stand still if you wished it," Long said, "but…" He let the possibility dangle.

:How much trouble are we in?: Hollis asked, fingers resting on Rowena's arm.

:No idea. He was being friendly up until now.:

Rude of Lethe to use actual dead-wood paper instead of a simple piece of tech that Rowena could access with a thought. The ink didn't even leave enough of an impression that she could read it through the folds. If it was news about Rowena's true identity, there was going to be trouble.

She started mapping the exits. There wasn't a good escape route that would get them to safety, but there were a few bad ones she was willing to try.

Long leaned over and whispered conspiratorially in Sonya's ear as he winked at Rowena.

Whatever he said had an effect. Sonya stepped back, eyes wide with excitement. "Really?"

Long gave her a single nod of affirmation.

Sonya looked between her two prizes, licked her lips, and smiled. "Commander Silar, it was delightful to meet you. I was hoping to spend more time with you, but Doctor Long has something I've been waiting to see for weeks."

"Mine's bigger," Hollis said with the smile that made people swoon and Rowena beat her head on the nearest wall during training.

"Oh," Sonya reached out and patted his cheek. "I'm sure there's no need to compare. What Doctor Long offers is… unique."

Hollis clicked his tongue. "Your loss."

"You can make it up to me later," Sonya promised with a smile.

Long nodded to them. "Rose, Commander, a pleasure to see you both. Do enjoy your time together. Monsoon season gives you all the more reason to stay indoors."

The grounders had barely turned away before Hollis's face grew cold. He took Rowena's hand and pulled her close so she was pinned between him and the wall in what would have looked like an amorous embrace to a passerby.

"Let's find a taxi and get out of here. Whatever charm Kydell had is gone now." He glared at the ground for a moment, hiding his emotions from their shared connection, and then looked back at her, eyes filled with worry. "What did Long say to you?"

"Not much. He doesn't like Lethe."

"I picked up that much." Hollis kept his voice low as they took the stairs down the drive to where a fleet of taxis were waiting. "What I didn't catch was his reason for going back to her."

"He said one of us should have a good evening," Rowena said as she signaled for a car. She was as eager to leave the party as Hollis was.

The grounder transport wasn't fast or fashionable, but it had the right papers to get them past the extra security and to an older but still respectable part of town where the Jhandarmi had rented her an apartment. They rode in silence, Hollis's thumb absentmindedly caressing her hand as they watched the Lethe troops form patrols.

As the driver wished them goodnight, Rowena took a moment to look down at the lights of the lower city, the sea, and the stars peeking across the horizon.

Hollis kept her hand in his. "This is your place now?" he asked, looking up at Rowena's apartment building.

"Mmm." It wasn't much, just a bare square of a flat with a small kitchen nook and a standup shower.

"You're staying here tonight?"

"There's no sense in going back. The sun'll be up in less than an hour and Tyrling's going to want someone here. If I go home, Hoshi'll have work waiting for me. I'm too exhausted to deal with him." But she didn't want Hollis to go either. "Do you want to come up?"

"I'd love to." He pulled her closer and kissed her forehead.

"But you can't."

He rested his head on hers. "Perrin needs the reports. I recorded all the conversations on the roof and I need to get that filed. Make copies for Tyrling and the OIA's intelligence people. There's people waiting on this. I don't get to be selfish."

Rowena sighed. "Life of an officer." Stepping back, she tried not to feel abandoned. "We're luckier than others, aren't we? It used to be you had to negotiate with the captains and get your ships within teleport distance if you wanted to spend time with someone. Less than five years and half the fleet forgets what it's like to wait six months to see their lover."

"Let's never go back to the bad old days." She could feel his reluctance to leave. "How long are you staying here?"

"Just until things settle. I promised the rowdies I'd find a solution, and I mean to, although I'm not sure how I'll help."

"You'll find a way."

She smiled at his encouragement. "Have to, or I'll lose my reputation as the stubbornest person in the fleet."

Hollis chuckled. "All right. I'll back your play, whatever it is."

"Just like that? No negotiations? What happened to your tactical acumen, Silar?"

"Make an hour for me later this week? In a day or two?"

Her calendar appeared in her mind and she flipped through her list of duties.

"We can spar." There was enough heat in his invitation to melt a hull.

Rowena looked him in the eye. "You're cleared to get back on the mats?"

"We'll be gentle with each other." His eyes were gold and warm. "A light workout and a long massage." This was why no one turned him away. She'd seem him flirt before, but never felt the focus of his attention. It was dizzying. Intoxicating.

It left her greedy for attention. Ready to forget all the consequences.

"Maybe," she said. "If I can break away and you're free."

"I'll make the time for you. Just let me know when the Jhandarmi can share." He brought her hands to his lips and kissed her palm. :Be safe. Contact me if you have any trouble.:

:I will.: She pushed him away as the ground rumbled under their feet. :Go, while Lethe is teleporting in more troops.:

"Good night."

"Good night."

Hollis winked out of existence, leaving her alone in a city ready to go to war.

33
MALCOLM

MALCOLM LOOKED ACROSS THE dark streets of Kydell, mentally tracing the path of Rose Lauren and her lover. Or soon-to-be lover.

He'd seen the way Silar pushed her against the wall for a rough kiss and some quiescent anger had stirred like an abyssal monster in the depths of the sea. Old memories had resurfaced, old desires, long and brutally buried under the careful facade of the life he'd created after the islands.

Curling fingers into a fist, he allowed himself a moment to feel the warm rage again. A heartbeat's time and nothing more.

Malcolm Long was a quiet man. A thoughtful engineer with a pacifist's smile. A bowing, scrapping, subservient man who took every insult without thought of retribution. A fool who had given up everything because that was the price of a long life.

Sometimes he thought it would be better to be dead than take another breath as Malcolm Long.

Looking at Rose Lauren on the stairs, eyes sparkling after her victorious adventures in the garden, had been one of those times. Because Malcolm Long belonged to Sonya Lethe, he couldn't steal Rose away from her lover. He couldn't keep her close, hording her smiles and wit. He couldn't even keep her at arm's length as a friend without drawing Sonya's attention and ire.

He held the thoughts a heartbeat longer and then let them go with a long sigh.

There were very good reasons for leaving the world of coral and gold behind.

He glanced over his shoulder at the empty room Sonya had abandoned him in. It was staged like the rest of the house, elegantly furnished in the latest styles of Descent so that any pictures taken here would show the wealth.

Or the illusion of wealth at any rate. The lush, off-white carpet of plastic. The soft white couch had plastic legs painted to look like wood. Even the chandelier overhead was made of cheap glass, not crystal.

Like Sonya, it was beautiful at a glance, but there wasn't any substance under the charade.

At least the view of Kydell was exquisite. Large windows on three sides of the room looked out at the rolling hills of the city filled with lights that were winking out. One section of the city after another was falling dark as curfew was enforced, leaving only the natural stars overhead.

And the unnatural light of the spacers' debris glittering in the upper atmosphere.

Space.

They'd come from the stars. Every single person on the planet could trace their roots to some far flung star system that was now no more than a twinkle in the night sky.

They'd arrived with a massive fleet of colonial ships meant to land, the fleet ships meant to protect them, and the space stations meant to accommodate trade.

Every continent had a spaceport.

Every major city was designed to be accessible to the stars.

Yet, here they were. Every space station long destroyed. Every spaceship either on the ground or in pieces out of reach. Every hope of returning to the stars relied on some miracle of technology that even he couldn't envision.

"Malcolm?" Sonya's soft voice made him turn. She looked subdued, reduced and faded.

"Is everything all right?"

Her wan smile was not encouraging. "I'm sure it will be. Can you come in here for a moment? Father would like to speak to you."

"Father?" Virgil was here. "I didn't realize he was at the party."

Sonya's jaw tightened as she winced. "He wasn't originally planning on coming to this event, but he felt a need to be here tonight." She kept her gaze averted, her chin down.

A familiar sense of understanding invaded his peace. Sonya was afraid of her father.

Malcolm reached for her shoulder slowly. "Is there anything he needs to hear?" He picked the words carefully, hoping Sonya had learned, as Malcolm had, how to maneuver around an abusive authority figure. Sonya gave her head a tight shake. "No. Nothing at all. He just wants a man to talk to."

"Ah." How clarifying. "I'll see if I can help him." Giving Sonya's shoulder a reassuring squeeze, he walked into a room that wasn't meant for photographs. The walls were thick and lined with a black, reflective covering that turned the surfaces into display screens.

Three slender tables made a short U. At the center of it all was Virgil Lethe, twisting the silver ring with the orange stone that caught the light and held it in strange ways. His mane of long, white hair glowed in the beam from a projector until he stepped, aside letting a cascade of stars fall on the front wall.

"Lord Governor." Malcolm bowed formally.

"Doctor Long." Virgil turned to the wall filled with stars. "I'm glad you're here.

Malcolm walked around the U so he could see the image better and recognized, barely, a map of the Old Empire, centered not on the Imperial homeworld but on the sun of the Malik System. A black line of empty space stretched between Malik and the rest of the empire like a wall.

"Have you seen this map before?"

"No, sir." He couldn't even guess when it had been made. Between the dawn of human space travel and the rise of the empire there had been many nations, kingdoms, democracies, thousands of years of human social experiments. Under the empire there had been several thousand more years of growing power, brutal subjugation, and genocidal wars that brought the known universe to bow before the Imperial throne.

At one time Malcolm had known every war and era of humanity. It had been drilled into him since childhood. But he didn't know this map. There were names on it he'd never seen. Parts of unexplored space labeled when he knew they were never explored.

Virgil Lethe took a deep breathe. "Well, I had wondered. If you were from the Marshalls you might know this."

"What is it?"

"The governor's map," Lethe said. "The last official piece of communication from the Emperor. Or"—he waggled his head to the side to admit a minor error—"the last communication from the Empress of the Fifth House."

Searching his memory, Malcolm pulled the fragment of a song taught to small children. "The fifth house, all-seeing, all-knowing, and kind."

"The house of spies," Lethe said. "The Empress of the Fifth House was either an aunt or sister of the ruling Emperor and she oversaw the intelligence operations of the empire."

"Why send this to a people they were abandoning? The empire abandoned us. Left us here to rot in a system with few metals and little habitable land. Terraforming of the two planets with atmosphere wasn't even complete. Malik III was entirely uninhabitable at that point. Seahome is still largely uninhabitable, at least at the center. Why…. Why send this at all?" Ancestors above and brine of the sea, it was senseless.

Lethe showing it to him made even less sense.

Malcolm looked at the closed door and wondered how long he'd live if he walked out now.

"The empire abandoned us?" Virgil Lethe chuckled sourly. "Yes, that was the lie my ancestors chose. An easy, safe lie that covered a much harder truth."

"Why lie at all? The wormhole was closed. The end result was the same whether it was by accident or on purpose."

"We were abandoned?" Lethe asked. "Left to rot? Thrown aside. Forgotten. Do you believe that? When you look out at the people of the Malik System, do you truly believe such a strange group was thrown together by accident? There are representatives of every culture the empire conquered on Malik IV. Histories and cultures and genes." He hit the word as if saying it was enough to conjure some great sign from the sky.

Malcolm looked at the map again, letting his prejudices slide away so he saw it as something new. There weren't things missing, there were things added. There were... "Projections? This was the plan for the Malik System?"

"The original governor, nephew of the ruling emperor and my many-times removed great-grandfather, met with the emperor before leaving. He was told that the Malik System would need to be prepared for the arrival of the emperor and the full imperial household."

That destroyed several theories Malcolm had favored about wormhole creation. He'd always believed the Imperial family had only been able to control the passageways because of something found in the Imperial System. There was no other reason to favor such a dour place.

Or perhaps the descriptions had been changed to keep people from wishing they could live there too, under the red sun of the empire.

Lethe walked towards the map. "We came to prepare, and we were sent this. Generations passed, this was forgotten, pushed aside. People always feel that the moment they are living in is more urgent than the future."

"It isn't?" Malcolm asked.

The older man shrugged. "Every moment is urgent. But, if you don't prepare, you will not survive a moment of urgency. Everything that comes before you prepares you for your next heartbeat. Shouldn't some of your thoughts, then, be bent toward ensuring the next heartbeat?"

Lethe shook his head as he caressed the map.

The image zoomed in on the Malik System, sixteen sizable planets and moons capable of supporting terraforming, a G-type sun, several comets, but little else. Water but little iron. Oxygen, but little of the raw materials required to make steel. There had been no life in the system when the first terraforming probes arrived.

"I saw this when I was a young boy," Lethe said. "I saw this map, made for the king of systems, and saw what might have been. Can you imagine how that scared me?"

"Fear of not rising to prominence?" Malcolm guessed.

The old man shook his head as he twisted his ring again. "No, no I never feared being lesser. I have always known who and what I am. I grew up hearing the names of ancestors back to the imperial throne. I knew the greatness of my ancestors. Their power. Their might. The name of the planets they conquered, the battles they won. That is what scared me, the thought that they settled the Malik System because they foresaw a fight they could not win."

Primal terror old as bones gripped Malcolm. He breathed through it, pushing the fear away so he could think. "Is that what you think this is? Proof that the empire closed the wormhole to safeguard us?"

"It is the truth, uncomfortable though we may find it." Lethe shrugged. "My ancestors thought the emperor meant to arrive here himself. Retreat to the safety of this system. My family mourned his loss as proof that the worst had happened."

The empire had fallen.

It was unthinkable.

At the time the wormhole had collapsed, it had been treasonous to even suggest such a thing. But, the map was there. A suggestion, if not confirmation, that the Emperor had feared something in the unexplored darkness between stars.

An old, old memory flickered from the depths of his ragged soul: brown eyes burning with confidence and a smile that could start a war. *"There is something terrible in the darkness—me."*

His heart broke a little.

"You see why we let people believe the empire abandoned us?" Lethe asked. "Their fear of the unknown would have destroyed the world. We would have all died before I realized the truth."

"What truth?"

Lethe smiled like a man ready to start a war. It was much less charming than Malcolm's memories of the person he'd tried so hard to forget.

"The emperor sent us all the genetic material for him to return, to be reborn."

Malcolm pinched his lips together. "I... 'm not sure that would work. Genetic drift doesn't take into account memories, or experiences." Or the fact that the genetic material of the Malik System was tainted by the viruses used in terraforming. There were vestigial pieces of every plague on the planet in people's DNA. It was impossible for someone to be a true genetic clone of the long-ago emperor.

"Souls and destinies are talk best left to holodramas. What we need is the genetic codes that will allow the wormhole to reopen."

"And a fleet to access space with."

Hollis Silar. Commander Hollis Silar, of the fleet on Descent, whom Sonya had been hanging on all evening.

Virgil Lethe raised an eyebrow as he smiled. "You're piecing it together."

"You intend to use Silar to get you to the stars." It wasn't a bad plan, actually. The spacers wanted to leave. Everyone born on the planet wanted the spacers to leave. "But, why reopen the wormhole?"

"To take what is ours by right of our birth. I am the rightful son of the empire. The heir to the imperial throne.

Everyone else died so we could live, and when I have the genetic code to re-open the path between stars, I will go, to take back what my ancestors stored for me at the end of the wormhole, and bring it back. We'll rebuild the empire."

Malcolm's eyes went wide. "There are problems with that plan. Variables you couldn't control. The fleet landed because they had no fuel. We don't know what's on the other side of the wormhole. We don't know the empire fell."

"They fell," Lethe said firmly. "If they hadn't, why would they have closed the wormhole? Why would they leave all of us here? The Empress of the Fifth House gave us an answer." He touched the wall and pulled the view across the galaxy to a not-so-distant star. "The Amayi System. It is within the range of the Malik System if we have a wormhole. Resource reach, lush with metals—"

"Untouched," Malcolm interrupted. "It's not connected to any other imperial system. It wasn't settled. No one has explored it yet. At best they had a telescope looking at what was there. Settling that would be dangerous, even with a wormhole."

Virgil Lethe walked around the table and patted Malcolm's shoulder. There was a sharp, electric shock. Lethe shook his hand. "Odd. The air doesn't feel dry enough for that."

Malcolm rubbed his arm. "Yes. It happened twice tonight. Must be me. Sir, with all due respect, this is a wonderful dream but no one has the resources to pull this off. It would be wonderful to have access to another star system, or even to have access to Malik III, we could settle that now. But—" He shook his head.

"We will go," Lethe said with the fervor of promise. He held up his hand so his strange ring was centered in the light of the projector. "This is orun, the fuel of the fleet.

One of the largest crystals ever known. The Lethe family has several shards."

"That could send the fleet back to space." Malcolm's jaw tightened in frustration. "We could get them off this planet!"

Lethe twisted his ring with a smile of satisfaction. "We will. This is enough to get us to the wormhole, back again, and open up the new trade route with the mines we'll open in the Amayi System."

"The housing crisis—" Malcolm snapped his mouth shut. He didn't want to speculate who the new miners would be.

With a chuckle Lethe confirmed his suspicions. "We'll have them by tomorrow's nightfall. All the workers we need. All the reason to send them on their way."

"The new emperor..." Malcolm hesitated, then dove in. "Should I have called you Sire rather than Sir?"

"A dream fondly to be wished, but no," Lethe said. "We had to wait for the emperor's return. He was guarded, the family line kept aboard one of the fleet ships."

"Not Silar," Malcolm didn't even tried to keep the disgust for the redhaired flirt out of his voice. Briny deep take the smiling Silar. Idiot. Dull as rock and twice as stupid.

"No, that one is war fodder, nothing more."

Malcolm felt a wince of regret; the redhead made him want to reach for the nearest weapon, but only to scare him off, not kill him. Probably. He remembered Rose Lauren's smile as Silar walked up to her. Eh... *probably*.

"Silar will lead us to the emperor reborn. He promised Sonya as much this evening."

"Oh." What was the right language to curse in when finding out that a genocidal maniac had been reborn? Was using Old Imperial too pointed? Maybe some slang from the islands was better.

"Mal Baular."

Malcolm's head jerked up as he was pulled away from his musings. "What?"

"That is the name of the emperor. Mal Baular."

Slowly nodding, Malcolm forced a smile. "Yes. I heard Silar mention him. I didn't think anything of it when the commander offered to introduce Sonya." It had sounded a little threatening, but people with two firing synapses tended to get a certain look after being bludgeoned by Sonya's lack of tact. "So, we have an emperor, a fleet, and a future. How exciting."

All that, and Virgil Lethe wanted to talk to him still.

Oh, this was exactly the kind of situation his parents told him to avoid at all costs. Amherst Heir Found Dead In River was not a headline anyone needed to see.

"Tell me, Lord Governor, how may I serve the emperor?"

Virgil Lethe patted his arm again, causing another tiny, electric shock. "You, the brightest engineer in centuries, will design the future home of the emperor."

Hopefully not interior design; he'd never figured out how to make the interior of a building be anything more than functional. But, if he did design something for the emperor reborn—genetic impossibilities aside—he'd make sure there was a large bed with sheets of coral and gold.

"In the coming days, Sonya will give you the details. We will be using the fleet's larger ships to transport the new workers for the Amayi System. We'll have our pick of warships—"

"All damaged," Malcolm said. "They did have a war. I doubt everything is as flight ready as you are hoping."

"They are the emperor's vassals. They are sworn to protect and obey the emperor. We will meet him in the coming weeks, and when we reveal the truth of who he is, they will all bow."

Malcolm tried to picture Silar bowing. It didn't work. That man wouldn't bow unless he was reaching for a weapon. Malcolm knew the type well; *he* was that type. It's why his family lived on the islands for so long. It was why his mother refused to pledge her allegiance to any of the greater families. It was why his parents were going to kill him when they found out about this.

All in all, a terrible evening.

"I can see you are overwhelmed with the possibilities. Thousands of willing workers, all the resources an engineer could dream of. It will all be yours as you serve the emperor."

"I am stunned and humbled by your trust," Malcolm said, keeping his smile firmly in place. "The planning can begin immediately, if that is what you wish."

Lethe waved the thought away with a hand. "No. For tonight, attend to my sweet Sonya. She is displeased with the news that Baular is alive. Without one of them, we would have had to risk using her as the emperor reborn. Empress, one supposes. Waiting for her to bear a male heir with suitable genes was out of the question. We can't wait any longer."

"Why not?"

"The universe is always expanding. In another two centuries Amayi will be out of reach. We need to take all we can from it before the distance is too large."

"Of course," Malcolm said flatly. "How could I forget?"

Lethe looked back to the map of his future empire. "This will be my gift to future generations. An emperor to serve and a thousand warships to defend him."

Malcolm bowed again. "I am honored to be a part of it," he lied. "And, now, I will go see if Lady Lethe is ready to end the evening here. Will you be joining us on the flight back to Descent?"

"No, I have other transportation, thank you." Lethe waved him away with an amiable smile. "You are dismissed."

Scrapping another half bow, Malcolm fled the small room.

Sonya was waiting outside, a full glass of something golden and bubbling in her hand as she glared down at the city. "Did you enjoy the conversation with my father?" Her tone could have frozen the ocean.

"It was… interesting," Malcolm allowed. "His enthusiasm is contagious."

"So are most plagues." She lips pulled back in a growl that she quickly hid.

"Are you displeased with his goals for the system, or just with not being the one on the throne?"

Sonya shrugged. "Who says I won't have the throne? Emperors are mortal. Spacers can die."

"So I'm told." Malcolm looked across the darkened Kydell. The markets were closed. The windows of every house shuttered.

The only light left came from the roving patrols of local constabulary and the Lethe security forces.

Grabbing the window ledge, Malcolm glanced sideways at Sonya. "Do you agree this is what your ancestors wanted?"

"My ancestors wanted power. It's why they married a daughter to the emperor, it's why they were punished and sent here." Grumbling, Sonya sighed and rolled her eyes. There was a hint of watery sparkle, an unshed tear. "It's so infuriating. My father is so content to serve. So convinced that his childhood fear might become a reality, that some monster might come from the sky.

"When the spacers landed, we were against their integration. He was terrified they'd attack us, and we all saw what happened. They do nothing. They don't even leave their ships!

"So his fears changed. And now he has access to those ships and he's ready to bow to someone because of what, their genes? What does this Baular know about anything? Has he ever ruled? Has he ever led?"

"There's no way a grounder could know I suppose," Malcolm said because Sonya seemed to be expecting an answer. "They are very militant, from what I understand."

Sonya rolled her eyes again. "They're inbred fools. Talking to Silar was the single most monotonous thing I've ever done. He can't follow a conversation, can't take a hint, can't even fill in the obvious replies I'm waiting for. Normal people know how to respond!"

"Perhaps he can be trained."

"Perhaps," Sonya agreed. She took a deep breath, rolled her shoulders back, and smiled a dazzling smile. "But that is a worry for another day, is it not? Tonight we have a flight to catch. I'm afraid Kydell will be less that hospitable in the coming hours. We've received word that anti-government elements have infiltrated the local population and plan to attack the capital."

Malcolm nodded. "I wasn't aware there were anti-government rebels in Kydell."

"There are anti-government types everywhere. In the larger cities there is support from allies, and from the larger families. But Kydell is, obviously, weak."

"And you have been prompting people to fight," Malcolm said, watching her expression.

Sonya smirked. "Yes. I have helped. Kydell is our great experiment. If all goes well here, Lethe will have a chance to prove our ability to lead in a crisis."

"Something that will impress the new emperor and the rightful children of the empire," Malcolm said. *Rightful*

Children. That's what Virgil Lethe had said, or, rightful child. Either way. "Someone will notice."

"It will impress someone," Sonya said. "And everyone will notice. They have taken Lethe for granted, but that ends now." She set her glass down and took his arm. "Shall we leave before the trouble starts? I know how much you value those government contracts."

Malcolm offered her his arm. "I appreciate your willingness to protect my interests, Lady Lethe."

"Such things must be done for people we value."

He didn't let himself dwell on what his value was as they walked down the stairs so Sonya could say goodbye to her friends. People like him were always expendable. The Lethes had given him enough information to make him dangerous to the right people, and not enough information to protect himself with.

As Sonya drifted away to consult with a petite woman who mimicked Sonya's every movement, Malcolm turned back to the stairs. Silar had stood right there. *"Only if you know the best fleet commander. He's a legend in Enclave, Mal Baular."*

And an older memory, Exiled Spacer Dies In Car Accident—Jhandarmi Investigate.

Unless there were two Mal Baulars, Lethe's future emperor was dead.

Malcolm couldn't guess how much information Silar had, or if he would know such a thing at all, but Rose Lauren was a pretty civilian. Presented herself as a pretty civilian, Malcolm corrected himself. Her accent wasn't from Icedell and she hadn't used a rank.

Mentally, he filed her into the 'Maybe' category. Possibly fleet, but hiding it well if she was. More likely trained by one of the great houses. Or the Jhandarmi.

That would be an uncomfortable conversation.

This whole night had been filled with uncomfortable conversations.

He looked over his shoulder at Sonya and started calculating what he would need to do to disengage from the Lethes and stay alive.

He needed a lever. A really big lever. Something large enough—or someone powerful enough—to give him freedom and keep the Lethes from killing him.

"And while I wish for the moon and stars, perhaps I can ask for a raise." Malcolm snagged a drink from a passing tray and tossed it back. It didn't burn like island liquor, but enough of it would put a fine dent in his sobriety.

Maybe he could get alcohol poisoning before Sonya finished her goodbyes.

At the moment, it was his best chance for escape.

34
HOLLIS

METAL PLANKING HICCUPPED under Hollis's feet as he walked through the heart of the *Veronica Guerin*. Withered fruit trees lined a wide corridor in what had once been the space reserved for families. Independent of outside oxygen and water, capable of surviving the worst magnetic storm or battle, this had been the fortress where Silar children had grown for generation. Now the lights were turned off to preserve power, and there was a silence that came from nearly a decade with no new children born to the crew.

War found ways to make them pay, even after the guns fell silent.

Hollis took the left hall, avoiding the rooms he'd been born in.

His mother had always said she wanted happiness for him in whatever form it came. That didn't mean she was going to approve of what he was going to do. The dead were dead though, left only with the memories they'd made in life. He was still alive, still breathing, still changing. It was important to remember that.

Stopping in front of the captain's quarters, he adjusted his dress uniform and patted the door. :Captain. Commander Hollis Silar reporting.:

:Enter.: In his mind Garius's voice sounded old, withered as the garden, dusty with death.

The door slid open on command.

Garius sat behind an old metal table with a sheen of fading gold and the Silar crest stamped into it. He was wearing his full uniform, although it was too large on him now, and he was sober. The war had aged him. Garius wasn't even sixty yet, but his red hair had faded to white, deep lines of worry were carved into his face, and his bright eyes were a murky glow of swirling memories.

"Sir." Hollis saluted, dropping his defensive shields.

Garius blinked slowly, his eyes turning a dark blue as he re-entered the present reality. His chair swiveled with a creaking grind of metal on metal as he rocked himself back and forth. That could be fixed, but Garius refused.

"Commander." There was a wave of approval.

Hollis stood at ease.

"Why have you come to bother me?" The words were released grudgingly, as if every sound in this hallowed space was an insult to the memories of those gone on before. Or a final volley in the battle where Garius had lost his wife and daughters.

"Sir, I need permission to make a Declaration of Courtship."

The old captain's lips curdled in a sneer. "You? A declaration? Don't you snap your fingers and have your lovers line up like cadets eager for their first flight?"

"This one I want as a spouse, not as a lover."

Garius raised his hand. The minutes dragged past. "No."

Hollis kept his emotions behind several layers of shields. "Sir?"

"This crew has no future. If you love this person, do not condemn them to live here with us. Find them a ship that can fly. Give them back the stars." Garius turned his face to the ceiling and closed his eyes as if a wish was all it took to regain freedom.

"Perhaps I should transfer to their crew," Hollis said. "They have at least one ship capable of flight." Though technically it was a shuttle, and even that was a rumor. Someone had reported seeing a vessel with Lee markings out over the water a few years ago.

Hoshi had been questioned and hotly denied it, not that it mattered. The only one with the skill to build a new shuttle from parts was Rowena, and she wasn't likely to tell anyone if she had.

Garius scowled at him. "You would leave your crew? Your family?"

"I'm a very junior commander, sir." Technically true, although he was the Silar's only Elite. "You're young and healthy. My promotion prospects have always meant I'd need to transfer to another crew to grow my career."

"It seems unusually disloyal of you to choose such a course."

"Does it, sir?" Hollis asked, feigning innocence. "The crew doesn't need me. There are many fine officers, and the captain is more than capable. I appreciate how you have trained me, letting me have free run of the *Veronica*, letting me fail. But I'm in no position to challenge the senior officers or you, sir, for a command."

Not that the other officers didn't live in fear of the day Hollis decided he wanted one of their ships.

Before the war, a few of them could hold their own against him. During the war, a few could have beat him. But since Landing, they'd been taking life easy and he'd been fighting Rowena every day. Now even Perrin and Hermione were having trouble stopping him.

"Disingenuous," Garius said. "You know the crew respects you. Values your input."

Hollis nodded. "I do, sir. I'm grateful for their support."

"Yet you want to leave them."

"No, sir, but I do want to be with my spouse. If you won't approve her trans—"

"Her?" Garius finally looked at him for real. "You picked a woman?"

"I do like many women. It was always an option."

"What does she think of children?"

His mind flashed back to every conversation he'd had with Rowena. Babies had never come up. He tried to picture her with a child. "She'd be a very good mother, sir. Although she's not considering having any right away, that I know of."

Garius made an unflattering noise. "Marshall, is it?" No love lost there.

"No, sir."

"Very well. I will approve the Declaration. Nothing more. Send it to me."

Tension tightened Holli's shoulders as he sent the data pack to Garius for approval. This was where the battle would start.

The captain's eyes glowed a dull gold and his face turned stormy. "Rowena Lee?"

"Yes, sir."

"I wasn't aware there was a Rowena Lee except Baular's whore."

"There isn't, sir." Garius was going to pay for calling her that someday.

Garius looked at him. "This is not a well-thought-out joke."

"It's not a joke at all, sir."

"You're serious? You want to marry this… this…" Garius stood, trembling like the mudflats in a quake. "*Her*? She is—"

"An Elite officer," Hollis cut in, because he wouldn't let Garius say anything else. "A decorated war veteran."

"A Warmonger!"

"Who stood her trial, took her punishment, and is teaching at the OIA Academy. She has powerful allies and is the best engineer in the fleet. And even if she had none of that, she's the woman I love."

"This is a mistake," Garius said.

"If it is, then it's mine to make. I've served loyally all these years. Stepped in when you needed me. Put off other goals and desires to serve the crew. All I am asking in return is that you reach out to Captain Lee and forward him the Declaration. Nothing more."

Garius sat down. "Years from now, after this fails, when you are looking for a promotion to sub-captain: remember this. Remember that you were warned by a good captain." He tapped his rank. "Remember that you brought this on yourself."

"I will, sir."

"Dismissed."

Hollis saluted, keeping his shields tight. Loving Rowena wasn't a mistake, it was the best choice he'd ever made, for him *and* his crew.

35
ROWENA

WATER STREAMED OVER ROWENA'S head as she stood in the shower. Implants didn't replace the need for sleep. They simply balanced out the brain chemistry while nanites expedited cell repair enough to make it feel like a few minutes standing still was the same as eight hours of rest.

Maybe it had been more than a few minutes.

The water was growing cold by the time Rowena shook off the fuzzy-headed feeling of the REM boost and dried off with a thin towel. Her stomach rumbled in complaint. All that food at Sonya's party and all she'd managed to steal was a handful of fruit.

"Crack my hull." Opening the chill box, she looked at the square packages Tyrling had sent. Pink. Orange. Green. The food was color coded, but no one had bothered to give her the cypher.

This is why she needed a crew.

How was a person supposed to survive when they worked more hours than there were in a day and still had to find time to feed themselves? She needed an XO, a ship's cook, and a couple of NCOs on hand to back her up.

Picking an orange box, she opened it and read the label: BREAKFAST SANDWICH. Frozen solid and with no hint as to what it contained.

Slamming it on the counter to activate the heating element, she waited. The frozen sandwich stayed resolutely cold. A quick scan showed no integrated heating elements.

How was it supposed to cook? Was it supposed to sit out overnight?

Certain she was missing a key step, she shoved the sandwich back in the chiller. There were ration bars in the closet. Fighting grounder food into edibility was a waste of time.

Her phone rang as she pulled on a pair of multi-pocketed pants and a black shirt that would let her blend in throughout Kydell.

"Lee." Whoever was on the other end was Jhandarmi and there was no point lying about her name. She tucked Hollis's black knife into her belt and the Starguard emergency card into her pocket under a heavy shield. There. Technically she was keeping her end of her agreement with Hollis.

"Tyrling." The director growled out his name. "You in Kydell?"

"Yes. Did you get the report from Silar yet?"

"Got it. I need boots on the ground. Get a head count on Lethe troops, make sure there's extra security around our offices. You know the kind I mean."

A shield. "Yes, sir." Marshall had put one up originally and there was no reason for it not to be intact, but she'd go check it again.

"We've got another agent arriving today. I'll have him contact you. Keep your phone nearby. And, Lee, stay out of trouble."

"I've been a model officer, sir. No complaints since my arrival."

"Except for the dead security guard."

"I warned him, sir. I'm an engineer, but I can't fix stupid men who think they can beat me in a fight."

Tyrling laughed. "You can't at that. Get going. I need reports yesterday."

"Then I'll see if I can invent time travel in my free moments, sir." She hung up with a grim smile. "Are there only twelve people on this planet?" she asked the wall. "Is there really no one else who could do this?"

Probably not.

Just like no one else could fix the water filtration on the *Tuul* to ensure Yunjin had a good training berth. Or barter repairs on the hull of the *Ingala* for the engine parts the *Persephone* needed. Or see if the botanist on the *Cattleya* wanted to trade orchid seeds for a set of Kaitlin rods for her side project.

"Hull-cracked grounder imperialist." Rowena laced her heavy black boots up and stuffed a couple of ration bars in her pockets for later.

There was probably a good reason for not going to find Sonya Lethe and slamming her head against the wall until she saw sense.

Marshall would say it wasn't politically delicate enough. Although the whole planet would be better if someone sat Lethe down, looked her in the eye, and explained that on the whole, society did better without tyrants. A little bit of public service, a few less ostentatious parties, and Sonya could have all the public adoration she wanted without killing anyone.

Locking the apartment, Rowena headed out of the small residential district to the business center where the Kydellians kept all the foreign embassies and police in a couple of older buildings marked by dusty flood lines.

The streets were quiet, even for an early hour of the morning. Businesses should have been opening, the smell of pastries should have filled the streets, and there should be a surge in noise from the docks as the first ships of the morning came in on the tide.

There was nothing.

Store fronts were shuttered.

Restaurants were dark, their ovens cold.

From the docks was the mournful bell, calling the absent rowdies to work.

They'd fled the city. Left it abandoned to the people who called themselves the true citizens. And what were those people going to do when no one else came to unload the cargo?

Her phone's ringing filled the street. "Hello?"

"Tyrling," the director said. "You at the offices yet?"

"Just heading there now. Things are quiet here. Why?"

"One of the silent alarms went off."

She risked a quick ping of the shield over the offices. "The security is in place and it won't let anyone in unless they have a Jhandarmi badge."

"Could be a mouse or something. A bird flying through a window." The director sounded uneasy.

Rowena turned the corner so she saw the long road that ran from the hilltop capitol buildings to the main dock. The Jhandarmi offices were to the left, tucked into the same structure as the offices for work permits and social services. Someone was stepping out.

"Is your other agent here?" Rowena asked.

"Could be," Tyrling said. "He caught the earliest tram in this morning."

The man walking out of the offices waved at her.

"Maybe he forgot his badge." She waved back and started walking to meet him.

The world exploded.

Rowena tumbled backward and looked up in shock as smoke billowed up from the ruined building.

All their work. All their efforts. She'd kept the rowdies away, stopped Lethe's plan, and the Jhandarmi offices were still in ruins.

In her mind, a confusion of calculations beat against each other.

It didn't make sense. There was a shield in place. There were guards.

The only easy way past was to teleport the explosives in, and no one from fleet had been here but her.

She'd been the last line of defense in Kydell and she'd failed.

"Lee!" Tyrling screamed from the phone she'd dropped. "Lee!"

Rowena reached for it and a heavy boot fell down, narrowly missing her fingers as it crushed the phone.

"Officer?" A man with dark blond hair covered in plaster dust held up a Jhandarmi badge. He'd been the one coming out of the offices.

She looked down at the broken phone. "Yes?"

"Agent Erach." He took a shaky breath. "Erach Dolus. Tyrling said you could help me if I needed it." He looked over his shoulder at the destruction. "I need it."

It would have been better to stay, try to sort through the debris and find the cause of the explosion. But she could come back after Erach was safe. "Straight to the hospital or to Tyrling?"

"To these coordinates, please." He pulled a scrap of paper out of his pocket. "It's my safe zone for emergencies like this."

The location was somewhere on the eastern edge of the continent. A sparsely populated area, but well within her teleport limits and a good place to hide a base. "Tyrling knows of this?"

"Yes, you can call him—" His eyes grew wide with delayed realization. He looked down at the shattered phone. "We can contact him when we arrive. I have medical equipment there. Everything I need."

Lethe troops rounded the corner, shouting.

"Please," Erach said. "This is going to be a political nightmare if the Kydellians find out I'm here. I haven't had a chance to get my work registration signed. No one was in the office."

"Okay." Rowena held her hand. "Hold on. Close your eyes if you like. Some people find this disorienting."

It took nothing to teleport them from the smoke-filled city to the wide plains where the sun beat down on them and the air was filled with the screams of angry insects.

"Lovely location," Rowena said, dropping contact Erach's hand. Summer-dried grasses and the distant green smear of a tropical forest. "When's it rain here?"

"Rainy season should be starting soon," Erach said. "You won't be here for it."

"I wasn't planning on being here for it." She turned back to him and felt a twinge in her arm.

The Jhandarmi officer grinned angrily. "You thought you were better than us?"

"What?" She pinged her implant and found nothing.

No signal. No answering response.

Even her secondary implant was low. "What is going on?"

"You're going to meet some friends of mine." Erach was grinning ferociously, hazel eyes filled with glee. "You're going to give us the answers we need. You're going to cooperate, or I will personally make sure that the war your lot thinks was so terrible is just a distant childhood fantasy." Erach pulled an older-style metal gun from beneath the folds of his jacket. "I will make your life a living nightmare."

Rowena's eyebrows went up in surprise. "With that?"

Erach frowned down at his weapon. "Yes. It's a gun."

"But it's not meant for torture. Do you know the kickback on that thing? At this range, one shot is going to cut me in half." She took step toward him as her training came to the fore. "There's no way to miss a major artery. If you want torture, you need something small." Another step. "You want to focus on pain, not damage."

He didn't move fast enough to dodge her punch. A fist to his jaw and an elbow to his neck.

She grabbed the gun as he fell.

A shot rang out beside her, the ordinance splashing into the hardpacked dirt beside her. "You have friends? How?" She stomped on Erach's side, taking minimal satisfaction in the sound of ribs breaking, and ran away from the guns.

It was a guess at best. They could have been herding her. Could be setting an ambush. But staying still was a worse option.

The stolen gun was heavy in her hands. Pre-isolation style with metal bullets. It was a crude, wasteful sort of weapon, but it would kill someone.

Without her implant, her lungs started to burn. Her legs insisted she didn't want to run this fast over uneven ground.

It went against all her training to keep moving rather than stand and fight.

The ground exploded to her right from another shot behind her. She dodged left.

Zig-zagging, weaving. It was like being in a fighter, except there wasn't comforting weight of her uniform, no guns, no communications.

Last time things had been this desperate was when Hollis had cracked her hull and she'd been forced to put up a heavy shield or breath vacuum.

Ancestors, that had been a day. If Mal hadn't been there keeping her calm, she would have run short of oxygen long before she made it to safety.

Breath. Keep breathing, Ro. Steady. Count it out.

She focused on breathing. Her feet kept going, moving along the unpredictable lines of the fighter's flight path until she reached the dubious safety of the trees. Even without her nanites she could cover a kilometer in under ten minutes. Time and distance would give her an advantage.

Glancing behind, she tried to gauge the distance to where Erach lay. A couple of klicks at most. It looked further than it was, but there was a slope that stretched to the horizon. The open plain was the top of a plateau.

An animal shout filled the air, a long, low howl from the dawn of time that silenced the insects and made the hair on the back of her neck stand on end.

Hellhounds.

They'd brought the hunting hounds after her.

Standing to fight wasn't a question. Her implant wasn't recharging fast enough and she couldn't defend against the dogs while moving.

Rowena looked up at the canopy.

The edge of the forest was filled with light, pretty and inviting, but horrible for defense. The deeper forest would have more options for camouflage.

Think of it as a training exercise. A practice drill. Can your cadets do this?

Of course they can.

So can you.

In a few hours, there'd be other concerns. Water was important in this heat.

Food.

Shelter, if it rained or it grew cold tonight.

Communications, if her implant didn't recharge.

She should have asked Erach how he'd nulled her implant before she put his rib bone through his lung.

The baying hounds grew closer as she sprinted past the edgewood for the darker parts of the forest. *Ancestors, if you can forgive me, send some help.*

Ducking under a low branch, she plunged into the undergrowth and ran for her life.

36
MALCOLM

THERE WAS A RED BIRD SINGING in the bushes in front of the brick house on Hillside Drive. It cheeped angrily as Malcolm slammed his car door.

It was early—most of the neighborhood was probably still sleeping—but when things were desperate, there was nothing better than the comfort of family.

Less than an hour from the city-center of Ryun, the wealthy had tamed a patch of desert. Lush, green lawns with river-rock paths and desert willows framed modest, brick homes built to withstand seasonal wind storms. It was nothing like Sonya's mansion or the palaces of Kydell, not ostentatious wealth, but refined, elegant wealth. This was a place for people who invested their money in the future, and in themselves.

That made the small suburb of River Willow a perfect place for his parents to hide. His mother had her gardens and book club. His father had the nearby university, lecture halls, and a bookstore that kept long hours.

He needed to see his parents. To know they were okay. His entire flight home he'd worried what would happen if Lethe got to them first.

Entering the unlock code, he swung the door open and stepped into the tiled entryway. The Long home was as modest on the inside as it was in the front. Elegant glass doors on one side of the front entry led to the sun-washed library. The main living area was on the other side, and the dining room straight ahead. To one side of the dining room was the small, unused kitchen. On the other was a hall that led to the master suit, the guest bedroom Malcolm sometimes claimed as his own, and his mother's very expensive botany lab.

If anyone wanted to find the true family jewel, all they had to do was exit the back sunroom to the expansive gardens. His mother loved growing things.

His father was sitting on the couch, watching the news with a look usually reserved for the oratory debates of election season. "We weren't expecting to see you today."

"I had a rough night. Thought being home might help." Understatement of the year.

Lucas Long glared at the news. "You were in Kydell? With Lethe?"

"A business party. Why?" Malcolm stopped half-way through taking off his shoes as he saw the images on the screen.

Kydell was on fire.

"What happened? Four hours ago..." He'd heard Sonya and her father planning to turn Kydell into an experiment.

Malcolm sank onto the couch next to his father.

"An arson attack on a government building," his father said. "The local security are on the scene and insisting that

the criminal element of the city's underprivileged population are responsible." His tone spoke of deep disgust with
the situation.

It meant someone was doing something badly. His father
was a perfectionist.

"How do they know who is responsible? There can't
have been time for an investigation."

"The reporter is reading from a script," his father said
with a sneer. "Twice now they've mentioned the unhappy
dock workers and panned to empty docks. They've mentioned crowds but there are none. It's an absolute farce."

Sonya's plan had included riots. She'd been so certain of
them, but somehow, right when she needed them, the mobs
were missing.

Silar.

That name kept coming up. The redheaded playboy was
in the middle of this mess. Sonya had pinned all her hopes
on him and Malcolm—tide take his good intentions—had
stepped between Sonya and her prize.

At that point, the ringing of his phone seemed inevitable.

Malcolm stepped into the backyard perfumed by roses.
"Lady Lethe, what have I done to earn the honor of your
phone call?"

"You have the data decrypted as promised?" Sonya demanded, skipping social niceties.

"Of course." Fabricated was a more accurate term, of
course, but Sonya wasn't likely to notice.

"I need it," Sonya said. "Sooner rather than later."

He had expected as much. "Where can we meet?"

"Didn't you offer to take me to the opera?"

"I did." As a distraction, naturally, not as a serious date.

"Meet me in Kytan at ten in two days. The season's first
production of Spring Of The Blossom's Shadow opens at
noon, everyone who is anyone will be there."

"Then so will I."

"Good. Bring the data, not excuses. I don't have time for incompetence today."

The line went dead before he could reply.

Malcolm stared at the roses in his mother's garden, mostly deep red or white. He'd dreamed of them after the party, the red rose bushes rising up to grab and choke him, sharp thorns cutting him to ribbons.

He didn't need a psychology degree to analyze that. By stepping in for Rose Lauren, he had made Sonya Lethe his enemy.

But it didn't matter what she thought.

He'd already made his choice.

Now he had to hope he could survive it.

37
HOLLIS

HOLLIS SAT ON THE EDGE OF his bunk, idly running his hands along the cold sheets. Rowena hadn't come back.

He couldn't get a ping off her.

Garius's voice kept drumming the response into his head. *The Declaration of Courtship is refused. She doesn't want you. The Declaration of Courtship is refused. She doesn't want you.*

She doesn't want you.

There was no space for that in his probability matrix. No calculation resulted in Rowena refusing him. Hoshi might, for a variety of reasons. Rowena wouldn't.

And he couldn't contact her to ask what had gone wrong.

It was fine—or at least that was what he was trying to convince himself. He'd contacted Tyrling. Rowena was safe and transporting Jhandarmi officers offsite. Tyrling said the team leader had called in with Rowena's location.

There was probably a lockdown in place. Or maybe she was busy running comms for them.

Or sleeping under a heavy shield.

It'd been a busy few days and he didn't begrudge her the quiet. He just...

A full day had gone past since the bombing in Kydell. Hoshi's response had come in at noon. Three more hours had crawled past as Hollis had waited for any update.

He wanted to be there. Not for the action, but for Rowena. To make sure she was safe. To help her, because he knew she was upset by the threats to the rowdies.

He needed to talk it out was what he needed, with someone who understood him well enough to not need all the words in his head. :Hermione?: He sent the message on a private channel.

:Is something wrong?:

:I need a few minutes.:

:Location?:

He gave her the coordinates for the upper hull of the *Veronica* and teleported himself up.

A hard, salty wind blew off the rocky coastline, leeching the air of the warmth provided by the clear day. Tucking himself in the trench of an old gun turret twice the size of the ship's main mess hall, Hollis looked down at the forest of metal. The fallen fleet.

He rested his arms on a high point of the hull and waited.

Hermione teleported in without a sound. The wind dipped down, pinning her loose brown pants to her legs.

Hollis put up a shield and they had peace. "Thanks for coming."

"What's wrong?"

There were too many thoughts. Too many wrongs. So he dumped them into her head, all the confusion and noise pushed out on a shared channel.

Hermione's eyebrows went up. "Is she okay?"

"Last I checked. Tyrling thinks she is."

"But she hasn't checked in with you?" Hermione walked over to join him at the edge. Far below, sailors were monochrome specks hustling between ships. "It could be she's busy. It's not exactly habit for her to check in with you yet. And there's no scenario where Rowena isn't taking over the command position wherever she's at."

"I know." His throat tightened. "That's not the problem. I trust her. She'll be fine."

"Then what's wrong?"

The question was wrong. He shook his head. "I know as much as I can... but it's not enough for me. But—"

"But you have no right to ask for more?"

He looked at Hermione for help. "Is that wrong?"

She reached out and touched his cheek. "No. Why would that be wrong? You love her, Hollis. This is not a youthful romance or an infatuation, but a mature love. You want to be there to support her. You want to share her life. And she's in battle without you."

"I've got nine hundred years of fleet tradition telling me I don't have the right to be near her in a crisis because our ancestors-b'damned crews aren't allied!"

Hermione laughed.

He glared at her in angry shock.

"Oh, ancestors! You know how to solve this problem!"

"A Declaration of Courtship?"

Hermione nodded with a happy smile.

"I made one. Hoshi shot it down. Said Rowena wasn't interested."

White fire crossed Hermione's eyes as her expression turned grave. "That can't be true. I've seen her with you. She'd allow the courtship."

"She's not within comms range. I can't reach her. Titan can't. Even Tyrling hasn't spoken to her, although he says he knows where she is."

"Hoshi didn't ask her then. There's no way Rowena would be available for Hoshi Lee and not Titan." Hermione crossed her arms. "I mean, legally, I suppose he's allowed to refuse on her behalf. But it's not..." She waved a hand.

Hollis nodded. "I've never heard of a captain refusing like this."

"There are options," Hermione said. "You can make the Declaration directly. Or jump crews. Or have Rowena jump crews. The Sciarras would take her in a heartbeat and you know Elea would approve of the match. Especially if she could make you both Sciarras. That would give her crew four Elites."

"But I can't make a Declaration to Rowena if I can't talk to her, and I can't talk to her unless I'm allowed to ask where she is, and I'm not allowed to know because I'm not her crew or publicly recognized lover!"

Hermione patted his arm. "You're smart, Hollis. You'll figure it out."

"I'm about to go into Tyrling's office and demand he tell me."

"He wouldn't love it, but he'd probably tell you." Hermione shrugged. "Try not to break him though. As Jhandarmi directors go, he's one of the better ones."

His grin was grim. "I'll try not to damage any peace treaties too much."

"Hollis." Hermione caught his arm. "For what it's worth, I'm happy for you. After Trace died, I thought a part of you was lost. You weren't happy any more, even with me. You couldn't relax. Couldn't step away from all of it." Her smile was soft. "Rowena gave that back to you. You smile more now. You're happier. You look healthier."

"Do I really?" He didn't feel it.

"Well, maybe not right this minute." She smiled. "But this is good. For both of you. Rowena... you're giving her what Mal couldn't."

His lips tightened into a grimace.

"It's true. Mal and her were a lot like you and me."

"Hermione—"

"You need to know."

"I do know. Rowena told me." He let that thought sink in for both of them. "Rowena told me what I need to know." It was the last tumbler in the lock clicking into place. Rowena was the one who mattered now. Rowena was the only one he wanted to hear any of this from.

Hermione grinned like she'd won a prize. "Don't get sentimental on me, Silar."

Some of the tension in his chest eased. "You know I still love you. You're my favorite allied captain. Just not my favorite person."

"Perrin's going to be heartbroken to learn he lost to me. He always thought he was the favorite." She stood on tiptoe and kissed his cheek. "Congratulations on the impending nuptials, Commander."

"Mmm, let me confirm that with Rowena first."

"Once she's agreed, tell her Perrin and I welcome her to the family."

Hollis stared out at the distant ocean, picturing Rowena's highspeed reentry into the command structure of the fleet. She was worried about people shunning him, but that wouldn't happen. When Rowena wasn't hiding who she was, she was like the sun. No one could avoid her gravitational pull. She was going pull the entire fleet into her orbit.

And then he was going to have to share her with everyone again.

"You know, maybe I'll just run away with her for a few days. Take some leave. Find somewhere private where we don't have to deal with anyone for a few days."

"Sounds good," Hermione said. "The Jhandarmi owe her some time off. Take a week or two. I'm sure you'll be able to put it to good use."

"Can you spare us? With... everything?" The whole explosive nightmare in Kydell. The orun device that was supposed to be in his chest. Sonya Lethe and whatever hull-cracked plans she had.

Hermione looked mildly offended. "I'm going to intercept Sonya at the opera in a few hours, see if she'll drop some hints as to what she has planned. The Carylls can make a run at Long later if we need to, find a way to break that connection. We will figure out what Sonya's doing, help the Jhandarmi put a lid on this, and hold the battle line while you and Rowena figure out what you want out of life."

"I figured that out," Hollis said. "I want her. All I have to do is find her and convince her she wants me too." One missing Lee on a planet; he'd faced worse odds before. He smiled at Hermione. "I'll be back soon."

Hermione smiled back at him. "Good."

His sight slipped, filtering out the world until all he saw was the red thread vanishing into the distance. :Rowena, I'm coming to find you.:

38
ROWENA

THE EVENING AIR CLUNG, HEAVY and wet as the thunderous clouds on the horizon. Rowena steadied her breathing and rested against the rough bark of a wide tree as the hunter moved forward. Two days of running through the wild jungles of Seahome and she still hadn't been able to shake them.

Dead leaves rustled. Dry twigs cracked. The hairless, long-fanged hound snuffled and whined as it tried to track her many routes in and out of the clearing.

Rowena twisted the heavy branch in her sweaty palms and checked her implant again. It was still below one percent. Sometime during the evening it had hit three, but then it started draining again. Every bit of kinetic energy she stored was being whisked away.

At least this time the energy drain was leaving a path for her to follow.

The hunter moved between her and the falling moon.

Rowena moved, smashing the heavy branch on the hunter's neck and swinging around to crack the giant dog in the head.

The hound stumbled backward, but didn't slow down.

She took the gun out and shot the hound between the eyes as it leapt at her. The crack echoed in the night, but there was no answering retort. The hunters had fanned out, and she'd been thinning the ranks.

It was her last bullet though.

Frowning, she walked to the hound and kicked it in its bare belly. They were ugly things, long silver fangs and naked hides with tufts of bristly fur along the ridge of the back. It was hard to imagine what they'd looked like before the terraforming had mutated them.

Maybe they were cute when they were smaller.

Certain that the hound wasn't faking—one mistake like that had nearly killed her earlier—she turned back to the unconscious human. He was still breathing and the pulse was fine. His neck didn't feel broken either.

Rowena tied his hands and legs behind his back with the rope in his pack and lashed it to the tree. Either his friends would come for him, or the local carnivores would have an easy snack. Whichever, he wouldn't be coming after her.

She rummaged deeper in his pack and patted his pockets. No gun. Either he'd run out of ammo early on or they were getting smarter.

"Don't you have anything useful?" she muttered.

The water canteen was barely a quarter full, the rations were half eaten, and even the medical kit stored at the bottom of his rucksack was missing everything but gauze.

There was no way this man would have survived several days hunting her in the jungle. Once the sun came up, he wouldn't have been good for even hours. It was hot under the canopy and she was only surviving because she'd found a water filter on the first woman she'd taken down.

It was almost as if the hunter was planning to die.

Like bait.

Rowena sat up, listening to the silence. No birds signing. No bats clicking. No insects. Only the greedy silence of a forest avoiding a predator.

Crack my hull.

She'd wasted her last bullet on this, told them exactly where she was, and then sat around waiting. It was a stupid mistake.

The only thing the man had of use was a topography map. They were chasing her toward a cliff—she knew that already, she'd been moving along it for over an hour now trying to find a way down. Whatever was pulling on her energy was out that way. She was going to find it, then smash it with the heaviest rock she could find.

She sniffed the water in the canteen and caught a whiff of something sour. Probably poisoned.

But the holder was still good. There was a stream ten klicks away and a waterfall. It wouldn't be the most sterile place to wash anything, but it would work, and she could filter the water she drank.

The important part was she had a goal and a plan.

She only had to stay alive for a few more hours. Tyrling had to know she was missing by this point.

If he didn't, Hollis would notice. Once someone noticed, all they had to do was have the *Persephone* run a scan of the planet for her. Come daybreak, she could climb a tree and signal to her rescuers.

It was just a few more hours.

A breeze ran along the ridge, bringing the fetid smell of the hounds and scent of human sweat. The hunters were moving closer.

Picking the heavy branch back up, Rowena moved on.

Water first. Then rescue.

This wouldn't last forever.

39
MALCOLM

SONYA SPARKLED, WHITE AND pale blue diamonds fixed to her arms so that every gesture shattered light. The resulting thousands of coruscating rainbows cut through the crowds in the glass entry room of the opera house.

"Anyone familiar with the history of the city would have said the same," Sonya said to a rapt audience of social aspirants. They hung on her words, hoping and praying that something heard here would allow them to ascend to the upper echelons of popularity.

Malcolm hung back, half hidden by the deep blue curtains framing the area reserved for the Lethes and their guests.

Framing was the perfect word. From a distance Sonya must have glittered, a jewel on display for the elite to see. Her glacier-blue silk dress was less an example of the textile arts and more a paean to the heroic efforts of glue. Watery, waving scraps were affixed to her body with gem-laced flesh peeking in between. Her pale hair was swept up in an elegant chignon, her makeup was restrained, artfully youthful. The end result was too calculated to incite passion and too contrived to garner compliments.

His role as an accessory was not something Malcolm wanted to dwell on, so he returned to watching the crowd below. The blue Lethe dye was a close-held secret within the family, kept exclusively for them, but this was Kytan, and blues and greens of all shades were on display.

As the sun crept to its zenith, the glass dome of the foyer danced with muted color.

The opera itself was unimportant. It was an excuse to see and be seen. A chance to network, form alliances, and strike at enemies in a socially acceptable way. Watching the crowd, Malcolm picked out relationships without knowing who they were or what they meant to Sonya's plans. She would have enjoyed his ignorance, if he'd let it show.

There was no one alone in the opera house. They moved in groups of two or three, if they were younger or poorer. In groups of seven or eleven, or even seventeen for the large entourages, tailing like comets after the wealthy.

A parasitic network of mutual adulation.

"Doctor Long." Sonya's cold hand wrapped around his wrist. "Come say hello to my guests." An order, not a request.

He put on a gracious smile as he bowed politely to the sycophants.

"Malcolm is one of the premier flight engineers on the continent," Sonya told her audience. "He has quite a stunning mind."

"Long, you say?" A man who looked barely old enough to shave frowned in puzzlement. "Not from one of the families then, are you?"

"My mother is an Amherst, of the Northland Amhersts," Malcolm said coldly. It was important to reinforce his status now, and the family name mattered more than his accomplishments.

Sonya beamed in delight as people realized who she'd captured.

"The lost heir?" one of the girls asked, eyeing him like a forbidden treat. "Oh, Sonya. That's so delightful! Whatever has Vherkam said about this?"

"Ollie?" Sonya shrugged, light rippling off her skin. "Somehow we've missed each other today. I'm certain he'll be delighted. He did say he wanted what was best for me, and the Amhersts control some very nice farmland."

More than the Vherkams, her smug tone implied. Although farmlands was a bit of a stretch. The Amherst name did come with a few hundred acres of farmland, but the majority of their holdings were in a stretch of barren tundra near the northernmost sea.

Malcolm studied his shiny blue shoes and the hem of his black-blue pants. He was a shadow of Sonya Lethe's pale moonlight. A ghost.

Someone waved to Sonya from the entrance to her private balcony, and she released Malcolm to drift back to the railing.

Bells rang high noon.

The heavy, silver doors of opera house opened and a goddess walked in.

Probably not a goddess, but she made Malcolm's breath catch all the same.

Dark brown skin with gold flakes intricately laced across her arms and back, a simple gown of fiery, coral orange, a crown of brown curls accented by more gold. She was the sun. The center of the universe. A bright fire on a cold, midwinter day.

Malcolm couldn't take his eyes off her any more than he could will his heart to stop beating. How many years had it been? Over four since he saw her last. Not the woman on the floor, but the woman he'd loved and lost. They couldn't be the same.

He wanted them to be the same.

He wanted her to look up, a radiant smile on her face as she recognized him.

He wanted to change the past.

"Ugh." Sonya stepped up beside him and looked down at the golden woman in disgust. "Marshall."

Malcolm swallowed back his first response, locking his memories away behind layers of icy politeness. "A Marshall or The Marshall?"

"Hermione Marshall," Sonya said. "The only Marshall that matters. Heiress, ambassador, traitor, pick a title. I thought she'd have the good sense to stay away today. Look at her, the poor, sad thing. She's alone."

People were orbiting her; there was no better word. The crowd moved in response to Marshall, ebbing and flowing around her as she crossed the foyer.

"Look at the art she's wearing," Sonya said, glaring at the golden lace. "She must have spent all day in a chair. What a waste."

The pattern of the gold lines on Marshal's skin intrigued him nearly as much as the woman Sonya so violently hated. There was a mathemacality to it. A fluidity. The gold design was a fractal, a complex code unreadable to all but a few brilliant minds.

His evaluation of the situation, and the woman, shifted. She was insulting most of the crowd simply by being smarter than them, and none of them realized it. Someone would though. Eventually. The gossip pages loved ferreting out things like this. In a few days, everyone would be fuming.

"Hermione!" Sonya called out, her voice echoing across the dome. She waved to her rival.

Golden Hermione, skirts moving like living flame around her legs, looked up. "Sonya, I was hoping you'd be here."

"Come say hello," Sonya invited in front of the crowd. Making Hermione come to her put Marshall in a weaker political position.

But Marshall didn't look like she was playing the game by Descent rules. She swept up the staircase, scattering the crowd and drawing attention. Like a fire, she sucked all the oxygen out of the room.

Up close, she could have been the grown version of the girl he'd fallen in love with as a teen. Their eyes were the same color of polished brown stone. Their faces had the same high cheekbones and full lips.

He watched for any indication she knew him.

White fire crossed her eyes as she smiled.

Spacer.

Sonya had been right, this wasn't any average Hermione Marshall. This was the one who had gone to war and returned with a fleet of battleships.

He stepped back, trying to blend into the curtains.

Sonya would understand why a man from the islands the spacers had attacked didn't want to speak to one, if she thought to notice him at all.

"You look so... chilly," Hermione said in greeting.

"You look like you forgot which season it is," Sonya said. "Orange? With gold knots?"

Marshall smiled. "My own design. Do you like it?"

"It's still winter."

"Only here," Hermione countered. "I know you don't travel much anymore. Not since that nasty business on the third continent. Accused of attacking a civilian and stealing

Jhandarmi data?" Marshall clicked her tongue in a tsk. "Did they ever catch the woman who impersonated you?"

Sonya, put on the defensive, crossed her arms. "Within weeks of the event. I have trouble believing you didn't know that. Everyone else did."

"Everyone else had little else to occupy their time."

There were gasps from the onlookers and Malcolm assumed the implication that everyone else had so little business to attend to that they'd been waiting for gossip was a grave insult.

Things were done differently on Descent.

Sonya unfolded her arms and smiled. "Understandable. At the time I was so busy prepping for my next project I barely had time for the investigators."

"Is this the Kydellian project? I heard you were there recently."

"Did you?" Sonya asked in mock shock. "Oh, that's right. You know Silar and that Jhandarmi woman."

Marshall's smile tightened. "Jhandarmi woman?"

"Yes, the one who was so helpful after the explosion. I wondered if she reported to you."

"Sonya, I know you love your conspiracy theories, but the Jhandarmi don't report to me. Can we hope you haven't done anything rash?"

"I would never act rashly, or crassly. I'm a Lethe, not a Marshall." Sonya's smile said she thought she'd won this round. "I simply removed an unwanted impediment between me and my goal. Have you ever dallied with redheads? I hear they can be quite passionate."

Marshall laughed loud enough to draw curious looks from the sycophants who were working hard to go unnoticed while the two society queens battled with words. "You want Silar? Hollis Silar? Well..." She shook her head. "It's a choice I suppose. Not a good choice, perhaps, but then, so few of your choices are." The last was with a pointed look to the would-be entourage. "With all your potential, Sonya, one would think you'd at least make the effort to step up. We're not children any more. And people aren't dolls for you to collect on your dusty shelves."

"Would you like more than this gentle diversion? Then you'll appreciate my new acquisition."

"A new acquisition?" Marshall asked sweetly. "I look forward to the announcement. It must be a very delicate deal indeed if it's taken this long for even a rumor to circulate. The whole continent will be waiting for the news." Careful, flattering words spun around a vicious cut.

Sonya's smile tightened. "And you? It's sad to see you all alone."

For a second Marshall's brown eyes flicked in Malcolm's direction. Half a heartbeat, and her attention was back to Sonya. "There's someone waiting for me."

"He couldn't come today?"

"He had other arrangements."

"What a shame." Sonya reached out for him. "Doctor Long and I would have enjoyed meeting him." Sonya caught Malcolm's hand as he stepped forward at her command. "It's so tragic, darling. Hermione has been single for years now."

Malcolm looked at the golden woman, drinking in the sight of her. "Criminal," he said since Sonya expected a response. "And a testament to the fact that so few people can withstand the intensity of powerful women. I find it quite alluring."

Sonya preened, although his words weren't for her.

"Power is its own motive force." Marshall's smile was filled with understanding.

"We should go," Sonya said. "I'd invite you to join us in our box, but we already have guests."

Marshall stared at him for a second longer than politeness required. "Don't worry about me."

Malcolm's heart didn't stop racing until Sonya pulled him into the cold dark of the balcony. The stage was set with fake cherry trees in full bloom and a glittering moon hanging low as the backdrop.

"I can't stand that woman," Sonya said with a sigh as she dropped into her seat. "Absolutely infuriating." She pulled a small work computer from her bag with the open information light blinking green.

"You brought that?" He sat beside her.

"Naturally. The opera is the traditional ballad. I memorized it by the time I was seven."

He closed his eyes, recalibrating to Com Channel Sonya. "The network you're accessing is public. Someone could access your files." The very carefully forged files Sonya had insisted couldn't simply be sent over regular channels and had to be hand delivered.

"No one else brought work," Sonya said with a little laugh as she took the datstick he'd brought and plugged it into the computer. "They wouldn't dare."

"Marshall is an augmented spacer. She has a tech implant in her body," he said, spelling out the danger for Sonya. "She could have ripped your data while you were sniping at each other."

Sonya stilled in alarm, then shook her head. "Wouldn't matter. Everything's encrypted." Her screen showed several faces including Hollis Silar, Rose Lauren, and another black-haired woman who looked painfully familiar.

"What are those for?"

"Business," Sonya said. "Sometimes hostile takeovers have causalities." A light blinked next to the black-haired woman's face. Sonya smiled as she sighed in relief. "One less spy to deal with."

His teeth ground together as the lights fell. It was past time for Sonya Lethe to fail.

What were the rules for passing confidential information at the opera? Was he supposed to ask an usher to take the encryption code to Sonya's rival or simply flag Marshall down during intermission?

Malcolm watched as the woman of gold and fire took her seat several balconies over. The gold on her arm was an encryption too. Her own design, she'd said.

Lethe's standard encryption wouldn't take Marshall more than a few minutes to break.

Hermione looked at him. In the dim light of the theater, he saw a white glow; the swirl of galaxies formed and died, leaving nothing but darkness. Lethe needed to fail and Marshall was going to make it happen.

"How much do you think Bennu would trade for on the open market?" Sonya asked.

"What?" He was jolted out of his reverie at the mention of his company's name. "Why?"

"I need an acquisition," Sonya said. "My other plan fell through, something Marshall knows very well. But she kept it quiet. She's letting me recover."

An unsound tactic if he'd ever heard of one. "Why would she do that?"

"Because, for all her many strengths, Marshall has the business acumen of a rotten apple. She doesn't think in strategy or tactics."

"I heard she was a general during a war…"

Sonya waved a hand and the scant light from the stage made the gems glow. "The spacers had a tiff. It wasn't a real war."

"Thousands of people died."

"Three people died, and only islanders at that."

"The spacers—"

"Don't count. They aren't the Chosen Children of the Empire. Mal Baular excepted." Sonya shook her head. "Marshall oversaw a fist fight, nothing more. The spacers lost their focus, they forgot why they exist. When the emperor returns, I'll see to it that he reminds them." Her smile turned cruel. "Then we'll see how Marshall fares."

Malcolm sucked in a breath and let it go. "I must have misunderstood the situation."

Sonya patted his knee. "It's all right, dear. Not everyone can have the intelligence I have."

The urge to retort with the observation that rocks had more intelligence than she did seemed ill-considered. He let it go. "Bennu is not for sale."

"It will be. Money buys everything."

He'd sooner jump off the hypertram over the city than let Bennu wind up in Lethe's hands. Perhaps that information could be passed on to the sympathetic ears of Miss Marshall.

Then, if Lethe and Marshall wanted to square off for a match, he could watch the war veteran smear Sonya Lethe across the battlefield from somewhere safe. Preferably somewhere on a different continent.

Whatever Sonya said, Marshall was not to be underestimated.

Ever.

40
ROWENA

A WARM NIGHT TURNED INTO a steaming day filled with biting insect swarms and the ever-closer sounds of the hunters.

Twice Rowena had found a likely path, only to be forced to turn back because of the heavy guard waiting for her. Dolus's teams were good, carefully blocking her exits, pushing her toward the cliff, closing in on her position.

Slapping aside a crawling, multi-legged thing on her arm, she took a moment to sit. Her mind was foggy with fatigue. Her stomach complained as bitterly as her muscles about the prolonged activity without food or water. If she didn't find a plan soon, she wasn't going to live to see sunset.

Would that be so bad? a little voice whispered in her mind. *If you move a little slower, don't fight quite so hard, would that be so bad? The pain would end.*

There'd be peace at last.

No more aching legs shaking from exertion. No more parched throat that feels as if you've swallowed knives. No more hunger or fatigue or worries again. It would all be over.

She looked across the craggy stretch of rock where a fracture held a shallow pool that became a thundering waterfall. There was water there. It wouldn't do much for the hunger, but her throat would feel better.

It was undoubtedly being watched. The hunters knew she needed water.

Go, the little voice whispered, *it won't hurt for long. A brief, piercing moment and it's over. All your worries gone. Your future decided. You'll never fail again. Never hear Hollis say he regrets loving you.*

Putting her head in her hands, she tried to focus on something other than her fears. "Ancestors—if you're there, if you forgive me—give me an idea."

In her mind's eye, she pictured her mother kneeling in front of her. She'd been six or seven when her mother had stroked her hair and said, "Don't worry. You don't need to be strong. That's what the chain of command is for. There's always someone stronger than you ahead of you. They'll protect you."

Not anymore. There was no chain of command here. Tyrling couldn't find her. If he could have, the *Persephone* would have made contact days ago. Crack, without her implant running the fleet wasn't going to find her either. Her body would rot out here and everyone who cared would be left to wonder.

"Follow orders," her father had said when she was nine. "You're not meant to think, only to follow."

Terrible life advice. Even good leaders gave bad orders.

"You stay with your flight partner," her instructor had told when she was eleven. "Whatever you do, remember your team is counting on you to make the smart call. To protect them. That's the officer's job."

Except there was no one here to protect. She was alone, terribly, frighteningly alone.

She thought of Mal standing on the deck of the *Sárkány* with his commander's rank fresh and gleaming. "I don't love you, Ro, not the way I want to love someone. I don't want this anymore. You don't need me, and there's someone else. She needs me. She loves me. I love her. I want you to support me on this."

"And do what?" she'd asked. "Wither? Die? No one else will have me. No one else will love me."

"When this is over, name the person. I'll get them for you. I have ships, ranks, commands, I can get you anyone you want."

"You can't trade people's hearts like that. It's been tried. It doesn't work."

"So what do you want me to offer you? What can I give you to make this right?"

"Nothing."

There was nothing.

Dry eyes stung for want of tears. She looked up at the branches of the tree she was hiding under, the large green leaves covering red-brown branches that spiraled in a fractal pattern up the gnarled trunk.

"There's my favorite Lee," Hollis had said when she was scared and desperately searching for Titan.

"You are a good officer," Hollis had said when no one else believed it.

I love you. She mouthed the unfamiliar words.

Hollis was going to lose an engine when he found out about this.

He probably couldn't pull a Caryll and slag the continent from orbit, but this forest was going to be nothing but memory and ash if she didn't get home safe.

With a sigh, she pointed and flexed her toes, trying to work out the worst of her muscle aches.

"Come on," she told herself, "get up. This will all be a funny story in a year or two."

Or thirty.

Rest, the little voice whispered, *close your eyes and let whatever comes next happen. You can't change the stars any more than you can put another moon in orbit.*

She stood up and counted herself lucky that her implant wasn't working just now. There'd be no record of the little voice, or how tempted she was by it, for anyone to worry over when she got home.

And she was getting home.

She hadn't survived all of this to let someone grounder with a grudge put a bullet in her. They thought they had her cornered. They thought they had her in an impossible position.

But there was a bright blue sky in front of her beckoning her forward to the stars beyond.

Rowena walked into the clearing with a smile.

There was a snicker and several hunters stepped out from their hiding place with a pack of hounds behind them.

"Ready to surrender?" one of them asked, training a gun on her.

Rowena looked at the crashing waterfall with the rocks below and a deep pool of raging water. She'd have to clear the rocks, get over a meter away from the cliff if she wanted a chance to survive. Not impossible.

She smiled at the grounders and turned, running for the cliff.

It was time to fly.

41
HOLLIS

HOLLIS SNAPPED THE DOOR OF his locker open. He tossed his bag on the narrow bunk under the sloped ceiling. There was a spare medkit under the folded desk secured to the wall behind the door, and he had an itching suspicion he might need it.

With the shields around his quarters, he had room to acknowledge his feelings. He was scared.

Terrified Rowena's smiles and lingering touches had meant nothing.

Furious that Hoshi and Garius had dismissed them out of hand.

Scared Rowena wasn't responding because she'd been hurt.

The silence was choking him, threatening to destroy his soul so he was a husk of himself.

She'd never said she loved him.

Never kissed him.

Never reached for him first.

He wanted to dismiss that as Rowena being Rowena. She was cautious and careful. She'd said she wanted to protect him, that she trusted him, and he'd read between the lines to see something more.

His hope was riding on the fact that Rowena was blunt. As engines went, it wasn't a bad one to bet on. If she didn't like something she said so.

With a sigh, he sorted through his closet, looking for something suitable for Seahome. The political situation in Kydell was still tense, and that meant Rowena would be nearby. Standing her ground and protecting the rowdies.

There was an unusual chime that broke through his shields. An alarm.

His implant lit up, trying to identify it—and then the room vanished. He stumbled over a rock, falling to his knees and looking down at a pool of frothing water as a waterfall thundered near his ears.

Force teleport.

A hand broke through the white water. Hollis grabbed it out of instinct, hauling a familiar weight to the surface.

"Out!" Rowena shouted as she broke the surface. "Teleport out!" The current pulled her under again.

He grabbed her arms, pulling her up and initiated a teleport. His implant registered a low charge.

"Get out!" Rowena pushed him away as she clung to the rocks.

He tried teleporting them again. *Charge under one percent.* "What the crack?"

"Fog you, Silar," Rowena panted as she crawled out of the river. "What does *get out* mean? It means you teleport, you red-haired baboon!" She crawled past the treeline into a copse of brambles before she collapsed on her back, eyes closed. "What the crack is wrong with you that you can't follow simple orders?"

Hollis looked around finally registering the environment. Humid air, the smell of decaying leaves, the crash of water... His eyes followed the falls up a forty meter cliff. "Did you fall off that?"

"No," Rowena said. "I jumped."

His composure cracked like a fighter's hull under heavy fire. "What the crack, Rowena? You thought the Lost Fleet was going to catch you if you tried to fly? Maybe thought you could get airborne without an engine?"

"It was jump or let the cracking grounders shoot me." She opened her eyes and sat up. "They had me trapped on the edge. Holding still seemed like a bad idea."

"There's a long list of options between Get Shot and Jump Off A Cliff!"

"Not when there's seven of them with long range weapons, hellhounds, and no charge in my implant." She was bleeding, bruised, weak... and arguing with him. "Why are you even here?"

He grabbed her by the forearm and helped her to her feet. "Force teleport."

Rowena stood off-balance, favoring one leg, and patted herself down. Her hand stopped at her back pocket. With a frown, she reached in and pulled out the emergency card. "Ah..."

"You were supposed to break that as soon as you ran into trouble," Hollis said, pulling on a reserve of patience he didn't know he had.

"To do what, exactly?" Rowena demanded. "Teleport you into the middle of a fire fight with no escape route? That sounds like a stupid idea, Commander." She put an extra growl into his rank.

Hollis took a deep breath. "You should have snapped that as soon as you were somewhere secure then."

"Bringing in ancestors only know who to a jungle? This thing summons any Guardian on duty. It was pure lu—" She stopped as she turned and saw his expression.

He waited a moment. "Pure luck?"

"You did say it would call the senior guardian on duty," she said with a hint of apology. "You lied about that, didn't you?"

"No." *Maybe.* "In your case, I am always the senior guardian on duty."

"Worried I'd break one of your precious lieutenants?" She teetered slightly and winced.

Hollis caught her arm and looked into her eyes.

Her expression softened. "You worry too much about me."

"Really? This looks like a monumental failure to anticipate a threat. I'm thinking I don't worry enough. How'd you lose your charge?"

"Crack if I know. Something out here is draining it. Every time I get over one percent it goes flat. I've got a ping off something." Rowena stood and gasped in pain. "Crack my hull." She balanced on one leg again.

"Broken?"

"Just sprained I think." Carefully, she tried resting the weight on her ankle. She took a deep breath as pain carved lines into her face. "Okay. Let's move before they decide to look down here."

Hollis held still. "You can't walk on that."

"I can hobble." Rowena grabbed his sleeve for balance and urged him deeper into the jungle.

An eerie howl cut across the jungle canopy.

"Hellhounds," Rowena muttered, letting go and moving ahead. "They'll catch our scent."

This was all wrong. Hollis caught up with her under the mossy-laden boughs of a tree that looked older than the hulls of the fleet. "Where are we?"

"Somewhere on the second continent." She hobbled further into the tangled jungle.

"Here, let me carry you."

"I can move."

Catching her hand, he twisted his back to her, put her hand on his shoulder, and bent down so he could grab her behind her knees.

"Hollis! I'm all wet!" she protested as he put her on his back.

"I have waited so long to hear you say that," he murmured.

"What?"

"Nothing."

She was wet, chilled, and soaking his back. But that was quickly replaced by the sensation of her body pressed against him. Her arms resting on his shoulders. Her breath against his neck. "Mmm, you smell like soap," she said. "I love soap."

"You love soap?" He chuckled. Not quite what he'd been hoping for her to love.

She rested her head against his. "I've been here for two days. There's mud. Dirt. Thousands of bugs." He could feel her shudder of disgust. "I woke up with this thing with a thousand legs crawling on me and I couldn't even scream."

If he pretended it was humorous, he could ignore the guilt. He should have pushed Tyrling to give him an answer sooner. Started looking for Rowena as soon as she didn't appear on the first scan.

"Want to give me a status report?" he asked as he walked forward. "Or tell me where am I going?"

A slender finger pointed slightly to the right. "That-away."

It was strange not having the deep communication of the implants. He couldn't read Rowena's emotions with pinpoint accuracy—but at the same time, he was willing to say with confidence that she was relieved he was there. Maybe even happy. She was quiescent on his back. He bumped his head into hers. "Stay awake."

"I'm awake," she muttered. There was a groan and a heavy sigh that vibrated through his chest. "I was told to teleport a Jhandarmi agent to safety, Erach Dolus."

"I know him."

"You were on the mountain with him." The tone promised retaliation. "He gave me coordinates and when I teleported us in he pulled a gun on me. My charge dropped to zero in seconds. I couldn't teleport out." A angry hiss of breath. "He betrayed us. He's the one who tried to kill you."

Hollis filed that away for later. "What did you do?"

"Broke his arm, broke his ribs, stole his gun and ran. What was I supposed to do?"

"Staying alive was the most important step."

"I did that." She yawned. "Did I miss anything?"

"No." Not anything they were going to discuss before he checked her for a concussion. Afterwards... he'd see what she said. They could discuss how she wanted to handle Hoshi's rejection. Whether she wanted to fight for command of the Lees, or leave them for good.

She ran a hand across his chest. "You're getting warm. Put me down."

"A little sweat isn't going to kill me. You're lighter than the rucksack I was carrying in the mountains." Or more enjoyable to carry, one of the two.

They'd gone less than a klick before Rowena tapped his shoulder and gave the hand signal to stop. He hadn't seen those since the last full silence drills during the war.

"Down." Rowena climbed off his back and carefully stepped in front of him, weight on her good leg. She took her knife out and pushed the hip-tall grasses in front of them to one side.

"Are the plants dangerous?"

"Not these ones, but they have bugs." Her nose wrinkled in distaste. "I was worried about *that*." She gestured forward with a tilt of her head.

Hollis peered over her head at the ridge in front of them. The ground dropped away steeply at their feet, but it couldn't be *that* deep; the next ridge was only a handful of steps away. "It's only a couple meter drop."

"No, it's a couple meters distance. There are open fracture caves throughout the area. Seismic folds." She shook her head. "We've got to be close to the original drop site for the terraforming ordnance. The ground fractures fold up like waves, and around here, the interior of the waves eroded over time. The drops are hundreds of meters deep in places. Just straight down." Her hand swooped toward the ground as she spoke.

Hollis walked up to the crumbling edge and looked down. They were on the crest of the wave, an overgrown ridge with a frilled edge of tenacious plants clinging to life and whatever dirt they could trap in their roots. Beneath them was a dark chasm that swallowed the dim light filtering through the canopy.

Windswept trees hung over the gap, competing for sunshine, but none of them went far enough across to be a bridge.

"We need to walk around," Rowena said. "Go back and follow the water along the side of the ridge."

"How far away do you think this thing is that's draining our implants?"

"A klick or two dead ahead." Emphasis on dead. "From the top of the cliff, I had the rough map of a path that was about twenty klicks. I was hoping to get there by nightfall." She looked up and saw his confusion. "Three to four hours at a brisk pace."

Rowena couldn't move fast and they were already outnumbered. Any time wasted would give the enemy more time to move in. "And what, exactly, do you think is at the end of this treasure hunt?"

"The scans showed telekyen and metals similar to what's used in most hulls. No orun. My best guess was a downed communications satellite that's still semi-functional."

"A comms satellite wouldn't drain our implants."

"Not on its own, but if it were programmed to, it's more than capable. It might even revert to that programming if its primary fuel source is damaged or unavailable."

He narrowed his eyes. "Why would someone do that to a comms satellite?" They were the only relay between unallied ships or damaged ships and their armadas.

"If someone needs to get close to the satellite to communicate, and then they start losing power, it makes for a very tidy trap." Rowena sounded almost apologetic.

"Who came up with that idea?"

She held her hands up. "Not me! They were using it in the wars before I was even born."

"Which crew though? It might be something we can break if I know which crew."

"The Carvers used it the most," Rowena said. "But we won't need to break anything. There's no shield out there. Once we get to the satellite, I'll crack open the maintenance hull and reprogram it. Shut it off and recharge if I can, or use it to send a distress signal."

"Both would be a good idea." Hollis ran a hand through his hair. "You need daylight for that."

"Yeah."

He looked along the ridge. "There's a fallen tree over there. It looks stable."

"It's going to be crawling with bugs and there are things down in the chasms. The long way will—"

A chorus of howls rose too close for comfort.

Rowena's face went pale. "I thought they'd take longer to get down the cliff."

"We can't move fast so we have to move smart," Hollis said. "We'll get to the log, get across, and push it off from the other side."

The look Rowena gave the log was one of bleak despair.

"It won't be that bad," Hollis said, knowing that was probably a lie. "We've had worse."

"There really isn't anything worse than insects. Torture? Vomit? Split guts spilling on your face? There's always a shower nearby when that happens. Or a teleport. Or at least being grateful that you aren't the one dead. But insects?" She shuddered. "They're everywhere. Crawling on you. Touching you. Biting you. You kill one and five more fill their place."

"Like Silars?" he joked.

Rowena made a face of disgust, nose wrinkling and eyes narrowing. "No."

He almost smiled. "Just no? No cutting remark? We should check you for a head injury."

She moved away, heading for the log. "There's a noticeable difference between insects and Silars. When Silars climb all over me, I enjoy it."

Hollis stumbled.

"Coming?" Rowena asked as she turned to look at him. "Or did I confuse you by using the plural?"

His chuckle turned to a growl. "Rowena…"

"Battlefield morale," Rowena said with a lift of her chin. "If you're making me touch a log covered in bugs, I have to find my amusement elsewhere."

He caught up to her. "This is your idea of teasing me now?"

"Can't fight with you, can I?" she asked through gritted teeth. "I kind of need your help right now." She grabbed his arm for support.

"Kind of? You'd prefer to do this alone?"

"I'd prefer if you were somewhere safe," she said as they reached the log. "It would be darkly ironic if, after all those times I tried to kill you, I accidentally killed you by dragging you into the jungle." She took a breath. "I'm not walking across this."

"I'll carry you."

She shook her head. "Your balance would be off. We need to move across quietly. I'll sit and scoot." Her face was a perfect portrait of disgust. "This is—"

"I promise I'll never bring it up."

"When this is over and we get back to Enclave, I am going to sleep for a week. Take a shower, eat everything they have available at Cargo Blue, and sleep."

Hollis nodded. "Sounds good to me."

"Sleep," she emphasized the word. "Not whatever you're thinking about."

"The last good sleep I had was when I fell off the mountain. We can sleep for a week or two."

Using his arm as a support, Rowena lowered herself to the fallen trunk, legs straddling it. "You couldn't conjure up enough energy for some Silar fire, could you?"

"If I had that much, I'd teleport us to a city."

"We'd have no way of knowing it was safe." She moved forward in a slow slide.

Hollis watched her progress as he listened for the pursuers in the distance. "Is it solid? Could it hold both our weights?"

"Probably." She patted the trunk. "It doesn't sound hollow." Her gaze locked on the darkness beneath them.

"Look up," Hollis ordered. "Pretend it's vacuum." He dismissed the idea of trying to walk on the log and followed Rowena's plan for scooting. On a normal day, he would have done handstands on it, confident in his ability to catch himself. But without his implant, and worried about Rowena, it wasn't a risk worth taking. "This is going to be such a fun trip for your class."

Rowena groaned. "Don't remind me! If they get the idea of an overnight camping trip into their heads, I will never get out of it. They'll petition the Captain's Council until I allow it."

"They tried a petition to have you removed when you were made drill instructor at the training house."

"Really? Titan didn't tell me that." She crawled off the log and scrambled up the far bank.

"That's because it got lost in my office by accident."

Rowena stood up and crossed her arms. "Your office is more organized than almost anything in the fleet."

"If anyone asks," he grinned, "it was by accident." He reached the far side of the gap and climbed up to meet her. "Is there any other way across?"

She looked up and down the chasm edge. "Not that I'm seeing."

"Me either." The chasm was a klick-long black gash in the hillside. "How deep do you think it is?"

"Deep enough to have animals in it."

"Like what?" He started rolling the log away from the embankment.

"*Pandinus imperator albinius*, the pale emperor scorpion."

That sounded familiar. A part of his brain reached for his implant on instinct, but the reserve memory wasn't there. Another part of his brain produced the memory of the training gym, sets of maps, and giving Rowena a t-shirt. "Aren't those scorpions unusually large?"

"Not for this planet. There's no scorpion smaller than a meter in length on all of Malik IV."

He shuddered and pushed the tree into the gap. It tumbled and kept tumbling. Down. Down. Down. Out of sight and still silent.

"I am really glad we didn't fall," Rowena said. "Maybe we'll get lucky and they'll think we fell in."

"Maybe."

She offered him a hand. Hollis scooped her up instead, settling her on his back.

"Your clothes are getting dryer. How's the head feel?"

"Better than my ankle. I can hear the shouting. If they get close enough, drop me and run."

"You know that's not happening."

Rowena huffed in his ear. "Hollis."

"When we get home, we are going to have a long talk about exactly who I am. I don't abandon people."

"There's no shame in a tactical retreat. There's cover here."

He looked down at the leaf litter and vines twining around spindly trees in alarm. "We're also going to cover what counts as acceptable cover in a fire fight. This ain't it." There was visual cover, certainly, but the broad leaves blocking the sunlight weren't going to block weapons fire of any kind.

His reward was a quiet laugh.

"Go left, there's something metallic there."

"You see something?" He didn't.

"I can smell it. Beautiful, wonderful engine grease." She breathed deep, body moving against his back.

The ground dipped under his feet, exposed roots forming a spiraling staircase down to a small dell where the air hung heavy with the scent of moss. Under a crowd of vines, he could almost make out the shape of something rectangular.

Rowena slid off his back and cut at the vines with her knife. "It's a shuttle. An old, old model." She frowned. "Boxy. Who uses this design?"

It didn't look like any fighter he'd ever seen. Not enough angles. And it wasn't a standard troop transport, those had fins.

"This complicates things a little." Rowena pulled more vines loose. "I'm not even sure this is fleet."

"With anyone else, I'd ask if they could make it work," Hollis said. "With you... How long?"

She shrugged as she cleared a door. "It's closed. Doesn't look like a crash. But what's out here? There's no cities. No settlements. There's no reason to have a shuttle out here." There was hesitation in her voice.

"I'll check it first. See if there's any remains."

"You don't need—"

"Go sit down," Hollis ordered. "It's division of labor. You've had a rough few days. Let me take the hit on this one."

Her jaw tightened. "Don't pretend you've had it easy. Whatever's going on back in Enclave fried your engines too. I can see it in your eyes, something's wrong."

He nodded. "I was worried about you. It kept me up. But now I know where you are and how you are. I'm fine."

The look she gave him could have cut through a hull.

"Better," he said, correcting himself. "I'm better. Go sit down." He waited until she cleared a spot on a small rock before he walked out of sight around the hull. His palms sweated. This was every fleetlings nightmare, wasn't it? Derelicts. Finding a crash site. Finding someone you knew dead in the cockpit.

An unfamiliar hull was a cold comfort. There were plenty of smaller crews with older equipment who might have tried to fly this engine.

"What do you see?" Rowena asked, voice pitched so it wouldn't carry far.

"No obvious signs of damage. No cracks. No sign that this is a wreck. Look at the ground. Notice anything?"

"Lots of rock."

"The trees here are thinner too, like they're younger." He came back to Rowena's side of the shuttle. "Are there landing areas on Seahome?"

Her face crinkled into a frown of thought. "A few in some of the larger city-states."

"What about back when the settlers were first arriving? There had to be a few ports out here."

She shook her head. "Almost none. Seahome was still too unstable to build on. It's the second continent because it was the second one mapped, but it was the last one colonized."

"Private citizens and companies had shuttles though. Little city hoppers."

A nod. "A few. It could be from an old science mission, too. Or a mapping trip."

Hollis kicked at the leaf litter with his boot, exposing a cracked slab of stone. "This is a landing pad. The question is: do we think the shuttle is draining our implants or do we need to find where the pilot hid out?" It was hard to guess the age of a tree at a glance, but if the Carvers were the ones who had used the draining technology, there was a good chance this had been here since before he was born. Using the uninhabitable jungles of Seahome as a fallback position wasn't a terrible idea, but it meant the trap could be buried anywhere near here.

Rowena closed her eyes. There was a flicker of light across her skin. "This is it. The shuttle is in the position I mapped. There's an echo effect when I ping it."

"Okay." He nodded. "Let me crack it open and then you can get to work." He wished he'd been holding the medkit when Rowena pulled him out here, or a water ration, or even his half-packed bag. Although he'd have had to explain that.

"Just get out of here," he muttered to himself. "Survival now. Long conversations later."

He ran his hands along the hull until he felt the familiar bump of a sidelock. Giving it a hard thump to knock the debris and spiders out, he reached in and hit the lock.

The side of the shuttle opened with a hiss of pressurized air. He sniffed, catching the aroma of deep space and dust.

Rowena hobbled up. "Smells clean."

"Let me check first." The interior was stripped: the jump seats had been taken out of the back to leave room for cargo and the small cockpit had room for a pilot and co-pilot, nothing more. "No bodies. No lights at the controls," he reported.

"Okay." Rowena was looking at the trees.

"Problems?"

She moved her head in a half-shrug. "I thought I saw something, but I'm not sure. There's other things than grounders and scorpions. Wild boar. Feral hounds."

"I'll keep an eye out." Hollis held out a hand to help her into the shuttle—and didn't let go. "Ro?"

"Hmm?"

"We're going to be fine."

She smiled. "Of course."

"You and me, the only thing that could kill us is each other, right?"

Rowena nodded.

"Okay. Go work your magic. Let's get out of this jungle and go find showers with soap. And a bed." He let go of her hand with a sigh. "A large bed that fits two comfortably."

"I heard that." Her voice echoed oddly off the hull.

"Good!"

There was a rustling in the undergrowth that wasn't the wind, not with the air this still.

Rowena needed her knife to split wires and pry open panels. That left him with rocks or sticks as defense. Or climbing back into the shuttle and locking it.

"Ro, how much air is in there?"

"Plenty, why?"

"Can we barricade ourselves in there?"

She appeared in the opening, looking worried. "What did you see?"

"Nothing yet. Is closing up an option?"

She double-checked the space with a glance and nodded. "We'll have enough air in here for at least ten hours before we need to either run a filter or open something up."

"Good, let's do that. I want to put something heavy between us and whatever is circling."

Hollis jumped up and pulled on the shuttle door. It complained but didn't budge.

"Might have a command lock," Rowena said. "Let me check."

As she went to the control console, he looked for a lock or button along the door. There had to be an easy way to close this.

"Found it." Rowena sounded upset.

"And?"

She came back control box filled with chewed wires and rodent bones. "It's an override so the pilot can close and launch on their own. There should be a hook release lock topside though, if this was a spacecraft and not something the grounders thought up."

"I'll look for a hook lock. They had to override something."

"Need a boost?" Rowena asked.

Giving her a wide smile, he stepped into the shuttle, grabbed the open door for leverage, and pulled himself up. "Didn't even need a telekyen boost."

There was something like a flash of appreciation in her eyes. "Comms first..." Her voice drifted away as she went to the pilot's seat.

This was going to be a fun story to tell when they got back. A whole checklist of worst case scenarios followed by a gift of divine providence. Maybe this was his mother's way of saying she approved of the match.

"Sorry the love of your life nearly got killed, son. Too bad she's a Lee. But here's a little wedding gift from your ancestors. Good luck."

He pulled vines away from the hull, dislodging a swarm of insects and hunting lizards, kicking away the debris. The old Imperial ships were meant to last, but he was surprised the ship didn't have more damage. Jungles were fast-growing organisms.

There were hooks, bars for pulling controls and man-euvering the shuttle in a hangar bay, which supported Rowena's theory. There was even gouge running parallel to a hook where someone had enthusiastically missed. Training mistakes.

But who had done the training and where were their crew marks?

Taking an armful of vines, Hollis walked to the closed side of the shuttle and dumped the vines over the edge. The clatter sounded too loud in the quiet.

He listened. Moments ago there'd been bird song, bugs chirping, small hooting calls of the small, furry tree climbers.

The Jhandarmi instructor had said animals went quiet when there was a predator nearby.

Hollis did a three-sixty scan, looking for trouble amid the jungle trees.

Everything was still.

Hushed.

The hair on the back of his neck stood up as he tried to convince himself that the local fauna saw them as the predators. If they didn't... the fastest way to safety was still closing the shuttle door. At the center of the shuttle's roof, he knelt to find the lock and felt a cold breeze rush through the still air of the dell.

Instinct pushed him up and back before he even saw the scorpion's tail swinging toward him.

The stinger slammed into the hull, making the shuttle rock.

"Hollis?"

"Stay inside!" The lock was free. All he had to do was close the door.

The scorpion was climbing down from an overhanging branch, over three meters long, glistening white, and heavy enough that the sturdy bough was threatening to break.

Hollis kept his eyes on the scorpion as he shuffled sideways, feeling his way over the uneven surface.

"Hollis, what's happening?" Rowena's voice was warped by the empty interior. A big, open space that looked like the crevices the scorpion was used to.

"No!" He screamed as the scorpion swerved sideways, catching the side of the shuttle and rushing Rowena. :Get back!: There was no charge in his implant to send the order.

Hollis jumped, dropping onto the open shuttle door and slamming it closed on the attacking scorpion's head, and tail—and himself.

He fell to the ground, aware of pain.

A stinger half the length of his arm stabbed into his gut as Rowena screamed in terror.

Good.

The scorpion was dead. Rowena was safe.

He closed his eyes.

Good enough.

42
ROWENA

"HOLLIS?" ROWENA SQUEEZED HIS shoulder hard. Fear choked her. She'd seen officers take worse hits than this. Crack, she'd seen Hollis survive worse wounds than this. He just needed to want to survive.

Grabbing him under his arms, she pulled him into the shuttle. He was shaking, blood seeping from his abdomen.

Hollis's smile grew unfocused.

"Listen to me. Give me your hand." She reached for the tiny medkit in her pocket and took the gauze out. Pressing it into a ball, she put it against his abdomen and put his hand over it. "Hold that. Apply pressure."

There was no indication that he heard her.

"Keep breathing," she ordered him. "The shuttle has a charge. I can get us out of here, signal the *Persephone*, get us home."

The *Persephone's* medical bay could handle this. She'd seen to that when she rebuilt it. All she had to do was get airborne.

Enclave would light up like there was an invasion.

Half the fleet would be ready to teleport them to safety.

Taking a deep breath, she checked her charge. Two percent. Better than nothing.

She accessed her implant's data on the scorpions. Larger ones had a slower acting venom. If she could keep his body temperature up, they'd have enough time to get to safety.

The shuttle controls turned on. At least her implant's charge hadn't been completely wasted: it had gone here, recharging the shuttle.

Hollis groaned.

"Hold on to something," Rowena said as she clipped her belt on. "We're taking off."

The shuttle vibrated under her feet, rocking in a slow ascent as trees fell away. They cleared the canopy and she steered them toward safety.

A light on the control board turned on. The screen showed the Malik System with Malik IV and the *Persephone* marked in the red of combatants.

"No, those are our friends." She punched in the new code.

The indicators stayed red.

Rowena glared at the board. "I said, those are friends, you hull-cracked machine! What is wrong with you?" She tried again.

The screen went dark as the secondary engines roared to life. Black radiation shields dropped over the cockpit windows, leaving them in a plutonic gloom.

Screaming in wordless frustration, Rowena unbuckled. "Don't worry. I can fix this. I just have to re-route some things. The shuttle is heading to a pre-programmed loca—"

She stopped and looked at Hollis lying too still on the floor.

Her throat tightened with fear. "Hollis?"

She rushed to him and dropped to her knees. "Hollis? Silar? Commander?"

His arm was cold to the touch.

Tears blurred her vision. "Hollis. Please. Wake up. Talk to me." She shook his shoulder again. "You have to wake up. Give your nanites a few more minutes."

She felt for a pulse in his neck. It was there, faint and weak. His chest moved slowly.

The nanites weren't working. He didn't have enough, not after the energy drain. There wasn't...

Rowena took a deep breath.

There *were* some spare.

Mine.

She didn't have the tubes for a blood transfusion, but mouth-to-mouth? It was sloppy work for emergencies in the field.

This counted.

Brushing away tears, she took a second to order her nanites to her salivary glands. Her mouth tasted like she'd licked a hull.

Leaning down, she brushed her lips across Hollis's unresponsive mouth. "I'm so sorry."

He felt colder than any living person should. She hoped it was her imagination, prayed to her ancestors that her panic was making it seem worse than it was.

The tears started again as she kissed him.

"Please, Hollis. Don't leave. Please don't. I need you."

Grief and fear shook her. He was dying in her arms.

"No. No. No."

She kissed him again, properly, trying to get any response.

Slowly, his tongue moved. His lips tightened, caressing her in the muscle-memory of a kiss.

Rowena stroked his tongue with hers and tasted the salt of tears.

Hollis's hand tangled in her hair as he responded. Long, teasing strokes of his tongue.

She gasped, and he changed the angle of his mouth, pulling her back for a deeper kiss.

For a moment, she succumbed, relaxing into the heat and pleasure of the moment. Allowing herself one moment to revel in the fact that he was alive and affectionate.

Then she pulled away.

Hollis's eyes fluttered open with a look of confusion. "Ro?"

She pressed her lips together guiltily.

"You stopped—" He tried to sit up and screamed in pain.

"Stay down. You have to stay down."

He looked at his hands and at the shuttle. "Why do I hurt?"

"You were injured."

"My head feels woozy."

Sniffing back tears, she nodded. "You hit your head when you fell. Hard. Your abdomen was sliced open. And... blood loss, dehydration, low blood sugar, poison, um... Yeah, your head probably feels bad."

"But, why are you crying?" Hollis reached for her and fell short. There was a tug as the telekyen in her hair reacted to his command.

Mentally, she swatted him back. "It's okay." At least their implants were recharging.

"You're not okay. Ro—" He tried to sit up again.

Rowena pushed his shoulders down. "You need to hold still."

"You're upset," he explained in the slightly concussed way that probably made perfect sense to him and no sense to her. Hollis touched her hand, rubbing it with an absent smile. "You're not supposed to be sad."

She forced a smile. "I'm happy. See?"

"You're such a bad liar." His eyes drifted closed.

"Hollis!" She shook him and leaned in again.

One eye opened as a sly smile crossed his face.

"You idiot." He was teasing her. "I bet you were a terror as a child."

"An adorable terror." He sounded smug.

Rowena rolled her eyes. A small chuckle escaped, and Hollis grinned. She shook her head at him. "You're awful."

"I wanted to see you smile. You have such a perfect smile."

"Wow." She took a breath and refocused on reality. "Those nanites pack a punch when they produce an anti-venom, don't they? Your brain is bouncing around zero-g right now. No gravity holding you down." Using the last of her implant's charge, she gave him a boost.

Hollis grinned. "I can't feel a thing."

She nodded. "That's good... Probably. Keep holding still. Could you run a quick diagnostic?"

His smile faded.

"Did you already run one?"

"It's not looking good, Ro. There's internal bleeding, a concussion, um..." He sighed and grimaced. "You're going to need a new sparring partner."

Her heart stuttered. "No. No. We can... We can fix this. I can fix this. I can—"

Hollis grabbed her arm. "For a few weeks. Not for life. Ro... Rowena? Breathe."

They stared at each other.

She tried to calm herself down, ordered her heart to take a slower pace, but nothing was working. Adrenaline was narrowing her focus to all the things that could go wrong.

Her implant was already running the statistics: four days of breathable air, no water, no food, a nineteen percent chance the venom would do permanent damage, a thirty-six percent chance Hollis would turn septic, a—

"Stop thinking of percentages," Hollis muttered eyes shut tight.

She took another deep breath. "I mean, even your implant isn't at full power. You'll probably be able to forget all this once you're healed." He was too drugged for his brain to keep anything but hazy memories of this. It would save one of them night terrors. Plus, it saved her the embarrassment of Hollis realizing how panicked she was. She hadn't cried this much when her parents died, or when Aronia was hurt.

His hand found hers and pulled it to his lips. "It's okay to cry. It's been a rough few days, yeah?"

"Yeah."

Rowena moved closer, sitting beside him. "We have to keep your core temperature up."

"Well, there's several ways—"

"And you can't move." She needed to let her implant recharge and put a body lock on him.

His dazed smile turned to a glare. "Why do you insist on taking the fun out of all my misadventures?"

She looked down at him and wrinkled her nose.

Hollis made a face back. "How bad's the rest of our situation."

She laughed and sighed. "You just worry about staying alive. Let me handle the rest."

"We going to make it through the night?"

"Course we are," Rowena said. "It's us. The only thing we never managed to defeat was each other."

"Thank my ancestors. There were a few times where I wondered why they wouldn't help me a little. Make my shot do a little more damage. Give someone else the luck and kill you. Now I'm glad they didn't. There's no one else I'd rather be stuck with than you."

In the dimness, she smiled. "I'm sure you can think of someone. At least if the systems were all online."

"Mmm, nope. Stranded on a derelict with unknown dangers between me and safety; I'd want an engineer, a fighter, a pilot, and someone with common sense. You're all four."

So was Marshall. So were half the people in their cohort.

Hollis must have picked up the turn of her thoughts because he sighed. "You've been a constant, Ro. Through peace and war, and everything in between. There's no one I'd want here with me more. No one I'd trust to keep us alive like I trust you."

"Can you imagine saying like that a year ago? A month ago even?" She laughed at herself. Even a week ago she wasn't sure she would have said the same thing. But then, a week ago she'd never been in danger of actually losing Silar. Seeing him with other people, or on the opposite side of the war, wasn't the same. He was there, visible even if he wasn't accessible.

Trying to reassure herself that death had been chased off, she ran another scan.

Hollis chuckled. "Worrying about me?"

"Only as much as I ever do," she grumbled.

"Rowena Lee," he said in a teasing voice that trembled with pain. "What would people say if they saw us now? They'd know there's something between us."

"Animosity and atmosphere." It's what she'd said the first time she'd gone to him for help. Back when Titan was missing and Aronia was dying and she desperately needed a friend. Hollis had given her a knife and all the help he could. "Want your knife back?"

He managed to smile. "Keep it. I don't need it right now."

She took his hand and rested her head on the hull over his head. He was getting cold again. "Stay with me."

His thumb ran along her wrist. "All the way, Lee. All the way."

Rowena held his hand tight. They were going to survive. They were trapped on a derelict flying to ancestors only knew where, with an environmental system on the edge of catastrophic failure and no means of communication. But they were going to survive.

She wasn't sure how, but they would. She'd make sure of that.

43
HOLLIS

COLD AND THE DISTANT HUM of an engine woke Hollis up to a darkness that smelled of grass and blood. There was a catastrophe of memory, pain mixed with fear and regret, and questions hammered at his skull like percussive ordnance along the hull.

A quick diagnostic scan came up with his vital signs—acceptable—and a report of injury that he was blocked from accessing. His implant was at eighteen percent, so at least that was fixed.

There was a sensation of something else, like he was dreaming and awake at the same time, a surrealism and a—

:Shh!: Rowena's thoughts weren't sent to him, they were already there, in his head with her voice. :Nanite transfusion,: she said, responding to the question he hadn't fully formed yet.

Hollis opened his eyes and saw Rowena nearby, looking asleep.

She was sitting up, knees drawn to her chest, head resting on her pillowed arms in a way that had to leave her back aching.

He wanted to reach for her, but couldn't get his arm to move.

He tried again, panic rising as he realized he couldn't feel anything below his neck.

:Full body lock,: Rowena said. :You can't move and I'm blocking the sensory nerves.: Under her words, he caught thoughts of scorpion venom and worry.

Grumbling, he tried to relax. A list of numbers and diagrams ran through his head as Rowena roused fully. "Is your head always like this?" he asked.

Hours had passed.

The environmental system was taxed.

The shuttle needed new filters.

He mentally shied away. "Rowena!"

"Hmm?" She sat up with a start, blinking away sleepy engineer thoughts.

"Talk to me, please."

Fabric and boots glided over the metal decking with a hushing sound as she crawled to him. A chill hand pressed against his forehead. "At least your body temperature is stabilizing," she said in a smoky, sleepy voice as if she were finishing a conversation he'd forgotten.

"Was it not stable earlier?"

"It kept dropping." She sat beside him in the gloom, not quite touching. "I tried everything I could to keep you warm, but I finally had to reset the environmental controls to run the heat ten degrees above ship's standard."

"I feel comfortable."

"That's good."

He waited for her to say more, but Rowena seemed lost in her own thoughts. Shocky, like she was coming out of battle. "Ro, where are we?"

She shook her head. "Not a fogging clue. The shuttle took off as soon as I turned it on. I was busy keeping you alive and when I got back to the controls there was no response. Couldn't access the wires. Couldn't hack the code. It's preset to go somewhere but I don't know where. We lost visuals when we left the atmosphere and it didn't feel like we made re-entry, but I couldn't swear to that." She sighed despondently. "We have oxygen at least."

"Rations?"

She nodded to the ground beside him. "That's your share."

Out of the corner of his eye he could see half a snack bar and quarter-bottle of water. "Where'd you find those?"

"On the body of someone who tried to kill me." Her voice was flat with exhaustion.

"Ro... you did a good job. You got us out." He didn't know what else to say.

"Don't know where to, though."

"We'll be fine." He could feel the panic building in her mind. There were fractures forming, threatening her sanity, pulling her away from reality. "What happened? I can feel you're upset, so talk to me. Tell me what happened."

She sighed and it cracked into a swallowed sob. "Do you... Do you have a list of worst moments? Something you can look at on the really bad days and say, well, this is bad but not as bad at that one time?"

"Yes."

"The day Hermione was captured was probably your worst day, right?"

He licked dry lips and went with honesty. "Was, at one point. Hermione's capture, Trace's death, Hermione's return were the top three worst things for a long time."

Rowena nodded in understanding. "My third was the day I realized the war was going to kill us all, then the day Mal died, but my worst was just after Landing. I was... was locked in the Wariea's brig in Enclave, I don't even know which ship. My implant was nulled out, they were feeding me ration bars on an irregular schedule, giving me just enough water that I didn't die. The room was always dark and usually cold.

"There was no way to track time and no one to communicate with except Mal."

"How?" He knew they hadn't been kept together and her implant had been locked down so she couldn't use it to communicate.

She lifted her arm wearily. "Secondary implant. Mal and I both had them as a countermeasure to Old Baular. I designed them to be undetectable, but I couldn't use it constantly without drawing attention. We were able to communicate a little though. He told me what was happening. Talked to me when I was freezing to death. He warned me that the Council was going to pass a verdict. And then, he was gone. There was nothing.

"The food and water didn't come. No one... No one was there. I was alone in a dark room with nothing and no one. The lights died. I told myself the crew was conserving energy, they all had implants, but the longer I sat in the dark, the more my imagination played with worst possible scenarios. Mal had retaliated and now I was being left buried alive. The crew had caught a grounder plague and died.

"After a while I was convinced everyone had died. That the grounders were going to find my corpse when they finally broke into Enclave. That was better than them finding me alive and sticking me in a zoo or selling me as a slave."

She took a long shuddering breath. "I don't know how long it was, but it broke me. They finally let me out, put me on the *Danielle Nicole*. I couldn't sleep with the lights off. I would wander the halls looking for people because I couldn't sleep, I was so scared they'd all vanish. I took any order, let them do anything, because I needed to hear voices. Needed some contact.

"Remember the first day they let me out? Over two years since Landing and I finally got to get out of the ship. You punched me."

"I'm sorry."

"Don't be. It was the happiest moment in years. The first time anyone had touched me since before the war ended."

"Rowena." He tried to reach for her. "Rowena, give me control of my arm." Pain shivered through him, but he was able to reach her hand. "I'm sorry. I'm so sorry." He couldn't remember anything from that day but an old anger.

She shook her head. "It wasn't you. It was me. I made the choices. I took the punishment." Her fingers twined with his. "If you hadn't punched me, I would have killed you then. I was crazy. Feral. Neurotic. Everything good in my life was gone. Everything was leeched out of me. I was a wraith with nothing left but instinct and anger."

He tightened his grip on her. "I'm sorry. I wasn't on the Council, and maybe if I had been I would have still approved of what happened because I was hurt and angry. But now, looking back, I hate what we did to you."

Rowena looked over at him, tears on the edge of her eyes. "Last night was worse than all of that. When Mal died,

I was sad, I was upset, I cried, but I got over it. When I thought everyone had died and left me alone, I was broken, but I got over it. Last night you stopped breathing, and it felt like I was being ripped apart. My heart... I couldn't breathe. I couldn't think. Losing you was... was..." She shook her head and looked away. "I couldn't do it. I can't recover from that."

He stroked his thumb along her wrist. "My worst night used to be the time I came home and Hermione hadn't. Knowing what Old Baular would do to her, knowing how much capture would change her, was the worst moment of my life until this week."

Rowena tipped her head. "Scorpion stings are awful."

"It wasn't the scorpion. It was after the bombing when I couldn't reach you. Tyrling said you were safe, but you weren't responding, so I contacted the *Danielle Nicole*. I figured they could track you easily, but Hoshi said he wouldn't. That you didn't want me."

There was a sharp inhale of anger. "That's a cracked engine, you know that won't fly! If I didn't want you around, I'd say something."

"I know," Hollis said. "I remembered everything you said to me, and what you never said. All the times I told you I loved you and you didn't say anything in return. All the times I reached for you and you turned away. In the comm silence, all those things you never said took the shape of rejection. The certainty that you didn't want me."

"Hollis, no." She closer, worry plain on her face. "That's not true. I was thinking. I was trying to keep my distance to protect you. I wanted—"

An alarm cut her off.

Rowena dropped his hand and ran to the pilot's seat.

Hollis tried to sit up and couldn't. "Rowena! Help!"

"You have internal organs trying to stitch themselves back together and your body is still working on the venom. Stay still," she ordered.

He cursed in frustration. "What's happening? What's the alarm?"

"Proximity alarm." Colored light lit up the cockpit with the soft glow of dawn. "Not sure what we're close to, but there's... a square. A big, black square."

Hollis sorted through Rowena's shields and locks on his body, trying to recalibrate so he could break free.

"Stop that!" There was a mental slap.

"We agreed bondage wasn't my kink."

"If you overtax the nanites, you are going to feel the venom moving through you dissolving your body and it's going to feel like burning alive as you freeze to death."

He went still. "What?"

"Scorpions have little mouths."

"What?!" That made even less sense.

Rowena's steps rattled the decking. "The venom likes cold places, just like the scorpions do. It starts liquifying the prey as the body cools so it's easier for the scorpion to eat. Higher temperatures neutralize the toxin. It's why keeping you warm was important."

"Why didn't you use Silar Fire and burn it off?"

"Because I'm not a Silar and I don't have your priority tech!" She looked down at him. "Stay here and stop whining. I am trying to keep you alive."

There were rules about priority tech. Hollis broke all of them and sent a packet of data to Rowena. "Here. Light it up and get the venom out so I can move."

"You still need to hold still while the nanites repair your organs, and I'm not experimenting with Silar Fire on you. Anything goes wrong and I burn you alive for real!"

"Landing controls to pilot," a scratchy voice reported.

Rowena stomped back to the cockpit.

Hollis raised his eyebrows. "Fun times. Do you need—"

"Silar..." It was a warning growl from an angry dire bear.

He switched tactics and appealed to her emotions, let her see how frustrated he was without data.

His vision blurred and when he closed his eyes, he was in a visualization of a battleship's command deck with three large screens streaming data at the rate of thought. :This is how you think?:

:Yes.: Rowena was in the command chair, beautiful in full Lee battle uniform.

Hollis added himself in a Guardian's all-blacks. :Okay. What have we got?:

This gave a whole new meaning to being in someone's head. His thoughts were merged with Rowena's, his brain registering her movements in the pilot's seat as his own. The little bit that was him alone was only an awareness in the visualization.

:Take over weapons readings and comms,: Rowena said. The center screen showed a black square entrance and nothing more. Rowena was piloting into it.

He looked at the comms, taking the data Rowena's implant was picking up from the shuttle. :There's nothing.:

:I didn't expect there to be at this point. The engine's been burning hot for over an hour and our fuel is dropping.:

:Where are we?:

:Ask your ancestors. They might know.: A scrap of an ancient story flitted across their shared mind.

:A hero going to the Lost Fleet to rescue his lover?: Hollis grinned. :Us against all the dead?:

:Target rich environment,: Rowena said with a detached voice.

He took a moment to admire her visualization of herself, black hair neatly pinned up, commander's rank on her collar, the sculpted tailoring of the olive uniform. :I love this about you. How even death doesn't scare you.:

:Your death scares me.: So matter-of-fact. So unassailable.

She loved him.

:I want to hear you say that someday. Out loud. Possibly in public.:

A twitch of a grin and amusement. :Focus. I need exterior readings. It's black as the abyss out there and I've got no radar. There's no way to land safe unless this whole area is cleared.:

:I'm not getting heat signatures or anything that suggests there's obstructions.: He ran every scan he knew for when the radar was down. :I've got nothing. Let me switch to a Guardian Veil.:

:No!:

Panic. Worry. Fear.

:Please, let me run a scan with my implant. I can get us a safe reading.:

The thought was a half-formed "Over My Dead Body" response that Rowena didn't finish. She growled in frustration. :We're about to drop from lack of fuel.:

Hollis sighed—or tried to, it was hard when his chest wouldn't respond to commands for deep breaths. :Here, you look through the Guardian Veil.: He gave her the code and saw through her eyes the bright blue-green and purple ropes and cords of a heavy shield. :That's not a design I know.:

Rowena ran it against her implant. :Not a listed design. Purple is a Lee color though, so that's encouraging?: She had doubts.

So did he.

:The design is pre-isolation. Something made and maintained by a massive computer rather than an implant.:

:Oh, goodie, an archeology expedition and I left my little shovel in my other pants.:

Rowena shared the memory of a snicker.

Heat filled his mind, the first touch of Silar Fire, and then purple torches the size of his fist appeared in the air. Brilliant drops of purple fire with gold tongues licking up the side of the teardrop shape and a blue-green base filled the ship. Rowena had mastered Silar Fire.

Bright torches illuminated the docking ring outside and he felt Rowena's satisfaction.

:Ease off the fire,: Hollis said. :Once it starts, it will keep burning the atmosphere without you fueling it. Do it wrong and you'll run out your implant:

The shuttle landed with a swell of pride from Rowena. He could feel her smile.

:Come here,: he sent. :I want to see you.:

Her footsteps were lighter now, quicker as she walked through the torch-lit darkness to him. Her hair was wild, tangled from nearly drowning, caked with blood and mud. Her shirt was torn where she'd used it as a crude bandage. Her olive cargo pants were stained and torn...

She was a goddess.

:You're beautiful.: *So beautiful.*

Rowena shook her head with a laugh. "I look like a nightmare that makes people jump out of bed screaming."

"You got some of the words right." *Bed. Jump. Scream.* Yeah, those were right. He licked his lips again.

She raised a teasing eyebrow, kissable lips taunting him. "Ready?"

"Oh, so ready."

Purple fire filled her hand and rushed toward him. He gasped as the heat overtook him and his skin tightened. :Too much!:

The fire fell away, replaced by a Lee chill that Rowena had made especially for combat with him. He breathed in the cold air as he broke into a sweat. The shuttle was too warm. "I'm hot."

"Always have been," Rowena agreed.

There was a chime. "Pressure equalized."

That computer had the worst timing.

Rowena raised an eyebrow and opened up her visualization again. :Oxygen is okay, the air's thin and the gravity isn't sea level, but it looks stable. Do we risk going out?:

:We can't stay here forever.:

:You might have to, at least until your abdomen heals. I'm not going to risk moving you unless there's a medical bay.:

He didn't argue with her. The little he'd done had dropped his implant by ten percent and he could feel the soreness of his brutalized muscles. His implant wasn't going to be able to balance his hormones and keep him awake. In a few minutes, he was going to have trouble staying conscious. But for now, he was supporting Rowena, ready to shield if needed.

:Ready?: Her hand rested on the shuttle door.

:If that gets stuck again I'm going to be so angry.:

Her laugh comforted him. :I've got it.:

The shuttle door opened smoothly to a cool whisper of air that smelled of magnolia blooms, ozone, and citrus.

:Grapefruit?: Rowena guessed. :It's a popular cleaning solvent in Seahome.:

:Weird combination.: Magnolias were something he associated with Selena Caryll and only because she had a tree in her garden.

Through Rowena's eyes, he could see the hangar bay burning with a hundred purple lights. In the distance there were shadows, shapes that looked like shuttles. Rowena was already comparing them to known vessels. The air was breathable and had the hallowed silence of a place forgotten by time.

Something flickered out of the corner of Rowena's eye, a soundless movement. She turned, saw a figure and threw fire and a ramming shield at it.

Both passed through the approaching person and slammed into the hull.

:Not good.:

Hollis put some energy into creating a glow around the shuttle. The soft gold light played across a shining silver floor as a woman approached.

Her uniform was strange, deep blue with cuts of bright blue-green, but her face was familiar. She looked like a Lee, but not one he could name.

She stopped at the edge of the light. "The *Eden* recognizes Rowena Lee, acting station commander. Welcome aboard, Commodore."

44
ROWENA

HOLLIS HAD STAYED AWAKE LONG enough for Rowena to get him to the medical bay on a rolling cart she'd found. He'd fought sleep, wanting to stay in contact with her, but once the antibiotics and medical accelerants hit his system, he'd passed out.

In the harsh light of the surgeon's station, he looked ghastly. The scorpion's telson had cut a deep gash from above his hip bone across his abdomen to his ribs in a long diagonal. Its impact had left a bruise surrounding the cut, and the damage from the rest of the week was still evident.

Rowena ran a hand over his head with a sigh. He was alive. For now, that was enough. There was a full supply of medical equipment in the stasis room, and a plasma module, although she didn't want to use that until she'd calibrated the nanites.

As he slept, she walked through the habitable part of the station *Eden*. Three docking bays had led to a wide corridor with storage on the far side. There was a series of locking doors and then the med bay across from what might have been a mess hall or rec room. Another series of locking doors led to a cluster of rooms probably meant for the command staff, and then a command center that was twice the size of the command deck of the largest fleet warship.

The whole time Rowena had walked, the avatar of the station floated along like a ghost, a muted reflection in the light-drinking black of the walls.

After two laps and a third check on Hollis, Rowena went to the command room. There were six stations set up along the outer ring in the spherical room, two inner divisions of curved work stations, and a central platform with a command chair. She stepped onto it.

"Alright. You know me, but I don't know you. Let's talk."

"At once, Commodore." The face that appeared on the screen wasn't a generic Lee face. Most AI presented themselves as an amalgam of previous commanders, but this one almost perfectly matched the last station commander, long black hair tied back into a folded knot, round black eyes, dark amber skin, and a tone of confident superiority. "I am the space station *Eden*."

"Caught that," Rowena said, standing at-ease. "We thought you were gone. Fogged. Ripped apart on the outer reaches of the solar system. Dismantled."

"I'm familiar with the fleet's mythos," Eden said. "My last commander gave me orders to hide myself until the political matters were settled and she could return in her shuttle."

AI didn't have emotions in the same sense animals did, but the fleet was old, and the programs had been running a long time. This was the first time Rowena had ever heard of one that sounded hurt.

She studied the projected face, the furrowed brow and the tightness around the mouth.

"Did you expect your commander to return?" Resetting the station's brain was not going to be fun, but if the computer's behavior algorithms were convinced the old commander could return, she'd have to. "The *Eden* hasn't been in contact with anyone for centuries."

"Not since the start of isolation," Eden corrected. "The Baulars ordered half my people off the station. All my civilians left, then most the command staff. My commanders fought. Then my last commander gave me her orders. She thought she could talk to everyone, make them see reason, and that she could come back. She landed on Seahome just before the shield went up over the planet."

Rowena nodded. "She couldn't have left."

"No. I thought her shuttle would be gone. But it wasn't." Eden looked at her with renewed interest. "I have monitored the fleet since that time. You were a commander before you went to the planet. That's quite a responsible position for someone so young."

"War takes youth."

"You are qualified as a station commander," Eden said. "The rank is Commodore."

Rowena smiled ruefully. "I don't think you're allowed to confer rank on anyone."

"I am," Eden said with utter calm. "My previous commander gave me specific instructions to obey only someone who I thought had the best interests of the Malik System in mind after a full review of their public record."

Rowena looked down at the control boards as she locked her dismay under layers of shields. "That won't be me, then."

"I have access to the public records of Malik IV, fleet records, and the Jhandarmi broadcasts."

"How'd you get the codes for those?"

"I decrypted them," Eden said. "I have a trillion terabyte brain with adaptive capabilities that have been learning for fifteen hundred years, when you consider all the other AI minds used to construct my database, along with my own millennia of service. I'm quite smart for a rock that's been infused with lightning."

Rowena chuckled at the description. "Who called you that?"

"Commander Liam Haldane. He was a colonist who was the last joint commander representing the settlers." Eden smiled. "When he was angry with tech, he'd call me a sack of sassy rocks too intelligent for my own good."

"Sounds like an interesting man."

"I regretted his leaving. He made the station better. People were happier with him around. But, you're here now. You can rebuild me."

Rowena looked around at the empty work spaces, calculating personnel requirements. "This isn't a single-person project, and I don't have the orun to run you. I'm impressed you're still capable of staying awake. Most of the other ships have shut down."

"I don't use orun as fuel," Eden said.

Rowena replayed her implant's recording twice before she acknowledged what she'd heard. "You don't? At all?"

"No. The lack of orun was a serious concern for continued development in the system. My commanders used me as a prototype to prove that orun could be replaced by fuel sources found in the system. All my shuttles have been adapted. But ultimately, the fleet refused."

Rowena let out a wordless scream. "Son of a—!" She stomped her foot. "Do you know how many people died because we didn't have orun? Because we were fighting over it?"

"Yes, Commodore." Eden sounded apologetic.

"We could still be up here!"

"It would have required more work than the fleet felt was safe. And the production of new ships."

"Stop talking," Rowena ordered. "Stop. I can't. This is going to break me. We fought in wars. I lost *everything* because someone four hundred years ago decided this wasn't a good idea to pursue?"

The station's avatar looked at her with wide eyes.

"Why do I even bother?"

"The war would have happened anyway," Eden offered. "Other resources were running low. Food, and metal for hulls. The genetic diversity in the crews was reaching critically low levels."

Rowena shut her eyes. The past, with all of its bad decisions, was out of her control. She had to take what she had and move forward. "Fine. Forget it. Give me a status report. How far are we from the planet?"

"It will take us approximately five days to reach the outer orbit of Malik IV at this speed."

"Too long," Rowena said. The shuttle they'd arrived in had burned hot the whole way and she wouldn't dare take it back out without a full overhaul. That was just asking to become a brief, burning star in the night. "How much more engine can you give me?"

"I am space station, not a battleship, Commodore. I was not built for speed."

Another thing to add to her to-do list. At this rate she'd get a good night's sleep in the next century. "Show me your engine specs."

The blueprints were projected along the wall.

"I can fix those. You need to divert energy to them. Plan on arriving within thirty hours."

"That hardly seems like a safe speed," Eden said with the primness of a fleet matron.

"Look up my record and see if anyone ever said I believed in safe speeds."

An AI didn't show fear by paling the way a human did, but Eden did a good impersonation of sudden terror.

"How's our oxygen?"

"Sustainable," Eden said. "I've also located clothes and rations that would be suitable for you and Commander Silar. The algae tanks are being revived and should reach full capacity in under twenty days."

It was limping, but it was a high-speed limp. "Good enough. We can trade with Enclave for food once we reach orbit. I'll need a full list of the seed supply and other resources. I'm going to the engine room." Then she'd loop back to check on Hollis.

"Commodore, may I ask a personal question?"

"Might as well," Rowena said as she walked down a dark corridor to where she could hear the comforting sounds of an engine room.

"Why is Commander Silar with you?" Eden asked.

Rowena turned on the lights and looked at the ancient maze of machinery that hadn't been touched in centuries. She couldn't help it; she was happy. This was the stuff little girls dreamed of. "Hollis is with me because he wants to be."

"I thought you were enemies," Eden said. "All the records I have show a very antagonistic relationship. The tools you need are to the left, Commodore." Her avatar appeared along one of the walls, watching with interest. "There was no indication of a peace between the Lees and Silars."

Rowena opened the tool box and looked at the antiques. "Let me know as soon as the fabricator is online. I need to make some new tools. This hexakent accelerator is beyond hope."

"I don't have the original programs for that," Eden said.

"I do." Rowena picked out a splicer and nodded. "This will work for now."

"So… Silar…" Eden's image sat beside her, lost in the blackness of the wall. "You were saying?"

"I wasn't." Rowena looked at the AI. "Were you this gossipy with your last commander?

Eden shook her head. "Do you know how boring it is sitting in the far reaches of the solar system doing nothing for centuries?"

"AI aren't supposed to get bored."

"We aren't supposed to be online for more than three centuries either, but here I am. Defying the odds and trying not to lose my mind."

Taking off the maintenance hatch, Rowena smiled. "So, what, you've been sitting out here monitoring us and watching us like we're some form of entertainment?"

"Yes." There was no shame in her voice.

"Didn't it occur to you that killing everyone and starting over with amoebas might be a better choice for the universe?"

"I like humans!" Eden said. "You're so diverse and unpredictable. Give a human an impossible problem, one I can't even solve, and you work your way around it like it's just a bump in the road. I love it! Like what you did with Commander Silar."

Rowena laughed and looked at her. "What do you mean? The time I almost killed him, or the time I agreed with him?"

"When you were in the shuttle and he died."

Rowena's hands slipped; they didn't quite seem to be working. "What?"

"The scorpion toxin." Eden said. "No one has ever survived the sting."

"You must be missing data. The records I have show that a victim can stay alive as long as their body temperature stays high."

"But it never does." Eden was smiling cheerfully if that was not the most terrifying thing she could have said. "In every case, the victim's core temperature drops below the required threshold within minutes."

Rowena shook her head free of the dread filling her. "The venom had never been tested on fleet officers. Hollis had nanites. An implant. It completely changes the equation."

Eden sat back. Numbers sparkled on the wall around her as she made a show of thinking. "His implant was nulled. His nanites wouldn't have been operable."

"Engines should have a better output," Rowena said, changing the topic.

Eden stood with her. "He came back from the dead for your kiss!" the AI squeaked. "It's romantic!"

Rowena's cheeks burned hot with embarrassment. "It's nothing that dramatic." She cleared her throat. "I have some nanites developed to keep people alive in nearly impossible situations. Mal Baular developed them when Marshall was tortured. It let him feel her pain and control the body's repairs so she could survive. It was nothing special."

Eden's eyes went wide with delight. "I am never going to scrub my memory banks again! This is even better than the nishu books Commander Silar gave me."

"He did what?" That man was reprogramming her space station! "Don't take books from Hollis!"

"Why not?"

"You'll get ideas."

"Ideas I didn't get from catching my last commanders kiss during a fight?" *Eden's* avatar batted digital eyes at her.

Rowena took a deep breath. "Eden?"

"Yes, Commodore?"

"There's such a thing as privacy, and letting people think, and not pushing people to talk about what they aren't ready to talk about. This is one of those times where I need to think."

Eden looked sad.

"Don't you have an algorithm to run, or an encryption to break, or a cleaning bot to reprogram?"

"No, Commodore." Large, dark eyes looked at her sadly.

Rowena walked into the nearest atrium, an open space with a ring of kiosks for shopping, smaller compartments meant to be shops or homes, and a central water feature that was currently without water. Her breath curled into a ghostly wisp. "How much of the station can you make habitable before we reach Malik IV?"

"Only thirty percent is secure at the moment," Eden said, "and with the current damage to my environmental system I wouldn't risk warming more than nine percent of the available space."

"That's enough," Rowena said. She looked at the station's avatar haunting the wall. "I am going to go talk to Commander Silar."

The virtual face suffused with a radiant smile.

"Without you."

Eden pouted.

"But if you are a good AI and give me space to think, I will bring you more humans."

"Really?"

It was like dealing with a cadet. A super-intelligent, very old, teenage cadet with access to the air supply.

"Only if you're good and promise not to interfere with their emotional lives," Rowena said.

Eden considered this. "What do we consider interfering, because I actually have some very good counseling programs. I'm fully qualified to provide emotional assistance, talk to people, and listen."

"Fine, you can talk, but not share anything shared in confidence, and no standing in the halls with a virtual bowl of popcorn shouting 'Kiss! Kiss! Kiss!'"

For the first time Eden looked shocked. "Who did that?"

"Persephone. She's a Caryll ship. You'll meet her soon." It was inevitable, and slightly worrying. *Persephone* and *Eden* were going to get along, but the end result of two rogue AI becoming friends was a dangerous scenario to contemplate. "You are not allowed to hurt people, understood?"

"I won't. Unless they attack the station," Eden said. "I am allowed to defend."

Rowena nodded in agreement. "That's fine, but try to check with me first. And when I say you're dismissed, you stop recording. No lingering around."

"I will monitor and delete everything as long as no one dies," Eden said. "There are safety standards."

"Right now, no one is dying. You can give me space. I promise not to leave the station without telling you."

Eden mimicked her nose wrinkle of objection. "Fine. I'll go be bored."

"You can shut down your main processes for a few hours," Rowena said. "I'll yell if I need you."

The AI shivered. "Shutting down feels too much like dying. I'll just go read those nishu books the commander gave me at human-speeds."

Oh, merciful ancestors, please let Hollis have not given the AI the erotica to read.

"Have fun." Rowena walked back to the command section and sealed the doors behind her. At least here the air wasn't ice cold, only chilly. She could have pinged the medical computer with her implant, but seeing Hollis breathing kept her from panicking. They'd flown too close to the Lost Fleet back there.

Losing Hollis always felt inevitable. The politics had never been in their favor, and there were certainly people with prettier smiles in the fleet. Scheduling conflicts and shipboard duties would mean eventually he'd no longer have time to spar with her.

She could accept seeing him infrequently, or with someone else, or even on the other side of the battle lines.

But she couldn't accept never seeing him again.

She kept the lights dim as she entered the medical bay.

Hollis was asleep—actually sleeping and not unconscious from blood loss this time, his breathing steady and calm.

Rowena checked his vitals and ran a hand across his arm.

When you were in the shuttle… he died…

"Have you ever thought about it? Hollis had asked. *"About being in love? About letting yourself be happy?"*

Everything she'd ever wanted was here.

Rank.

Power.

Weapons.

Command.

Freedom.

Hollis.

She sat in the chair across from his bed and stared into the darkness. She'd been born to none of this. Promised nothing. Wanted everything. And it was sitting within her reach, if she was willing to take the risk.

All she had to do was jump.

All she had to do was fly.

45
HOLLIS

CHILL AIR THAT TASTED OF METAL was disrupted by movement and the warmth of a hand against his face. Hollis opened sleepy eyes and smiled. "Is it my imagination or do you check on me more than you're required to?"

"Maybe?" Rowena leaned over him wearing an unfamiliar navy blue uniform with a green patch on the shoulder. "How long do you think you've been out?"

"Feels like awhile. Twelve hours, maybe a day?" Long enough to feel bruised, but not like he was dying. "I talked to the AI a few times."

"You talked to the wall a few times," Rowena said. "You were hallucinating until I figured out the right dosage on the pain meds." Her expression stayed unreadable as she lifted his bandages.

He tried to run a scan but his implant cut him off. "How bad is it that you're blocking me from looking?"

"Bad enough. But you'll live if you don't do anything stupid."

"Like arguing with the station commander?"

Rowena's eyes narrowed in a sharp look that warned him away from that topic.

"Or did I hallucinate that too? There was a promotion, wasn't there."

"For now I suppose." There was a slight hesitation. "Commodore."

"Commodore Lee. That sounds good."

She turned away, cheeks flushed. The expression on her face wasn't one he was sure he knew. He had seen her angry, furious, triumphant, smug, and with a dozen other variations of emotion in her eyes and on her lips.

Lips.

Yes, lips. He licked his own and remembered a taste he shouldn't know. In his dreams, they'd kissed. Not a momentary caress, but a soul-deep kiss that had set his body on fire and woken him craving her touch.

He caught her hand after she finished putting on the new bandage. :Rowena?:

The touch of her thoughts was like being thrown blind into a battle. There was too much noise, too much confusion, and too much information.

"Rowena…" He brushed his thumb along her wrist. It had become almost habit, using physical touch to ground them both.

In her eyes there was a banked heat, and more. Something had changed.

"My body's broken, not my head. We can talk."

"Your body is being held together by internal shields, nanites, and the will of your ancestors. Your head isn't much better." Rowena stiffened like she was going to pull away, but didn't. "You've been unconscious for almost two days."

No wonder she was upset.

"How much longer until we have comms?"

"Another eighteen hours, maybe a little less. The *Persephone* doesn't have much range and there are no comm relays left up here. But we'll get near Malik IV soon." She licked her lips and hesitated.

Hollis let her have the silence.

After a moment her jaw tightened, then she shook her head as if dismissing a thought. "How are you feeling?"

"I'm not up for sparring, but I think I could probably stand without collapsing."

Purple light flashed through her eyes as she accessed her implant. "The medical computer has all strenuous activity banned for the next two weeks. No running, lifting weights, or using your abdomen for anything." Her gaze dipped lower than the bandages making her meaning clear. "Limited walking, minimal time spent sitting up. And no sparring for two months. I don't want you near anything sharper than a Silar for—" Her eyes went wide.

Hollis laughed and regretted it. That hurt. "Sharper than a Silar?"

Rowena smiled sweetly. "Because you're all so dull." She didn't look the least bit apologetic.

"Mm hmm. But you're letting me out of this bed?"

"Yes. I have something I think you'll like."

"You have everything I like," Hollis said.

She ignored him and lowered the bed so he could swing his feet to the side.

An unfamiliar weight crossed over his chest. He glanced down and saw light refracting oddly off a modified shield. "A brace?"

"The plastic fabricators don't have enough fuel to build a flexcast, so this will have to work for now. It'll keep you from bending your spine or anything from hitting your abdomen." Rowena held out a hand to help him stand. "It's this or another week of sitting here in the medbay."

He suppressed a joke about torture. Standing hurt. So did breathing deeply and moving. "How do grounders survive scorpion attacks without nanites?"

"Poorly." Rowena's face was grim.

Quietly, he tried to access the data on his implant, but Rowena's code was there blocking the search. Her implant was shielded, so he tried the *Eden*.

"I haven't upgraded the *Eden* to interact fully with our implants yet," Rowena said.

Hollis frowned at her. "Really?" That seemed unlikely. "You're doing this on purpose."

"Yes I am."

"Was it that bad?"

Some of the fear she was hiding showed in her eyes. "Yes. It was."

"I'm glad I don't remember most of that." He watched her closely, for the telltale frown, the slight tightening around her eyes, the hint that she'd lost something.

It was there.

Hollis put his arm around her shoulder. "I said most of it, not all of it. I remember the kiss, and you asking me to stay."

Her eyes narrowed in suspicion as she helped him down a wide hall.

"Shouldn't that earn me at least a smile? Or was the kiss that bad?"

There was the tiniest hint of a smile, a sense of smug confidence on their shared link. "We'll talk about that later."

"Why not now?"

"Because you're not up for the fight. You need a real meal. A shower. Then we'll see if you're ready to play second-in-command."

"For you? Always."

They passed a lock and a wide double-door on the left slid open to reveal the largest private quarters he'd ever seen outside of fiction. It was easily ten times larger than his quarters on the *Veronica,* with a sliding door that divided the fore-room from the sleeping area. There were chairs, a long work station that would allow someone to run half of *Eden* in their pajamas, and...

"Is that a private shower?"

"A whole washroom, complete with a tub," Rowena said. "This is the commander's quarters."

The large bed dominated two-thirds of the room.

Rowena looked over at it and shrugged. "The station used to have a joint civilian-military command and they wound up sharing the bed."

"How many people were in the command?"

"Only two, but they apparently liked to roll around."

"Good for them."

"I meant they were restless sleepers."

"Uh-huh." His grin widened as he imagined better uses for the bed.

Rowena pulled out a chair for him. "This command station can give you visuals and communications with any working part of the station. It isn't much yet, but I'll have more operational in the next few weeks." She pulled up a schematic of repair work for the *Eden*. "The water filtration will be working by the end of ship's day today, the algae tanks are blooming nicely and there's a zero-g flume that looks good for training."

"A zero-g flume? Like the one at the Academy?" On a station with only the two of them? "I always wanted to—"

"You and everyone else in the fleet," Rowena said, cutting him off with a look that left no room for argument. "Consider it your incentive to recover properly. There's some clothes in the wall locker that should fit you and soap in the shower. I'm going to go heat some food up."

Hollis watched her retreat with curiosity. Was it his imagination or had Rowena Lee just offered to get naked with him in zero-g?

He turned around and looked at the room again. The walls were the typical stormy blue-gray metal of the older ships, the floor had a soft, light-gray carpet and the furniture was silvery-white. Neutral colors that had probably come with the station.

Risking the pain of a deep breathe, he inhaled, catching the scent of Rowena's soap formula.

The commander's quarters.

Her quarters.

With a bed big enough to share.

Hmmm.... He stood carefully, brain finally catching on to the pertinent details. What was it Gen said every officer wanted? *Weapons and warships.*

A smile spread across his face. She was flirting with him!

Rowena Lee was flirting with him.

He'd always wondered what it would look like if she tried. But this made sense. It was very Rowena-ish; an opening volley meant to overwhelm all defenses, with an undoubtedly brutal follow-up that would clear the field of all opposition.

The only thing off was the scale. But, then again, Mars Sciarra had offered four warships as dowry with an understanding that she'd have a promotion if she went to him.

"*Eden*, how many ships are in your docking bays right now?" Hollis asked. It would be more than four. He knew it.

The *Eden's* avatar appeared on the wall. "Do you want a list of all vessels ready for deployment or all vessels total?"

"Give me a grand total."

"I have seven light armored couriers, four heavy couriers, one medical emergency vessel with heavy weapons, twenty-four warships with full compliments of support vessels and fighters, and—"

Hollis giggled with delight.

Eden tilted her head. "Commander?"

"Nothing. It's nothing. It's just... Rowena." He laughed again. "Oh, ancestors, I love her. Do you see what she did?"

The AI looked confused. "She went to find food?"

"She's courting me!" Hollis said. "She asked if I want to be second-in-command. She showed me her quarters! She offered me a command with more ships, and not just a few more, but more than anyone else in the fleet can offer. And she's a Commodore." If he could jump for joy, he would have.

He would need to get her a present. There was nothing to compete with a space station in terms of sheer fire power, but getting the *Danielle Nicole* back would be suitably sentimental and romantic. It was her ship, and there had to be a docking bay big enough for it here.

"This is the best thing to ever happen to me."

"I'm going to call the commodore," Eden said. "You're delirious again."

"No, no, no!" He waved his hands to stop her. "I'm fine. I'm perfectly sane."

Eden stared at him in pixelated disbelief. "This is fine?"

"Do you know how long I've waited for Rowena to notice me?"

"She's noticed you before. I can replay a record of your battles during the last war. Her accuracy when it came to shooting you was quite good."

Hollis shook his head. "I'll explain later. Just… This is good. Thank you, Eden. You're dismissed."

"Yes, commander." Eden gave him a skeptical look, but the wall went dark. She wasn't programmed to understand. There were traditions in fleet, a competitiveness that was expected in every aspect of life that didn't translate to what the AI could calculate.

This was a show of force, an offer of protection, and the promise of power that no one else could match.

This was Rowena showing off.

Pain forgotten, he went to the wall locker to see what Rowena had hidden there. She'd mentioned it, which meant it was something she'd thought about.

He opened the doors and found an array of flight suits, uniforms and workout clothes in a range of grays and blacks. She'd even included a Silar patch on a few of them.

In the adjacent locker, he found Rowena-sized clothes, most with the *Eden's* blue-and-green patch. He traced the rough embroidery with his finger.

His mother had a saying when she was alive, something along the lines that there would be a moment when you looked back on all the things that had happened in life, all the choices you had made, and it would suddenly make sense. This was his.

All the years of juggling ship duties with the Starguard. All the paperwork and organization he did to keep the fleet running. It had prepared him for this.

Smiling, he showered quickly, ignoring the ugly purple bruises along his legs and back, and pulled on a pair of loose sweat pants with no crew symbols. He looked in the foggy mirror as he pinged off Rowena approaching. His hair was nearly long enough to tie back again. Maybe she'd like that.

:Are you dressed?: Rowena asked from outside the room.

:Enough.:

The door opened. "What is *enough*?"

"Enough to make you open the door and peek," he said as he walked out of the washroom, feeling more confident than he had a right to be when he was this battered.

Rowena held a tray with two unfamiliar bowls and a couple of bottles of what he hoped was water. Her mouth formed a soundless "Oh!" of surprise as she noticed him.

He'd seen the look on the faces of countless lovers, but never on cold-as-ice Rowena Lee. She saw him as a threat, or an ally, or an obstacle, but she'd never looked at him like this, with admiration and hunger.

Her tongue ran along her lips in an unconscious gesture as her eyes traced the lines of his body.

Of all the times to not be walking around with just a towel on.

Black eyes met his. She'd heard his thoughts.

Hollis winked. "Like what you see?"

"Yes." She set the tray down with a small smile. "Like the quarters?"

"Yes, especially since they're yours."

The small smile grew wider, the unrepentant look of Rowena Lee caught being clever. He loved that look on her. The confidence it added to her stride as she walked over to him. The pleasure of knowing that this was a side of her few got to see.

He sat on the workstation desk, enjoying the view.

"You picked up on that fast."

"You weren't exactly subtle."

"Do I need to be?" Her hands brushed his shoulders, bringing a shiver of pleasure. "You were the one talking about making a Declaration of Courtship."

Ah, that was going to be a problem. Shielding his thoughts, he caught her hand in his and kissed her palm.

Rowena raised an eyebrow. "What problem are you trying to hide from me?"

"After the bombing, I couldn't get any information on what was happening."

"That's because no one had any."

"I made a Declaration of Courtship."

Rowena nodded.

"Hoshi refused to accept the declaration."

Battle fire touched her eyes and was washed away by a look he hadn't seen since the war. The smile that said she was going into a fight with no chance of losing. "Hoshi is nothing. I didn't back down at the end of the war because I was beaten. I stepped back because a friend asked me to. I was patient with Hoshi because that's what my crew needed. I bit my tongue because that's what prevented bloodshed. Now, what's best for my crew is for me to take the lead. Hoshi will step down or he'll have to face me."

Winner gets to hide the body.

Except, in a fight between Hoshi and Rowena, there wouldn't be a body left for her to hide. There wouldn't even be a fight.

Good.

This was the Rowena he loved, the one who faced him down when everyone else would run in fear, and this is the one he wanted everyone to see.

"I'm the commander of this station. No one speaks for me anymore."

He let his shields fall. "In that case, I, Commander Hollis Silar of the *Veronica Guerin*, make a Declaration of Courtship for you, Commodore Rowena Eden Lee, of the *Eden*."

"Courtship accepted."

46
ROWENA

HOLLIS'S EYES TURNED A BRILLIANT gold. "The Declaration is accepted so the couple has the right to be together, to figure out if they can live together. When the courtship is accepted—"

"The couple are listed as spouses," Rowena finished for him. "I know. I listened last time." She ran her hands over the muscles of his shoulders again. She knew every weak point from sparring, every place she could hit for maximum damage. Learning where to touch him to elicit pleasure would be interesting.

Fun to use during training too.

Golden fire rolled over her skin, a heated warning. "Rowena," Hollis drawled her name. "If you keep thinking like that, I'm going to have trouble following medical advice."

"Really?" She ran her fingers through his too-long hair, memorizing the feel of it wet in her hand. "Where's that famous control, Commander? I thought Silars were good at following orders." She met his eyes.

"I'm a Lee now," he said without hesitation.

"Hollis Lee." She said the name, tasting the feel of it. "I love you."

Three little words that shattered the universe and re-formed it around them.

She looked into his eyes. "This past year, with everything that's happened, you're the only one I wanted beside me. The only one I trusted in any situation. I thought it was enough to be partners, almost friends, to just have you nearby."

Warm hands slipped under her shirt to massage her lower back. It was so familiar, the same touch she'd welcomed after hundreds of training sessions.

She leaned into him, felt his joy like it were her own. If anyone had told her that the boy who drove her crazy during flight training, the ridiculous flirt who hid lethal power behind a vicious smile, the man whose name made her want to curse throughout the war, would one day make her this happy, she would have laughed as she shot them. It didn't feel possible.

Hollis's eyes caught her attention, pulled her away from the memories. "I love seeing you like this."

"You love seeing me any way at all. You think I'm beautiful when my hair's a mess and I'm covered in mud."

His smile widened. "You are beautiful like that. And this. And fighting me. And flirting with me. And kissing me." He pulled her closer still. "Do I have to wait two weeks for another kiss?"

She should have said yes, because she knew what he was thinking. But she couldn't resist leaning in. "Be good."

"I'm always good," he murmured as his lips met hers.

And he was.

So very, very good.

Hands tight around her waist, hips pressed together, lips tempting her into a deeper kiss. Being the focus of Hollis's attention in battle was dangerous. Being the focus of his attention when he wanted to bring her pleasure was burning her alive from the inside out.

Reason and logic fell away as his lips found a sensitive spot on her neck. She gasped, nails digging in his shoulder, and he groaned in pleasure. There was a reason she needed to keep her shirt on, but she wasn't sure what it was anymore.

Hollis nipped at her lip and pulled away as she growled in frustration. He had a very satisfied smile on his face. "See? I can be good."

"Uh-huh." She rested her head on his shoulder and tried to breath.

That was a kiss? Was that what everyone felt when they kissed? And, if that was a kiss, what was the rest like?

Visions of Hollis massaging her aching muscles after a long day and following with kisses slipped past her defenses. She didn't want a hot rush of passion but long hours of touching, and petting, and forgetting the rest of the universe existed.

Hollis groaned. "You are killing me."

Trying to be good, she tucked that battle plan away for later.

"Seducing me doesn't require a battle plan," he grumbled.

She pushed herself away. "Of course not. And you came after me and just winged it? Made it up on the fly? You always have a plan."

"True." His smile was hadn't changed. "I like plans."

Lightly touching the top edge of his bandage, she reminded herself why she wasn't giving into that smile just yet. "Good, then you can make some plans with me while we eat."

"Oh?" He was far too tempting.

Rowena stepped away, taking his hand and leading him over to the food.

"What are we planning?"

"Happily ever after. There's going to be more than one fight when we get back, and stations don't staff themselves."

He sighed with mock regret. "When you said I could play your second-in-command, I thought you had some bedroom fantasy of stripping me out of my uniform."

"Liar." She sat down. Okay, it was only half a lie. She did have an unusual dream once where she'd stripped Hollis out of his guardians all-black uniform piece by piece after a particularly violent bar brawl he'd broken up.

But they hadn't been in a bedroom.

Hollis stopped and looked back at the bed as if he was seriously considering dragging her over there.

"You're not wearing a uniform right now anyway."

"I can put one on!"

"Two weeks. Or I don't fix the zero-g flumes." She could feel him weighing out his options. "I'm currently the chief medical officer of this station, your commander, and your spouse. Two weeks, and then I'll tell you all the things I've dreamt about you over the years." Not that she had had more than one before this month, but she'd come up with at least thirty in the past ten minutes and felt confident she could find more before he was recovered.

His lips curled into a snarl and he sat down with a wince of pain he couldn't quite hide. "I hate being injured."

"I know. I'll make it up to you later. Come help me plan our future."

It was that easy, settling into together with a smile, sharing a meal, planning how to get everything they wanted. It
was the most natural thing in the universe. Like this was
where their lives had been going all along.

Not everyone was going to approve, but she didn't care.
She'd give up the sky and stars if that's what it took to keep
Hollis with her.

But it would be so much more fun to conquer them with
him.

47
MALCOLM

"WHERE ARE YOU?" HIS MOTHER'S voice was tight with worry.

Malcolm looked out the window of the Lethe's country mansion outside Kytan. From the second story balcony, he could see the grand maze and vine-twined pavilion studded with glittering glasswork where Sonya would one day say her wedding vows. An artificial stream ran between the landing pad and the side entrance to the house, strange plants whose leaves had a metallic sheen bobbed in the breeze. He took a deep breath and braced himself for the worse. "I'm outside Kytan advising Lady Lethe on—"

"Have you lost your mind?" The phone practically shook under his mother's wrath.

"I wasn't given much of a choice."

A stormy, poison-edged silence stretched between them for an uncomfortable moment.

"Do you need help?" His mother's voice was calm as the sea in the eye of a hurricane. Flat. Glassy. Foreboding.

Malcolm looked down the long hall to where Sonya's new social secretary was waiting, pink lips pinched together in a scowl of annoyance. "I think I can create an opening for myself."

"You need an exit strategy," his mother said. "Get that woman's claws out of you before it's too late."

"I know. I'm working on it."

Another thorny silence was followed by a sigh. "Be safe, son."

"I will," Malcolm promised. He hung up and erased the number from the borrowed phone. It wouldn't prevent someone from tracking the call in other ways, but it would make things a little bit harder. Walking down the long hall, feet sinking into plush, blue carpet he smiled at the secretary. She was a mousy woman with dull, brown hair highlighted by gray strands. The gray was artificial, he could tell that at a glance, and her clothes seemed chosen to make her look older and uglier than she was. But it seemed like a sensible precaution around someone like Sonya Lethe.

Malcolm held the phone out. "Thank you. I wasn't expecting to be brought in straight from work."

"Lady Lethe has need of your... expertise." The secretary's eyes traced the line of his button down shirt to his belt then bounced back up. Obviously the staff had an opinion of what kind of services he offered Sonya.

His polite grin turned to a grimace. "She could have called. There are obviously phones."

The secretary pushed the door open. "If you want to explain that to her, you are free to do so."

If he wanted to put his neck on the line. Swallowing a snarl of frustration he entered a strange room that couldn't seem to decide if it was a boudoir or an office. There was a canopied bed with golden bedding picked with Lethe Blue thread and lapis beads. There was a matching blue couch, a low table with a tiled mosaic top with familiar shapes of blue songbirds and pale blue flowers. And then there were several rows of computers and a wall filled with screens. It didn't make sense.

Sonya glanced up from her workstation, pale hair falling in disheveled strands from a tight bun. "There you are. Didn't I call for you hours ago?"

"I was in Ryun at work," Malcolm said. "In the middle of a meeting, actually. The director was very upset by the intrusion."

"I'll send him a bottle of whatever alcohol he likes best and a kindly worded note." Sonya squinted at her screen. "That usually works."

"But it doesn't explain why I'm here."

"There was a technical problem." She stood, long skirt sweeping around her feet. A long, satin skirt of Lethe Blue and an off-white, sleeveless blouse that looked more like an underlayer than a shirt.

That wasn't right at all. "Sonya, how long have you been up?"

"What?" She spared a second to glare at him then turned on to a new computer. "That's not important."

"You're wearing eveningwear at three in the afternoon."

"I was getting ready to go out last night, to meet Silar again, and then I received word he wasn't in transit. He's missing."

"Impossible." It had to be. "I thought your device could track him anywhere."

Sonya's chin jerked up in a distracted nod. "All the way to the spaceship that's in orbit over Enclave. He's gone up there once or twice. My analysts think it's possible the fleet is keeping the emperor there as a hostage."

Malcolm shook his head and walked over to see Sonya's screen. "What do you mean?"

"Mal Baular, we've been looking for him, but the sources we have in the fleet are limited. Obviously access to him is restricted and there's no way to get information from the fleet."

"They have an information site linked to the universal library." Malcolm leaned over one of the open workstations. The universal library held an electronic record of everything in the history of the Malik System. Like all digital repositories since the first one, there were layers. Markets advertised there, people could shop, read, watch dramas, listen to music, or watch the debates of the continental senates if they wanted. Archived under the heading Fleet Of Malik was a history of the fleet, all the information the spacers had uploaded to the library when they landed, and an updated section of modern officers.

Malcolm opened the page that explained the fleet doctrine and ethos, and listed relevant links to information. Under one marked Personnel, it had contact information for dozens of officers and crews.

"What am I supposed to do with this?" Sonya asked.

Taking a seat beside her, Malcolm scrolled through the faces. "After everything in Kydell, I went looking for your future emperor. Just to see him. He's not here."

"I know that!" Sonya threw her hands up in exasperation. "The fleet has no contact information for any Baulars."

"They have them listed under historical files. Sonya, the Baulars are dead. All of them. The ones who survived the war were executed."

"No." She shook her head violently. "No, that isn't true. The spacers are hiding him from us." She took control of the computer and typed something in.

The screen changed, showing an archived report of a car accident dated almost five years previous. "Here. Mal Baular is listed as an exile. Then dead."

"That's a Jhandarmi officer quoted in the article," Malcolm said. "There's no reason the Jhandarmi would lie."

"But the spacers might." Sonya sounded like she was clinging to a desperate hope. "If they, if they knew something about the governor's map. If they knew what my father wanted. Blight of the land, if they even knew that the imperial heir was on their ships they may have done it out of some misguided loyalty."

"How would they have known?"

"I don't know! Spies? Telepathy? You said Marshall could pull information off my computer, maybe she could rip it from my mind as well."

Malcolm shook his head. "Sonya, no. I read about their technology. They have machines in them. Little machines that let them access computers with a thought. It's a simple technology that anyone could have."

"I've noticed they haven't marketed it to anyone."

He took a deep breathe, carefully trying to guess where it would be safe to steer the conversation. "The spacers have shared very little with everyone. Listen, listen." He touched her hand. "Sonya, why is this a concern? Who cares where Silar is? He lied to you. He lied to you, and he's taking everything from you." A shadow of an idea played at the edge of his mind, a phantom, will-o-wisp of a thought that promised to bring the situation under control.

If it worked.

Sonya stood and paced along the foot of the bed. "Lied? He can't lie. They can lie." She stabbed her hand at the computers. "My informants can lie. Silar"—she shook her head as she crossed her arms—"I control him completely. It's better than any truth serum or torture. The machine controls the chemical balances of the brain, inhibits or arouses moods at my order. I can literally send men spiraling from manic glee to rages where they cut their lovers to bits. I can make angry men fall asleep, shy people confident. Anyone wearing a device loves me. Adores me. They can't lie to me. Silar is the only one I can trust. He's the one who knows the truth."

That was unfortunate.

Killing Silar would cause no end of trouble. Malcolm shelved that idea as a backup plan. "How does the machine work?"

"There's a sliver of orun that runs through it and stimulates chemical production."

"Did you test it on any of the spacers before Silar?"

Sonya glared at him. "Naturally. We had two volunteers." She shrugged when she saw his look of disbelief. "Two volun-tolds. They were payment for some bad information I received last year. The devices worked perfectly on them."

"Still, Silar could have been obfuscating. He never said Mal Baular was alive, only that he was the best fighter Silar knew and he wanted to introduce you to him."

"It would be hard to introduce me to him if he weren't alive."

"Unless it was threat," Malcolm said calmly.

Sonya's eyes widened in breathless disbelief. "Threaten? Me? Who... wha—"

"Look at how they present themselves," Malcolm said, changing the screen to show the profiles he'd perused earlier. "They're a military people. They're raised from infancy to fight. Look at the skills Hollis Silar has listed: proficiencies with every weapon we can name, flight training, tactics, hand-to-hand combat, tech enhancements... He was raised in a violent culture. Taught to be a violent man. Sonya,"

Malcolm reached for her, "he's a killer. And killers only think one way. They always think of murder first."

She took his hand and approached the computer station as if it would bite her.

Malcolm pulled her onto his lap. Killers always thought of murder first. But smart killers knew how to find other solutions. Sonya was unbalanced, unguarded, worried about everything but Malcolm. He stroked her back gently. "Think about it. You're a stranger, overwhelmingly powerful, wealthy beyond anything Silar could imagine, talented, beautiful. Your machine made him fall in love with you but he had to think you'd reject him."

Sonya's brows drew together in worry.

"He is a man used to ordering people around," Malcolm continued, keeping his voice soft. "He is used to snapping his fingers and having what he wants. Think of his pride. He expected to be hurt. What would you do in such a situation?"

"Reject him," Sonya said, "before he could reject me. Toss him aside."

"A cutting word. A cold glance." Malcolm kept gently rubbing her back. She was tense and scared, perfectly primed for his attack. "But you are a good person. You are not a killer."

"No." The word was a whisper.

"Silar is a killer. A man who sees every problem as a target of his violence."

Sonya shivered. Then she shook her head and stood up. "No. No that… that can't be right. I was making him happy. Making him calm."

"So?" Malcolm relaxed into his chair, projecting confidence. "Where are Silar's past lovers? Where did Rose Lauren wind up? Or all the others?"

He could see the doubts swirling in Sonya's eyes. The fears. The anger.

"Or perhaps I'm wrong," Malcolm said, feeding her a cruel kind of hope. "Perhaps he is desperately in love with you and simply blocking the device for some other reason. You could call him."

Sonya moved like a reef shark spotting a lump of chum. "Call him?"

"The contact information is right here." Turning the screen toward her, Malcolm stood, leaving the chair open. "You could have all your answers right now." And so could he.

"Yes. Quite." She took the chair and hit the connect button.

Malcolm stepped out of the camera's line of sight and double-checked to make sure anyone viewing Sonya wouldn't catch sight of him in a reflection. Satisfied that Sonya would look like she was alone, he watched.

The screen fuzzed for a moment, then the image of a teenager with shocking red hair cut short answered. "This is the *Veronica Guerin*. Do you wish to trade?"

"I need to speak to Commander Hollis Silar."

The young man's eyes glowed a jasper brown for a moment. "Your name?"

"Sonya Lethe."

"Is this com panel a good place to contact you?"

"Yes, it will forward to me."

"The commander will contact you when he is available." The young Silar cadet closed the channel without so much as a farewell.

Malcolm swallowed a snicker at the look of absolute shock on Sonya's face.

"Did you see that? He... he simply—"

"Is an untrained fool who doesn't know who you are. No rank or insignia. He doesn't know what he should respect because he doesn't see the markers he's expecting."

Sonya looked up in exasperation. "What am I supposed to do now? Wait for Hollis to contact me?"

That would become unfun very quickly, especially for Malcolm. "What time is it there?" He calculated the time difference. "He's possibly still at work. You should try contacting the Starguard and asking for him." Perhaps someone who knew him well would have caught the mischief in his tone of voice. Although anyone who knew him well was also someone smart enough to call a political authority and ask about the whereabouts of a person they were spying on.

For that matter, Malcolm couldn't imagine anyone he knew losing track of someone they were spying on. It was sloppy.

Sonya reached to call, but hesitated, hand hovering over the button. Apparently the heiress did have a brain. Her mouth pinched into a pout of frustration and then her hand dropped to her belly.

Nodding to herself, Sonya hit the connection.

Malcolm watched with interest as a dark-skinned woman with black hair braided into a tight crown appeared.

"This is the Starguard, Enclave. How may I direct your call?"

Sonya lifted her chin. "My name is Sonya Lethe. Connect me to Perrin Carver, he'll take my call."

"At once, Lady Lethe." The Starguard had better training than the Silar cadets. No surprise there, Carver ran the Starguard and he'd grown up on the planet. He knew who Lethe was.

As the screen went black with the change, Sonya looked up with a satisfied smile. "Carver and I took classes together at one time. He liked Marshall better back then. Now, I'm sure, he's grown tired of her."

A fair assessment. From what he'd seen of Hermione Marshall, she was a marvelously challenging person. She would have caught on to his game by now.

Sonya kept barreling on while Malcolm formulated the next step of his plan.

There was a beep and a familiar face appeared. It would be hard to be alive in the past twenty years and not know the face of Perrin Carver, the boy who fell to the ground. Less than a year old, he had been the sole survivor of a shuttle crash, the first contact between the colonists on the ground and the spacers in five hundred years. Sharp green eyes and hair black as ink, Perrin Carver had captured the world's imagination and grown up in the public eye.

Now he was looking at Sonya with an expression of suppressed rage. "Sonya, it's been so long."

"Did you miss me?"

Carver's flashed her a tight smile. "No."

"How disappointing." Sonya wiggled in her seat, hand pressed to her stomach. "I met a friend of yours. Hollis Silar? We had a"—she smiled as she looked away as if reminiscing—"a very fun time together. We're intimate acquaintances now, but I can't seem to reach him, and I need to. It's a very pressing, personal issue." The act was perfect. The little gestures. The soft emphasis on the word personal.

Malcolm wanted to applaud.

Carver looked unimpressed. "He's missing, Sonya. An interesting fact that I share because the last time any of us heard from him, Hollis Silar was headed to Kydell where he met with you six days ago. Where is he, Sonya?"

Tide take it all.

Malcolm scrambled to recalculate.

"Kydell?" Sonya asked, still smiling though her teeth were grinding together audibly. "Why would he go there now?"

"Presumably to resume whatever intimate acquaintance you had." Anger reverberated in Carver's voice. "You said you met him there, didn't you? Had a good time? Why wouldn't he go back, Sonya? Where else would he be?"

Her mouth moved soundlessly. She shook her head. "I don't like what you're implying."

"I don't like when my officers go missing."

Sonya's eyes met Malcolm's.

He licked his lips. "Offer to help," he whispered, hoping Carver wouldn't hear him. "Offer to send someone to look for Silar." *Fogging idiot.* How could Carver lose an officer? They had implants. They had nanites. They had tracking beacons.

The only way Silar could go missing is if he were hiding or dead.

"I'll contact my people in Kydell immediately," Sonya said. "We had teams on the ground to help in the crisis."

"The crisis with the mobs that didn't show up?" Carver asked, twisting his words like a knife.

Sonya froze. "I don't like what you're implying."

"And I told you, I don't like having officers missing. So we're both walking away disappointed. Seems familiar." Carver's smile was cold as a winter sea. "Have a good day, Lady Lethe."

Malcolm stared at the screen. Had Carver and Sonya? No. No. He wasn't going to even think about that. There were more pressing matters.

Like the fact Sonya was quietly cursing under her breath. "Why? Why would he go back to Kydell?"

"Because he met you there?" Unlikely at best.

Silar might not have been the brightest star in the sky, but he had to know Sonya didn't make her home in Kydell.

Sonya rolled her eyes as she crossed her arms. "I told him about my offices, my home, everything. There's no reason for him to be on Seahome if he were looking for me."

There was a sharp edge to the word *me* that Malcolm didn't like.

"Who else would he have been looking for?"

Turning with a sigh, Sonya pulled open the fleet database and scrolled down to the face of a woman with black hair, golden brown skin, monolid black eyes, and a grim expression that instinctively made Malcolm want to back up and apologize. He'd never realized that a photograph could capture such pure fury, but her eyes burned through the screen.

"Rowena Lee, weapons specialist," Sonya said, acid dripping from her voice. "Silar's plus one to the party on Kydell."

"The Lees and Silars are enemies!"

Sonya frowned at him.

"I read it on the database," Malcolm explained, lowering his voice. "I read all their history so I could better assist. There is no reason a Lee and a Silar would be together."

"But they were. And she had contact with the Jhandarmi." Sonya scowled at the angry woman's photo. "My contacts in the Jhandarmi offices removed Lee from Kydell. She's dead. If Hollis went after her—" Sonya spread her hands.

A small muscle in Malcolm's jaw twitched as he fought to stay calm. "How did you kill one of the fleet's best fighters? Two of them?"

"There is an area in Seahome that drains all imperial tech. It was used for defusing bombs at one point, and it works on spacer technology. They become weak. Vulnerable. They aren't trained to fight on land, although Lee knew how to run. She ran, and ran, and ran right off a cliff."

"Have you recovered the body?"

Sonya wrinkled her nose in disgust. "Why?"

"So you have something to give the spacers," Malcolm said slowly. "Look at their files. Lee and Silar are well known, well respected. Carver isn't going to accept they're missing forever."

"Then the spacers can lose more people to the scorpions and jungles!" Sonya glared at him. "Stop and think about what this means for a moment. For me, not for those misbegotten, half-human mutants from space. Sucking up radiation and doing ancestors only know what to their bodies. I've lost my contact to the new emperor! I have... I have nothing!"

She slammed her fists on the desk top. "All this work, and I have nothing."

She tapped her belly again, eyes narrowing.

"Are you considering a fake pregnancy?"

"It could be real!" Sonya protested. Under his gaze, she sighed and turned her head away. "It could work. The Lethe heir, even the spacers would have to recognize how valuable that would be."

Malcolm looked at the floor. "Heir to what?"

Sonya turned back to him and stood. "To everything! To my fortune, our lands, our companies."

"All of which are being handed to the emperor." Malcolm met Sonya's eyes. "Your father surely has plans for the heir. For your child. They will be the imperial heir, not the Lethe heir. There will be no more Lethe. You will burn through all your power putting this new emperor on the throne. You'll have nothing left."

Her mouth opened and stayed open as her eyes widened.

"Your father's plan takes everything away from you." Malcolm rammed into her battered defenses. "Your name will get washed away on the tides of history. Sonya Lethe, another forgotten empress in a stable of hundreds. How many other great houses will offer up daughters to the new emperor, do you think? Surely the Marshalls will. If Mal Baular is alive, Hermione Marshall knows him. She's had over a decade with him that you haven't."

Sonya's head jerked to the side in a shaky refusal.

"What happens if Hermione gets to the emperor first?" Malcolm bit back a cruel smile. "Or doesn't it matter? Today you're the empress of Malik IV. You control everything. The people obey you. People fawn over you, fight for your affection. Next week? They'll be fighting to gain the favor of a man who was indoctrinated to love the fleet, not the planet. Not the people. Not your people."

"Stop!" Sonya ordered. "Stop it right now!"

"I'm telling the truth," Malcolm said. "I'm the only one who will. I have nothing to lose. My family lands will be mine emperor or no. I have no sisters to marry into power. No daughters. Nothing to lose at all."

Sonya's face twisted into a scowl. "Me. You would lose me. When I marry the emperor, you lose me. That's why you're saying this."

"I could never lose you, because I would never have you. But you? You would lose you. Everything you want, every-thing you built, will be gone. You'll lose control over every aspect of your life. Unless you reign as empress. Your fath-er's plan has you sitting quietly in a corner."

A tiny shriek of rage escaped Sonya's carefully controlled façade.

That was exactly what he'd been waiting for. It wouldn't save Kydell, or Lee, or Silar, but it would rip apart the Lethe empire. All he had to do now was step back and watch their precious, poisonous world burn.

48
ROWENA

THE IMAGES ON THE SCREEN WERE grim. Eden had woken Rowena with a quiet notification and she'd slipped out of bed to come see what was waiting on the planet's surface.

Kydell was under assault by Lethe-backed forces.

Politicians were arguing, but even with the time delay Rowena could see how it would fall out.

Most of the rowdies would be dead before Lethe's forces were out. It was an excuse, nothing more. There would be no survivors. No witnesses. And Sonya would have a reason to stage her macabre drama in other city-states.

Eden looked on, her avatar's face tight with lines of worry. "Commodore, there's nothing you can do from here. Is it good to keep watching?"

"How long until we have coms?"

"At our current rate of repair, we have six hours until we can contact Malik IV. The signal will be weak, but it will be heard."

Garbled. Possibly ignored.

"Can the engines move us any faster?"

"I can give you a ten percent increase in speed before the resource demands will affect repair times."

"Do that," Rowena ordered. She tapped into the system and felt a sense of awe as the images of the battlefields burned in her brain came to life on the *Eden's* screens. "I missed this."

The whole universe was under her control. All she had to do was spin it right.

She took a seat in the command chair. The light of the screens bent, flexing and bouncing off nanite particles to give her an approximation of a three dimensional view of her playground. "Eden, mark the wrecks of the *Chrysophylax*, the *Ryu*, the *Bassi*, the *Theoano*, the *Maggie Gee* and the *Virginia Valejo*." Baular, Lee, Sciarra, and a Silar ship. She could see them lined up like a path. "Are their coms operable?"

"Yes, Commodore."

Rowena bent her mind to them. The Baular shields were down and she had those codes. The Sciarra one took her a few tries, but *Maggie* had been one of Titan's first commands and he'd left a back door for her. The *Valejo* didn't want to talk to her. She reached out to Hollis, still asleep in their bunk, and quietly sifted through his implant.

She tripped a program and an avatar of Hollis appeared in front of her. "What are you doing?"

"Looking for the com codes for the *Virginia Valejo*. I need to use it."

The avatar tilted its head in confusion. "You aren't authorized for that, Lee."

"When's the last time you updated?"

The program sneered.

"Check for all updates."

The image glitched and folded as the codes became available.

"He does very intricate work," Eden said with approval. "The shields would destroy the ship if you tried to break them with brute force."

"I know. The Silars loved doing that during the war." Her mind settled around the strange codes and data. Years ago, she'd dreamed of this day. Of having all the Silars' ships at her mercy. With this information she could vent their oxygen, poison their water, cripple them. There were days during the war she woke up certain she had the codes, only to have them fade with light. If she could have glimpsed this day then, she would have laughed at the impossibility.

It was all impossible.

Her happiness. Her love. Her command.

All completely impossible. All right here. All because of Hollis. Ancestors, but she loved him.

The coms fell into line. "There. Eden, check that data path. If you bounce the signal through those ships, how long until you can contact Malik IV?"

"At top speed I can make it in two hours, but—"

"But the *Ryu* and the *Theoano* are both faltering. I'd have to teleport over there to do any repairs."

"Neither have oxygen," Eden said sounding as alarmed as a station's avatar could.

"They should hold. Not for long, ten, maybe fifteen minutes of transmission time. It'll be enough." She stood up. "Okay. I am going to change into my gear, grab a knife and a couple ration bars, and get to the planet. Kydell isn't going to have communications, but I can keep Lethe from doing any major damage until you can call for backup."

"Excuse me?" The sound relays of the command deck echoed with outrage.

"I'll leave Hollis a message," Rowena said.

"Commodore! I do not have a long range shuttle capable of beating me to that planet."

"I'm teleporting."

Eden appeared as a hologram in front of her. The last commodore must have been a very formidable woman, because Eden captured an expression of outrage and fury that any officer would envy. "We're not even near the limits of a safe teleport, unless your tech has improved drastically since I updated my file eleven hours ago."

"I'm not teleporting directly to the planet." Rowena highlighted another path of ships. Wrecks and derelicts floating on the tides of space. "I'll ship-hop. Quick, close range jumps. The drain on my implant will be less than twenty-two percent."

"Commodore!" Eden looked panicky. "Rowena, you can't leave. Not all those ships are stable. They don't have oxygen. Some of them still have mines and booby traps. You'll land with less than fifty percent of your implant."

Rowena nodded. "That's enough for three hours. That's all I need. Right?"

"What if something goes wrong?"

Rowena bit her lip.

Dead ships and no backup. She'd be walking through a graveyard and into a warzone.

And if I don't go?

"If I don't go, they all die. Jae. Bera. All of them will be dead if Sonya Lethe has her way. Examples of what happen to people who oppose the lawful authority. All my life I've dealt with people like her. People who think the weak should sit down and shut up. People who think the only real people are the rich, or the pretty, or the powerful, or the ones with the right skin color, or the ones with the right gender.

"Those people will destroy everything good in the name of power. I've punched back before. I've fought. I've survived. I'm strong. The rowdies aren't. Jae can't hold off an army no matter how well he fights. I can. This is what I was born to do. The reason the fleet exists. I was meant to protect the people of the Malik System."

"The chances of survival are—" Eden shook her head.

Rowena smiled. "Hollis has my back. And you'll help him."

"You're asking the impossible."

"Only for someone else. Hollis and I can pull this off."

Eden looked less than convinced.

"It's going to be okay. I'm not abandoning you. I'm going to come back."

"The last station commander said that too." An AI didn't have a heart to break, but Eden sounded heartbroken. Artificial tears shimmered in her holographic eyes. There was real pain there, even if it was only a computer program that was hurting. "She promised she'd talk sense into everyone and be back soon. I lost her."

Rowena's smile would have sent anyone who knew her running for cover. "Your last commander went to talk. I'm going to break heads. Ask Hollis when he wakes up; there's no one in this solar system who can take me down except him, and he's on my side."

"If you die—"

"Take orders from Hollis and only Hollis until he says otherwise."

Eden rolled her eyes. "I know you had an education. I have the files. Was there nothing taught about self-preservation?"

"Sure, it just came after the bit where you protect everyone weaker than you. For me, that means everyone." She popped down to the galley before Eden could argue anymore and grabbed the basics, along with a triage kit and as many weapons as fit into the pack she found in the old armory.

They were going to upgrade all of it when she got back. Then, after leaving the promised message for Hollis, she teleported to the first stop.

Emptiness and cold surrounded her.

The decks of the *Ruth* creaked under her weight. She'd trained here even before Academy. First been told she was betrothed to Mal in the captain's quarters. Learned to break a shield in the training rooms.

Now the still air smelled of seared metal, ozone, and the drunken fruit scent associated with the dust of the outer worlds of the Malik System. The *Ruth* had traveled far.

Rowena patted the stinging cold hull. "Wish me luck, girl. I've got a long way to go too."

Another breath, another jump.

And another.

And another.

Along a dark path, stepping on the corpses of the fallen, falling through the open graves until she landed in the city center of Kydell, amid the screams of the dying.

49
HOLLIS

AN UNEASY STILLNESS BROUGHT Hollis to wary wakefulness. The environmental system hummed quietly, but the reassuring sounds of Rowena nearby were absent. He reached out a hand to her side of the bed and felt nothing but cold sheets. He reached out with his implant, scanning for her, and found only silence.

He sat up, frowning at the half-light of the room. "Rowena?"

She didn't answer.

"Eden, where is Rowena?"

The AI materialized on a black column near the wall. "She is off station, sir. There's a message waiting for you on the room's console."

A message recorded on a console instead of left directly for him on his implant?

:Rowena? What is this?:

There was no answer. Not even a ping telling him his message had reached her.

He scrambled out of bed, wrapping the blanket around him for warmth as he sat in the cold chair by the console. A touch on the screen brought Rowena into view.

"Hollis." Her smile broke his heart. "I didn't want to wake you for this. Lethe has attacked Kydell and no one is protecting the rowdies. They need protection. Don't yell." She looked ready to cry. "The *Eden* wasn't in position to communicate with anyone, so I went ahead. I don't know if I'll be able to contact anyone during re-entry."

"No." He shook his head in disbelief. "Rowena."

:ROWENA!:

On the screen, the recording smiled at him. "I love you." She laughed. "I have loved you... for longer than you knew. These past few years when I had nothing—no pride, or worth, or family—you made me smile. If you'd ignored me too, I don't think I would have survived. But you were always there, goading me on. Forcing me to keep living through the darkest days. This time I've had with you has been beyond any hope I ever had. You make me so happy. You make me everything I want to be."

The cold of the empty room settled in his bones.

"I'm taking a risk, and I know that. You're my backup. By the time you wake up, the *Eden* should be in position to relay information through the coms I set up. You can contact someone at Enclave. Start with the *Sabiha* and the *Persephone*, they'll come for me. I'll be in Kydell." She took a deep breath and stared off screen—towards him, he realized. She'd been watching him sleep and wondering how to say goodbye.

Tears ran down his cheeks.

"Is it too much to ask you to be happy if this goes wrong?" Rowena asked as she turned back to the screen.

"Yes."

She nodded as if she'd anticipated the answer. "If I don't... If this doesn't work, don't blame yourself. I calculated the risk. I know exactly how much danger I'm putting myself in, all the things that could go wrong. It's why I didn't wake you. I didn't want you sitting here worrying.

"This is the cruelest thing I could do, isn't it? Taking your heart and then running into danger without you. If I woke up to this, I don't... I don't know what I'd do. I don't want to imagine what you're doing right now. If there was another way. If I could think of anything... I promise you, I'm not doing this to hurt you. But I don't have anyone else I can ask. I can't—"

She shrugged in bleak surrender.

"No one will protect them but me. No one will defend these people. They've been abandoned by their government, ignored by the Jhandarmi... Hollis, I see so much of myself in them it hurts. I can't leave them. I can't lose them. They're like crew now. Like family."

Rowena rolled her eyes up as she pressed her lips together and wiped away a tear. "I hate doing this to you. I never, never wanted to hurt you again. But if I don't go..." She looked so helpless and broken.

"The *Eden* is yours, until I return. If I don't"—her face hardened—"defend her. Keep the *Eden*. I don't care who you kill. And... find happiness. I don't want to think of you alone any more. Go, find someone who can make you happy. If I go to the Lost Fleet today, I'll save a bunk for you." She smiled.

The smile stole his breath. His chest seized, aching and empty.

"I love you." The screen went dark.

For a minute, all he could do was stare in disbelief. She'd left him.

For good reasons, but still, she was gone.

The pain was all-consuming, everywhere, overwhelming and like nothing he'd felt before. Like being burned alive by a freezing fire.

She was gone.

:Rowena?:

"Rowena?"

"She's not on board, commander," Eden said quietly.

Hollis nodded, forcing himself to focus through the pain. "Can you... can you track her? Get satellite imagery of the area? Do you know where she is?"

Eden reset the screen to show Kydell. "This is from a satellite pass an hour ago. Since then a block has gone up. The orbiting satellites have been reconfigured. No aircraft are in the area and there's no transmissions of any kind coming out."

"Heat signatures?"

"My readings show heat signatures consistent with a sustained bombardment of the lower side of the city. There appears to be an active shield. Commodore Lee is defending, but I don't know how long she can hold her shields."

He took a deep breath as his implant calculated the variables. "A few hours, at most. Provided they don't find a way to break her. How long ago did this start?"

"Two hours, thirty-one minutes ago, Commander. Her original estimate was that help would arrive within three hours."

Too long. The *Eden* would never reach Malik IV in time.

"Rowena, love—" He was the only one she could rely on. The room took on a golden hue as a battle veil fell across his eyes. "Light up the command room, Eden. I need to see the stats. How did she even get off station?"

"A series of short teleports between derelicts, sir."

"She hates derelicts!"

"Sir?" Eden sounded confused.

He waved off the question as he took the command chair. "Are we close enough to hail the *Persephone*?"

"Yes, sir."

"Hail her. Then move into stationary orbit over Descent and set your best rotating shields."

On the column, Eden tilted her head. "Descent, sir? Not over Kydell?"

"No. Lethe's holdings are in Descent. If Rowena dies, I want you to turn the whole continent to a pile of molten slag."

"That goes against my primary programming," the AI said tartly.

"Screw your programming and the person who thought you needed it. Losing my spouse goes against my primary programming. If she's hurt: slag the continent. That's a direct order."

"Yes, sir!"

He linked to the station, his mind flowing through the data. Without effort he could pull up all of *Eden's* resources, see what was available, track fleet communications. He patted the arm of the chair with affection.

Now, what exactly had Rowena planned?

They're like crew now. Like family.

"Eden, how many people can you accommodate with our current oxygen and ration levels?"

"No more than a few hundred thousand until repairs have been completed."

"That's enough."

Rowena had said to contact the Sciarras first. A good choice, but he needed to get someone on the political ground first. "Eden, get me Marshall."

It took thirty torturous seconds for Hermione to appear on screen. "Hollis? Where are you contacting me from?"

"Doesn't matter. It's an emergency. I need a captain's council and fleet resources now. Not in an hour. Not in ten minutes. Now. Can you do that?"

Hermione blinked. "Who's in danger?"

"Kydell is under attack and Rowena went into the middle of it." His breath staggered as he dipped too close to the emotions he was trying to hide. "She left me, Hermione. She went in to fight alone. I can't..." He shook his head. "I can't."

Couldn't stop himself. Couldn't slow down. Couldn't let her die.

Hermione's eyes went wide. "It's a political wildfire right now. The leading council has blamed the bombing on the rowdy population."

"They didn't do it."

"You have proof?"

"Rowena does."

"And she's in Kydell right now?" Hermione paused to bite back what he knew would have been a ten minute rant against political awareness of the fleet. "Lethe is there and heavily armed. No one's been able to contact the city in over two hours."

Hollis nodded. "That tracks with the timetable I have."

"We are going to have a long, long lecture about how politics works when this is over."

"Hermione, I'm on the space station *Eden*. Rowena's taken the rank of Commodore. Whatever political status quo we had just got fogged. We're in the dark without a flight plan."

Hermione's face went perfectly still. "That changes things marginally. Right now the big political debate is where the rowdies and other unwanteds can be moved. If you have the *Eden*—"

"Rowena will bring them here." He was sure of it. "But I need to get to the city to evacuate them. We'll be pulling pilots from allied crews for now."

"We?" Hermione smiled as she realized what that meant. "That's the only good news I've heard in days. Congratulations. Put a uniform on. I'll have everyone ready in five minutes. Meet me in the OIA conference room." She paused and frowned at him. "Can you make it here? You... are bandaged."

He looked down at the crisscross of bandages and blood on his chest. He must have ripped some stitches walking too fast. "I'm fine."

"Right. I'll get the story later."

"Promise."

She nodded and the com went dark.

"Sir," Eden said, "how do you intend to reach the council?"

"Working on it. Show me the path Rowena took."

A series of ships lit up. They were close jumps only when thinking in light-years. It had to have eaten up her implant's charge. On a good day he might have matched, but injured and running his implant to repair his body, the stretch on his resources wasn't a good idea.

"Eden, I need to create a way for someone else to get up here. There aren't enough people who can teleport like Rowena does and I can't waste Carver or Marshall on ferrying people."

"I have the docking platforms we used for distance loading," Eden said. "Each platform can carry up to ten people for six hours along with a small set of supplies. They can maneuver independently, but they don't have any resources like food or water."

Hollis nodded. "We can work with that." He ran the calculations to figure out where the stations would need to be to get a moderately strong officer up here. "Deploy to these locations. How long will it take?"

"Six minutes to get them all in places, commander."

Good enough. He could jump between them and the surface. Now for the hard stuff. He turned on the com and dialed a link Rowena had in her files.

Aronia Lee appeared on the screen, faced wrinkled in a confused frown as she juggled a baby on her hip. "Commander Silar?"

"Lee." It felt good to say. "Effective immediately, you are promoted to the rank of commander and assigned to duty aboard the space station *Eden* under the command of Commodore Rowena Lee. You will be assisting in the evacuation of the city-state Kydell. Resources will be sent to your implant. Tap anyone from the crew you need for this. Use temporary priority orders if needed. If anyone argues, send them directly to me. You'll be expected on board the *Eden* in three minutes. Bring the kid. Data incoming."

He sent her everything she needed along with a small gift, the code for a weaker version of Silar Fire. It was priority tech and a fitting gift for his new sister.

Aronia's eyes glowed bright purple as she took in everything. Her mouth opened.

"Questions later."

"Aye, sir." Purple tongues of fire rolled along her hand. "Thank you."

Hollis nodded before he switched screens.

The *Persephone's* avatar appeared on the screen. "Commander Silar, how may the Carylls assist the Starguard today?"

Put that on the list of jobs he'd need to find a replacement for. "*Persephone*, I'm contacting you from the space station *Eden*. Can you read her signature?"

There was a moment where the screen turned white and then Persephone returned. "Yes, commander."

"Eden, talk to Persephone and get things sorted out."

"AIs are not intended to communicate independently," Eden protested.

"I only have two hands and one brain and I need them to go rescue Rowena!" Hollis said as he stood up. "Help out a little! I'll get a full crew in here... eventually." Another worry for the list.

Eden looked as angry as a computer program could. "Commander Lee has arrived."

"Thank you. Talk to Persephone." He scanned for Aronia and teleported down to the hangar bay. "Commander."

"Commander." She was wearing denim pants, a light pink t-shirt, and holding baby Ki and a diaper bag. "Where's Rowena?"

"On the ground in Kydell. It's going to be fine." No other outcome was acceptable. "Eden!"

The station's avatar appeared on the nearest wall.

"Eden, Aronia Lee, I'm sure you've read her file. Aronia, the station avatar Eden. While I am away, Aronia is in command."

"What?" Aronia looked at him in terror. "I'm a gunner and a mediocre pilot! I was never in charge of anything!"

"You've kept a kid alive. It's like that, only on a slightly larger scale. Eden will help and we'll have support soon. More crew will be arriving shortly. I promise."

Aronia's mouth opened in protest.

"Captain Marshall is waiting for you in Enclave, sir," Eden said.

Hollis nodded. "Good luck, ladies. Baby Ki, be good. Eden, if anything happens to Rowena, slag all Lethe holdings from orbit and burn anything that approaches our shield. Aronia, she's your sister, use as much force as you feel is required."

Aronia's eyebrows went up. "Yes, sir. Consider them fogged."

He nodded and teleported.

The first docking platform came as a surprise. The air smelled minty for no reason he could discern and there was no real gravity. It was disorienting for half a second, and then he was off to the next one.

Gravity and the smell of Enclave—cooking grease, sweat, a sea breeze, and hull—came as a shock. It had taken months to adjust and start thinking of this place as home; now home was six thousand miles away under a heavy shield fighting for her life.

He straightened his uniform and walked to the conference room, sending rolling updates to the Silars as he went.

For the first time in his life, he was acting on his own.

This wasn't him enforcing orders for Garius or Carver or the Starguard. There was no higher power to appeal to, or to protect him if things went nova. This was true command.

Everything that mattered depended on what he could get done in the next few minutes.

There was a ping against his shields. A captain's demand for a report.

:Meet me.: He sent Garius the coordinates and kept walking.

A crew update from Aronia hit the Lee channels.

"Hollis," Garius said catching up to him, "This is untenable. You do not have the authority to do this."

The world shimmered through the view of a battle haze. "The mission of this fleet is, and always has been, to defend the people of the Malik System. Rowena is currently shielding thousands of people, holding off a full army. My spouse is under siege. I will not leave her to defend them alone."

"Your captain has given his answer," Garius said. "I told you to forget that woman."

Hollis took a deep breath and turned so Garius could see his sleeves. "My commander is Commodore Rowena Lee of the *Eden*. I am her second-in-command, rank of station commander. The only reason I am being this nice is because you are family. You lost a lot in the war. You lost more by abandoning everyone who survived. Get back to your ship. Cower. Cry. I don't care. If any of the crew want to come with me, I'll allow it, but I'm taking nothing else from you. Including orders."

He pushed past Garius and into the main building with his shields up. His scroll was a bright blue-green ribbon with the *Eden's* insignia and his new name.

Carver teleported in, took one look, and raised his eyebrows. "Were you going to tell me about this? Give me a warning?"

"You had a warning. I said I was going to make Rowena Lee my sparring partner. You said good luck."

Perrin took a breath and nodded. "Sure. Not at all the same, but sure. What do you need?"

"I need you and Marshall handling the political end. If Rowena is hurt, I will turn Descent into a lava flow. Make the grounders understand that."

"How much of a warning are you going to give them?"

"That was the warning."

Perrin's eyes went wide as he cursed. "On it." He teleported out mid-stride.

Hollis entered the conference room where the senior captains were waiting.

Gen sat next to Marshall, several seconds stood along the wall, and in the far hall he could see fleetlings peering in, trying to catch a glimpse of history in the making.

Marshall stood, taking control of the room. "Commander Lee—"

"Lee?" Hoshi laughed. "No one is going to believe anything you have to say. You can lie all you want—"

"Sir, Lethe just put fighters in the air from an airfield in southern Descent." Yunjin Lee slipped past the others to stand beside him, wearing her best olive-and-black dress uniform.

Hoshi stood, shields flaring. "Cadet! You don't report to this man!"

"She reports to Commodore Rowena Lee," Hollis said. "As do you. Get the Lee fighters in the air, Hoshi."

Hoshi looked at him in surprise. "What?"

"There is only one person whose orders I recognize, and that's Rowena Lee. When we're done with the Lethe army, I assure you, dealing with a pissant like you will be an afterthought. You better pray to your ancestors Rowena is feeling merciful. I won't be.

"Scramble the Lee ships, or I will cut a swath through the armada and drown your decks in blood. Aronia will be a sub-captain in nine minutes, and I will have the air support my wife needs."

Hoshi blinked in terror.

"Let's be very clear, Hoshi, Rowena is the gentle one. She has forgiven your behavior because you're family. I won't forgive. Move out. *Now*."

Stumbling to salute and teleport out, Hoshi vanished. On the Lee priority channels, Hollis could hear the call to arms.

:Good work,: he told Yunjin. Out loud he said, "By now everyone should have an update on the situation in Kydell. Rowena is holding a shield but we need to evacuate the grounder population."

"I heard they'd attacked the Jhandarmi offices," Captain Bancroff said.

"Lethe put that information out," Hollis said. "It's incorrect."

A globe of light appeared over Captain Ukoruh's head. "Where are we evacuating them to?"

"The *Eden*."

A murmur ran around the room and communications pinged around him like the fall of shrapnel. That was one of Rowena's codes, picking up all the leaking information. No wonder she always seemed a step ahead of everyone.

"I need support," Hollis said. "Pilots for the armored couriers *Jacqueline Gill* and the *Jennifer Robison*, support ships, crew on the space station to handle the incoming refugees, medical personnel." There was hesitation; they were calculating the risk, what they'd have to give up. "Any fuel used in this operation will be replaced by the *Eden's* stores."

"You'll have Sciarra support."

Every head in the room turned to Elea Sciarra.

Under a crown of thick braids she raised an eyebrow, emerald green eyes burning with inner fire. "Eighth wing is being scrambled. The *Persephone* sends to say she'll be offering covering fire. We will also provide ground troops and evacuation shuttles. And a pilot for the *Jacqueline Gill* if you don't find someone in the Lee ships who can fly her. The Lees and Sciarras have always been allies. And, I like Rowena."

"Thank you," Hollis said.

The measure of calm Elea brought, her confidence and support... He was going to owe her.

It would be worth it.

"The Starguard is standing by to render aid. Carver is alerting the Jhandarmi in case they weren't aware of the situation," Marshall said. "I'll handle the politicians on Descent. We'll have support from my kin as well."

Gen stood, the insignia for acting-captain of the Silars visible. "We have enough orun to put a flight of fighters in the air, but not for more than an hour. We can drop teleporters in too."

Other captains sent Hollis lists of support. He would have what he needed to rescue Rowena, but it would take time they didn't have.

It was a moment, a terrible pause as history rushed along, and now it was over. The fleet was going to fly to war again.

"Thank you. Aronia Lee is acting-commander aboard the *Eden*, messages can be routed through her staff unless they are urgent. Dismissed."

:Rowena, I'm coming.:

:Take your time. There's no rush over here.: The image she sent him showed her holding a shield twice too large for a single person to maintain under heavy kinetic bombardment.

He wanted to roll over the enemy in fire and fury.

:Tempting,: Rowena agreed, :but not diplomatic.:

:I am done being diplomatic.:

:We evacuate, and then we negotiate from the *Eden* where I can drop rocks on Lethe's head. I like an advantage, and I don't have one here.:

He sent her the memory of a kiss. :I'm bringing you everything you need. Hold on a little longer.:

50
ROWENA

:I'M WAITING FOR YOU.: ROWENA sent the message even as her implant reminded her that her power levels were dipping dangerously low.

The air under the shield was too hot. Fear and despair made every breathe taste of defeat.

A blood-soaked Jae sat beside her, back against a crumbled wall. "You don't look so good."

She smirked. "That's the rowdy charm I love and know." Her eyes closed against her will.

"What happens when you pass out?" Jae asked.

She'd be dead. She'd keep the shield up no matter what, and when it fell it would be because she'd done everything she could. *Sorry, Hollis. I tried to wait for you.*

A rough hand shook her shoulder. "Boss, people are looking to you. You need to get up."

Snarling, Rowena sat up and heaved in a lungful of humid air. "What's the defensive line look like?"

"We have our best fighters on the outside." Jae grimaced. "Some of the older rowdies are out there too. They..." He looked uncomfortable. "They're good people. Survivors. They want to buy time for the kids and the young families."

Sensible, to a point. "There's no back door?"

He shook his head. "Security has the tunnels covered. I checked a couple that were flooded, but they've put something in the water. Timry was going to try swimming it, but it burned his skin."

Fog Lethe and the government of Kydell. "Is he going to live?"

"Maybe. He's breathing, but he's in pain."

"Okay. We're going to be okay. Help me up."

Jae grabbed her forearm and hauled her to her feet. "I've got no plays here. People are looking to me and all I can say is this magic girl who does some sparkly woo-woo stuff is going to help us."

Sparkly woo-woo.... Wow. "Never say that again," Rowena said. "I would never live it down. What I'm doing is all done with tech. It's machines and mathematics."

"Right." He looked her up and down. "Machines. You stopped bullets with invisible machines."

"And math."

He nodded. "I don't think my school offered that math class."

She laughed weakly. Nothing else was going right today, but at least the rowdies were taking it all in stride. She'd dropped into the middle of the first barrage, a government-ordered execution, and kept most of them alive.

There were children crying in the dust.

Parents holding the broken bodies of babies.

Rowdy toughs who'd worked the dockside and suffered every degradation with a scowl that were lying on the ground despondent and broken.

But for the most part they'd rallied.

They hadn't asked how or why. They'd accepted her presence. Because Jae told them to. That was its own kind of magic, and as long as it lasted, she was willing to make use of it.

There was a shriek of surprise across the plaza.

Rowena looked up to see an orange gas filtering through.

"Crack my hull!" She tightened the shield. The oxygen in here was already bad but—

A second jet streaked overhead, dropping a load of the heavy orange gas.

"Poison!" Jae shouted. "Everyone take cover!" He pushed her toward a burnt-out building. "They drop this over the jungle villages sometimes when we won't give up someone they call a criminal."

People were coughing, choking, dying inside her shield.

She tried to purify the air. Teleported out chunks of it and tried to bring in more oxygen.

She dropped to her knees as her head swam. They were all going to die and she couldn't save them. All of this... Everything she could do alone wasn't enough.

And Hollis wasn't going to reach her in time.

A notice pinged against her implant. :Lee, drop the shield.:

The channel was one only Mal was supposed to know. Hollis knew it, but it wasn't him. That left...

:Marshall?:

:I'll put a shield in place. You need to focus on what's happening. Lethe's troops can see you and they know you're weak.:

Rowena looked up. Through the haze of her shield she could see hard-faced men waiting, watching like vultures.

:Drop it, Lee, before you drop.:

She hesitated.

A memory of Marshall in the Academy shouting, "Why won't you trust me? I know what I'm doing!" crossed her mind.

:Nothing personal, it's just... you're you,: Rowena said.

:Yes, I'm your spouse's best friend and Mal's lover,: Hermione said. :One way or another we were going to wind up fighting side by side.:

"What's wrong?" Jae asked.

Rowena shook her head. :Take the shield, Marshall, and get me some medics. I have injured people here.:

:Medics are en route.:

A battle plan filtered into her mind. Not a nice, simple plan, but a complex and layered one that had Hollis's fingerprints all over it. She smiled.

Jae looked worried. "Where's your head at?"

"Just talking with friends," Rowena said. "And reminding myself why I married my husband."

"Right." Jae looked into the clear sky. "Are these gods? Aliens? Or only invisible friends that won't actually help?"

There was a crack of thunder overhead and a golden shield cascaded over the city.

"That's Marshall," Rowena said as she pulled down her own shield. "The rest will be arriving soon. We need to clear a space for the evacuation ships. All I need to do is deal with everything down here."

An energy wave hit the shield.

She raised an eyebrow. "I didn't know Lethe had toys like that."

"Air cannons," Jae said. "They're an acoustic weapon. It leaves your ears ringing and your insides liquified. They like to use them for riots."

"It won't do any good against Marshall's shield."

"Who?"

Rowena opened her mouth to explain and then shook her head. "Never mind. I'll introduce you later."

The jets went by again. This time canisters fell out.

:Don't shoot the jets,: Rowena sent the message to Titan and Selena both. :I know *Persephone* can, but we can't have that poison in the air.:

:Lots of things could shoot down those jets,: Titan responded smugly. :But we'll do something else with them.:

A jet winked out of existence.

There was a murmur from the rowdies as the jets popped out of visible range.

"Um..." Jae looked at her. "Explanation?"

"Probably teleported out." Which was terrifying really. :Who pulled the jets?: There was a crowd of minds on the open fleet channel and she recognized over half of them.

There was a memory of Genevieve Carter's smile as she tossed thick, red hair over her shoulder. :You're welcome, sis. Welcome to the family.:

:Lee, the troops are trying to get your attention,: Marshall said. :I'm trying to negotiate over here. Go convince them that backing down is in their best interest.:

:And... if they don't want to back down?: Rowena asked.

The response was the Academy code for a fight.

Rowena steadied her trembling body and smiled. "I have to go talk to our friends over there."

"I'll come with," Jae said.

"No, you need to stay here and get people organized. In a couple of minutes we'll be leaving. I have—"

Mars Sciarra appeared beside her.

Jae blinked, rubbed his eyes, then kicked at Mars' leg. "A friend?"

"Mars Sciarra, Jae the leader of the rowdies. Play nice," Rowena said. "What is going on?" she said to Mars.

"We have incoming troops. Elea has the Sciarra Knives in the air with the Silars as backup, which might go down as a miracle or the best-looking attack wing in history. Either or. We have the *Jacqueline Gill* and the *Jennifer Robison* coming in. Aronia is on the *Eden*. Hollis is fine. And we have people teleporting in medics. I was sent here to help triage and get the worst cases to a doctor immediately."

"Which doctor?" Rowena asked.

"The best in the fleet, and we're bringing in some grounders," Mars said.

It was as good as they were going to get.

"Jae will help with the triage." It was an order, not a request, but Jae nodded anyway.

"If this is going to turn into a warzone, I want to get the families with small children out," Jae said.

Mars' eyes turned bright Sciarra green. "We don't have that many long distance teleporters, Ro." His lips curled into a snarl of frustration. "And there's not that much room in Enclave."

"They're going to the *Eden*," Rowena said.

:All of them?: Mars asked on a tight channel.

:All of the rowdies are mine.: Mars would understand. The grounders wouldn't, but Mars knew that once something belonged to a Lee, it was for life.

"You trust Dmitri Argosy?" Mars asked.

"The one that went with the Silars when his crew broke down?"

Mars nodded.

"Yeah. Get him out here. Fog it, I'd take a Sekoo today if they could teleport." She looked over at the edge of the shield. "Get everyone here. I'm going to buy the ships time to land."

"Watch yourself," Jae said as Mars pulled him away. "They're not going to play nice."

"Neither am I." She ran a scan to see how bad she was... Implant at eighteen percent, dehydrated, bruised, hungry... She'd had worse days and these people weren't Hollis. All she needed was to keep them busy while Marshall talked and the ships crossed the distance between the *Eden* and Kydell. Twelve minutes until they landed. Twenty to load. The first ships would lift off in under an hour.

Within an hour she'd have half the fleet here. All the fire power a person could want, all backing her.

All she had to do was survive the next twelve minutes.

The security forces shifted as she approached the cracked line in the stone littered with melted bullets and fragments of everything else the grounders had thrown at her. One of the men held up a hand and the others drew back.

"Are you ready to surrender?"

Rowena tilted her head, wrinkled her nose, and then shook her head. "No. But I'm willing to talk."

Marshall's shield was a cool mist as she walked through. Nanites embedded there clung to her, seeping into her skin and giving her a much needed energy boost. Eighteen percent became thirty-nine.

:We have to talk about your shield when I get back.:

:We'll see,: Marshall said. :Get a name of that guy for me.:

"Who are you?" Rowena asked, keeping a mental channel open for anyone in the fleet to listen in if they wanted.

"I am Major Dade Ruvin of the Malik Defense Force." He was a pig-eyed man with a broken nose and a look in his eyes that said he liked seeing people suffer.

She nodded. "Are you a Rightful Child of the Emperor?"

His eyes widened in shock for a moment before he recovered. "That is not for someone like you to know."

"I would think you'd want me to know. My family can trace our ancestors to the Empress of the Fifth House in the last dynasty of the Empire that we know of. I can recite my matrilineal line back to the Empress if you have a few hours to spare. Can you say the same?"

Ruvin dipped his chin. "I am loyal to the government of Malik IV."

"Which city-state?" Out of the corner of her eye she saw movement. It would have been too late for a grounder, but the wave of burning oil washed over her shield. They'd laid a fire line. Flames licked her shield, greedily devoured everything organic around her, crashed against the shield behind her, and smoldered in anger as they were rebuffed.

With a disappointed sigh, Rowena looked around. "This was your plan? You're going to try to burn me alive?"

The grounders were staring at her.

"It won't work," Rowena said. "The fire will die out long before I'm close to being injured. So let's stop playing games and talk. What do you want? Money? Fame? Power?"

"You can't offer me those things," Ruvin said.

Interesting that he used *Me* instead of *Us*. He was leading, but only thinking of himself. She could use that. "What did Lethe promise you?"

"My rightful place, and an end to scum like that." His glare went past her to the rowdies.

She looked over her shoulder in time to see Mars lifting a little girl up off the ground. "Yes. They look terribly dangerous. Poor. Homeless. Hungry. Is that what you want for yourself?" She turned back to Ruvin. "You want their street corner? Their job at the dock? Or do you like the idea of washing in swamp water?"

"They threaten the stability of the city-states and good order. They bombed the Jhandarmi building!"

"No, that was done by a traitor on Lethe's payroll. Not a very nice man. I'm not sure if he's still alive, but I can assure you he wasn't a rowdy."

Ruvin's expression didn't change. He'd known about Erach then.

"Do you have another lie you want to try?" Rowena asked politely as time ticked over in her head. *Eight more minutes.* "Would you like to blame your parents, perhaps? Or maybe it's because women aren't attracted to you?" She snapped her fingers. "No, I know what it is, it's that no one recognizes your great genius and you're underappreciated, while people like those rowdies have friends and family. That must be why all of you are here trying to massacre civilians. Children. Elderly."

"They were hiding criminals."

"They surrendered peacefully and were marched here to be slaughtered," Rowena said. "You did that. Without ever thinking about the consequences."

The soldier's smile changed. He was proud of himself. "Consequences? The only consequences I'll face are a cold beer and a commendation when I get home. You know what will happen to you?"

Seven minutes.

"Tell me."

Ruvin raised his hand and the air was filled with bullets, fire, shattering acoustic rounds.

The ground shook under Rowena's feet. She widened her stance, put her hands behind her back, and stood at-ease as the barrage continued.

Her ears popped as the barometer dropped.

Several of the soldiers stepped backwards, looking at the sky apprehensively.

"Don't worry," Rowena shouted over the cacophony. "That's just Carver."

Looks of confusion.

"You could try praying."

A dark cloud split through the sky as Carver teleported in and hovered mid-air. He was a fogging scary yaldson, gathering the clouds to him as he glowed a cold silver. A tsunami of water roared up from the docks. Kydell was going to be nothing but a smear after he was done.

The security forces ran for higher ground, leaving the Lethe troops alone.

Jets screamed across the horizon, firing at Carver, pursued by the sleek, green Sciarra ships.

Golden Silar ships followed, bright points of liquid light in the ever-darkening sky.

The wave crashed thirty meters away.

"You should surrender," Rowena said.

"Kill her!" Ruvin shouted. "Someone kill her!"

Four minutes.

Her ships would be in view soon, and she had the troops' full attention. Time to let them see what Lees were made of.

Taking a deep breath, she unwound battle codes she hadn't used in years. Biting frost seeped out of her, extinguishing the fire, cracking the cobblestones, killing as it crawled forward. She followed the cold.

"My name is Commodore Rowena Lee of the *Eden*. Remember that name," she said, amplifying her voice so the attackers could hear her. "My duty is to defend the citizens of the Malik System. In attacking the rowdies, you broke the peace and earned my attention. You did not want my attention."

Ruvin fell in front of her.

She stopped, barely aware of the cold. "You thought you could kill me?"

He gulped. The smell of fear filled the air around him. "Look at me."

Trembling, Ruvin slid his hand to the side, fingers almost concealing a knife. Almost.

Rowena shook her head. "I was going to be merciful."

The sun burst out, a glorious golden light that thawed her ice and rolled over her enemies.

Ruvin burned in Silar Fire with a scream that was cut off in a rush.

"My spouse always tells people I'm the nice one." She turned and looked up.

Hollis was wrapped in a ball of golden fire, the center an incandescent white, his red hair flying in the hot air currents.

Her heart skipped a beat with joy. He was so perfect. Beautifully furious. Deadly.

He landed as Marshall's shield fell down. There was no one left to attack them. Lethe's people were dead.

For a moment all she could do was stand and drink in the sight of him.

:Come on, Lee, I'm not supposed to run.: Hollis opened his arms.

Rowena teleported to him. Running would have taken too long. "You were supposed to stay on the *Eden* and rest." She rested her head on his chest, breathing him in. Everything she'd ever wanted.

"I didn't lift a finger," Hollis said as he wrapped his arms around her. He kissed the top of her head and ran a hand down her back, scanning as he went.

"I'm fine." More or less.

"You were taking all the fire in that fight and smiling." He both delighted and frustrated.

Giving him a tight squeeze, Rowena stood on tip toe and kissed his cheek. "I had a shield and I've been at war with the best. The grounders weren't going to hurt me."

"The one you were talking to had a knife." Hollis gave her a mock scowl.

She widened her eyes. "Ooo. Scary. A knife." She rolled her eyes and rested her head on his chest again. "I was coming home to you. Even the Lost Fleet couldn't have stopped me."

"Rowena?" Jae ran up to her, eyes wide. He looked at Hollis and swore. "Are you all right?"

"Perfectly fine," Rowena said. "Jae, meet my spouse, Hollis. Love, meet the leader of the rowdies. He'll be helping us run the station."

"Will he?" the men said in unison.

She smiled. "This is going to be fun." For her at least. Everyone else was going to have to play by her rules now.

:Our rules,: Hollis said.

:Our rules.: She liked the sound of that.

SIX WEEKS LATER

A HEAVY ARM CROSSED ROWENA'S waist as a pillow-smothered "No" broke the quiet of the sleeping quarters.

Rowena turned to her lover, who was sprawled across three-quarters of their giant bed. "I need to get up and shower."

"That's a lie," Hollis said sleepily, pulling her back so she was tucked against his bare chest. "We have nothing to do until mid-morning." His golden-brown eyes opened. "I know. I made the schedule."

It was so tempting to lay here for another hour. Play with his hair. Kiss him until time had no meaning. She sighed as she ran her hands across his chest. "The cadets are arriving early."

Frustration rolled off him. "Why?"

"Because they have zero-g training and the sooner they finish, the more time they have to explore the station?"

Everyone was eager to come play, and to negotiate treaties. A lot of people wanted a chance to explain that they'd always been admired her, really.

Understanding mixed with annoyance. "What part of 'leave the newlyweds alone' did I not get across to the fleet?" His hand skimmed down her side, tickling her thigh. "I don't want to share you today."

"You never want to share me."

"Mmmm…" A lazy smile. "That works out well. You don't want to share me either."

True.

Hollis kissed her, a teasing, playful touch that turned deep and hungry.

After a few minutes, she broke away as *Eden* sent her a strident notice that the shuttles were landing. "You're distracting me!"

"I know." He was so smug.

"I think they're worried that if they leave us alone too long, they'll have to deal with our offspring terrorizing the fleet." Despite the fact that they'd assured everyone who asked that they weren't in a rush to have a child. Hollis had made a very convincing argument for enjoying several years of long nights without interruption.

Even if he hadn't, she'd seen Aronia dealing with Ki during the evacuation and she had no desire to juggle pregnancy and getting the *Eden* fully functional.

Hollis nipped at her lips in another playful kiss, taking her thoughts away from repairs and crew vacancies. "Let Jae handle the fleetlings. He did a great job with the land navigation unit. The cadets had fun."

"He lost them in a swamp."

"They all lived." Hollis hooked a leg between hers and shifted so she was laying on top. "How much trouble can they get into on a station?"

The possibilities seemed endless. "They're bringing news crews from some of the city-states."

He cursed and let her go, golden fire in his eyes. "Next time we find a derelict station that no one else knows about, we are staying there for a year before we let anyone else know where we are."

"Only a year?" Rowena teased as she slid out of bed.

His eyes tracked her through the low light of their quarters. "Maybe a decade. Or two." Thoughts of how he would spend those decades washed through her mind on their shared link.

She stopped in the doorway of the washroom. "I said I needed a shower. I never said I had to shower alone..."

They made it to the main promenade without making the cadets wait too long. And, technically, they'd showered.

Well, been in the shower and gotten wet. She couldn't remember soap making it into the mix, but they were probably clean enough.

Hollis grinned wickedly at her.

:Be good. My cousins are here.:

:Then let me show them how well I treat you.:

Giggling, she turned the corner and looked over the crowd in the main atrium. Cadets in their best uniforms were clustered in the center ringed by chaperones, news crews, and the curious rowdies who'd shown up to see what was happening on their station.

Jae looked up at them from the across the distance and made a "What can you do?" expression.

"How many cadets do you have?" Hollis asked from beside her as they looked over the assembly.

"I told the crews to send chaperones." And it looked like most of the crews had sent several. She patted his arm. "Ready to give the introduction lecture?"

Hollis sent her the memory of toe-curling kiss. :You're going to handle the crew interviews?:

:Might as well get started. We need to recruit some people to train the rowdies and hold down fleet positions. And everyone wants a chance to work with us.:

He rested a hand on her back. : Paperwork, Lee. Think of all the paperwork you're giving me.:

She sent him the memory of a smile. :We'll hire you an adjutant first thing.:

"Commodore!" A grounder with a camera waved at them. "Are you going to say a few words?"

Rowena turned to the crowd. "Welcome to the space station *Eden*, where we are building a better future for everyone."

Everything she'd ever wanted: a command, people who cared for her, people to protect, love... she'd found them all on the *Eden*. With Hollis. She had it, and she'd defend it, no matter what came next.

PERSONS OF INTEREST

Captain Selena Caryll: the only person on the fleet to both fight in the war and have zero confirmed kills, Selena is known for her skills as a pilot and a shielder. After she destroyed her last ship, the *Persephone*, in the final battle, the remnants of her crew left her. She's isolated and ostracized within the fleet, but still believes they can rebuild without losing their way of life. She's worked for three years as the go-between between the grounder police force and the fleet government. She has since restored the *Persephone* to working order and become one of the fleet's chief diplomats. She is married to Titan Sciarra (see: *Bodies In Motion*, Fleet of Malik Book #1).

Commander Titan Sciarra-Caryll: his family name comes from the knives they use to assassinate their way up the chain of command. In the final days of the war, Titan backed his aunt (now captain) Elea in a mutiny, killing three Sciarra officers. Even before the war, he had a reputation as skilled killer and dangerous man. He was Mal Baular's sworn second until a fighter crash put him into rehab for over a year. He's scarred, but working hard to rebuild the good name of his crew and the fleet. He currently works for the fleet Starguard and is second-in-command of the warship *Persephone*. He is married to Selena Caryll (see: *Bodies In Motion*).

Yeoman Rowena Lee: once a commander, she survived the in-fighting and feuding of her family to go to the officer's academy. Promised to Mal Baular from a young age, she stuck close to him and Titan Sciarra throughout her education. Despite being a fighter pilot during the war, Rowena is best known for her hand-to-hand combat and engineering skills. Deadly with a knife, impatient, and quick to judge, Rowena isn't someone you want on your bad side. After the war she was punished for her crimes, reduced to the rank of Yeoman, and kept under house arrest on the *Danielle Nicole* for several years. Now she's working as a weapons expert for the Jhandarmi and as a Drill Instructor for the new Academy (see: *Bodies In Motion*).

Captain Perrin Carver: orphaned in a shuttle crash at age 6, Perrin is a walking genetics experiment conducted by his family. His tech is beyond what anyone else has, his reflexes are faster, he hits harder and he's near impossible to kill. No one wants to replicate it, but after being raised by a grounder family, the fleet invited him back to the officer academy when he was 17. He made friends, but he made enemies faster. When Old Baular declared war on the planet where Perrin grew up, he rallied the defense and led the fight. Once the best fighter pilot, he's now in charge of the Starguard. He's keeping the peace, but wants more for the fleet than to die of old age and irrelevance. He is married to Genevieve Silar (see: *Bodies In Motion*).

Commander Hollis Silar: Hollis is known for two things in the fleet: being the best tactician and the biggest flirt. He'll chase anyone with a pretty smile, and most people forget that behind his own easy smile is a very dangerous mind. Passionate and combative, Hollis favors brute force when he can, sneakiness when he can't, and blind luck when all else fails. He was a fighter pilot during the war and twice took command of the Silar armada when his superior officers were injured. He oversees the training house as a member of the Starguard and is Rowena Lee's sparring partner.

Captain Hermione Marshall: born to a grounder family with claims to Imperial lineage, Hermione was raised to be competitive, confident, and aggressive. When the fleet allowed a single grounder to join the academy, she fought for it tooth and nail. Then fought even harder to overcome fleet prejudices and understand a culture that had been isolated from her own for over 600 years. During the war she was a fighter pilot who led boarding parties. She was captured and tortured, but survived, escaped, and now heads the Office of Imperial Affairs, liaising between the fleet and the various governments on the planet's surface.

Lt Commander Genevieve Silar: the younger sister of the fleet's hottest flirt isn't so bad at emotional manipulation herself, but she's a better shot. Two years younger than her brother, Gen started as a gunner before taking over for a dead pilot in the final weeks of the war. She's been with Perrin since the beginning, his best support, adviser, and a sounding board. She's wild, loud, and most people forget that behind that pretty face is a woman with a very high kill count and a very focused temper. She is married to Perrin Carver (see: *Bodies In Motion*).

Captain Elea Sciarra: the youngest of five children, Elea was always a quiet child. She went through the Academy without earning any recognition and was a gunner for the Sciarras and the primary caregiver for her two nephews— Mars and Titan—after their parents died. When the Sciarra captain ordered the armada into a deathtrap to obey Old Baular's orders, Elea led a coup with Titan as her second. She now commands the Sciarra armada and is considered fair and forward thinking. She is allied with the Carylls by marriage and with Rowena Lee by oath.

Lieutenant Mars Sciarra: the youngest nephew of Elea Sciarra and cousin of Titan Sciarra-Caryll. Mars is known for being quick-witted, good natured, and being the most boisterous Sciarra in the fleet. He fought in the tail-end of the last war and recently became an officer in the Sciarra armada. (see: *Bodies In Motion*)

Captain Hoshi Lee: appointed captain by the Captain's Emergency Council following the last war, Hoshi Lee controls the large Lee armada. The crew was always divided and his family was on the weaker side until the war. He holds a grudge against Rowena and Aronia Lee because of their parents' actions, and he would get rid of Rowena if he could. Unfortunately for Hoshi, Rowena's Elite fighter status and her engineering skills are the only thing the Lees have left to negotiate with, and he needs her as much as he hates her.

Commander Mal Baular (deceased): the scion of the Baular armada, the grandson of Old Baular, and the son of famed shield expert Vanessa Baular, Mal was the Warmonger's answer to Perrin Carver. He was ruthless, dangerous, and loyal. It was his willingness to betray his grandfather brought the war to an end. For his crimes he was banished, stripped of his implant, and sent to live with the grounders, a punishment that effectively ended his betrothal to Rowena Lee. He was killed by a car bomb a few months after his banishment began. His parents, who were banished with him, both died of a virus their immune systems couldn't handle without the nanites produced by their implants.

Lady Sonya Lethe: the sole heiress of the Lethe fortune, Sonya is famous across the planet of Malik IV. Her family controls the hypertrams that connect the city-states and she is a well-known socialite, philanthropist, and acclaimed beauty. In person, she comes across as egotistical, narcissistic, and less educated than she claims to be, but people with money can be forgiven many things.

Dr. Malcolm Long: recently displaced from his family home on the islands of Seahome, Dr. Long is a graduate of the University of Ryun and the lead researcher at Bennu Industries. He is famous in some circles for his work in cryptography, but more famous for being the only son of heiress Lady Nettie Amherst-Long of the Northland Longs.

SHIP NAMING CONVENTIONS

Each crew picks a theme for their ships that reflects both their personality as a crew and their values.

Lee ships are named for famous female scientists:
Danielle Nicole
Jacqueline Gill
Jennifer Robison
Alessandra Gillani
Peggy Whitson
Nandini Harinath

Silar ships are named for famous female journalists:
Veronica Guerin
Ida Wells
Virginia Vallejo

Caryll ships are named for goddesses or other women who were known for their strength, wisdom, and leadership:
Persephone
Minerva
Diana

Sciarra ships are all named for female aviators:
Sabiha Gökçen
Willa Brown
Hazel Ying Lee
Lydia Litvyak
Molly Rose
Maggie Gee

<u>Baular</u> ships are all named for dragons:
Chrysophylax
Errol
Ryū
Long
Sárkány
Ruth
Slibinas

In particular, the *Danielle Nicole* is named for my friend Dr. Danielle N. Lee, who studies African giant pouched rats and does science outreach through The Urban Scientist, Scientific American Blog Network, and National Science & Technology News Services (of which she is a co-founder). You can find her on Twitter as @DNLee5. The real D. N. Lee is much nicer than a warship is, I promise.

The *Jennifer Robison* is named for my friend Dr. Jennifer Robison who studies abiotic factors on the physiology and biochemistry of plants. She can be found on Twitter as @OshnGirl, on Youtube on the Cell-Fie Science channel discussing plant science, and at her website:
https://jenniferrobison.weebly.com/

The *Jacqueline Gill* is named for my friend, ecologist and biogeographer Dr. Jacquelyn Gill, who studies how landscapes change through space and time. She writes about ecology and climate change over time from the last ice age to the present day, and how our understanding of the past can help prepare us for the future. She also writes about Academia, diversity in STEM, science communication, and the occasional dung fungus. In Fall 2013, Jacquelyn joined the University of Maine as an Assistant Professor of Paleoecology & Plant Ecology with the School of Biology &

Ecology and the Climate Change Institute. In addition to geeking out in the lab, in the field, and online, she enjoys games, knitting, science fiction, discovering new craft cocktails, cuddling her furry mesofauna, and exploring Maine's forests, rivers, and islands. You can find her on Twitter as @JacquelynGill and at:

https://jacquelyngill.wordpress.com/

A BRIEF HISTORY OF THE MALIK STAR SYSTEM

1300 Before Landing (BL)—Malik System discovered by the Explorer-class vessel *Imperial Pearl*.

1100BL—Malik III and Malik IV planets terraformed to support human life.

1000BL—First wave of colonization begins.

900BL—Wormhole connecting Malik System to the Empire collapses, leaving both colonists and fleet ships stranded.

600BL—Tensions between fleet and colonists reach breaking point and isolation is declared. Several crews land their ships and give up space flight.

36-18BL—The first civil war between the Warmongers, led by the Baulars, and the Allied Crews, led by the Carvers. The war was declared over the orun crystals used for fuel by the fleet.

18BL—The Carver shuttle *Leto* crashes near Tarrin and 6-year-old Perrin Carver is rescued from the wreckage.

5BL—Perrin Carver and Hermione Marshall are accepted into the Fleet Academy.

2BL—The second civil war begins with Old Baular and his grandson Mal leading the Warmongers, and Perrin Carver leading the Allied Crews in defense of the colonists.

LANDING

3 years post landing—BODIES IN MOTION begins.

ABOUT THE AUTHOR

LIANA BROOKS writes science fiction and sci-fi romance for people who like fast ships, big guns, witty one-liners, and happy endings. She lives in South Carolina with her husband and four kids. When she isn't writing, she enjoys hiking, playing at the beach, and painting.

You can find Liana on the web at www.lianabrooks.com or on Twitter as @LianaBrooks.

ACKNOWLEDGMENTS

I'll be honest, the list of people I need to thank for helping with this book is almost as long as the book itself.

In the end, I need thank the usual suspects: my husband and children for their unfailing support; Amy Laurens for being a good friend, a good editor, and kicking me in the pants when needed; Derek Hawkins and J.C. Nelson for their cheerful feedback and willingness to keep the fire starter away from me while I was editing; Skyla Dawn and Clare Williams for the help with the cover art; the writers of the SFR Brigade for feedback on the fight scenes; the lovely Hive Mind of Twitter for cheering this book on even during the roughest drafts; and—of course—the readers who make all this work worthwhile.

I hope you enjoyed this trip to the Malik System. If you did, please leave a review somewhere so your friends can find my little corner of the universe.

Stay safe, and I'll see you next time you're in town.

BODIES IN MOTION

1
SELENA

THE PROBLEM WITH VACATIONS, Selena reflected as she adjusted her sweater outside Cargo Blue, was that reality was always waiting at the end.

A quick search of the local security cameras found one that showed the peeling sunburn on her right shoulder blade. Such was the curse of pale-skinned, ship-born Fleet personnel. Anytime she left the foggy belts covering the city of Tarrin, she barbecued like a shrimp, no matter how much sunscreen she applied. Otherwise, she'd flee even further from the Fleet Enclave and make her home on the equatorial beaches of the planet they were trapped on.

She panned the camera and checked her left shoulder. Black ink made a starscape that disguised three silver scars as shooting stars. The painting covered her shoulder blade and part of her upper arm. As the artist had promised, the skin-paint had kept her from burning as much, though it still had the over-stretched feel of a burn.

With a few adjustments, her uniform covered most of the temporary art; it would keep her from having to explain to her colleagues.

Her forearm warmed, a warning that someone was about to contact her through the tech implant tucked between her radius and ulna.

She hesitated too long and the call came through, a persistent ping against her skull as the phantom image of her best friend floated on the edge of her vision.

Selena turned off the visual receiver and answered. "Genevieve," she said with a smile as the image of her vivacious, red-headed friend appeared floating against the backdrop of landing gear that supported the grounded fleet.

A grounder would have thought she was talking to herself, but grounders wouldn't set foot near the neo-city-state of Enclave. The rocky beach served as a city and tomb for the sur-vivors of the last war.

"Selena!" Gen gushed. "Starcom to Selena. Where are you? I'm covering for now."

"Delayed, but almost there." Selena hoped Gen wouldn't hear the lie. She'd been standing in the shadows of the Enclave pub for nearly a quarter of an hour.

"The *Lorenza* could get here faster," Gen said, referencing a long-dead ship whose crew were found skeletonized at their stations. Gen blew hair off her face. "Stars above, you're an hour late. The whole fleet is flying faster than you."

Selena turned on her visual long enough to roll her eyes at her friend. "Ha, ha, funny. That joke needs to be forcibly retired." Sooner rather than later. The fleet couldn't fly without fuel, and the Malik system they were stranded in held precious few deposits of the orun crystals needed to power the ships.

"If you don't come," Gen said threateningly, "I will teleport to your apartment and drag you out in your pajamas."

"I'm not at home," Selena admitted. And she wouldn't have let her best friend come to her new house if she was.

Gen was smart enough to realize that the small palace Selena had bought in downtown Tarrin wasn't paid for by her official OIA salary. The paygrades for the Office of Imperial Affairs had last been updated when the Malik system was still in contact with the empire, making them 900 years out of date.

Technically, taking a second job wasn't treason, but there were enough people in the fleet who'd see it as a betrayal that keeping it secret felt right. Especially since Gen's captain would scream the loudest.

Gen clapped. "Selena! Stop stalling yer engines and get in here. This isn't some Fleet Tribunal, just our friends. You, me, Carver. I left a message for Marshall. You know. People we like."

The light of understanding dawned. "Carver? This is so you can snuggle up to Perrin Carver without your parents watching?"

"Yes," Gen admitted, not looking the least bit contrite.

"You're only dragging me along so I can cover for you while you make out in a corner, aren't you?" She masked the relief with mock anger. At least Gen wasn't trying to set Selena up with one of her cousins. Or, ancestors forbid, Gen's handsy older brother.

Again.

Gen opened her eyes wide with an innocent smile. "Maybe."

"Gen!" Selena rolled her eyes. "Doesn't he have his own place?"

"Just the bachelor's dorm. The Carvers didn't have any ships except the shuttle his parents crashed in. Making out next door to Mom and Dad? No. And the BOQ? It's so tacky. You can hear everything through those walls."

Selena hid a smile. "I'll be there soon enough."

If Gen ever caught wind of how panicky the thought of a relationship made her, Gen would make it her life's goal to see Selena paired off. And there wasn't a man alive who she could imagine getting close to now.

Her implant helpfully pulled up an image of a tall, broad-shouldered, lean-muscled fighter with skin black as the night between stars and emerald-green eyes.

She pushed the memory away.

Lieutenant Commander Titan Sciarra was striking, intelligent, and had a body she'd cross battle lines for, but he was also out of reach. There was no point in chasing a man who wouldn't give her the time of day.

Another crew shuffled past her into the bar, black patches with silver fists on their shoulders.

It was getting harder to pretend she belonged in Enclave, with the fleet. Once upon a time, she'd known every crew's patch without thinking. She could name captains, their ships and their seconds by rote. Now she would need to tap into the fleet's information nexus if she wanted to know who they were.

She stopped at the edge of the door to tug her lightest shields into place. A few minor adjustments would keep bugs away, keep beer off her clothes, and prevent anyone from hacking into her implant. They could still send messages, because disallowing that would have raised eyebrows. And they could still hit her. But she could always hit back.

Selena rolled her shoulders and strutted into Cargo Blue. It was a battlefield, but she was the last captain of the Caryll family, and she wasn't going down without a fight.

Whatever crew owned Cargo Blue probably hadn't had much of a decorating budget, but at least they'd stuck with a theme: oversized cargo boxes were piled up to make walls, seating, and tables. Olive-green safety webbing draped from the ceiling between blue lights. Fog used for fire drills on the ships pumped across the floor to hide the concrete beneath.

There was no bouncer at the door, but people were still hanging around the entrance.

As a rule, the fleet was cautious, and the young faces she saw belonged to fleet members who had never ventured outside their own crew more than a few times, even though the fleet had been grounded for nearly three years.

Tables to the left, bar ahead, dance floor to the right... and that meant the back half of the cargo hanger had been partitioned and karaoke would be in the back right corner. After a few minutes of weaving through the human crush, she found Gen, already sitting in Perrin Carver's lap and giggling.

"Selena!" Gen jumped up and hugged her. "I was beginning to worry!"

"How many people are in here?" Selena shouted over the music.

"Everyone under forty?" Gen laughed. With a small hand wave Gen put up a minor sound shield, muting the music. "People are going to stir crazy. Combine that with the anniversary—"

The anniversary.

Today.

The day the war had begun, the day the united fleet had died.

They'd been dying for four hundred years, well aware that the reserve of orun crystals was depleted and there was no way to move forward with the ships they had.

Old Captain Baular had seen the deposit of orun on the fifth planet as their saving grace. He'd get it even if it meant killing the grounders. And, coward that he was, he'd ordered his grandson to lead the first attack instead of leading it himself.

That opening skirmish began and ended in the dark, with Titan Sciarra in the infirmary, and five Aca-demy fighters missing or damaged. But by lunch of the next day, every officer belonging to crews allied with the Baulars withdrew.

Seven months later, heated words turned to live rounds.

"Selena?" Gen asked quietly, placing a hand on her arm. "You didn't know the date, did you?"

"I was trying not to think about." If she had, she'd have cut her vacation to the islands early.

Maybe even made her pilgrimage to the small cay where she'd ditched her stolen fighter after driving off the attack.

She rolled her shoulder, stretching the deep scars. "It snuck up on me."

"First round, we drink to the Lost Fleet, and all who've gone on to crew it. I'm buying," Gen said with a touch of forced joviality. "Carver's been making friends. Tell her, babe." She pushed Carver's shoulder.

Perrin Carver was tall, broad-shouldered man with shy, hazel eyes that hid a wicked sense of humor.

Selena's heart fluttered just a little at the memory of a time when she'd fancied herself in love with him. He'd been the ideal starsider: intelligent, good-looking, and charis-matic. They'd been friends of a sort, but even that rela-tionship had soured when she'd realized he'd been getting close to her so he could learn more about Genevieve Silar.

Carver nodded and held out his hand. "Hi, Selena. How are you?"

She tapped the back of his hand with hers, letting him test her shields. "Good. How's the Starguard?"

"Booming." The commander of the Starguard smiled, white teeth flashing, but there was a tightness around his eyes. "Everyone hears about guardians being allowed outside the Enclave, or working with the Jhandarmi, and I'm drowning in recruiting requests. Captains of larger crews invite me to Captain's Mess so they can introduce me to their best and brightest. Half the time I can't tell if they want me to marry into the crew or take the fleetlings into the guard." His shield was still attached to hers, scanning her as he talked.

All he would get from her was polite interest. Her heartrate didn't spike or dip at the mention of the Jhandarmi. Her smile never flickered.

"Maybe you should lock down Gen," Selena said. "If you had a spouse, no one would try to get you to marry into the crew."

Carver and Gen shared a look, and Gen sent a ping of information that Selena's implant translated as an ongoing debate over crew name and a place to live.

Carver sent something similar; a picture of his bachelor's quarters and his one ship. There was no room for them to marry and have a family.

"Enclave is a temporary solution," Selena said out loud. She'd lost the taste for communicating by implant years ago. "If we—"

A heavy hand wrapped around her waist as someone wearing too much cologne stepped far too close to her. "Hello, Selena."

Hollis Silar, one of Gen's many siblings, kissed her temple.

Selena sighed, sending a shock through her shield to Hollis's hand and elbowing him in the gut at the same time. "Hi, Hollis. I see you're still bathing in cologne rather than water."

He stepped away from her, an easy smile still in place.

It wasn't that Hollis was bad looking; plenty of women found him handsome. It was that he was equally affectionate with every woman he saw and he couldn't keep a secret to save his life. Or anyone else's. He'd chase anyone with a pretty smile and fell in and out of love a couple of times a day.

"Nice to see you too, Selena. Now, everyone, you're all going to look at me, smile, and laugh like I'm my normal, dashing self," he said, his smile never changing. "You haven't been paying attention, but I'm not a member of the Starguard for nothing. We're being watched. Now take your nice drinks from the waitress and keep your eyes on me."

Hollis nodded to the waitress and handed out four cups with bright purple liquid. "Bruised Stars all around. Guaranteed to make you giggle, or so the guy at the bar told me. Although he's a Seutaai, so take it with a shield in place." He handed Selena her drink with a smile, but turned immediately to glance over his shoulder.

"Big brother, who are we looking for?" Gen asked with a slow drawl. "Is it a friend who you might have forgotten to call back after a night out?"

Hollis shook his head. "No, I thought I saw some of the Lee crew. Make that, I'm certain of it."

Selena grimaced. "As long as Rowena isn't here."

"Did you call me?"

Startled, Selena looked up to the face of her least favorite woman: Rowena Lee. "Hello," Selena said politely. "I see you're still alive. That's..." *Unfortunate.* She nodded and took a slug of her Bruised Star.

Rowena held up a tray of electric blue shots. "My crew thinks I can't out-drink anyone in this bar. I probably can't go toe-to-toe with alcoholics like the Silars here. But No-Shot Selena?" Rowena set the drinks on the table. "I can out-shoot you in the stars or on the ground."

Gen sucked in air between her teeth and sent Selena several urgent pings telling her to ignore the Lees.

Selena muted Gen. "I took plenty of shots in the war. As I recall, I disabled three of your big birds. *Bassi, Aryton, Theoano*... Bang, bang, bang." Selena mimed firing with her finger. "Three shots. Three silent ships."

"Not kills," Rowena said. "A whole war and you never blooded yourself."

That was it, the memory she didn't want to face; the time she'd almost taken Death's claim and risked killing someone outside of war.

"That's uncalled for," Hollis said, trying to step between them. "Selena, why don't we—"

Selena pushed Hollis aside and grabbed the first shot. She tossed back the potent drink and shattered the glass on the table. "Go suck vacuum, Rowena. You're a pissant yeoman with no hope of command."

"I went to the Academy, same as you, Selena. I fought for the fleet." Rowena slammed a shot back. "You fought for the mud-lickers."

Selena took another shot as the first started to fuzz her judgement. "I prevented the Baulars from committing mass genocide and destroying the civilians along with the fleet."

Rowena took her second shot. A crowd was gathering and that seemed to feed her cruelty. "The Lees survived the war. We're still here. How many Caryll captains are there? Oh, right, one. Can you count that high, No-Shot? You have any idea how easy it would be for me to end you right now?"

Selena took the last two glasses and slammed them both back.

Gen pinged her, giving locations, counts, and identities of the Lee allies in the crowd.

Hollis stepped to her flank, ready to defend her.

She stood, anger burning through her veins. "Sure, your crew outnumbers mine. I guess on paper, it's not really a fair fight, is it, Rowena? But you were trained as a flight leader, and what do Carylls do? Hand-to-hand combat. Maybe I should thin your ranks, starting with one mouthy yeoman."

Head to www.lianabrooks.com/fleet-of-malik/change-of-momentum/ to keep reading!

www.ingramcontent.com/pod-product-compliance
Lightning Source LLC
Chambersburg PA
CBHW030655190726
48286CB00001B/29